NEVER CAN SAY
GOODBYE

NEVER CAN SAY GOODBYE

Christina Jones

WINDSOR
PARAGON

First published 2011
by Piatkus
This Large Print edition published 2012
by AudioGO Ltd
by arrangement with
Little, Brown Book Group

Hardcover   ISBN: 978 1 4713 0406 4
Softcover   ISBN: 978 1 4713 0407 1

British Library Cataloguing in Publication Data available

Printed and bound in Great Britain by
MPG Books Group Limited

For The Toyboy Trucker, Elle and The Doctor
with all my love

With many thanks to Broo Doherty, my agent, and Emma Beswetherick, my editor, for not even trying to talk me out of writing this book.

And with thanks to Linda, whose pendant-twirling in the pub gave me the idea in the first place.

Chapter One

'... and to Francesca Angelina Maud Meredith, I bequeath my—'

'Hang on, Rita,' Frankie Meredith, perched on the wide and highly polished wooden counter of Rita's Rent-a-Frock shop, interrupted. 'I think I might have spotted a teensy bit of a flaw there.'

'Really?' Rita, Frankie's middle-aged friend and employer, salsa'd between the claustrophobically crammed clothes rails in a too-tight, too-short, scarlet silk flamenco dress. 'And what's that, then?'

'You can't bequeath me anything. You're not dead.'

'Well spotted, love. No flies on you.' Short and stocky, Rita gave a wobbly mock-curtsy. 'But actually, not being dead doesn't come into it.'

'Doesn't it? I'd always thought being dead was a vital part of bequeathing. And are we adding that dress to the shop or are you buying it?'

Rita smoothed down the riotous ripples of scarlet silk. 'Sadly, much as I love it, under the circumstances, once it's been cleaned it'll have to go into the stock. I'm trying to rid myself of clutter—hence the bequeathing. And even though it's a very beautiful frock, it's just a tad too tight.'

Diplomatically, Frankie said nothing. The dress, donated by one of Kingston Dapple's ladies-who-lunch, was probably a small size twelve, and Rita certainly wasn't.

Rita's Rent-a-Frock was warmly cosy on this cold, grey, autumnal afternoon, and Rita was indulging in her favourite pastime of trying

1

on newly donated dresses to while away the customer-free moments. The fictional bequest-making, Frankie assumed, was a new game invented for much the same reason.

'Anyway,' Rita continued, fluffing at her heavily hennaed hair, 'with me being a titian, red's not really me, is it? Red's more your colour. You can get away with red seeing as you're dark and dramatic and look exactly like Joan Rivers.'

'*What?*'

'You do, love. You know you do. Loads of people have said so.'

'Have they? Lord ... Well, OK, she's very glam, but she's also about four decades older than me, and blonde, and with an American accent, not to mention a caustic turn of phrase. I'm not sure we're that similar, actually, are we?'

'Maybe you're not, then.' Rita looked doubtful. 'You know me and names ... P'raps it's not Joan Rivers. Maybe I mean Joan Collins, do I?'

'Well, she's still ultra glam, and at least she's brunette, but, er, again, slightly older than me.'

Rita frowned. 'Yes, OK—you know I don't do the celeb stuff. Oh, who am I thinking of?'

'Claudia Winkleman?' Frankie said hopefully. The vague similarity had been mentioned rather flatteringly before. Especially the hair.

'Who?' Rita shook her head. 'No, definitely not him. You look like a famous *Joan*. Brian from the kebab van always says so.'

Frankie laughed. Brian from the kebab van said a lot of things. Most of them wrong.

'Brian says,' Rita continued, 'you look like that black-haired rock 'n' roll woman who looks like Alice Cooper only much prettier and with a heavy

2

fringe and more make-up and—'

'You mean Joan *Jett*?' Frankie sighed. 'Oh, I wish ... OK, our hair is much the same and there's a bit of a physical resemblance, but I'd look terrible in leather—and you'd have to add gangly and gawky for a fuller and truer description of me.'

'So you're tall and a bit on the skinny side. So are the best-paid catwalk models and you don't hear them complaining, do you? And don't knock that retro rock chick look, love. It's refreshing in these days of WAG-orange clones. That hairstyle and your panda eyes will make a comeback soon, you wait and see.'

'You say the sweetest things.' Frankie grinned.

'What I mean is,' Rita said, 'when it all comes round again, as it will, you'll be way ahead of the trend. Until then, you have a unique, um, style all of your own. Joan Jett dressed by Barbie.'

'I'm not sure that's even a compliment, now,' Frankie laughed. 'I just seemed to drift into the primary-coloured, flouncy, girlie look early on. It must have been an amalgam of all those Goths and New Romantics when I was growing up ... they were so glamorous to a plain Jane like me. As an eighties child, I'm only surprised I wasn't born with a fixation for *Dallas*-type shoulder pads too.'

'Shoulder pads!' Rita clapped her plump hands. 'Oh, I loved them! They gave a girl balance and style. We don't get enough of them in here, do we? I loved the eighties. Like you say, such amazing outfits. And all that *Dallas* stuff too—huge hair and glossy lippy and skyscraper heels and big, big bling—it was a fabulous decade for fashion.'

Frankie smiled. Rita thought every decade had been a fabulous decade for fashion. It was a shame

3

that Rent-a-Frock didn't reflect her passion.

Rent-a-Frock was more like a haphazard Saturday jumble sale in the Kingston Dapple scout hut. Rita never turned anything wearable away. She accepted any item of clothing anyone brought in, with the result that everything was crammed in everywhere with no regard for style or era or colour or even size.

'Anyway,' Frankie said, 'what did you mean earlier by "under the circumstances" and decluttering? Are you having a life-laundry moment? Is that what the bequeathing is about?'

Rita stroked the red frock again. 'No—and if you'd stop interrupting, I'll explain exactly what's happening.'

'OK.' Frankie settled herself more comfortably on the wide counter. They weren't busy; the shop had been empty all afternoon. 'I'm all for a new game.'

'It's-not-a-game.' With a further swish of red silk, Rita continued her stumpy dancing round the rainbow-crammed rails. 'Right, where was I?'

'You were making bequests. So far, you'd apparently left all your shoes to Maisie Fairbrother and your Mantovani vinyl record collection to Twilights Rest Home.'

'Maisie Fairbrother has always been the Imelda Marcos of Kingston Dapple and a good friend even if she's a bit, well, odd and has never set foot inside this shop.' Rita twirled round a box of mixed gloves and socks. 'And Twilights have tea dances every Friday afternoon and must get tired of foxtrotting to the same old music. So, that's two bequests satisfactorily made. Now . . .'

Frankie leaned forwards. 'Once you've made all

your bequests, can I start on mine? Not that I've got much to show for someone who's very nearly thirty. Half a very small rented house complete with ditzy flatmate, fourteen shelves of books—all paperback chick lit, not an improving literary tome in sight—a very small telly, an ancient DVD player, an even more ancient sound system, a laptop, one stack of rom-com films, three cases of girlie CDs, a wardrobe of second-hand dresses, a much-loved but moth-eaten teddy bear ...'

'Frankie.' Rita stopped shimmying. 'Are you going to listen to me or not?'

'Yes, OK.' Frankie grinned, unabashed. 'It's not like we're snowed under with customers, is it?'

'Hardly going to be are we?' Rita glared at the relentless rain lashing across Kingston Dapple's deserted market place and hammering against the shop's 1950s windows from a pewter sky. 'Early November—terrible time for us. Always has been. In a couple of weeks' time, once you get towards December, now that's when you'll be really busy, when everyone wants a new party frock for Christmas, ditto New Year's Eve, and then on into the post-festive diet period when no one wants to spend a fortune on new dresses while they're between sizes, and then the spring weddings and ...'

Frankie scrunched up the layers of her purple wool skirt and drew her black-opaque-tighted knees up to her chin. 'Mmm, I've been working here for three years—I do know the trading pattern—but you just said "you" there a lot. "You". Singular. Not "we" ... You're being weird.'

'Because,' Rita said, executing a twirl, 'that's what I'm trying to tell you. I'm making the

5

bequests—getting rid of everything I no longer need—because I won't be here in December.'

'What?' Frankie stopped smiling. 'Why? Why not? Oh, God, Rita, you're not ill are you?'

'Good Lord, no. I'm as fit as a fiddle. Now, if you'd just stop interrupting and let me do this before we get sidetracked again. To Francesca Angelina Maud Meredith, I bequeath my shop ...'

'*What?*' Frankie clutched the counter. 'Are you mad?'

'Not as far as I know, love. So, listen. Rita's Rent-a-Frock will be closed down and renamed Francesca's Fabulous Frocks next week. I'll be gone, and you will be the sole proprietor from next weekend.'

Frankie gawped. 'Are you joking? You are joking, right?'

'Wrong, and don't gawp, love. You're a pretty girl, but it's still not a good look.'

Frankie snapped her mouth shut, then frowned. 'OK—now—please can you just repeat what you've just said?'

'About the gawping?'

'About not being here and bequeathing me the shop.'

Rita repeated it.

'God, Rita, you are ill! You can't be ill! You're not, um, going to, um ... ?'

'Die?' Rita chuckled. 'Goodness me, I hope not. At least not for another eighty-odd years. No, as I've just told you, I'm as fit as a lop. Well, a few pounds overweight maybe, but otherwise I've just passed my MOT with flying colours.'

'Thank goodness for that.' Frankie heaved a massive sigh of relief. 'But please stop messing about. You can't give me the shop—even in a game.'

'For the umpteenth time, it's not a game and yes, I can. And as I won't be here for much longer, it seems eminently sensible to tie up all the ends now and—'

'Stop, please. This is just too bizarre for words. And what do you mean you won't be here for much longer?' Frankie gulped. 'That sounds really awful. Rita, you're honestly OK, aren't you?'

'Never better. Now, do you want to hear about your future or not?'

'Well, yes, of course, if you're being serious.'

'I'm being very serious. About my future—and yours.'

Frankie shook her head. 'OK, but to be honest, I didn't think I'd got one. I've been worrying for ages that you were going to make me redundant after Christmas. After all, a second-hand rental clothes shop in a Berkshire village trading badly in the teeth of this ongoing recession can hardly justify two members of staff, and now—'

'All gloom and doom.' Rita sniffed. 'You'll be fine. Second-hand clothes always do well when money's tight. I'm relying on you to carry on where I left off—and then some. I know you'll make a success of it.'

'But, why are you giving up the business? You love it. It's your life. You can't—'

'Can and am. I want you to have the shop. It's all arranged. You've been brilliant here, the customers love you, you're a great walking advert for the business with all those retro frocks you wear, you did the stonking deal with the dry-cleaners, you're ace at selling—and you're nearly thirty, you've got

7

no one permanent in your life and you're basically rootless. You need stability.'

Frankie sucked in her breath. OK, if the blush-making litany of entrepreneurial praise was more or less true, the last part of the statement definitely was. She was nearly thirty, with no significant other—there had been no significant other on the scene for years, and even the last insignificant other had been months ago—and nothing to show for her years of working in various retail outlets except a few paltry possessions that would fit into a couple of bin bags.

'But you can't just *give* me a shop!'

'Can and have.'

Frankie, still pretty sure this was just another one of Rita's jokes, nodded. 'So, come December, I'll be running Francesca's Fabulous Frocks, and where will you be?'

'Mykonos.'

'*Mykonos?*' Frankie blinked. '*Mykonos?*'

'Mykonos,' Rita said, beaming. 'Greek island. Glorious, laid-back, hot, one-time slightly risqué playground of the rich and famous, now just fabulous. Can't wait. It's going to be a million times better than spending yet another miserable cold winter in Kingston Dapple.'

OK. Frankie nodded. It was beginning to make sense at last. Well, some of it anyway. Rita hadn't had a proper holiday in all the time she'd known her. December in Mykonos would be wonderful. She'd misunderstood the rest of it. Rita *was* having a bit of a life-laundry moment and just wanted her to be in charge of the shop while she was away.

'Are you going on holiday for the whole month?'

'Nope.' Rita glowered again at the relentless rain

sweeping across the deserted market square outside the shop. 'I'm going to live there. For ever and ever.'

'But you can't go! I'll miss you!'

'And I'll miss you, too. But once we're settled you can come and stay with us in our beachside taverna.'

'What taverna? You never mentioned a taverna ... And there's a lot of "we" and "us" there.' Frankie frowned. 'Is this a sort of daydream to while away the grim grey hours of Kingston Dapple's November non-shopping? You're pretending to be Shirley Valentine, and Brian from the kebab van is going to be your Costas or whatever, and—'

'I'm not pretending anything, love. I *am* going to Mykonos, and none of this involves Brian from the kebab van ...' Rita paused and smiled dreamily. 'Although actually you're not a million miles off the mark with the rest of it.'

'Aren't I? Am I getting warmer? Goody. Anyway, I know you and Brian were, um, close at one time. And he's a really nice bloke, even if he's slightly childlike and smells a bit funny.'

'A touch fatty and garlicky, maybe.' Rita shimmied round the empty shop with an imaginary partner. 'Always a hazard in his line of work. And anyway, Brian as a beau is no more. He's been an ex-paramour for some time now.'

'Oh, right.' Frankie nodded. 'So, as you've never been solo for more than five minutes ever since I've known you, who—?'

Rita stopped prancing and waddled towards the counter, puffing. 'All in good time. And actually, although he won't be going to Mykonos, Brian does

9

feature in my plans. He's having my bungalow—poor sod, still living with that bitch of a mother of his at his age.'

'No way!'

'Yes, way!'

Frankie shook her head. 'This is all getting far too weird. Does Brian know? Come on—please tell me what's happening. Have you won the lottery or something?'

'I never do the lottery, as you well know. I've never held with gambling. And no, I haven't told Brian yet. It's all sorted out though, as is the shop. The bungalow's mortgage was paid off last year, so all he'll have to find is money for the bills and what have you.'

'You're kidding, aren't you?' Frankie shook her head in bewilderment. 'You going away and Brian having your bungalow and me having the shop? I mean, I couldn't afford the lease on the shop or anything—I don't even have a house to use as collateral and my overdraft is maxed out and—'

'No need to worry about any of that,' Rita said smugly. 'It's all taken care of. Change of name and everything. Lease, rent, business rates, utilities—all of it. Twelve months paid up front—or at least, the funds are lodged with my solicitor to take care of. You'll have a year, hassle free, to make this shop your own. After that it'll be up to you.'

Stunned beyond belief, Frankie simply stared.

'Say something.' Rita stood in front of the counter, still puffing slightly. 'I thought you'd be pleased.'

'Pleased?' Frankie swallowed. 'Pleased? How can I be pleased? You're leaving me!'

'I'm also leaving you the shop.'

'Yes, OK—right then—if that bit's true then I'm absolutely delighted and will never be able to thank you enough. But as I still don't believe a word of it.'

'Start believing, love. I'm off to Mykonos in two weeks' time. Most of my clothes will come here, everything else unnecessary is going to Biff and Hedley Pippin's charity shop in Winterbrook, and I'm bequeathing what remains of my life to those who I love best and who deserve it. And you, Frankie angel, deserve it more than anyone. Now, you go and put the kettle on and we'll have another one of Patsy's Pantry's rum babas to celebrate. I'm so going to miss those retro cakes from Hazy Hassocks when I'm in Mykonos—you'll have to send some out to me, won't you?'

In a complete daze, Frankie headed for the kitchen and watched the raindrops trickle in non-stop trails down the windows as she waited for the kettle to boil. Suppose it *was* all true? How fantastic would that be? The one thing she'd always wanted. Her own business. And not just any business, but this fabulous retro shop ...

But it couldn't possibly be true, could it? Things like that didn't happen to people like her, did they?

And, just supposing it *was* true and Rita was heading off for some Greek island paradise, which seemed impossible—she'd miss Rita so much. Rita made work seem like fun. Rita had given her a chance three years ago when she thought she'd never be able to work again after the horrors of leaving her fashion retail job in Masons under a bit of a cloud.

And would she, Frankie, ever be able to cope with running an entire shop on her own? Well, maybe, but what did she know about the business

11

side of this shop anyway? Rita had always taken care of all that. Frankie sighed as she sloshed water into the mugs—goodness, there were so many things to think about.

And if Rita went, nothing in Kingston Dapple would ever be the same again ...

Chapter Two

By the time the coffee was made and the rum babas glistened in gooey temptation on two plates and they were sitting in Rent-a-Frock's tiny kitchen, Rita, clearly seeing the confusion and disbelief on Frankie's face, obviously decided it was high time she made things crystal clear.

'Right—' Rita juggled a rum baba, fielding a spiral of syrup away from the scarlet frock '—now just listen to me. I went about that all the wrong way. I shouldn't have messed around with the bequeathing thing, I should have just told you. In a nice businesslike fashion. I thought it would be fun to spring it on you, but it was obviously just confusing. But you did get the gist?'

Frankie, her mouth full of rum baba, nodded.

'Good.' Rita beamed. 'As I say, all the legalese stuff has been dealt with. We can go through other things before I leave. Mind you, this has taught me something. When I tell Brian about the bungalow I'll just tell him straight, no messing about.'

'Good idea,' Frankie managed to mumble. 'Brian's not the brightest pixie in the forest. But please, please can you tell me like that, because I still don't really understand. Why exactly are you

12

going to Mykonos?'

'To make my dreams come true.' Rita managed to remove the rum baba traces from her lip gloss and smiled dreamily. 'I've bought a beachside taverna. I'm going to live in shorts and flip-flops for ever and ever. I've used my entire life savings. This shop has done me nicely over the years. I've invested well in the good times. I don't need the money from the sale of the shop or the bungalow. I love you, and in a way I love poor Brian, too. I want you both to have what I've been lucky enough to have but no longer need.'

'Thank you, but—'

'Don't tell me you've never had a dream,' Rita interrupted, 'because I know differently. How many times, since you've been working here, have you said your dream was to own your own clothes shop?'

'Well, yes, of course that was what I've always wanted. But I always imagined it was an impossible dream. I didn't expect you to make it come true—never, ever in a million years.'

'Just call me your fairy godmother, then. Making your dreams come true, just like I've done with mine.' Rita beamed happily as she poured more coffee. 'You see, Mykonos was my dream from the day I first saw a picture of it in my children's encyclopedia at the age of eight. It was as far removed from where I lived as the moon. I've wanted to live there ever since.'

'But you've never been there, have you?'

'No. Not yet. I never wanted to go there and come home. I just wanted to go there—and stay. And now, when I see it for the first time—really, really see it—it'll be because I'm going to live there

13

for the rest of my life.'

'But what if you hate it?'

'Hate it?' Rita spluttered. 'How could I hate it? I'll adore it. It's my destiny.'

'But you won't know anyone, and how can you have bought a taverna if you've never been there, and who's the "we" and "us"?'

'Well—' Rita's eyes sparkled '—that's the other exciting part of the story—Oh, damn, was that the door? Yes. Oh, sod it, I think we've got a customer.'

'Aren't you supposed to say, "Oh, goody, I think we've got a customer, on this very quiet trading day"?' Frankie grinned. 'Or have I got it all wrong?'

Rita frowned as they made their way out of the kitchen. 'No, you've got it right, but I did want to talk to you without interruptions … and the customer is bloody Biddy. You serve her, love. I want to get out of this frock, and Biddy always brings out the worst in me, I'm afraid.'

Rent-a-Frock's door was wide open and, in a torrent of horizontal rain, a small woman swathed in a dripping mac and flourishing an even more dripping umbrella, catapulted in.

'Black!' she announced from beneath the peak of her see-through Rain Mate. 'I need black!'

'Hello, Biddy. Nice to see you again. Nasty day, isn't it? Let's shut the door, shall we? Oh, and please try not to drip on the floor too much—health and safety, you know.' Rita paused on her way to the curtained-off changing cubicles. 'And for pity's sake put that umbrella down. You know it's bad luck to have an umbrella up indoors.'

Biddy, still dripping, complied with bad grace. The umbrella's shower managed to soak everything within a two-foot radius in the process.

14

Frankie, despite her head reeling, slipped automatically into her friendly, chatty shop-assistant default setting.

'You're looking for black?' she enquired. 'Lovely. Party wear for Christmas?'

'Hardly.' Biddy sniffed. 'Funeral. Tomorrow.'

'Ah, right ... Sorry. I do hope it wasn't someone close.'

'No, well, not family. More a sort of friend. Acquaintance, really. Ernie Yardley.'

Frankie looked vague. 'I don't think I know him.'

Biddy wiped away more raindrops. 'You wouldn't. He lives—lived—alone in Tadpole Bridge. His wife, Achsah died some time back—real lovely funeral she had.'

'Achsah?' Frankie frowned. 'That's a very unusual name. I've never heard that before. Is it Russian or something?'

'Goodness me, no. Achsah was Berkshire born and bred. It's biblical. Her dad was a bit of a fire and brimstone man by all accounts.' Biddy looked disapproving. 'All her brothers and sisters had really obscure Old Testament names. Silly, I call it. Anyway, Ernie belongs—belonged—to our Seniors Day Group.'

'Was he a good age?'

'One of the oldest in the group at eighty-three, but fit as a fiddle as far as I knew.' Biddy shook herself, drenching a row of nearly new but slightly shrunken cardigans. 'Apparently he'd had heart trouble for years, though.'

'Oh dear.' Frankie desperately hoped she looked and sounded sympathetic. All she really wanted to do was serve Biddy and get back to talking to Rita about the shop. 'Anyway, I don't suppose you want

15

to discuss it, so—'

'Shocking, it was.' Biddy's pale gooseberry eyes glinted. She obviously had no problems with talking about the demise. 'We had our usual weekly minibus trip to Poundland in Winterbrook, and Ernie got caught up in the melee round the retro foods. Went down like a sack of shit.'

Frankie bit her lip and stared hard at the floor.

Snorting with laughter behind her, Rita dived into the fitting rooms.

'Um ...' Frankie steadied herself with a deep breath. 'Oh dear, how awful.'

'Ah, it was.' Biddy nodded. 'He'd got his hands on the last of the Vesta beef curries too, lucky so-and-so. They're like gold dust, they are. Just reaching for a butterscotch Angel Delight to round his tea off nicely he was when it happened.'

Knowing there was nothing she could possibly say without disgracing herself, Frankie just nodded.

'Course we all had to stay put while we waited for the ambulance. I could of told 'em that was a waste of time, Ernie was as dead as a dodo, and pretty tedious it was too.'

Frankie, just itching to get rid of Biddy as quickly as possible, hoped she was still managing to look contrite. 'Er, so, are you looking for a coat for the funeral, or a dress or a suit?'

'Anything black and cheap to hire for the day.' Biddy wiped a raindrop from the end of her nose. 'No point in wasting good money on buying new just for the one day, is there?'

'Er, no. I suppose not. And, of course, hopefully, you won't be attending many other funerals.'

Biddy looked beady. 'Oh, at my age funerals are beginning to be top of the social agenda. I go to lots

16

of funerals, you know. But none of them stipulated black. Most don't these days. So if you could find me anything cheap as chips in black. I don't have anything black in my wardrobe, you see.'

'Yes, well, it doesn't suit everyone.'

Biddy nodded in a small shower of raindrops. 'It's so draining. I was told by Cherish, she's my colour palette advisor over at Hazy Hassocks, to avoid black at all costs. Cherish says I'm a blossoming spring person.'

Blossoming? Spring? Frankie blinked. Pale and gingery, Biddy looked like an anaemic squirrel.

'Teals, aquas and primroses are my hues, Cherish told me.' Biddy nodded, still dripping. 'Spring colours. But not suitable for this funeral, because—' she glowered '—this one stipulates wearing black. And I really wanted to wear my eau-de-nil two-piece. Or maybe my lemon duster coat.'

'Oh, dear,' Frankie said soothingly, thinking that any of the pale shades mentioned would make Biddy fade into even more insignificance, and wondering just what sort of warped sense of humour Cherish, the Hazy Hassocks colour-palette advisor, had. 'Right, let's see what we can find in black and a size ... what ... eight?'

'And in a petite,' Biddy added, trotting towards the overcrowded rails, removing her Rain Mate and shaking it across the floor. 'I don't want something trailing round my ankles.'

'Right ...' Frankie, practically jigging with impatience, started clawing through the disorganised rails. 'Let's see what we've got ...'

Frankie found it a dispiriting task. Apart from the fact that the whole shop was in a complete

17

muddle, and she was searching for funeral wear, Rita's astounding announcement was the only thing she could think about. Running the shop would be amazing, of course, but what would life be like without Rita? Frankie knew exactly what it would be like: unthinkable, that's what.

'How about this?' Frankie pulled a black coat with a mock-astrakhan collar from the crush. 'It's your size, and nice and thick, too. You're going to need something warm in this weather, especially if you've got to, er, stand around outside ... I mean, I suppose if it's a the crematorium it wouldn't be so, er, cold.'

'It's a cremation,' Biddy confirmed almost cheerfully. 'In Thatcham. We're having a minibus. Mind you, the wind cuts across there something cruel while you're waiting to go in if there's a lot on that day. Like a conveyor belt, it is sometimes. Once you're inside the crem it's better, mind. Nice and snug. And ever so warm.'

Frankie supposed it must be. Fortunately, apart from her grandad's funeral when she'd been very young, she'd never had to find out. 'Shall we try it on?'

'I will, you won't. There's no "we" involved here. You youngsters have no idea about syntax.' Biddy snatched at the coat and stared at it. 'Hmmm, not bad. And the right size, and it'll cover everything. So I can wear something more spring-coloured underneath it, can't I?'

Frankie nodded, stepping over the abandoned soggy raincoat and fastening the black coat round Biddy's tiny frame. 'Well, unless you have to take it off at the wake, I suppose. Maybe, um, the deceased's family will expect you to be all in black.'

18

'Ernie Yardley didn't have any family to speak of.' Biddy preened and posed in front of the shop's cheval mirror. 'Just a couple of nieces or nephews or something. They're organising the funeral, they're the ones who decreed black, but they never came near Ernie while he was alive, so no doubt they're just waiting for the pickings. And slim, they'll be. Poor old Ernie had nowt to show for his life but his old age pension.'

Frankie, simply itching to shove Biddy into renting the coat and shove her out of the door so that she could talk to Rita, nodded in sympathy.

'Still, the Motions are doing the send-off, so it'll be spot on,' Biddy continued, irritatingly still keen to chat. 'Old-fashioned undertakers, they are. None of this happy-clappy stuff. They know what's what.'

Frankie perked up a bit. 'Oh, I know Slo Motion. He and Essie Rivers have got a flat in my friend Phoebe's house. He's a lovely man. So funny.'

'He's a reprobate.' Biddy sniffed. 'Don't conduct himself proper for an undertaker. Living in sin at his age—disgusting, I call it. Still, he's organised the wake back at the Faery Glen in Hazy Hassocks, which should be a good do, they always do a nice spread. So, what I'm saying is, no one will care what I'm wearing underneath once the niceties have been observed at the crem, will they?'

Frankie, not well versed in funeral etiquette, supposed not and shook her head.

'Lovely.' Rita, having composed herself while shedding the red frock and now in black trousers and a turquoise sweater, emerged from the cubicles. 'That coat could have been made for you, Biddy. Frankie always has a good eye for what suits.'

19

'Yes, I suppose she has,' Biddy admitted grudgingly as she continued to twirl and admire her reflection. 'Yes, yes, this will do nicely.'

'Will you be needing a hat?' Frankie asked. 'I think we've got some black berets somewhere … and gloves … and a scarf? If you don't wear much black, you may not have the accessories, and if, as you say, the, er, wait will be chilly …'

'Well, now you come to mention it.' Biddy unbuttoned the black coat and reached for her soggy raincoat and still-soaking umbrella. 'I don't have any of the folderols in black—Cherish advised no black whatsoever—so, yes, that's a good idea, as long as they won't cost much.'

'Nothing costs much here,' Rita said. 'You should know that by now, Biddy. OK, so while Frankie sorts you out, shall we do the paperwork?'

Frankie, rummaging through several large cardboard boxes of jumbled accessories, glanced across at the counter. Rita, chatting to Biddy as she filled out the rental copybook in triplicate, flicking the carbons into place, looked just the same. She didn't look like someone who was just about to run off to Mykonos.

'Here we are.' Frankie placed beret, gloves and scarf on the counter. 'All in black. Rita will sort out the pricing for you.'

'Two days rental, if you bring them all back by close of business on Friday.' Rita added the accessories to the handwritten accounts book. 'You'll have to pay an extra day if you leave it until Saturday.'

Frankie quickly folded everything into a large Big Sava carrier bag.

Biddy looked shocked as she parted with her

money and gathered up the receipt and bag. 'Don't you worry, they'll be back in here first thing on Friday morning when I come into Kingston Dapple to change my library books. I'm not going to be caught by your gazumping, Rita Radbone.'

'And thank you too,' Rita muttered, as they watched Biddy struggle back out into the storm. 'And there goes one of nature's charmers.'

Frankie frowned. 'Why does she pretend to be so *old*, though? She must be in her fifties, and that's young these days. She should still be in jeans and heels. Why does she dress and speak like someone *ancient*?'

'Because she's a miserable cow,' Rita said comfortably. 'Some people are born old, and Biddy's one of them. Still, it was a clever touch of yours to get the accessories added in there. See? You've got a real flare for this business. You're a natural.'

Frankie shrugged. 'Every little bit helps, as they say.'

'Mmm.' Rita beamed. 'It certainly does. Anyway, where were we before Biddy chose to interrupt me?'

'You were going to explain about the "we".'

'Ah, yes.' Rita nodded, leaning her plump arms on the countertop. 'So, as I was saying, you were almost right earlier on when you mentioned Shirley Valentine. You see, I *am* going to be Rita Valentine in Mykonos ... I'm going to be marrying Ray Valentine the day after we arrive.'

Frankie shrieked with laughter. 'Ray Valentine? You're going to Mykonos with Ray Valentine, and you're going to get *married*? Dear Lord, Rita. For a moment there I thought you were serious. Ray

21

Valentine … Funny old Ray Valentine from the market flower stall. Who in their right mind would want to marry Ray Valentine?'

'Me, actually.'

Still laughing, Frankie looked at Rita's face. Whoops. Quickly, she tried to stifle her giggles. 'Er, well, I mean, er, um … Oh, dear. You're serious, aren't you?'

'Dead.'

'Um, congratulations then. But I didn't even know you and Ray were, um …'

'There's a lot you don't know about me.' Rita still looked very miffed. 'And as for the romance with Ray, well I've managed to keep that secret, and I would very much like to keep it that way.'

'Well, yes, of course,' Frankie said quickly. 'I mean, who wouldn't? Er, that is … well, I know he pops in a lot and you're friends and he takes you to lunch every now and then, but *marriage*?'

'I fail to understand why you think me marrying Ray Valentine is so impossible.'

Frankie pushed the 'He's fat, bald, the wrong side of fifty, wears terrible clothes, smokes a pipe, smells of compost', quickly away and smiled bravely. 'Well, I mean, he's been a fixture in Kingston Dapple's marketplace for ever, and I didn't know you and he were even, um, romantic friends, let alone, um, and, well …'

'Ray's a couple of years older than me but we were at school together. He was my first crush and my first love. My only real love actually. Then he got embroiled with the dreadful Deidre Muncaster and married her, and I just, well, I just amused myself with various other people in the many, many intervening years, but I never stopped loving

22

Ray ... Then after his divorce Ray and I sort of drifted back together.'

'Did you? When was that?'

'About a year ago. After Brian from the kebab van—he understood, bless him.'

As Brian seemed to rarely understand much that was happening around him, Frankie rather doubted this. 'Blimey though, you and Ray Valentine ... I can't believe I never noticed.'

'We were very discreet, love. I know I've always been considered a bit of a good-time girl in Kingston Dapple—I didn't want anyone laughing at Ray. I can be discreet when I choose.'

As 'Rita' and 'discreet' were two words no one in Kingston Dapple would have ever used in the same sentence, Frankie decided that sniggering at this point wouldn't be the best idea she'd ever had, so she attempted to look serious. 'Er, right. And Ray's happy with Mykonos, too?'

'Ray wants to escape from here as much as I do, so he's piled his money in with mine and we've bought the taverna.'

'Which neither of you has even seen?'

'Ray has. I've seen the photos. He's been over there and done the business side of things, I've signed the paperwork over here. It's only just been finalised—which is why I've not said anything earlier. Now, we leave in two weeks' time, and we get married on the beach the day after. Which is why I'm tying up all my loose ends.'

Frankie exhaled. It still all sounded totally implausible, but it might actually be true. Rita might really be going to Mykonos with Ray. Rita might really be giving her the shop.

'But, I'll miss the wedding ... Still, you'll be

having a leaving party, won't you?'

'Sorry, love, but no. We're going low-key on everything. And we've still got loads left to do before we fly off. You and I will have to go through all the Fabulous Frocks stuff, and I'll have to get Brian sorted out with my bungalow. And Ray has to see to his flower stall, too.'

'Has he sold it?' Frankie frowned. 'What a shame. There's been a flower stall in the marketplace for ever, hasn't there?'

'Yep. Valentine's Flowers are into their third generation. But Ray's got that covered. His nephew is taking it over.'

'Oh good. Nice to know there'll still be a Valentine selling flowers in the marketplace. At least some things will stay the same. Is he local, the nephew?'

Rita paused. 'Dexter? Um … no … Comes from up Oxford way. He's Ray's brother's lad. And lad's the right word, so Ray says. He's a bit of a havoc-maker if you get my drift. Lost his job and been in a lot of trouble by all accounts. Not sure what, I didn't like to ask, but I gather it was pretty bad. I think Ray's giving him the flower stall to run to sort him out before he goes right off the rails.'

Brilliant, Frankie thought, her head still reeling. Another fat and balding Valentine in the marketplace—only this time younger and more leery and without the saving grace of Ray's kindliness and cheerful demeanour.

She could just see Dexter Valentine—a sort of mini-Ray: overweight, scruffy, with tattoos and piercings to go with his baseball cap and hoodie, and this time he'd also be work-shy, aggressive and a troublemaker.

24

Dexter Valentine, the flower stall's heir-apparent, sounded exactly what sleepy Kingston Dapple could well do without.

Chapter Three

Three weeks later, towards the end of November, everything had changed except the weather. Bone-chilling rain still poured from a pewter sky and a biting wind still rattled relentlessly across Kingston Dapple's market square.

'I don't know where to start ...' Frankie stared round the dimly lit, cold-grey interior of the shop. 'I'm totally overwhelmed by all this. I haven't got a clue what to do first.'

'I'll put the kettle on,' Lilly, Frankie's housemate who'd been roped in on her day off for the reorganisation, said cheerfully. 'It'll all look much better when we're full of caffeine.'

'Will it?' Frankie, shivering inside a thick yellow jacket, a green woollen dress, thick tights, long boots and several scarves, twirled the shop keys in her fingers. 'I wish I had your optimism. It's only been closed for week but it doesn't look like Rita's shop any more. It just looks cold and cluttered, and it smells ... well, old and unloved.'

'Like you.' Lilly giggled, her bottom wiggling in her skinny jeans as she teetered away into the kitchen on her perilous heels.

'Thanks.' Frankie pushed her way through the cramped rails and leaned listlessly against the wooden counter. 'Thanks a bunch.'

And that was the problem, Frankie thought. It

25

wasn't Rita's shop any more. The lively, laughing place that Rita had made such a pleasure to work in for the last three years had disappeared with its owner.

Rita had gone. There had been gloriously coloured photos of the Mykonos beach wedding— with Rita glamorous in a vivid sarong and Ray in matching Hawaiian shirt and Bermuda shorts, both looking ecstatic—and the pretty taverna, emailed.

The shop was hers. All hers.

Outside, the sign-writers had emblazoned FRANCESCA'S FABULOUS FROCKS in huge curlicued gold letters across a facia of deep purple. She'd spent the last weeks meeting with Rita's solicitors, accountants and business advisors and signing umpteen pieces of paper. The shop was really, truly, hers.

And she didn't have a clue what to do next.

Without Rita she was rudderless. Without Rita's cheerful friendship, she felt both lonely and alone.

'There you go.' Lilly pushed a steaming mug into Frankie's hands. 'This'll warm you up. It's pretty darn cold in here. Don't you have any heaters?'

'Thanks, and there's central heating that works from a boiler in the kitchen. We turned it off when Rita left. I'll have to get it going again, especially if I want to open up next Saturday.'

'Mmm.' Lilly, snuggled in a vivid orange wrap-around sweater, leaned against the counter beside her. 'It's pretty depressing at the moment ... and I've just thought of something.'

Frankie sighed. 'Oh dear, have you? Is it gossip about a celeb I've never heard of having an affair with someone else I've never heard of? Or someone on Twitter? Or ... '

26

Lilly, her spiky blonde hair falling into her heavily kohled eyes, looked hurt. 'I do have other thoughts sometimes, you know.'

Frankie laughed. 'I know. Sometimes you think about men, and clothes, and men, and make-up and shoes, and men and more shoes.'

'Well, if you don't want to hear my idea ...'

'Sorry, yes, of course I do.'

'It's got to do with trade descriptions.'

Frankie gazed at Lilly in surprise. What on earth did Lilly, whose entire life outside her job as a receptionist at Beauty's Blessings in Hazy Hassocks, revolved around men and clothes and shoes and glossy magazines and clubbing and reality telly shows, know about the trade descriptions act?

'Go on ...'

'Well—' Lilly blinked inch-long blue eyelashes '—the sign outside says "Francesca's Fabulous Frocks".'

'Yes, and?'

Lilly looked round the crammed jumble of rails. 'Well, it's not, is it? Frocks, I mean. It's just, well, any old tat. If it says frocks then it should be just frocks.'

Frankie, excitedly slopping coffee, hugged her. 'Lill! You're a genius!'

'I know,' Lilly sighed. 'It's such a shame no one else ever realises it. Er, why?'

'Because that's what it's going to be. What it says on the tin.'

'What tin?'

'Oh, just a figure of speech. No, seriously, you're brilliant. That's what it'll be. Just a frock shop. A lovely, gorgeous, retro frock shop.'

Frankie sat in silence for a moment, just

27

visualising it. A frock shop. A fabulous frock shop ... *Her* fabulous frock shop ... Just like it said on the sign ...

She grinned. 'We'll sort out all the dresses, and clear out everything else and see if Biff and Hedley Pippin want it for their charity shop first before we offload it elsewhere, then we'll work on sorting out the frocks and—'

'You could sort of colour code them,' Lilly said. 'Or something like that, couldn't you?'

'Yes, I could.' Quickly Frankie drained her coffee and slammed the mug and the keys on the counter. 'In fact, what I could do is make this a proper vintage shop. We can sort them into decades—we've got stuff dating from the nineteen fifties and maybe even before that in here somewhere—then into sizes, then into colours, or something along those lines. Oh, Lilly, you're amazingly clever.'

'Bless.' Lilly beamed. 'I know.'

An hour later, with the heating working beautifully, half the rails denuded, and towering mountains of other people's clothes dwarfing them, Frankie and Lilly gazed at one another.

'We need a skip or a big lorry or something.' Frankie pushed her silky black hair behind her ears. 'And a lot of other people. We'll never get rid of all this ourselves.'

'Yes, we do and, no, we won't, but looking on the bright side you've got millions of gorgeous dresses hidden away, haven't you?'

Frankie nodded enthusiastically. They'd uncovered some real gems amongst the dross.

'And the shop itself,' Lilly said, 'isn't too manky at all, really. I thought the walls would be dirty

28

and dreary—but they're OK. Cream's nice as a background.'

'Rita had it decorated last year. With difficulty.' Frankie chuckled at the memory. 'Poor old Brian from the kebab van came in on Sundays and moved stock from one side to the other until it was all done. So, at least that's one thing I don't need to worry about. Although I'll need some other sort of decoration now if we're just going to be frocks, won't I? Posters and pictures and maybe things that relate to each of the decades.'

'Mmm. Sounds great. But—' Lilly hauled herself up onto the counter to survey the devastation '—what I don't understand is—well, loads of things really.'

Frankie smiled. 'Like the meaning of the universe? Nah, that always baffles me, too.'

'Like,' Lilly continued, 'how did Rita make this place work? How did she ever make any money?'

'Rita was pretty astute and she'd been running this for all her working life and been successful. Well, she must have been—she made and saved enough money over the years to be able to leave this—and her bungalow—and whiz off to Mykonos and buy a taverna.'

'Yeah, I suppose,' Lilly said doubtfully. 'She must have been very clever with her money, though.'

'She said she had savings and investments.'

'Really? How clever. I wish I did. My salary is always spent before it's earned. But, I mean, if she never sold anything, just rented it out, then took in more stuff, surely there must have come a time—like now—when there just wasn't room for any more things?'

'Quite often,' Frankie agreed, pulling herself up

29

onto the counter too. 'We used to have clear-outs sometimes. Stuff that never moved. We used to donate it to the charity shops, but Rita never turned anything wearable away.'

'Obviously. So, once she'd paid someone for it, you just hired it out over and over again?'

Frankie nodded.

'And—' Lilly frowned '—then you'd have to have it cleaned every time—which costs—before you rented it out again—so, why didn't she just sell it?'

'Because Rita didn't like to part with anything. And she thought renting, hiring, whatever, offered a good service to people who couldn't afford, or didn't want to, buy.'

'Right.' Lilly flicked through the pile of duplicate accounting books on the countertop. 'And you did all the transactions in here, did you?'

'Yes. Rita didn't trust computers. Not for the business. Even the till is manual. It's all very nineteen fifties.' Frankie shook her head. 'Which is nice and cosy and all that, and OK for what Rita was doing, but not for me and the twenty-first century. I intend to change all that.'

Lilly nodded. 'Mmm, Jennifer Blessing would have a fit. She's ace at business, is Jennifer. She sent me on all those IT courses when she updated her systems at the salon and ...'

Frankie wasn't listening. Jennifer Blessing's high-tech beauty salon was a million miles away from Rita's Rent-a-Frock. Except, of course, it wasn't Rita's any more, was it? And she'd already decided to buy a computer from the capital allowance that the accountant had told her was in the business account for exactly that sort of purchase. And she'd ordered a whole mountain of

Francesca's Fabulous Frocks carrier bags in gold and purple. She was getting there—slowly.

She suddenly frowned at the still-chattering Lilly. 'Sorry, but what did you say earlier?'

'About the courses Jennifer Blessing sent me on?' Lilly wrinkled her forehead. 'Oh, just that there weren't many men on them, but I did meet that really cute boy, Daniel, the one with the piercings, and—'

'No, what did you say before that.'

'I don't know.' Lilly looked anxious. 'I can't remember that far back.'

'Selling. You said something about selling.'

'Oh, yes.' Lilly beamed happily. 'So I did.'

'Exactly!' Frankie clapped her hands in delight. 'Because that's what I'm going to do. Sell not rent. It's not Rita's shop any more, so there'll be no more *buying* other people's old clothes. I'll just take donations of frocks. And no more renting or hiring, just selling. Paying for them isn't good business, selling them is very good for business. Simples!'

Lilly, looking slightly confused, frowned. 'Well, yes. You should be making money, not spending it. Jennifer says—'

'Jennifer Blessing makes Lord Sugar look like an enthusiastic amateur,' Frankie said, laughing. 'But of course she's right. And so am I. When this reopens as Francesca's Fabulous Frocks that's what I'm going to do. I'll take in the unwanted frocks and sell them. Which means—' she picked up the duplicate books '—that these can go straight into the archives. As soon as I get the computer later this week, I'll have to get a sort of stock-and-sale system up and running, and pricing and everything else.'

31

The new system may well alienate some of Rita's regular clients—people like the funeral-going Biddy—she'd have to work round that somehow and try not to lose customers, but otherwise it all made perfect sense.

Lilly slid from the counter. 'I can help you with setting up some of the computer stuff if you like. I do it for Jennifer.'

'Can you? Do you?' Frankie watched as Lilly swayed seductively between the heaps of clothes towards the blacked-out windows. 'Honestly, Lilly, you're full of surprises.'

'Because I'm an airhead?' Lilly looked over her shoulder. 'Yeah, well, Jennifer is dead scary let me tell you. I had to learn that data input stuff over and over again until I got it right.'

'Yes, sorry. I didn't mean to—'

'Yeah, you did,' Lilly said happily. 'I don't mind. I know I'm not as stupid as everyone thinks I am. Well, not really.'

Frankie laughed, then frowned. 'And they're terrible, too.'

'What are?'

'These lovely big double windows. All that space all piled with rubbish. Rita never had much of an eye for window dressing. She just piled stuff in there. She said everyone knew what the shop did so there was no need to make a meal of the windows. I'm going to clear it out and do a proper window display and change it regularly.'

'Yeah, right. In the spare time you've got between sorting out this lot and getting the place up and running.' Lilly pulled a face then peered out of the door at the rain-swept market square.

'Yes, but,' Frankie sighed, 'I'm missing so

many tricks here. It's nearly Christmas—I need a Christmas window display.'

'Yeah.' Lilly nodded. 'At Beauty's Blessings Jennifer has had a Christmas window display in place since October. So you'll need to get a shift on. You've only got a month.'

'I know.' Frankie nodded. 'Don't remind me. Christmas is obviously an optimum trading time. Everyone wanting to buy things, and that's what I've got to give them. Things to buy. I'm going to have to sort out all the party frocks and stick them in the window, drape a lot of twinkly, sparkly stuff round them, find some holly and baubles and—'

'Ohmigod!' Lilly suddenly shrieked. 'No way!'

'What?' Frankie looked at Lilly in alarm. 'What's the matter?'

'Out there!' Lilly turned wide-eyed. 'Come and have a look! Out there! Quick!'

Frankie frowned. She couldn't imagine anything remotely exciting happening in Kingston Dapple's marketplace. Nothing ever had or did.

Kingston Dapple's cobbled market square was really three-sided, with the fourth side opening on to the sleepy High Street. Traffic meandered up and down there, as did the village shoppers, and any deliveries to the rear of the marketplace's pre-war shops were made from a narrow horseshoe-shaped service road looping off the High Street. The buildings were Victorian, tall and close-packed, the roads hundreds of years old and almost single lane. The twenty-first century had had very little impact. In fact, Frankie reckoned, nothing much had changed in Kingston Dapple for at least a hundred years.

Apart from Rita's, no, *her* shop, there was

the Greasy Spoon caff, a small stationer's-cum-newsagent's, a shoe shop selling sensible sandals and cosy slippers, a toy shop, a gift-type shop selling postcards and collectibles of the rather ugly plaster variety, a greengrocer's and a butcher's.

And, of course, the Toad in the Hole pub.

The Toad had, for centuries, been the Kingston Arms Hotel, coaching inn and hostelry, until becoming very run-down in the 1970s. It had mouldered for quite some time before being bought by an up-and-coming brewery chain. As it was a listed building, outside the ancient architecture remained the same as it had ever been, but now alienated most of the village's beer 'n' a bag of crisps pub-goers by incongruously housing a very minimalist glass, chrome and spotlit gastro bar. The Toad currently provided Kingston Dapple's only nightlife.

Unless, Frankie thought vaguely, you counted the various weekend shindigs in the village hall. Which very few rational people ever did.

So, the only other additions to the market square were the space where Brian parked his kebab van every evening, after doing his rounds of the villages, from 'ten 'til midnight depending on the weather and the number of munchy-headed revellers staggering from the Toad', and Ray Valentine's closed-down flower stall.

There was nothing out there, especially on a wet and windy freezing cold November day, Frankie thought, likely to warrant Lilly's reaction. Then again, she thought as she negotiated the heaps of second-hand clothes to reach the door, Lilly was always a little bit OTT.

'Frankie!' Lilly urged again. 'Quick!'

34

'What?' Frankie peered over Lilly's shoulder. 'What am I looking at? Where?'

'There!' Lilly, wide-eyed, jabbed a midnight-blue sparkly talon across the square.

Frankie peered some more. A few hardy souls, heads down against the storm, were attempting to fight their way into the shops, but apart from them, she could see nothing.

'Look!' Lilly grabbed her arm. 'Him! Just opening up Ray's flower place ... Wow! What a body! What a face! Isn't he just the most gorgeous thing you've ever seen? Isn't he just sooo fit? I love all that layered hair and those cheekbones and I bet he's got just a hint of stubble. Sooo sexy. He's ... he's ...' She furrowed her brow and then beamed. 'Oooh, he's just totally Beckhamesque!'

Chapter Four

Frankie laughed. The description was absolutely perfect. Despite the weather, the very attractive man darting in and out of the flower shack's open door, managed to look elegant and golden and achingly cool. Dressed in jeans and boots and a battered leather jacket with the collar turned up, and with his sun-bleached streaky hair feathering in the wind, he was certainly extremely eye-catching.

'Wonder who he is?' Lilly pressed her nose against the glass. 'Any ideas? Is he the one taking over from Ray? Nephew or something, you said, didn't you? Oh, wow, if he is, how fab would that be?'

'Well, yes it would be, but no, I don't think he

35

can possibly be Dexter Valentine,' Frankie said. 'That bloke's probably someone from the council making sure Ray's stall hasn't been vandalised.'

'Shame.' Lilly pressed even closer to the door. 'Because he'd be just lovely to look at every day—even for a man-hater like you—wouldn't he?'

'I'm not a man-hater,' Frankie said quickly. 'I'm just a bit more picky than you are. And I'm sure he isn't Ray's nephew, because I sort of gathered from Rita that he was a Ray lookalike, only younger and a lot less pleasant. I'm guessing Dexter Valentine, when and if, he ever turns up, will be a fat slob with a beer gut and a builder's bum—in fact, a whole lot less attractive than that.'

'I know, you said.' Lilly gazed dreamily across the square. 'So it can't be him, can it? Sod it—because he is sooo hot. Maybe he is from the council then. Still, whoever he is, I'm in love.'

'Why aren't I surprised? Poor bloke won't stand a chance,' Frankie laughed, watching him standing outside the flower stall shack now in the storm, looking rather bemusedly at the rain bouncing relentlessly off the empty wooden decking tiers. 'But I wonder who he is? And what on earth does he think he's doing over there?'

'I'll go and ask,' Lilly said, tugging open the door and allowing the bitter wind and a lot of very wet leaves billow into the shop.

'Lill, noooo!' Frankie groaned.

Too late. Lilly, slipping and slithering across the cobbles in her ridiculous heels, had already gone.

Frankie grinned to herself. No doubt the Beckhamesque beauty—if he was available, or even if he wasn't, yet—would soon be a regular feature of their shared house, until Lilly fell in love with

36

someone else.

Sometimes Frankie wished she had Lilly's happy equanimity towards relationships. But then, Lilly had never been in love had she? Not really, really in love. And that was the problem: once you'd been hopelessly, besottedly, heart and soul, once and for ever, in love, it became very hard to settle for anything less.

As she well knew.

She watched in amusement as Lilly, her blonde spikes seemingly wind and rain resistant, bounced up to the golden David lookalike and smiled and started chatting, in typical Lilly fashion, with both her hands and her mouth.

Now he was laughing. And talking back. And Lilly was waving extravagantly towards the shop, and, oh Lordy, they were coming over ...

The door flew open again, with yet another flurry of freezing wind, slashing rain and wet leaves.

'It's *him*!' Lilly beamed, ushering the Beckhamesque beauty into the shop. 'He *is* Dexter Valentine! How amazing is that?'

Amazing, Frankie thought, blinking hard at Dexter Valentine who, despite being wet and windswept, managed to look even more gorgeous close to than he'd been from a distance. Totally amazing ...

In fact, so devastatingly amazing that if she wasn't careful she'd be joining Lilly in openly drooling.

How wrong had Rita got that then? And if she'd been wrong about Dexter's physical appearance, maybe she'd been wrong about the rest too? Maybe Dexter Valentine was hard-working and decent and ...

37

Quickly remembering her manners, she stopped staring and smiled in what she hoped was a warm and friendly but definitely disinterested way. 'Hi, then. Welcome to the entrepreneurial hub of Kingston Dapple. I'm Frankie Meredith, and no doubt Lilly has already introduced herself.'

'She has.' Dexter nodded, his tawny eyes laughing, and holding out his hand. 'Great to meet you.'

They shook hands. The first touch of flesh on flesh was tantalisingly electric. Dexter looked far more at ease with it than Frankie felt. His eyes were on a level with hers and she dropped her hand and looked away first.

'Not the best weather to see your new business for the first time,' Frankie said, trying to regain control, and immediately inwardly cursing herself for falling back on the weather as an opening gambit. She sounded like her gran. Damn it.

'It's not.' Dexter brushed raindrops from the leather jacket. 'But this—' he cast a slow appraising glance round the shop, and an even slower and more appraising one over her and Lilly '—is pretty cool. And to think I was really dreading coming here. I thought Kingston Dapple was going to be the carbuncle on the boil from hell. Now—' he grinned at them both '—I can't thank Ray enough for running off with your ex-boss to re-enact *Captain Corelli's Mandolin* or whatever it is he's done as a result of his midlife crisis.'

Despite herself, Frankie giggled. After all, it was pretty close to what she'd thought herself about Rita and Ray's romantic adventure, wasn't it?

And, oops, Dexter was not just a total havoc-maker and utterly irresistible, but he also clearly had a sense of humour. It was an extremely heady combination.

'I'll put the kettle on,' Lilly said happily, swaying off into the kitchen. 'I told Dexter you'd be surprised it was him. I told him you said he was a lazy fat thug.'

Frankie groaned.

'She did,' Dexter confirmed cheerfully. 'I was very hurt.'

'Sorry,' Frankie muttered, still trying not to stare too much at the streaky-haired, tawny-eyed gorgeousness. 'It's just that you didn't come with a very good build-up.'

'Hardly surprising,' Dexter said easily. 'I've been a huge disappointment to the family. Turning me into Berkshire's answer to Alan Titchmarsh is the last hope of any salvation, apparently.'

'Er ...' Frankie was still horribly embarrassed. 'So, do you like flowers? Um, horticulture? Is it your business?'

'I know slightly less about flowers than I do about nucleonics.'

'Right.' Frankie pushed her hair behind her ears again. 'So, why ... ?'

'Like I said—' Dexter stared round the devastation of the frock shop '—it was Ray's plan to rescue me from the bad place I'd, um, found myself in. And, to be honest, as I was out of work and needed to get out of Oxford—things had got a bit complicated—a ready-made business was too good an offer to turn down. Ray's left me a healthy float and loads of info about suppliers and markets and things. I'm going to sort out the restocking tomorrow. I expect I'll pick it up as I go along.'

Frankie thought that while Rita may have got

39

the physical side of Dexter completely wrong, she'd obviously been spot on with the rest of it.

'So, what about you?' Dexter continued, seemingly unembarrassed by admitting he was both escaping from some misdemeanour in Oxford, and totally inept as a florist. 'You seem to be in a bit of a muddle here.'

'Understatement. I'm hoping to reopen by the weekend but at the moment I'm a bit overwhelmed.'

'You've inherited all this from Ray's Rita, haven't you?'

Frankie nodded.

Dexter laughed. 'He told me a lot about you.'

Oh, Lordy ... Frankie took a deep breath. 'Did he?'

'He did.' Dexter gave her the lazy appraising glance again. 'And unlike my own pre-appearance hype, he seems to have got it dead right.'

Frankie was pretty sure she was blushing. How awful was that? She hadn't blushed since she was a teenager.

Dexter nodded. 'So, we've sort of been chucked into the same rocky boat, haven't we? Thrown in at the deep end, in the middle of winter, with businesses we have very little idea about running and which could easily go belly up in the present economic climate.'

Great, Frankie thought. Look on the bright side. 'Actually, I'm really excited about running this shop. I've got some great ideas and—'

'Coffee!' Lilly teetered back into the shop carrying a tray and plonked it down on the counter. 'Now—' she beamed at Dexter '—as you and Frankie are almost related by marriage you've obviously got loads to catch up on. Why don't we all go to the Toad later and do the lovely getting-to-know-you thing?'

'Not tonight, Lilly,' Frankie said quickly, before Dexter could say anything. Anyone as gorgeous as Dexter was bound to be already heavily attached and certainly wouldn't want either her or Lilly tagging along. 'I'm going to be here all night sorting this lot out. I'll need to rope in an entire army if I'm going to be open by the weekend.'

'OK,' Lilly said cheerfully, hauling herself up on to the counter, 'that just leaves me and Dexter then.'

'Sounds good to me.' Dexter used the sexy tawny eyes to their full advantage. 'Especially as I only have a lonely bedsit to go back to.'

'Really? In Kingston Dapple?' Lilly asked ingenuously. 'Me and Frankie live in Featherbed Lane. Are you anywhere close to that?'

'No idea.' Dexter wrapped his hands round his mug of coffee. 'I don't know anything about the village at all. Ray sorted out the bedsit for me—he's been pretty good on all fronts. I just dumped my stuff there an hour ago before I came to have a look at the flower stall. It's somewhere off the High Street. In Peep 'o' Day Passage?'

'Oh, lovely.' Lilly nodded. 'Really close. Well, nowhere in Kingston Dapple is very far from anywhere else so we'll be practically neighbours. Are you sharing with anyone?'

Frankie, her mouth full of coffee, spluttered.

Dexter shook his head. 'No. It's just me and the lonely bedsit.'

'Oh, great.' Lilly grinned. 'Another singleton! We can meet about eight in the Toad then if that's

41

OK with you?'

'Fine with me.' Dexter grinned back at her over the rim of his coffee mug. 'But won't you be needed here? If, um, Frankie has got to be up and running by the weekend I reckon she's going to need all the help she can get.'

Lilly pouted. She still managed to look cute. 'Oh, I didn't think of that.'

Frankie shrugged. 'Please don't let me interfere with your social life. I'll be fine. I'm going to call in as many favours as I can and get everyone here tonight to shift this lot.'

'That's OK then.' Lilly beamed at her. 'You can come over to the Toad and join us when you're finished.'

Dexter didn't look so sure. 'Perhaps it would be much better if we all mucked in and helped?'

Frankie looked at him in surprise. Maybe he wasn't all bad. Maybe the Oxford misdemeanours hadn't been *that* awful.

'Then,' Dexter continued, 'when we've got this place up to speed, we can all go for a drink in the pub, and maybe you two can help me get the flower stall sorted out tomorrow?'

Fat chance, Frankie thought, unless someone manages to make time stand still for a few weeks. But still, it was kind of him to offer to help her, and he was the most fabulous man she'd ever seen. Even more fabulous than . . .

'Oh, shame. I'm back at work tomorrow,' Lilly said, looking disappointed. 'But Frankie would love to help you.'

'I'm really not going to have the time.'

Lilly raised her perfectly threaded eyebrows. 'Then you should make time. Jennifer says

42

organisation is the only way to run a twenty-first century business. Jennifer says—'

'I don't care what Jennifer says.' Frankie shook her head. 'And unless Jennifer is going to magic up a whole makeover crew to get this shop sorted out then I don't think she's particularly relevant right now, do you?'

'Touchy.' Lilly giggled. 'You need to chillax big time. But yeah, OK—I s'pose if we all get stuck in here tonight it could be fun.'

Fun, Frankie thought ruefully, it wasn't going to be. Just an awful lot of hard work. And resulting in probably even more mess. However, with the addition of the totally devastating Dexter to stare at when things got really stressful she may just cope.

She reached for her mobile phone. 'I'll just make some calls then, and see who's up for a bit of hefting and heaving.'

Chapter Five

Three hours later, as the cold November night closed in and the wind and rain howled ever more viciously outside, Francesca's Fabulous Frocks was noisily filled with people.

Most of them, Frankie was sure, had only turned up out of rural nosiness to see what she intended to do with her unexpected inheritance. Her friends—and Lilly's—she knew, were there mainly to try clothes on and see if there was anything worth having in amongst the jumble, but several stalwarts actually seemed keen to help.

'Bit of fun, this, isn't it?' Brian from the kebab

43

van grinned happily as, with steam rising from his soaking duffel coat, he helped a delighted Biff and Hedley Pippin with armfuls of clothing to load their charity shop van. 'Like in the Blitz. All mucking in together.'

'As you're no m ore'n fifty-five you can't possibly have known what it was like in the Blitz,' Hedley Pippin said testily, tripping over a trailing violently coloured 1970s housecoat.

'Ah, no. But it's the spirit, see?' Brian said merrily from behind a mountain of other people's jeans. 'All walks of life brought together by adversity.'

'Hardly adversity—bugger it,' Biff Pippin muttered as the pile of socks, gloves, scarves and hats toppled from her hands. 'This is like manna from heaven for us and it's a wonderful stroke of luck for young Frankie—Rita leaving her the shop—and you too, Brian. You did OK, didn't you?'

'Ah.' Brian's pale-blue saucer eyes moistened. 'I did that. Rita was always so kind to me. I had hopes of us tying the knot one day, but I knew she still carried a torch for fat Ray really. Mind, it's really lovely being in that bungalow on my own and not having my miserable ma yelling at me morning, noon and night. You know, some mornings I can make me breakfast without even having to get dressed.'

'Far too much information,' Frankie giggled, straightening up from folding a heap of T-shirts.

'I mean—' Brian looked indignant '—while still in my 'jamas, gel. Ma would never let me have breakfast in my 'jamas. Always had to be properly washed and dressed afore eight in our house. And

44

she used to check that I'd got clean hands. Treated me like a kid, she did. Never let me wear my 'jamas downstairs even when I was ill. Now sometimes I wear 'em all day on a Sunday. It's lovely.'

Frankie smiled fondly after him as he and Hedley disappeared out into the storm to load the van again. Rita, bless her, had managed to spread an awful lot of happiness with her generous bequeathing.

Surprisingly, the disparate roped-in crowd seemed to be working quite well together. The shop was being rapidly denuded of everything that wasn't needed. The good frocks—all of them—had been locked away in the small room that passed as a stock cupboard until such time as Frankie could sort them out. The rest of the stock was disappearing nicely.

'Dexter hasn't shown,' Lilly said grumpily as she helped a large lady look for anything 'suitable for the gym in a twenty-four plus, duck, if you've got it'.

'Well, he did say he was going to get something to eat, and no doubt he's got his own unpacking and settling in to do, and, let's face it, this is probably hardly the type of nightlife he's been used to.' Frankie straightened up again with yet more T-shirts. 'And if he's interested in you he'll be here, you know that.'

Lilly sighed as she showed the large lady a pair of piebald harem pants in a size six. 'You're pretty useless at sign-reading, aren't you? He's not interested in me. What?' She frowned at the large lady. 'Won't they? Not even one thigh? Ah, shame … OK. Oooh, look, jogging bottoms. Extra-extra large. Go and try them on—in the cubicles over there. A snip at a fiver and they're

45

just your colour. Sorry? Well, OK maybe maroon doesn't suit everyone but they'll look lovely on, trust me.' She watched the lady lumber away towards the cubicles then beamed at Frankie. 'There—see? Saleswoman of the year—thanks to Jennifer. Now where were we?'

'You,' Frankie said admiringly, 'were just selling rubbish to a customer. I thought we were giving it away.'

'*Giving it away*?' Lilly looked horrified.

'Well, yes. I just want shot of it.'

'And you want money for it, too,' Lilly insisted. 'At least the stuff that isn't going to charity. You have so much to learn. Like with Dexter ... He really fancies you.'

'Rubbish.' Frankie frowned. 'Of course he doesn't.'

'Duh!' Lilly struck a pose. 'He was all over you, you lucky thing. I hardly got a second glance.'

'You got far more than that. And Dexter Valentine is definitely a player. He's sexy, gorgeous, and friendly, and amusing—and he knows it. He thinks he's irresistible and any girl is fair game. I bet he flirts with every female he comes into contact with. I've known loads of men like Dexter.'

'Really?' Lilly smiled gently. 'Why haven't I met any of them, then? We've been housemates for three years and—'

'You know what I mean,' Frankie said quickly.

'Yeah.' Lilly clambered over the discarded harem pants and gave her a swift hug. 'And if I ever meet the bastard who broke your heart I'll give him a good slap.'

'Thanks.'

Fortunately, Frankie thought, the chances of

Lilly, or anyone else, ever finding out about Joseph Mason were slim to nil. And the chances of them ever meeting were even slimmer.

She watched in amusement as the large lady emerged from the cubicles and beamed at Lilly, declaring the jogging pants were '... exactly what I was looking for, duck. You're a clever girl.' The lady then handed Lilly a five pound note.

'See,' Lilly said triumphantly as she passed, 'easy peasy. I'm putting the money in the biscuit tin in the kitchen. We've got loads in there already.'

The door flew open again.

'What's going on in here?' Biddy-the-funeral-goer demanded as she elbowed her way through the crowds, her pointy nose twitching, making her look even more like an inquisitive squirrel. 'I was just passing on my way to the bus stop and I saw the lights and I wondered if you were doing a late-night opening.'

'No, we're not,' Frankie said. 'I'm just having a clear-out. You're more than welcome to have a look round and see if there's anything that you'd like.'

'To hire? Why would I need to hire anything on the off chance?'

'We're not going to be hiring clothes any more,' Frankie said gently, noting with some amusement that Biddy was dressed in a duck-egg blue ensemble that made her skin look like putty. Cherish, the colour-palette advisor's choice no doubt. 'When I reopen the shop I'm just going to be selling frocks.'

'Selling? Frocks? Disgusting!' Biddy snorted. 'Where are we going to get our bits and pieces from now, then?'

'Biff and Hedley Pippin are taking lots of the

47

stock for their shop,' Frankie said. 'So if you catch the off-peak bus to go into Winterbrook I'm sure you'll find something really cheap to buy in there, and it all goes to a good cause.'

'I likes the hiring, not the buying. I don't want stuff cluttering up my maisonette. And the Pippins' shop's for animals.' Biddy sniffed. 'Bloody animal charity shop they run. I ain't giving my hard-earned to no animals.'

'Oh, dear, that's a pity.' Frankie decided she really, really didn't like Biddy. 'Please excuse me, I'm really busy, but now you're here, do stay and have a look round.'

Biddy snorted again. 'Bet you're charging an arm and a leg for it and—'

The rest of her disgruntled reply was lost in a gale of giggles from the far side of the shop where Frankie's friends, Phoebe, Clemmie, Sukie and Amber, were fitting a selection of woolly hats on each other.

Biddy tutted loudly and stomped away towards a tottering heap of mixed tops in vaguely unpleasant colours.

'Whatever she wants,' Frankie hissed at Lilly, 'make sure she pays loads for it. Miserable cow.'

'So speaks the entrepreneur of the year.' Lilly giggled.

'Guess who's on their way over to give you a hand, gel?' Brian's eyes glistened as he and Biff folded several ancient and rather pungent hacking jackets into a cardboard box.

'Barack Obama? Bob Dylan? David Dimbleby?'

'Nah, don't be daft, gel. It's a lady.'

'Oh, OK. Cheryl Cole? Lady Gaga? Holly Willoughby?'

48

'Never heard of any of them neither. No, it's Maisie.'

'Maisie?'

'Maisie Fairbrother—you know—she lives in them little flats out on the Hazy Hassocks road. Rita left her all her shoes.'

'Oh, yes. I remember Rita saying that Maisie loved shoes, but I don't think I've ever seen her in here. In fact I don't think I've ever met her.'

'Maisie don't get out much,' Brian said, nodding. 'She can't use public transport, see? Not with her trouble. But she felt she ought to make the effort to help out seeing as she got all them shoes. I saw her earlier and told her what we was doing tonight. She'll be here in a trice, will Maisie. She was getting a taxi as soon as she'd had her Toast Topper.'

'That's very kind of her,' Frankie said, wondering what sort of trouble Maisie had. Presumably it wasn't the same as Dexter's. 'I'll look forward to meeting her.'

'Ah, you just have to take Maisie as you finds her, gel. Know what I mean?'

'Yes, of course,' said Frankie, who didn't. 'Oh, steady with those ...'

She dived towards a couple of elderly women who were tottering towards the door with armfuls of clothing.

'Here, let me help you. I'll just open the door, shall I?'

The elderly duo smiled their thanks as they disappeared into the wild night. Frankie had to lean on the door to close it. Blimey, the wind was strong ...

'You can't keep me out like that,' Dexter panted through the gap. 'It's been tried before.'

49

Laughing, Frankie opened the door. 'Sorry, I didn't notice you.'

'And that's not a phrase I've heard very often, either.' Dexter, glistening with raindrops, grinned at her. 'Sorry I'm late. I got delayed.'

Frankie, attempting not to be impressed, again, by the devastating good looks, also tried hard not to speculate on what—or who—might have caused the lateness. It was none of her business. And anyway, she didn't care, did she? 'It's fine. It's good of you to even volunteer on your first night.'

'Wouldn't have missed it for the world,' Dexter said, his eyes lingering on her for just a second too long before looking round the shop. 'You've worked miracles in here.'

'Not just me,' Frankie said, noting with amusement that Phoebe, Amber, Sukie and Clemmie—all of whom had gloriously sexy partners of their own—had stopped trying on the woolly headgear and were staring admiringly at Dexter. 'I've got some really good friends, and so had Rita. They've all mucked in.'

'So I can see. Right, what would you like me to do?'

'Hi, Dexter—and ooh, where to start.' Lilly chuckled, sashaying towards the kitchen with the money box biscuit tin. 'And was that an open invite to all-comers or simply for little old me?'

'Ignore her.' Frankie laughed. 'At least until later. And actually we could do with a bit of muscle to carry out those bigger boxes to the van outside. Biff, Hedley and Brian are all nearly pensionable age and must be getting tired by now.'

'Fine.' Dexter slid out of the leather jacket, displaying even more of the fabulously toned body as he pushed up the sleeves of his black sweater. 'Just point me in the right direction.'

'Well, we've got a box ready for the Salvation Army to collect, and all those piles of clothes over there have been allocated to the Pippins' charity shop. Lilly's got the other stuff sort of cordoned off by the counter, and all the saleable frocks are safely out of the way. Biff and Hedley have just taken a vanload back to Winterbrook, so maybe you could carry the next lot over to the door ready for the return trip?'

Dexter nodded. 'Actually, I've got my car parked right outside—I didn't see any double yellows—so I could load it up and drive over to, um, wherever it is, if you like.'

'Brilliant. Thank you. You can have Brian as navigator as you don't know the area.'

'Brian?' Dexter screwed up the tawny eyes and scanned the crowd.

'The big bloke over there with the wild hair and the duffle coat.'

'Ah, right. He looks, um ...'

'Brian's lovely,' Frankie said quickly. 'Like a large child, kind, hard-working and very eager to please. He runs the kebab van in the marketplace.'

'Does he? I'll have to cultivate him then.' Dexter laughed. 'Nothing like a kebab after a good night out, and that means he's another one of us, doesn't it?'

'"Us"?'

'The Kingston Dapple market traders association.'

Frankie smiled. 'Yes, I suppose it does. Did you get settled in OK?'

'Into the soulless bedsit? Yes. I travelled light—

51

by necessity—so it didn't take long to unpack. And I found a late-opening supermarket to stock up on the basics in one of the neighbouring villages. There's nothing much in that line in Kingston Dapple, is there?'

Frankie shook her head. 'No, not really. Everyone goes to Big Sava in Hazy Hassocks, but there are Tescos and Sainsburys and proper shops in Winterbrook.'

'Big Sava! That was it.' Dexter beamed. 'They had everything I needed. I even managed to microwave a curry for my dinner, so I won't starve. And I called up a few of Ray's contacts. I'm getting my first delivery tomorrow. All seasonal stuff— poinsettias, holly, mistletoe, festive wreaths, that sort of thing. Apparently I'll have to go to the flower markets myself in future, but at least I'll have some stock to start with. It all took far longer than I'd thought, which is why I'm so late.'

'Great, er, I mean, I'm pleased you're getting stuff sorted out too. OK, now let me introduce you to Brian, oh, and it might be better if you don't mention Ray too much. Brian had, um, a bit of a romantic liaison with Rita for quite a long time.'

'Really? Did she jilt him for Ray?'

'Not exactly jilt, no. But I think Brian was more hurt than he lets on.'

'OK.' Dexter smiled. 'Poor Brian. We've all been there, haven't we?'

I may have, Frankie thought, but I very much doubt that you've ever been anything other than the cause of any amount of heartbreak. I doubt if you'd understand for a minute how Brian feels, or me, for that matter.

'I can be sensitive when needed, you know,'

Dexter said, as if he'd read her mind. 'I'm not as bad as people think.'

Not sure that she believed him, and very aware that every female in the shop stopped and stared at him as she manoeuvred Dexter through the throng towards Brian, Frankie decided to ignore what might be pretty dangerous ground. 'Whatever. Handsome is as handsome does, as my gran always says.'

'Mine too.' Dexter nodded innocently. 'I never understood it.'

Exchanging an eye-meet with a giggling Lilly across the shop, Frankie tapped Brian on the shoulder. 'Brian, I've got someone to introduce to you.'

'Have you, gel?' Brian peered at her. 'That's nice. I like meeting people.'

Dexter held out his hand. 'Hi, Brian. I'm Dexter. I'm new round here and I'm going to need your help.'

Nicely done, Frankie thought grudgingly, leaving Brian excitedly agreeing to be Dexter's navigator to Winterbrook.

In fact, she thought, looking round the shop, the whole evening was going very nicely indeed. It was far better than she'd ever hoped. Maybe Francesca's Fabulous Frocks really would be open by the weekend.

The door rattled and then swung open, allowing yet more of the storm to billow icily inside.

'Hello, sweetheart. Am I too late?' A plump and slightly bedraggled figure, draped in a voluminous raincoat with a massive hood over her cauliflower-head perm, and swaying on ridiculously high leopardskin shoes, peered into the shop. 'I couldn't get a taxi for love nor money. It's the weather, you see. Everyone wants taxis on nights like this. Still, I'm here now. I'm Maisie, sweetheart. Maisie Fairbrother.'

'Oh, yes. Brian said you were on your way. No, of course you're not too late.' Frankie pulled the door open wide. 'It's lovely to meet you and so kind of you to offer to help. Come along in and meet the crowd.'

Tossing back the raincoat's hood, Maisie Fairbrother stepped into the shop.

And screamed.

Conversations died. Laughter petered away. Giggles ceased. Everyone stopped what they were doing and stared towards Maisie and Frankie in the doorway.

'Are you all right?' Frankie asked anxiously. 'What's the matter?'

'Oooh,' Maisie gasped, striking her forehead with the back of her hand in a dramatic fashion. 'Oh my word ... I've come over all faint, sweetheart. Completely light-headed. It always happens ...'

This, Frankie reckoned, must be the trouble Brian had hinted at. Great. Maybe Maisie was shop-phobic or something.

'Let me get you a chair? A glass of water?'

Maisie shook her head weakly. 'No, no ... They won't help. Oh, my word, can't you see them, sweetheart? So many of them. They're everywhere.'

Was it agoraphobia? Frankie wondered. It must be the shop heaving with people that had brought on this panic attack. Maisie was still leaning heavily against the door for support.

'People?' She looked worriedly at Maisie. 'Well, yes, but they're all friends. They're all here to help.'

'I know that.' Maisie's voice was barely a whisper. 'That's not what I'm talking about, sweetheart. Oh, this is unbelievable.'

At a complete loss and mentally cursing Brian for even mentioning the clear-out to Maisie who was clearly not a well person, Frankie patted Maisie's damp shoulders. 'I'm sorry, I'm not sure what's wrong. Do you have a problem with crowds? Shall I get someone to run you home if you don't like being amongst all these people?'

Maisie shook her head, whimpered, and slumped a bit more.

'Maybe a nice cup of tea?' Frankie was rapidly running out of her caring repertoire. And everyone else was still silently staring. Surely someone was a first-aider or something? 'A cup of tea, with lots of sugar? Then we'll get you away from all these people, OK?'

'It's not the crowds that bother me.' Maisie sighed softly, eyes closed and still adopting the dramatic head-smiting pose. 'Not these living people in here, sweetheart. They don't worry me. They're not calling to me.'

'Aren't they? Oh, good.'

Maisie opened her eyes. 'No sweetheart, they're not. It's not the living, sweetheart. It's the dead. Ghosts, sweetheart. This shop is full of them.'

Chapter Six

Bloody hell, Frankie thought. This is all I need.

With a gentle groan, Maisie, still leaning backwards against the door, closed her eyes again and slowly slid sideways.

'She's fainted!' Frankie looked wildly round the still-staring shopful of people. 'Someone do something, please.'

'Ah, it often happens with Maisie. I said she had her troubles, didn't I?' Brian, still carrying cardboard boxes, lumbered towards them, dropped his cargo in a heap and elbowed Frankie out of the way. He grabbed Maisie's shoulders. 'Stand back, gel. I can deal with this. My old ma knew how to deal with faints. Head between the knees, that's what she needs.'

Brian tightened his grip on Maisie's shoulders and jerked her head forwards.

'Brian!' Frankie yelled. 'Not like that!'

Too late. Brian quickly had Maisie bent double and was trying to force the cauliflower head somewhere midway beneath the voluminous raincoat.

'Head-between-the-knees,' Brian panted. 'Head-between-the-knees.'

'Brian! Stop!'

Brian continued to thrust Maisie into a forward-bend gymnastic contortion.

The shop watched the manoeuvres in shocked and silent awe.

Frankie whimpered. She definitely wasn't insured for this, was she? 'Brian! You can't! No one

56

can bend like that! You'll kill her! I mean, if you're going to do head between the knees, surely she should be sitting down first. Oh, Lord.'

Maisie gave a little scream and suddenly fought back.

'There you go, gel,' Brian puffed, straightening up with a triumphal smile. 'That brought her out of it. Always works, that does.'

The shop gave a ragged round of relieved applause.

Maisie looked around her with vaguely blinking eyes. 'What happened? Did I make contact?'

'Only with Brian,' Frankie said, mightily thankful that Francesca's Fabulous Frocks didn't have a death on its hands before the official opening. 'Are you feeling a little bit better now?'

Maisie shook her head. 'No, sweetheart, I'm not. I'm still all of a flutter. I'm afraid I can't stay here, sweetheart, and neither should you.'

'What?' Perplexed, Frankie shook her head. 'What on earth are you talking about?'

'Spirits, sweetheart. Presences. The souls of the dead.'

The shop was gradually returning to normality. Frankie wished she was.

'Is she OK?' Dexter, followed by Lilly, clambered across the pile of boxes. 'Did she have some sort of funny turn?'

'Ah.' Brian nodded. 'She did. She often does. That's why she don't get out much. Her troubles make her a bit of a social piranha. It causes a lot of problems, see? Maisie's a medium.'

'She's never!' Lilly gawped. 'She looks like a large to me.'

'A medium.' Brian looked pityingly at Lilly. 'You

57

know, gel. Communes with the dead.'

Dexter laughed.

'It's no laughing matter.' Maisie did the back-of-the-hand head-smiting thing again. 'They're not laughing, the spirits in this shop, sweetheart. They're unhappy souls.'

'Bloody hell,' Frankie groaned. 'This is lunacy. Maisie, this is a perfectly normal shop. It's old, yes, but with no dodgy history. It was never an old hospital or a church or built on some prehistoric graveyard. There aren't any spirits here. There never have been. Anyway, I don't believe in ghosts.'

'Oh, I do,' Lilly said happily. 'And you must do, Frankie. You've seen the film. We watch it loads of times. Especially on duvet days. You always cry.'

'Patrick Swayze and Demi Moore are *acting*. It isn't a sodding documentary.'

Lilly looked crestfallen.

'And you—' Frankie turned to Brian '—should have told me about ... well ... about her, um, troubles.'

'You said you knew.' Brian sounded sulky. 'I said she had troubles and you had to take her as you found her and you said yes.'

Oh, God ...

'All I knew about Maisie,' Frankie hissed through gritted teeth, 'was that she has a shoe fetish and eats Toast Toppers.'

'Does she?' Dexter looked at Maisie with new interest. 'Lovely—I haven't had a Toast Topper since I was a kid.'

Frankie groaned.

'No, well—' Brian blinked slowly '—maybe I should have said. She sees ghosts. They make her come over all funny. But she says she can talk to

58

them. And they talk back to her.'

'Rubbish,' Frankie said sharply. 'And please don't tell anyone else that. Especially not here. You know what Kingston Dapple's like—it only takes one whisper to start the rumour mill grinding.'

'Ah, you don't need to worry about that, gel. Everyone local knows about Maisie. If she says a place is haunted then we just accept that it's haunted. We take it as read so to speak. We're all used to it. No one gets scared off by Maisie's ghost stories.'

'Is that because no one's ever seen one of Maisie's ghosts?' Dexter queried. 'Has there ever been a sighting?'

Maisie, still quivering, gave a soft sigh. '*I* see them, young man. And that's all you need to know.'

'But no one else does—has?'

Maisie looked piqued. 'Well, no, not yet . . .'

'Which is why, gel,' Brian whispered to Frankie, 'you don't need to fret too much over this. Look at 'em—all the locals. They ain't taking too much notice, are they?'

Frankie looked round the shop. OK, it was true that the crowd in the shop were definitely divided into two camps. Those villagers who clearly knew all about Maisie's 'troubles' had stared at her during the fainting episode with amused concern but little surprise; whereas those to whom Maisie the medium was a whole new phenomenon, had been shocked rigid.

Brian beamed kindly at Frankie. 'Don't worry, gel. She ain't the best in the business by a long chalk. Maisie's ghost-busting won't affect your little shop.'

'It might,' Lilly said. 'Especially if she eventually

59

manages to conjure one up.'

'I'm not damn Paul Daniels,' Maisie said huffily. 'It's not a magic act.'

'Course it's not, gel,' Brian said soothingly. 'We all knows that. Now, if them old spirits are giving you a bit of gyp here, shall we get you home?'

'That would be lovely, sweetheart. Thank you.' Maisie looked at Frankie. 'Sorry not to have been able to help with the clearing up. I wasn't expecting, well, to be taken over the way I was. And can I give you a word of advice?'

'Please do,' Frankie said faintly.

'Well, sweetheart. I'd suggest that you let me come back when the shop's empty and let me talk to the poor souls who are here. See if I can get them to leave, you know, sweetheart? I'm afraid you won't be successful until they've gone.'

Frankie sighed. 'Thank you for the offer, but honestly, no. And anyway, if you think this place is haunted, then why didn't the ghosts cause a problem for Rita? I've worked here for three years with Rita and no one's ever mentioned ghosts.'

'They were probably here all the time, sweetheart. I don't know. I never came here. And Rita wouldn't have noticed anyway, would she? Rita was very one-dimensional, sweetheart. No imagination.'

'Rita had loads of imagination,' Frankie said robustly. 'But not even Rita would have imagined she was surrounded by the souls of the dead or whatever they're supposed to be. It's complete nonsense.'

Maisie bridled. 'It's not nonsense. I can only assume that Rita's life-aura was very strong and blocked the spirits from making contact. Now she's

60

gone they're free to roam.'

'Like spectral ramblers?' Frankie sniffed derisively. 'And what you really mean is that Rita didn't believe in ghosts, don't you? Well, neither do I. The shop has obviously been unhaunted for years and years—there's no reason at all why it should be any different now.'

'But there is.' Maisie looked sorrowful. 'Because now we *know* there are unhappy souls here, don't we? Now I've made contact, now I've intercepted their spiritual space, they'll be waiting for me to speak to them and release them from their haunting hell to give them eternal freedom.'

'Well done.' Dexter clapped his hands. 'Very nearly as good as Stephen King.'

Despite everything, Frankie smiled to herself.

'Oh.' Lilly looked puzzled. 'Are they trapped, then? The ghosts? Oh, poor things.' She flickered the inch-long blue eyelashes towards Frankie. 'We shouldn't leave them trapped. It's cruel. Maybe Maisie should—'

'NO!'

'Whatever . . .' Lilly flapped her hands. 'But I still think—'

'And I think that when Dexter and Brian take these boxes to Biff and Hedley's they should pop Maisie in the car and take her home,' Frankie said quickly. 'Then maybe the rest of us can finish off in here and have time to go to the Toad before last orders.'

'Slave driver,' Lilly muttered, teetering away, every inch of her radiating irritation like a cross cat.

'Sounds like a plan,' Dexter said. 'OK with you, Maisie? Lovely—now let me fetch you a chair so that you can sit down and calm yourself for

61

a bit. You're obviously not feeling too well at the moment. We won't be long.'

Dexter climbed back over the boxes, disappeared into the kitchen and returned with a chair. Maisie subsided weakly on to it, the voluminous raincoat billowing out round her.

'OK now?' Frankie asked.

'As I'll ever be in this place.' Maisie's eyes darted fearfully round the shop, obviously still seeing things that weren't visible to anyone else. 'Or at least until you come to your senses, and let me sort out your unwanted visitors.'

'None of my visitors are unwanted,' Frankie said firmly. 'And please, Maisie, I don't mean to be rude, but can we just let the haunting stuff drop now?'

'You can if you like, I can't. It's my calling, sweetheart. I didn't ask to be blessed—or cursed— with this gift.'

'I'm sure you didn't. But I'd honestly rather not hear any more about it. Especially not tonight. I'm far too busy to cope with anything else.'

'Whatever you say.' Maisie pushed trembling hands through the cauliflower perm. 'But one day you'll need me here, that I can promise you.'

Frankie sighed, holding the door open against the storm and watching as Dexter and Brian started hefting the boxes of clothes into the boot of Dexter's car. 'And when that day comes I'll be in touch, OK?'

'OK, sweetheart.' Maisie seemed mollified.

The rain slashed icily against Frankie's face and she shivered. Someone walking over her grave, her gran would have said. Nonsense! All nonsense.

'There.' Dexter grinned, the wind whipping

62

his hair across his face, and slammed the car boot shut. 'All done. Let's get Maisie buckled into the back then we can squash some of those carrier bags round her.'

As Brian clambered excitedly into the passenger seat, Dexter, with surprising gentleness, helped Maisie up from her chair and out into the car.

It was a pretty swish car, Frankie thought. Especially for someone who allegedly hadn't got a job. Was it a BMW? Or a Mercedes? Or one of the new Jaguars? And how on earth could someone like Dexter afford a car like that? Was he into something else? A little iffy business on the side? Was that why he had to leave Oxford so quickly? Was that the cause of his troubles?

Oh, well—again, it was none of her concern, was it?

As Dexter blew her a kiss and started to drive away through the horizontal rain with the car's engine purring luxuriously and the windscreen wipers working overtime, Brian waved happily. Maisie didn't.

Frankie closed the door.

'Here!' A sharp jab in her ribs made her jump. 'What was all that about?'

Frankie glared down at Biddy-the-funeral-goer. 'Sorry? And that hurt.'

'All that malarkey with Maisie just now.' Biddy's pointy nose quivered. 'She told you this place was haunted, didn't she?'

Frankie nodded, rubbing her ribs. 'Yes, as you obviously well know, and I don't want to talk about it because it's all nonsense.'

'That—' Biddy fastened the duck-egg blue ensemble more tightly round her '—is where you're wrong. If Maisie says there are ghosts in here then there are.'

'And I'm telling you that there aren't. Now, did you find anything you liked?'

Biddy gave a mighty sniff. 'Actually, I did. There was a lovely little two-piece in oatmeal—Cherish says oatmeal is perfect on me, like a dewy sunrise on a spring morning—that would have done me a treat. But that ... that—' she jerked her ginger head towards Lilly '—little madam told me I'd have to pay twenty pounds for it. Twenty pounds! Daylight robbery! I told her I could get it cheaper in Marks and Sparks!'

'Oh dear.'

'Ah, mind you—' Biddy flourished a second-hand Big Sava bag under Frankie's nose '—I went into my bartering—good at bartering I am, ever since our seniors group had that day trip to Boulogne— and got it for a tenner!'

'Goodness.' Frankie peered into the bag and tried not to chuckle. The extremely ugly oatmeal suit had been languishing unloved and unhired in Rita's shop for at least two years. 'That'll teach her then, won't it?'

'Yes, it will.' Biddy straightened her shoulders and preened. 'And you, too. You can't pull the wool over my eyes. But you mind what I say—Maisie isn't as daft as she looks. If she's raised the dead in this place then you'll be out of business before you know it.'

Waiting until the door closed behind Biddy, Frankie pulled a face, and then returned to the seemingly never-ending job of sorting out years and years of unwanted clothes.

*   *   *

By ten thirty the sorting out was almost done. Everyone had gone. The shop floor was cleared, the majority of unwanted articles from Rita's reign had all found new homes, the dresses that still needed checking for flaws were piled beside the changing cubicles, and the frocks that needed to be delivered to the dry-cleaner's were stacked beside the counter.

Lilly, disappointed that Dexter had taken Maisie home *and* gone to Winterbrook and therefore wouldn't be available for a quick drink in the Toad, had left with Sukie, Phoebe, Clemmie and Amber for the delights of the Weasel and Bucket in Fiddlesticks instead.

Frankie leaned against the counter and ran her hands through her hair. She was so tired. And so grubby. The years of accumulated second-hand clothes had harboured more dust than she'd imagined possible. Oh, for the bliss of a long, hot soak . . .

The door opened, allowing the wind and rain to roar inside, with its usual accompaniment of whirling, dancing dead leaves.

'That's some storm.' Dexter shook raindrops from his hair and looked around. 'And you've worked miracles in here.'

Frankie nodded. 'Everyone was brilliant—we've done far more tonight than I thought possible—and I'm so grateful to them. All that's left to do before I open next week is to clean the whole place from top to bottom, decorate it, replace the clothes rails, sort the dresses into decades and sizes and colours, then fill the rails with frocks and make sure they're

65

all priced, oh, and start making the entire premises look festive, and do two huge Christmassy window displays, and—'

'Enough.' Dexter laughed. 'Stop right there. I'm exhausted just thinking about it.'

'Me, too,' Frankie sighed. 'I'm just hoping the adrenaline kick will keep me going for the rest of the week, and everyone has promised to help when they can.'

'Count me in then.'

Frankie looked at him in surprise. 'Are you sure? Won't you be busy with setting up the flower stall?'

'Not too busy to help you out. After all, I'm only just across the cobbles; I can nip backwards and forwards when I'm needed. No sweat.'

Frankie paused. Maybe she had got him wrong ... Maybe he wasn't so bad after all. 'OK then, thanks, but you may well live to regret that offer. And I certainly wasn't expecting you to come back tonight. Not after the round trip to drop Maisie off in Hassocks and then on to Winterbrook with the charity shop stuff.'

'I thought I'd see if you still needed a hand with clearing, and help you lock up.'

'Thanks, but there's no need. I'm quite organised now.'

'So I see, but I thought we were all going to have a celebratory drink in the Toad in the Hole.'

'Sorry, but everyone decamped to Fiddlesticks about half an hour ago. Country pub. Lax on closing times. I'm too exhausted to join them, but I can give you directions if you like.'

Dexter shook his head. 'No, you're OK. I'll give it a miss. I've had more than enough excitement for one night. That was some floor show ... Maisie's barking, isn't she?'

Frankie laughed. 'In a nice mad way, yes. Although I do think she sincerely believes she has some sort of spiritual gift. Anyway, thanks so much for taking her home. It was very kind of you. Was she OK?'

Dexter grinned. 'She was recovering nicely by the time me and Brian got her back to her flat. She seemed to accept that she'd made a bit of a fool of herself and that her pronouncements weren't exactly welcome, and certainly didn't say anything about making a return visit.'

'Thank goodness for that. The last thing I need is some nice-but-batty medium telling everyone that my new shop is haunted before I even get started. Hopefully, any rumours started tonight will just die a death. Right—I'm not going to even think about it, or the shop, any more tonight. I just need a long hot soak in the bath.'

Dexter's eyes sparkled. 'Sounds like a plan to me—as long as you get the tap end.'

'Alone,' Frankie chuckled.

'Spoilsport. But what about the drink in the Toad? Are you too tired for that, too? If we dash across now we should be in time for last orders. And honestly, I could do with a pint.'

Frankie hesitated. A relaxing, chill-out drink with Dexter, after the evening's hard work, was a pretty enticing prospect. And just one drink—because she was driving and so was he—wouldn't hurt at all, would it? It wasn't like a date or anything, was it? And it would be an opportunity to get to know him a bit more, wouldn't it?

And, all right, she admitted to herself, it would be just fabulous to be out with someone

67

as gorgeous as Dexter, even if it was just as sort of work colleagues. Although Dexter was clearly *exactly* the sort of man she shouldn't be going out for a drink with, but . . .

'OK.' She grabbed her coat and the shop keys before she could talk herself out of it. 'Lovely. Let's do it.'

After making sure everything was switched off and the shop was securely locked, they hurtled across the cobbles, almost blown off their feet by the ferocious wind.

Dexter looked around the interior of the Toad with some surprise. 'This isn't what I expected. From the outside, I thought it would be all beams and horse brasses and wall-to-wall rustics.'

'It should be,' Frankie agreed, as they picked their way through the minimalist pale bar furniture. 'Well, except for the rustics, of course. They'll never set foot in here again. They all get taxis out to the pubs in Fiddlesticks and Bagley-cum-Russet.'

'Can't say I blame them.' Dexter stared morosely at the Toad's solitary nod to the festive season— one very minimalist white and blue artificial Christmas tree. 'This is a bit of a travesty for a coaching inn.'

'A lot of a travesty. I've no idea how they got planning permission to mess about with it. And how it stays in business is something of a mystery to everyone in Kingston Dapple.'

'Yeah, I can see it's not exactly heaving.'

'It's always empty. Rita and Ray campaigned against the changes—loads of the villagers did—but it went ahead anyway. All anyone wants round here is a proper pub, serving proper pints and pub grub that involves recognisable things with chips.'

'They do sell beer?'

'Mmm, I think so. But it's not in casks or kegs or barrels or anything. It's in little dinky bottles with funny names.'

Dexter laughed as they approached the blue-lit bar. 'I'm sure I'll find something, but what would you like? No, let me guess. White wine? You look like a girl who knows her way round a nice Chardonnay.'

'A pint of snakebite, please. And a double Cointreau chaser.'

'*What?*'

'Don't assume anything about me.' Frankie smiled. 'Don't stereotype me, please. Just because I'm a female of a certain age, it doesn't necessarily mean I'm congenitally attached to a wine bottle.'

'Er, no.' Dexter looked slightly nonplussed as they negotiated the spindly-legged bar stools. 'OK, so I've learned my first lesson. What was it again, snakebite and ... ?'

'Actually, Chardonnay would be lovely, thanks.'

Dexter laughed. 'I can see you're going to be a worthy adversary.'

Several nattily dressed and very bored bar staff stood in a row behind the gleaming chrome and looked hopefully at them. Customers were, as always, very thin on the ground. As soon as it was clear they were going to order drinks, a sort of Mexican wave of barmen moved forwards to serve them.

Frankie thought it was sad that the bar staff never greeted any of the customers by name, and the customers had no idea who the bar staff were. Everything in the Toad was carried out with antiseptic anonymity. She was determined that

69

when Francesca's Fabulous Frocks was open she'd make a point of knowing names and using them.

Once Dexter was armed with the wine and a bottle of extremely expensive and unrecognisable beer, he peered round the Toad's emptiness. 'I don't know if we'll manage to find a seat—oh, look, there are about thirty over there.'

Frankie laughed, following him to the deserted island of chrome and glass and spiky legs.

'Here's to us.' Dexter raised his bottle once they were perched precariously on high chairs with very tiny, shiny seats. 'And the success of our new ventures.'

They clinked drinks.

'And,' Frankie said, having taken her first delicious glug of wine, 'to you settling in to your new home. Welcome to Kingston Dapple.'

'Thanks.' Dexter drained half his beer and examined the bottle. 'Oh, great, I'm not sure what it is, but I needed that.'

'So.' Frankie looked at him over the rim of her glass. It was no hardship. He was very, very beautiful. 'What really made you leave Oxford and take over Ray's flower stall?'

'Oh, you know ...' Dexter shrugged. 'This and that. Time for a change. Things had gone stale. Honestly, it's part of my life that's over and behind me now. I'm just moving on and starting over.'

Frankie sighed. Whatever the Oxford badness had been about, Dexter clearly had no intention of divulging it to her. It *must* have involved a woman, she decided. Oh, well, she had things in her past that she wouldn't want to make public knowledge either, didn't she?

'What about you?' Dexter's tawny eyes asked a

million questions. 'I know you live here in Kingston Dapple with Lilly, and I know you've worked for Rita for some time before you took over the shop, but what else makes you tick?'

'Oh, this and that,' Frankie said artlessly, determined that she'd could play Dexter's game as skilfully as he could. 'Nothing much. I'm not very interesting at all, really.'

Dexter grinned. 'Touché. And as I don't believe you for one minute, I think I'm going to have a lot of fun finding out the truth about you.'

Chapter Seven

'There!' Frankie smoothed down her short red wool ra-ra dress, and stood back and admired her handiwork. 'What do you reckon?'

No one answered. Which was hardly surprising as she was alone in the shop. She'd found, rather disconcertingly, that since Rita's departure she'd taken to talking to herself. Or the softly playing radio. Or sometimes even the dresses.

It was late Friday afternoon. Tomorrow she'd open the doors of Francesca's Fabulous Frocks for the first time.

And, thanks to the valiant efforts of her friends during the week, she may just be ready.

Rita's shop had been totally transformed. There was now an area for each decade, from the 50s onwards, with suitable pictures, posters and nick-nacks adorning the walls for each era.

Biff and Hedley had been wonderful in reciprocating the donated clothes by providing

71

some absolute gems.

Now the cream walls were barely visible as Audrey Hepburn graced the 50s with elegance and style and lots of swept-up hair and nipped-in waists, alongside a floaty, pouty Marilyn Monroe; Twiggy and Jean Shrimpton strutted their slender miniskirted white-booted stuff for the Swinging Sixties; Toyah and Siouxsie did the same for the punk 70s only with more chains and aggression; the ladies from Dallas graced the 80s with bright colours, power suits, massive shoulder pads and huge hair; and the Spice Girls and Princess Diana jointly illustrated the variations of the 90s.

The Noughties had caused some trouble because no one—not even Lilly—had been able to pin down what exactly that era had provided by way of style. In the end Frankie had decided to go for enlarged culled-from-the-internet pictures of the more outrageous designer collections—including Alexander McQueen and Stella McCartney—and anything since then currently sat beneath a huge poster of Cheryl Cole.

Frankie surveyed the shop again. She'd changed the lighting—well, she'd added spotlights in the areas where they were needed and used pretty pink bulbs to soften the harsher corners—and had old-fashioned hatstands for each section draped with hats, of course, scarves, bags, suitable jewellery and every other accessory she could find—ostensibly for decoration only. But if anyone offered her hard cash for them, she knew she'd sell them. She was determined to make a success of this.

The dresses, now arranged on hanging rails according to size in each section, were a wonderful riot of colour. From one side of the shop to the other, you could walk from the 1950s into the twenty-first century, savouring all the fashion glories of the intervening years as you went.

It looked, Frankie thought happily to herself, like a proper fabulous frock shop.

And she'd managed to sort out the computer system, so pricing, stock, selling—everything she needed—was to hand. And Lilly had also promised to talk to 'this really cute guy I know who owes me a b-i-g favour because I never breathed a word to his fiancée—not that I knew he had a fiancée at the time, the cheating slimeball' to design a Francesca's Fabulous Frocks website.

So, if the local paper did their stuff and sent someone to the opening, and the posters she'd made and plastered everywhere that wouldn't have her arrested for fly-posting, and the flyers she'd printed off and distributed round Kingston Dapple and the neighbouring villages on one of the nights when sleep was simply a luxury she couldn't afford, created some interest, then tomorrow should be one of the best days of her life.

In fact, it should be the best day of her life for, well, at least three years. Three years ago, when Joseph Mason had broken her heart and wrecked her life and her dreams, she had not thought that she would have had the resilience to clamber back, and rebuild not only herself, but also her entire future.

She wrinkled her nose. She'd come this far on her own. No one was ever going to take it away from her. Not again. The success of Francesca's Fabulous Frocks was the only thing that mattered now.

Walking across the shop, Frankie gazed at the two huge display windows in delight. In the absence of sourcing proper mannequins, although she was still looking, she'd plastered red crêpe paper everywhere and several waterfalls of long tinsel strands twisted and danced in the rising heat. Red, green and gold party frocks from all eras were draped artistically over festive boxes wrapped to look like the most enticing Christmas presents. The windows glittered in silver and gold, surrounded by baubles and more tinsel and masses of twinkling fairy lights.

Considering that all the decorations had been borrowed from her and Lilly's collection at home— even their ancient artificial Christmas tree had a place of honour—Frankie reckoned it looked almost professional.

And the rain had stopped.

Oh, and there hadn't been any sign of a ghost.

Mind you, Frankie thought now, staring out across the marketplace, the whole of Kingston Dapple looked pretty spooky today. The wind and rain had given way to a cold, dark sullenness and a dawn to dusk swirling pea-souper fog. The Christmas lights across the square gleamed feebly in the grey, shifting gloom and the shoppers were spectral figures as they appeared and faded in the murk.

Across the cobbles, Dexter's flower stall had also undergone something of a transformation. It looked, Frankie thought, like Santa's grotto, with cascading fairy lights, fat shiny swathes of holly and ivy and mistletoe draped everywhere, big glossy Christmas wreaths with crimson ribbons piled high on the decking, and scarlet poinsettias and winter red begonias studded like rubies between the dark green foliage. Inside, Dexter had used Ray's contacts well, and had massive vases of hardy cut flowers and ferns. From outside it smelled like a rural branch of Lush.

Frankie laughed to herself. In a very short space of time, Dexter had managed to attract far more customers than Ray had ever dreamed of. Female ones, of course.

The news of Dexter's arrival had spread, as everything did in the village, like wild fire, and the flower shack was almost always surrounded by women: Kingston Dapple's young mums with their babies snug in buggies, looking, giggling, texting, but not buying, the country ladies who seemed suddenly to need to turn their homes into Kew Gardens and every hue of female in between.

Dexter flirted and chatted with them all, and— even if he didn't know much about his stock— managed, Frankie thought grudgingly, to sell far more flowers than Ray had ever done.

She wondered, again, what jobs Dexter had done in the past. In fact she wondered what exactly Dexter's past had involved full stop. So far he'd been charmingly reticent about it, like the night in the Toad, and cleverly fielded any questions she or Lilly had asked.

Which, she thought now, she couldn't complain about as she'd managed to avoid answering his own questions about her. Two could play at being enigmatic. And anyway, what did it matter what they knew about one another, really, as they were never going to be involved in anything other than business? All that mattered was that her frock shop was a success so that she didn't let Rita down.

OK, she looked round the prettily lit interior, what next? Coffee, she decided. Before she tackled the last of the price tickets. And then, maybe tonight she could go home before midnight and catch up on some very much needed sleep.

Shivering, she opened the door, and managed eventually to catch Dexter's attention through the fading light and the cold, clammy fog, indicating with elaborate hand gestures that she was putting the kettle on.

As Ray's stall had no food or drink facilities, Rita had always included Ray in their refreshment breaks, and throughout this week Frankie had continued the practice, making Dexter a drink whenever she had one, carrying it carefully across the cobbles.

He grinned at her and gave her a thumbs-up sign. Several girls, clustered shivering round the holly and mistletoe, glared at her.

Minutes later, with the girls glaring even more, she hurried across the square with a steaming mug.

'Great, thanks.' Dexter wrapped his hands round the mug, staring at Frankie over the rim. 'And you look very, um, festive. Really pretty. That's a fabulous dress. Are you wearing the stock? If so, you'll be the best advert the shop could ever have.'

Frankie, unused to compliments, blushed and quickly shook her head. 'Er, thanks, but no, it's one of mine. From someone else's charity shop. Ages ago. Um—'

Dexter, clearly sensing her discomfort, smiled gently and changed to a universally safer subject. 'This coffee is ace. Freezing today, isn't it?'

'Mmm.' Frankie shuddered. 'I think I preferred the rain to this. It's real Dickensian weather. You can almost imagine how Kingston Dapple was in the old days when it's like this, can't you?'

'Full of ghosts?' Dexter laughed. 'Yeah.'

Frankie pulled a face. 'I never want to hear that word again. Hopefully, it'll all be forgotten now. I can't see Maisie making a return visit somehow.'

'No, I'm sure she won't.'

'You ... you don't believe in all that haunting stuff, do you?'

Dexter shook his head. The streaky hair moved silkily. 'No way. I'm with you on all things that go bump in the night. In fact I have a pretty low opinion of the majority of people who say they can talk to the dead. I'm sure there are genuine psychics out there, and possibly real mediums too. It's just that I've never come across them, and until I do I'll stay on the disbelieving side of the fence. But it worries me that the charlatans are simply trying to cash in on the raw grief of the bereaved. That is pretty cruel.'

'It is,' Frankie agreed. 'Although I don't think Maisie does that sort of thing, does she? I think she just thinks she can see ghosts in a kind of general way. Like we see living people everywhere, she says she sees the dead. I can't see her holding forth with random things like "I've got a message for someone here whose name begins with A from someone whose name begins with B and if you give me twenty quid I'll pass it on", somehow.'

Dexter laughed. 'No, neither can I. Barking she may be, but Maisie struck me as a kindly, well-meaning soul.'

'Me too. Anyway, I've got far more important things to worry about than Maisie the useless medium. Opening tomorrow morning and getting at least one customer through the doors being the main one.'

'You'll be fine.' Dexter looked towards the shop. 'The windows look amazing and you and Lilly have worked your socks off with the PR.'

Frankie laughed. 'Oh, Lill's been surprisingly brilliant. She's handing out flyers to everyone at the beauty salon where she works, and she's got our other friends doing the same. Clemmie runs a firework display business with her husband and she's popping my flyers in with theirs. Amber's got posters up at all Mitzi Blessing's herbal cookery outlets, Phoebe's plastered Cut 'n' Curl with them and Sukie has done a mail drop with her aromatherapy business. And they're all telling everyone they know, too.'

'Word of mouth is the best publicity ever,' Dexter agreed. 'I wish I had friends like yours. No, I just wish I had your friends—they're absolutely gorgeous.'

'Shame, because they thought you were a right munter.'

'Did they?' Dexter looked stricken. 'Bloody hell.'

'Oooh, what a delicate ego you have,' Frankie chuckled. 'Hands off my friends, Mr Valentine. They're all very happily and very firmly attached, but you'll be delighted to know that really they all thought you were pretty damn hot, too.'

Dexter preened.

Frankie gave him a mock-glare. 'You're truly terrible.'

'Thank you. Oh, excuse me a second.'

Causing a bit of a stir among the girls in their jeggings and skimpy tops and no coats despite the freezing temperatures and who were now going blue with the cold, Dexter pushed his coffee mug into Frankie's hand and moved away towards a pretty blonde in a long camel coat who was looking at the holly wreaths. After a lot of laughing and deep discussion she parted with several ten pound notes and waved goodbye.

'Sorry about that.' Dexter took the mug again. 'But as a fellow entrepreneur I know you'll appreciate that business comes first.'

'Funny business. She gave you money. You didn't give her anything.'

'Not yet.' Dexter's tawny eyes sparkled. 'It's my new service—home delivery. Saves the ladies having to lug heavy festive greenery all round the village. And so far they've all been, um, extremely grateful.'

Frankie shook her head. 'Unbelievable. Is that why you had to leave Oxford? Too many grateful ladies and lots of less-than-grateful husbands?'

'Something like that, yes.'

Frankie sighed. Just as she'd thought. 'Oh blimey, it's cold out here. I'd better get back and carry on with the pricing. And then I'm going to have to vacuum the shop from top to bottom before I go home.'

'Good luck.' Dexter took another mouthful of coffee. 'I think I'll be calling it a day soon, too. See you later.'

The girls clustered round the flower stall, Frankie noticed, looked no warmer but definitely much more cheerful as she hurried away across the cobbles.

'Oooh, lovely,' she said, relishing the heat as she pulled the door shut behind her. She picked up her own coffee and took a gulp. 'OK, let's just finish this, then I'll crack on with the pricing and—oh!'

Frankie's heart skipped a beat. She wasn't alone.

A small figure was standing on the far side of the shop, between the 1950s and 60s sections.

With her pulse racing, she tried to keep calm. 'Goodness, you made me jump. And I'm sorry—' still shaking, Frankie attempted a friendly smile '—but we're not open until tomorrow. I should have locked the door. Please come back tomorrow morning and have a proper look round then. We're opening at half past eight.'

'All right, duck.' The figure moved away from the rails of dresses and out of the pink-lit shadows, sounding very apologetic. 'I'll do that. I must have got it wrong. Sorry to have bothered you.'

Frankie frowned, relieved now that she wasn't about to be mugged, or worse. The man—it hadn't been possible to discern the figure's gender earlier—was wearing an old-fashioned shiny suit, and now he was in the light, Frankie could see he was really quite elderly, with grizzled hair and a cheerful-goblin wrinkled face.

Not an axe-wielding murderer, then.

'Um, now Rita's gone we're not renting stuff out any more. I'm just going to be selling dresses. Um, were you looking for something for, er, a lady?'

The man shook his head.

Oh great, Frankie thought, I've got Kingston Dapple's only geriatric cross-dresser.

'Well,' she said brightly, 'I'm sure you'll find something to suit you here. Tomorrow.'

'I know what I want.' The old man crossed the shop and beamed toothlessly at her. 'I've already found it.'

'Oh, good,' Frankie said, trying hard not to

80

laugh.

Well, she'd wanted customers, hadn't she? Who was she to be picky about their predilections? And anyway, her friend Clemmie's best friend, YaYa, was in a drag act and had promised to bring all his, er, her fellow drag queens to buy outfits from Francesca's Fabulous Frocks. One more— even if he was ancient—really wouldn't make any difference.

'Lovely,' Frankie said cheerfully, turning away and opening the door again. 'Well, make sure you get here nice and early so that no one else buys it.'

'Ah, duck. I'll do that. Sorry again for making you jump. Thank you.'

The fog swirled into the shop in a cold, steel-grey all-enveloping blanket.

'Mind how you go—oh, you've already gone.'

Frankie stared out at the marketplace. The elderly man had, like the few shoppers remaining on this bleak afternoon, been enveloped in the thickly churning mist. Frankie hoped he didn't have far to go. It was a really nasty night.

Still smiling to herself, she carefully locked the door, turned up the radio and started pricing.

*　　　*　　　*

*

'Oooh no—don't make me laugh!' Lilly giggled later that evening as, perched on Frankie's much-flounced pink and purple bed, in Frankie's much-flounced pink and purple bedroom, she waved her mascara wand away from her false eyelashes. 'I'll have me eye out!'

'It wasn't funny,' Frankie muttered, struggling wearily into her flower-sprigged Cath Kidston

81

pyjamas. 'I wasn't laughing. He scared me to death to start with.'

'I bet,' Lilly chuckled, surveying her eye make-up in the mirror. 'Typical of you, though. Your very first customer turns out to be an ancient Eddie Izzard.'

'I know. But he was really sweet, and very polite and seemed embarrassed about being there when he shouldn't have been.' Frankie yawned and stretched. 'I do hope he does come back in the morning. If he's found a dress he wants it would be such a shame if he didn't get it.'

'Yeah, I suppose it would. And you—' Lilly stood up as she added lip gloss '—should be more security conscious. Fancy leaving the door unlocked. Jennifer says—'

'I'd only popped across the square to Dexter's with a cup of coffee. It didn't occur to me that anyone would wander in.'

'Well, it should have done.' Lilly twirled round under the multiple ropes of rose and lilac twinkling lights that bedecked Frankie's boudoir bedroom. 'You were lucky it was only an old gentlemanly cross-dresser. It could have been a horde of hoodies. You could have lost all your stock and had the whole place trashed into the bargain.'

'Don't.' Frankie shuddered, as she snuggled underneath the soft downiness of her multi-frilled deep purple satin duvet. 'Oh, goodness, I'm totally shattered. Please, please, don't let me oversleep in the morning. We'll need to be at the shop by half past seven. If my alarm clocks and phone don't go off you'll wake me up, won't you?'

'If I'm home in the morning.' Lilly was wide-eyed. 'I've got a hot date.'

'Oh Lord—have you? But it's way past eleven o'clock.' Frankie peered sleepily at Lilly, in her skinniest jeans, her skimpiest top and her highest heels. 'I suppose I should have noticed you weren't getting ready for bed. Where are you going?'

'The Rinky-Dink. It doesn't get started much before midnight.'

'No, I don't suppose it does. Well, take care driving in this fog, and have a nice time. I just wish I had your stamina.'

Lilly wrinkled her nose. 'You poor old thing. It must be awful to be nearly thirty.'

'You're not that far off,' Frankie said drowsily, sinking her head into the softness of her pillows. 'Ah, bliss. So, who's tonight's lucky man? Do I know him?'

'Course you do,' Lilly giggled. 'It's Dexter.'

Chapter Eight

And, of course, Frankie thought the next morning, it really didn't matter at all. Lilly and Dexter: both flirty and flighty and game for a laugh. Neither of them looking for love or pretending to be looking for commitment—or probably even able to spell it—what could be better?

It wasn't as if she was even vaguely interested in Dexter herself, was it? Or he in her? And he'd proved, not only with his rapid dating of Lilly, but also with his "home delivery specials" that he was exactly what she'd known he would be: an irrepressible, irresistible, irredeemable womaniser.

So, on that basis, for her self-esteem and her

sanity—not to mention keeping her now-mended heart intact—it was much better that they were just friends. And therefore, she thought as she prowled round, nervously checking and rechecking the interior of Francesca's Fabulous Frocks, it didn't matter in the slightest that Dexter had asked Lilly out and not her, did it?

No, of course it didn't ... And even if he'd asked her she wouldn't have gone anyway, would she? No of course she wouldn't—well, probably not ...

Pushing the Everywoman/Lilly/Dexter combinations out of her mind for the time being, Frankie checked her mental tick-list as she walked round the shop. Every inch was gleaming. The frocks were hanging neatly on their rails, and all had price tags attached. Next, the lights—spots and dimmers, uplighters and downlighters—and the stereo system. All fine. Michael Bublé smooched softly into every corner of the shop, and the perfume diffusers filled the room with billows of summer meadow fragrance.

OK. Frankie stood back and took a deep breath. Everything was perfect. It was nearly eight o'clock. Everything was ready. But was she?

She checked herself again in one of the long cheval mirrors. Never totally happy with her appearance, she'd made a special effort for this morning. It was OK. The cobalt-blue 1970s skating-style frock looked fine. And the dark-blue tights and high boots made her long legs look even longer. Did she look like the owner of a frock shop? Frankie giggled to herself. Probably not. She certainly didn't feel like one.

She'd beaten both the alarm clocks and her phone and been up well before six to get ready.

84

And yes, she'd sneaked a quick look into Lilly's bedroom before leaving the house. Just to make sure that Lilly had got home safely. Not, of course, to see if Dexter was there too. Perish the thought.

And Lilly, alone in her minimalist pewter-framed bed, had peered bug-eyed over the edge of the white duvet and said she'd be up in a minute before promptly falling asleep again.

So ... in half an hour Frankie would be opening Francesca's Fabulous Frocks for business for the very first time. It was exciting and terrifying all at the same time.

She'd emailed details and photos of the refurbed shop to Rita and Ray and received ecstatic replies and a huge Greek good luck card. And her friends had promised to be there to help out by nine. All that was left to do now was wait and see if any customers actually turned up on this cold, grey, foggy morning.

'Hi.' Dexter, managing to look very fit in jeans and boots and a navy sweater under the leather jacket, despite also wearing a grubby money apron and fingerless mittens, pushed the door open. 'Good morning, happy opening day, you look beautiful—and I've brought you these.'

'Oh, wow.' Frankie took the massive bouquet of exotic rainbow flowers. 'Thank you so much. They're fabulous. Are they from Ray's, er, yours?'

'No.' Dexter looked hurt. 'That would be a cheap gift, don't you reckon? I haven't got anything like these. I ordered them specially in Winterbrook and picked them up just now.'

'Oh—I mean, that's really kind of you.' Frankie was a bit thrown. She'd rarely had flowers from anyone. And these were stunning. And Dexter had made a special effort to get them for her—even though merely hours before he'd been out with Lilly, and presumably previous to that, with the pretty blonde in the camel coat. 'Honestly—thank you.'

'You're welcome. You deserve them. And I brought this too. I didn't know if you'd arranged any sort of refreshments.'

Frankie blinked at the magnum of Krug. 'Blimey—no. I thought food was a bit of a no-no in case it got on the frocks, so I only got some cheap fizz and orange juice, nothing as fabulous as this. It's very generous of you.'

Dexter grinned. 'No problem. You can give the fizz to the browsers and the real stuff to the buyers. Or, better still, keep it for friends when today's over. I'll put it in the fridge, shall I? Oh, and have you got a vase in the kitchen? I thought the flowers'd look nice on the counter. Yet another splash of colour.' He gazed round the shop. 'This is truly incredible. Amazing. You've worked so hard.'

'Thanks.' Frankie tried not to stare too obviously at Dexter to see if he showed any traces of being out clubbing until the small hours. He looked, she thought, stunningly sexy, annoyingly bright-eyed and wide awake, and definitely not debauched in any way. 'And yes, Rita had some vases under the sink. I think they're still there.'

He took the flowers and champagne and disappeared into the kitchen.

Frankie watched him go, and sighed. He was lovely. But then, Joseph had been too, hadn't he? At least until the awful ending. And after Joseph she'd sworn there'd never be anyone else. And anyway, she'd already decided Dexter was clearly the worse kind of heartbreaking womaniser, wasn't he? Dexter was, she decided, best avoided in any sort of *silly* way at all.

Eight twenty. Still no sign of Lilly or the others. Maybe she should throw caution to the winds—or rather the icy clammy fog—and fasten the door back to welcome in the hordes of eager shoppers.

No, maybe that would rocket the heating bills sky-high and bankrupt her before she'd even started trading. She'd just have to hope that people would notice the windows and the lights and have seen the posters and the flyers and be curious enough to push the door open and step inside.

Once inside, Frankie was sure, no one would be able to resist.

'There you go.' Dexter plonked the huge vase of flowers on the edge of the counter. 'They look really nice there, don't they? Mind you—' he stroked the petals '—I haven't got a clue what they are. Obviously haven't got that far in my *I-Spy Flowers* book. I'm quite good on holly and mistletoe now though, and I know what a winter begonia is too.'

'Congratulations.' Frankie laughed. 'It sounds like you've made a good start. Um, and did you have a good time last night?' She groaned. She honestly hadn't meant to say anything.

'Last night? With my home deliveries?'

'No, well, yes—I meant after that really.'

'Oh, you mean at that Rinky-Dink place? Yeah, great thanks. It was a bit of an eye-opener. I didn't realise it was a drag venue until we got there. I spent most of the night trying to work out who was who.'

The pungent hothouse perfume from the flowers

87

was happily mingling with the sweet meadow scent from the diffusers. Michael Bublé was poignantly telling everyone he wanted to go home.

'Lilly often goes there.' Frankie wiped away imaginary dust from the counter and didn't look at Dexter. 'She loves it.'

'So she said. She's a funny girl—great company.' Dexter nodded. 'It was good to get out of the lonely bedsit and see a bit of local nightlife, to be honest.'

'Mmm.' Frankie looked for even more grime on the spotless counter. 'It must have been. Did you meet YaYa Bordello? She's a good friend of ours and the Rinky-Dink is one of her regular venues.'

'Yeah. What a character! And so glamorous. She introduced me to her friends, um, Cinnamon and Campari and Foxy—oh, and someone called Midnight who *had* to be female, but apparently isn't, and isn't even gay and is married with kids and drives a bus.'

Frankie laughed. 'The Rinky-Dink isn't to everyone's taste, but it sounds like you enjoyed it.'

Dexter nodded. 'I did. It was really kind of Lilly to ask me.'

'*She* asked *you*?'

'Yes. She had a couple of free tickets given to her at the beauty salon. She said there was no point asking you because you'd be too knackered to go because of this place, and everyone else she knows is boringly settled down with husbands, lovers and/ or babies to go out on the spur of the moment, so she asked me.'

Frankie suddenly inexplicably wanted to turn a celebratory cartwheel. 'Um, yes, that was nice of her. So, er, are you seeing her again?'

'Yes, of course.'

88

The cartwheel feeling rapidly collapsed like a bad soufflé.

'In—' Dexter looked at his watch '—about two minutes if she turns up to help you as she's promised.'

'Oh, right.' Frankie tried not to beam. 'Well, seeing the state she was in when I left this morning I'm not counting on it.'

'Nor me. I drove, stayed sober, and Lilly attacked the Woo Woos big time. She was asleep long before we got back to your place. I practically had to shovel her up your path and through the front door.'

Frankie laughed and hoped she looked simply amused and not relieved.

'Oh, yes,' Dexter said. 'And another thing, while we're on the subject of cross-dressing. She told me about your unexpected visitor yesterday.'

'Did she?' Frankie said cheerfully. 'Well, in hindsight it was really funny, but at the time I was a bit startled.'

'You should have shouted for me.'

'If it had been a six-foot bloke in a balaclava wielding a baseball bat, don't worry, I'd have been over to you like a shot. But he was a real sweetie. I do hope he turns up this morning to buy whichever dress he'd set his heart on.'

Dexter shook his head. 'It was never this exciting in Oxford. And to think Ray told me Kingston Dapple was a sleepy little backwater where nothing ever happened.'

'Even sleepy little backwaters must have their—um—oddities.'

Dexter nodded. 'And as far as I can see, most of them have already turned up in here—present company excepted, of course.' He laughed and shielded himself from her mock punch. 'I suppose I'd better go and open up. I'll tell all my customers to pop in here and buy a party frock, and if anyone asks about these flowers, please reciprocate and lie and say they came from my shack and point people across the square.'

'Of course. And thank you again.'

'Good luck.' Dexter suddenly leaned across and kissed her cheek. 'But you'll be fine. We'll catch up later, OK?'

'OK,' Frankie said quietly, trying not to let her fingers stray to her cheek as he left the shop.

'Hiya, and sorry I'm late. You should have woken me.' Lilly, dressed in the trademark skinny jeans and a fondant pink T-shirt and yellow boots, clattered through the door.

'I did. You went straight back to sleep.'

'I don't remember that. And it took me ages to find somewhere to park and I'm probably still well over the limit so I shouldn't have even driven. We could have shared a car if you'd woken me. And was that Dexter who just left?'

'Short-term memory loss already? So sad at your age,' Frankie teased. 'As far as I know you only parted company about three hours ago.'

'Oooh, don't.' Lilly staggered behind the counter. 'Hangover from hell. We had a good time, I think. He's such a flirt though. He really fancied Midnight. Was sooo gutted that she was actually a straight man. Think it almost turned him celibate.'

'That I doubt.'

'Mmm, me too.'

'It was really, really kind of you to ask him out with your free tickets.'

'He told you?' Lilly squinted. 'And is that sarcasm? Don't try to be clever. I'm too muzzy-headed to be clever.'

'OK.' Frankie shrugged. 'Why did you ask him out?'

'Why do you think? Because he's scorching hot. You don't mind do you?'

'No, why should I?'

'That's OK then. Because you're right about him. He's definitely a player. He was amazing to be with, but, well, for as much time as I can remember before the Woo Woos kicked in, he was aware of every other woman—and man, before he realised his mistake—in the club and giving them the benefit of the Valentine charm.'

'Always looking for the next good thing?'

'Yeah. Dexter is a fab guy, just not a settler. Any woman who goes out with Dexter would just be one of many. Which is OK as long as you *know*. Oooh, those flowers are lovely.' Lilly staggered along the counter and buried her face in the bouquet. 'Wow. Fabulous. Did you—?'

'No, Dexter did.'

'Cool. See, told you he fancied you.' Lilly pouted. 'Now I wish I hadn't just said all that other stuff. Sorry.'

'Don't be. I'd already worked it out for myself. I've seen him in action with his customers, and I still think he left Oxford because of a woman.'

'Or thirty.' Lilly nodded. 'Ouch. Remind me not to move my head. It hurts.'

'So, you didn't manage to find out why he had to leave Oxford? Or what he's done in the past or how come he owns a mega-expensive car or anything?'

'No. Trust me, I tried to do a Jeremy Kyle on

him. I asked all the questions, but he wasn't telling. He just clammed up. Maybe it's just really boring— like he split with his girlfriend and she kicked him out of their shared flat, and he got made redundant from whatever job he had but they let him buy his company car really cheap, all at the same time, so Ray's invite to come and sort himself out in Kingston Dapple came at just the right time and was his only answer to being homeless and jobless. Maybe he just wants it to all seem mysterious, because Ray gave him a real bad-boy build-up, and he's embarrassed that it isn't.'

Frankie laughed. 'That's pretty profound coming from you considering the state you're in.'

'It is, isn't it?' Lilly looked pleased. 'Now, if you want me to do any work at all today, I'm just going to drown myself in black coffee and take paracetamol and please don't shout at me for at least an hour.'

Chapter Nine

By nine o'clock Francesca's Fabulous Frocks was jam-packed. Everyone Frankie had ever known since she moved to Kingston Dapple had turned up, and many, many more besides. Her throat was sore from shouting greetings across the thrum, and her face ached from smiling.

It was absolutely brilliant.

'This is madness,' Lilly panted, as beside Frankie behind the counter, she rapidly folded dresses into the purple and gold carrier bags and took money or zapped cards. 'I think we might have overdone the publicity. I'm hungover, I've had about five minutes sleep, and we need about twenty more people serving in here.'

'I know.' Frankie nodded, scanning the queue in front of the counter while folding a black and white Mary Quant copy in purple tissue paper. 'It was one thing I didn't even think about. I'm just so used to it being me and Rita and a basically empty shop most of the time.'

'I think those days are long gone,' Lilly puffed as she juggled a Visa card. 'If it carries on like this you're going to have to get staff.'

'Are you applying?'

'No way. I'm more than happy at Jennifer's, thank you.'

'Good.' Frankie beamed at a girl from Bagley-cum-Russet who had just bought an exotically patterned Vivienne Westwood dress, and something in tartan and bedecked with chains, from the 1970s rails. 'Sharing a house is one thing, but working together is something else entirely. Anyway, I reckon things will calm down once today's over. This is just the typical village nosiness over something new. Once the novelty has worn off it'll slow down again. And I don't want to spend out on wages for someone who just sits around doing nothing all day.'

'Like you used to.'

'I never did! Well, OK, when we weren't busy maybe—sorry?' Frankie leaned over the counter towards a tiny woman in a brown coat and paisley headscarf, both misted with foggy droplets. 'Culotte-frocks? I'm not sure . . . ?'

'Eighties or nineties,' Lilly said, 'I think. Shall I go and look?'

'Nooo. Don't leave me. Amber is over there somewhere in the crowd, pointing people to the right areas.' Frankie smiled again at the brown-clad woman. 'The sections you need are over there and the girl with the blonde hair and the flashing reindeer earrings will help you—can you see her? Oh, good. Hopefully you'll find something there. If not, come back and I'll make a note of your phone number and get in touch with you when we have something suitable in. Lovely.'

Frankie watched as the woman made her way through the throng to Amber who smiled warmly and started searching the appropriate rails. Everyone had turned up. Amber and Clemmie were playing at personal shoppers and style advisors, Sukie was circulating with trays of Buck's Fizz and answering questions, and Phoebe was manning the fitting rooms.

It was all going perfectly. Frankie could hardly hear Michael Bublé above the hum of happy bargain-hunters.

'What about the stock?' Lilly queried. 'If you carry on like this you'll have an empty shop before Christmas.'

'I've had lots of donated dresses this week. They're upstairs in one of those rooms Rita never used waiting to be sorted. I'm not too worried about running out—yet. People seem delighted to be able to offload their dresses just before Christmas when they want to buy new, or, um, nearly new anyway . . . Yes, can I help you? You want to look like Brigitte Bardot? Your husband always fancied her, did he? Have a word with Amber and Clemmie—over there see, yes? They'll help you look in the nineteen fifties section—I think you'll find several little

94

gingham frocks in there, and some off-the-shoulder shifts too.'

'She'll never look like Brigitte Bardot in a million years.' Lilly frowned.

'No, but if it keeps her husband happy.'

'That's a bit anti-feminist. Jennifer says a woman must make herself beautiful for herself first and for everyone else second.'

'Quite the philosopher, Jennifer Blessing,' Frankie chuckled, then stopped as she was suddenly buried beneath a proffered pile of 1980s specials: three power suits, a batwing jersey dress and a shirtwaister in Margaret Thatcher blue, all accompanied by an agitatedly waving Amex card.

Two hours later, with the shop still full, a reporter and photographer from the *Winterbrook Advertiser* turned up and made Frankie pose in front of each section, surrounded by beaming customers all with frocks and hats and feather boas, then outside in the freezing fog in front of the lovely sparkly Christmassy windows, and then drape herself along the counter coyly holding a Francesca's Fabulous Frocks carrier bag, much to Lilly's amusement.

'Bet they'll get it all wrong,' Frankie said as the hacks departed. 'You know—"Fiona Merryweather, fifty-seven ..."'

'Yeah, they never get the names right, do they? And why are they so obsessed with ages?' Lilly frowned as she carefully packed a Princess Diana-type glittery number. 'And they always use the worst photo possible. The one that makes you look like a fat shoplifter just coming out of court.'

'I'm sooo looking forward to the next edition of the *Advertiser* now, thanks,' Frankie chuckled. 'Still,

95

I suppose it'll all help with publicity.'

'Not if they think you're a fat shoplifter.'

'True,' Frankie giggled. 'Oh Lord ... more customers coming in ... and my feet are killing me.'

'I think mine dropped off ages ago.' Lilly looked down at her stilt-heeled boots. 'I haven't felt my toes since half past ten. We should have worn slippers. Hello, can I help you?'

*   *   *

By lunchtime, Frankie felt as though she'd owned Francesca's Fabulous Frocks for ever. She was on a roll. The dark, cold, foggy weather didn't seem to have deterred anyone, and the waves of customers, busy doing their Saturday Christmas shopping in Kingston Dapple, had all popped in to have a look, and at least half of them had bought something.

In the middle of adding up a 60s mini shift, a 70s bo-ho maxi and an 80s backless cocktail dress, she was suddenly aware that a lot of her female customers had stopped raking through the rails and were staring at the door.

'Dexter alert,' Lilly chuckled. 'Every woman in the shop has turned into a meerkat. He must give off some sort of—what are they called?'

'Pheromones?' Frankie hazarded.

'Yeah—well, I think so. Whatever they are, the effect is pretty damn amazing, isn't it?'

Frankie smiled. It was.

'I know you said you didn't want food,' Dexter said cheerfully from behind several scarves, 'at least not for the customers, in case it messed up the frocks, but I guessed you and your friends must be hungry by now, so I've brought some refreshments from the Greasy Spoon.'

'Bacon rolls!' Frankie drooled, as the delicious aroma wafted across the counter. 'Millions of them! Oh, I'm starving. You're a star. Thank you so much.'

'It's so cold out there I had mine ages ago, so if you want to disappear into the kitchen for ten minutes or so, I'll hold the fort in here.'

'Are you sure?' Frankie frowned. 'I mean, it's a bit manic.'

'And he's Dexter and all the customers are women,' Lilly hissed. 'He'll be fine, as long as he stays one side of the counter and they stay the other.'

'I'll scream if I need you to rescue me.' Dexter moved behind the counter. 'Go and have these while they're still hot.'

'Thanks.' Frankie took the bags of gloriously scented, forbidden fat 'n' carbs. 'But who's looking after the flower stall?'

'Um, Giselle or Genevieve, I'm not sure what her name is. She helps out in the Greasy Spoon.'

'Ginny.' Frankie nodded. 'Student. Works part-time. Very, very pretty.'

'That's her.' Dexter grinned. 'I'll have to think of some way to thank her later.'

'Come on, girls,' Lilly yelled at Phoebe, Clemmie, Amber and Sukie. 'Tea break!'

Ten minutes later, Frankie was halfway through her third bacon roll, her fingers wonderfully greasy, when Dexter opened the kitchen door. 'Sorry to bother you but there's someone asking for you.'

'It's OK—' Frankie wiped her hands on a piece of kitchen paper '—I'll have to stop now before I pig out completely and turn into a roly-poly ball. Is

97

it male or female, or didn't you notice?'

'Do you think I can't tell after last night?' Dexter laughed as he held open the door. 'OK, after last night I'm not sure... Seriously, though, female. In fact, two females. Why?'

'Because,' Frankie said as she followed him out in to the shop, 'I was sort of hoping it was the little old man who wanted to buy a dress yesterday. He hasn't turned up this morning.'

'It's definitely not him,' Dexter said. 'Pity he hasn't shown, though. Maybe he couldn't face being outed in a shop full of people.'

'Hmm, maybe. Shame, he was sort of sweet—oh, bugger.'

'What?'

'You didn't say it was Biddy-the-funeral-goer and a pal.'

'You didn't ask. Why?'

'Biddy and I hardly parted on the best of terms after Maisie's, er, turn, did we?' Frankie took a deep breath and fixed her best shop-owner smile. 'Hello, Biddy. How nice to see you.'

'Doubt if you mean that.' Biddy, more gingery than ever and dressed in a faded apricot ensemble, looked like a wrinkled elderly peach that's been long forgotten at the bottom of the fruit bowl. 'But it's polite of you, I must say.'

'Oh, I'm always polite.' Frankie smiled a bit more. 'Oh, look, why don't we move over here to the end of the counter then we won't keep getting in the way of the customers. There. That's better. So, how can I help you?'

'It's more me that can help you.' Biddy's thin nose twitched and Frankie almost expected her to start cleaning her whiskers.

98

'Really?'

'Yes.' Biddy cast a beadily dismissive glance round the bustling, crowded shop and raised her voice above the continual hum and Michael Bublé proclaiming that he hadn't met you yet. 'I thought, seeing as you were going against everything Rita held dear, you could do with some help.'

Oh Lordy, Frankie thought, waving to Dexter as he exited the shop, and looking hopefully at her friends as they all skittered smugly replete from the kitchen and immediately disappeared into the throng, she's applying for a job.

'Well, I'm not actually looking to employ anyone yet. But if I do need an assistant, I'll certainly bear you in mind.'

'I don't want a job.' Biddy's tiny eyes narrowed into shocked slits. 'Not at my age. And I certainly wouldn't want to work for or with you, thank you very much.'

'Then what?'

'Cherish.' Biddy motioned to the even thinner and paler, nondescript woman wearing top-to-toe taupe standing bedside her. 'I thought Cherish would be a huge asset here seeing as how you clearly don't know nothing about colour and Cherish knows everything. She's my colour-palette advisor from Hazy Hassocks.'

'Yes,' Frankie said faintly, 'I remember you saying.'

Cherish, Frankie had imagined, would be at least larger than life, and definitely Jamaican: all big smiles and white teeth and warmly welcoming with a gutsy laugh and a massive sense of humour. No one this pale and emaciated could surely be called *Cherish*, let alone set herself up as a colour advisor?

99

'Um.' Frankie swallowed and forced a smile. 'Cherish, how lovely to meet you.'

'Nice to meet you too,' Cherish said in a soft burring Berkshire accent. 'And you don't want to be wearing that bright blue. Not with your eyes and that black hair.'

'Er, don't I? I thought it matched my eyes quite well, actually.'

'Ah, that's where so many mistakes are made.' Cherish drew herself up to her full five foot two. 'You want to match your colours to your inner self.'

Pink, red, bloody and gory? Frankie winced.

'You—' Cherish peered across the counter '— are a grey person. Gloomy. Almost colourless. You wants to wear a nice gunmetal or pewter or ash. You're a faded winter evening person. Grey, dear, that's what you are. There's not many of you about.'

Frankie blinked. Just her and John Major then?

'I've never really liked grey. I prefer bright colours.'

'Big mistake,' Cherish sighed. 'Bright colours stifle your true personality. You'll never find happiness and success until you match your colours to your soul. And your soul, dear, is totally grey.'

Oh, great, Frankie thought.

'Well, there you go.' Biddy twitched excitedly at Frankie. 'That's where you've been going wrong, isn't it? Stop wearing all those primaries and start wearing shades of grey. It'll transform your life.'

'I'll bear it in mind,' Frankie muttered.

Cherish beamed.

Biddy twitched a bit more. 'Told you she was good, didn't I? Now, what I thought was if Cherish stationed herself over there by the fitting rooms, she could nab people as they went in, have a look at

100

what they'd chosen and put them straight.'

'And I'd work freelance,' Cherish said enthusiastically. 'I'll be like a sub-contractor. You wouldn't have to pay me. The customers would do that.'

If there were any customers left after Cherish's downbeat and screamingly awful advice, Frankie thought bleakly. She upped the professional smile. 'Well, it's very kind of you to offer, and of course, maybe when the shop is a bit more established I might be interested in adding different aspects, but right now I'm still feeling my way and—'

'Are you turning Cherish down?' Biddy looked scandalised.

'Yes. Sorry. It's just not for me at the moment, I'm afraid.'

'If you don't take her now, then Dorothy Perkins in Winterbrook'll be snapping her hands off.' Biddy blinked furiously. 'I knew Rita was making a mistake leaving you in charge of this place. You don't know a good thing when you see it. You'll run Rita's lovely little shop into the ground afore Easter at this rate.'

'Shall I just leave my business cards here on the counter, dear?' Cherish looked hopeful. 'Even if I can't actually work in here at the moment, you might like to recommend me. I do most of my work from home anyway.'

'Er, yes, OK.' Frankie squinted doubtfully at the pile of dog-eared DIY business cards. 'Just leave them there. That's lovely.'

Biddy and Cherish elbowed their way through the shop, pausing to look at selection of pastel puffballs. Frankie somehow couldn't see Biddy in a puffball . . .

101

'What was all that about?' Lilly broke off from serving at the other end of the counter and dumped another armful of purple and gold carrier bags in a slithery heap. 'I didn't quite catch it.'

'Oh, just Biddy the misery introducing Cherish her colour advisor. Cherish wants to work here telling people that they're all insipid and boring and must match their colours to their inner selves. She says I'm a grey winter person, apparently.'

Lilly shrieked with laughter. 'You are so funny. I could never come up with a story like that in a million years. You have such a great imagination. Oh Lord, there's Big Stacey from Londis looking through the size six Bibas. I was at school with her and she's never been less than a generous twenty. We've got some lovely kaftans that would do her a treat. Are you going to tell her or am I?'

Frankie shook her head. 'Let's leave it to Clemmie and Amber, shall we? They're on style advice. We're on serving only. OK, who's next please …'

From the corner of her eye, Frankie watched Biddy and Cherish move mercifully away from the puffballs and start to push their way through the crowd towards the door. She scooped up Cherish's business cards and was about to drop them in the bin when Biddy turned round and scuttled back to the counter and stared at the handful of cards.

'Oh, um, I was just going to put them somewhere safe.'

Biddy's nose twitched. 'Good, but what I meant to say earlier was I've been to see Maisie Fairbrother. She's still in a state of traumatisation. And she still maintains this place is haunted. And despite the nay-sayers in this village, I know for a

102

fact that Maisie's never wrong when she's got an inkling of spirit infestation. So you watch your step, my girl. You needs Maisie in here to lay your ghosts, you do, before you've got more trouble in this shop than you know what to do with.'

Chapter Ten

Eventually, as the winter darkness fell, and the fog swirled murkily across the market square, the crowds disappeared. It had been a truly spectacular day. Frankie, utterly exhausted, shut the door, turned the sign to CLOSED, then leaned against the counter and thanked Rita from the bottom of her heart.

Francesca's Fabulous Frocks was established. It was up to her now to continue to make the business work. And she could do it. After today, she knew she could do it. Although, she thought drowsily, she may well need to employ an assistant—even just a part-time one—especially over the Christmas period if they were going to be this busy.

Frankie grinned happily to herself. When and if she employed someone, it definitely wouldn't be Biddy.

Lilly, Clemmie, Amber and Sukie had already staggered across the fairy-lit cobbles, through the wraithlike fog, to toast their involvement in the success in the Toad in the Hole. Phoebe, who was planning on having a cosy night in with her other half, Rocky, had made her excuses because of the worsening weather, and driven home to Hazy Hassocks.

'They're doing three Jägerbombs for a fiver tonight in the Toad!' Lilly had announced happily as she'd click-clacked towards the door. 'Shall I get you some in?'

'No thanks.' Frankie had shaken her head. 'Sorry to be a pooper, but honestly once I've locked up here, all I'll be fit for is a hot bath, a hot chocolate and bed.'

'You are getting sooo old,' Lilly had giggled. 'Where's that party animal I used to know and love?'

'Turned into a boring old fart,' Frankie had chuckled. 'A really boring old fart with her own business. And how can you face Jaegerbombs after your close encounter with the Woo Woos not that long ago?'

'Easily. Especially if Dexter's there to share them with.'

'Well, he won't be. He shut the flower stall down dead on five and went off with Ginny from the Greasy Spoon.'

'Bugger. Did he?' Lilly's face had fallen. 'How do you know?'

'Because I watched him go,' Frankie had said smiling. 'He waved and gave me the thumbs-up.'

'Oh, well. His loss. Expect me when you see me then. I might just have one quick drink with the girls in the Toad, then leave my car here, grab a taxi and go into Winterbrook.' Lilly had tottered back across the empty shop and thrown her arms round Frankie. 'You've been ace today. Done so well. You must have made a fortune. I'm really, really proud of you.'

'Thanks.' Frankie had hugged her back. 'I couldn't have done it without you, though. You were all really great.'

'That's what friends are for.' Lilly had wriggled free. 'Now I'm going to be a young free and single girlie about town, while you turn into Mrs Cosy Slippers. Don't wait up.'

And Lilly had clattered off out of the door and across the cobbles in the gloom.

Frankie looked wearily around the shop. The rails were pleasingly depleted—and in an awful mess. She really should tidy them up then go upstairs to the stockroom and sort out replacement dresses ready for Monday morning. She should, but she knew she wouldn't. She was far, far too tired. She'd come in tomorrow when she'd had a good night's sleep and the shop was empty and she could concentrate properly. And much as Lilly might disapprove, all she really, really wanted was the bath and the frothy chocolate and bed.

Making sure the safe was locked, and all the lights and plugs in the kitchen were switched off, Frankie hurried into the shop and reached for her bright pink coat and selection of lilac and blue scarves. Grey person indeed. Huh!

She paused for a moment and buried her nose in the flowers Dexter had brought. Fabulous. Rich and heady. Should she take them home? No, she thought, winding the last of her scarves round her throat: the flowers, bright and gaudy, belonged in the shop.

'Bright and gaudy—just like me, Cherish,' she said out loud, reaching for the light switch. 'Exactly like me.'

'Excuse me.'

The voice suddenly echoing through the emptiness made Frankie stop stock-still. Her mouth was dry. She tried to swallow but couldn't. Speech wasn't an option either.

'Excuse me, duck,' the little grizzle-haired man stood between the now denuded 50s and 60s frock sections. 'Sorry. I didn't mean to startle you—again.'

Frankie stared at him. She worked saliva into her mouth. 'Well, you did. Dear God, you really scared me. Why do you keep doing this? Coming in at the wrong time? I'm so sorry, but I've just closed up for the night. You should have been here earlier. I did look out for you.'

'I was here, duck, but you were too busy to see me. You've done nicely today, I'd say. It was very crowded, wasn't it?'

'It was,' Frankie agreed. 'But you didn't buy, er, the dress you said you wanted, did you? Or did Lilly serve you?'

No, as soon as she'd said it she knew Lilly would have told her. With a lot of wide eyes and gestures and exaggerated giggling.

'No, duck. It's still here. No one bought it today.'

'Oh, good.'

'They stole it from me, you know.'

'I'm sure whoever they are, didn't. We don't deal in stolen goods,' Frankie said firmly. 'I'm sure whichever dress it is that has taken your fancy was donated honestly by its owner.'

'No.' The little man shook his head sadly. 'It wasn't. It was mine and they stole it.'

Frankie sighed. She was too weary to argue. 'Who did?'

'Thelma and Louise.'

Oh Lordy ... Frankie closed her eyes. However sweet he was, she was far too tired to deal with some mad old cross-dressing pensioner living in fantasy land tonight. Maybe it was best to humour him.

'Really? That was naughty of them.'

'Naughty? It was downright bloody wicked!'

'Well, yes. Stealing is wicked, of course. And because this Thelma and Louise stole—allegedly, stole—the frock from you and must have donated it here, you want it back?'

'Yes, but—' he shook his grizzled head '—it weren't *my* frock, duck. I don't wear frocks. I ain't no Danny La Rue.'

Not a cross-dresser then. Just barking.

He looked anxiously at Frankie. 'It belonged to my wife. She's gone now. Dead.'

'Oh, I'm sorry.'

'Ah, me too, duck. I thought I'd be joining her soon but it don't seem like that's going to happen.'

'Oh, don't say that! It must be awful for you, of course, but life does go on. Honestly. My gran eventually managed to have quite a nice life after Grandpa died. She joined clubs and went on trips and—'

'I tried that, duck, but it ain't no fun any more. I just want her dress back. Let me show you which one it is.'

'Ok.' Despite her tiredness, Frankie felt desperately sorry for the lonely old man. She'd switch on the till for him and just make one last sale. 'And then I've got to lock up and you really must go.'

Frankie followed him to the 1950s rails and watched as he pointed to a cream silk shantung dress. It was very Audrey Hepburn: slim-fitting, sleeveless, high waisted with a flamboyant bow.

'It's very pretty.'

'She wore it on our wedding day.' His eyes grew distant. 'And she had a cream rose in her hair. Her hair was as dark as yours back then, duck. Beautiful she was.'

'She must have been.' Frankie suddenly wanted to hug him. So what if he was slightly deranged and a bit deluded? He wanted his wife's wedding dress back again. It had huge sentimental value. What was so wrong with that?

'I was only seventeen when I met her at the village hop over in Tadpole Bridge, and we were wed when I was twenty-one. We had fifty wonderfully happy years together.'

Frankie sighed. She'd have to give him the frock, she knew she would. She couldn't ask him to pay for it—however it had turned up in the shop, he had every right to want it back, didn't he?

'Nineteen forty-six it were.' He looked at her. 'Just after the war ended. Things were just getting back to normal. It was nice to have the village dances and that after all the misery. I went over to Tadpole Bridge with a couple of pals. They always had a good band over at Tadpole Bridge village hall. A proper little dance band, you know?'

Frankie, whose understanding of dance music was clearly light years away from his, nodded anyway.

'Ah, it was a right good do. A smashing band with a couple of singers—crooners we called 'em back then. Anyway, I saw her as soon as I walked in. Beautiful, she was. Standing there in her pretty red and white frock, her hair like black silk. She was with some friends but I didn't notice any of them. Just her.'

Frankie, still just wanting to go home and sleep, could sense his deep sadness. It wouldn't hurt her to listen to him for a little while, would it? Not if it helped him?

'And did she notice you, too?'

'Not straight away, duck. I was right shy, and she was so lovely, I just sort of stared at her, with my heart going like billy-o. My pals were straight over to the girls and asking them to dance, you know, but not me. I hung back. Anyway, she just shook her head when anyone asked her to dance. My pals danced with her pals. They were jiving a bit—and I was never any great shakes at that, but the girls loved it. The GIs had taught 'em all the moves when they were stationed over here, see. And then the band started to play "Twilight Time", and everyone stopped jitterbugging and I could see her across the floor . . .'

'So,' Frankie asked, seeing this all unfolding in her mind like an old black and white movie, 'you plucked up the courage to ask her to dance, did you?'

'Ah.' He grinned. 'I did. And I was shaking like a leaf I can tell you. Why she'd dance with me when she'd turned my pals down, I wasn't sure. But I had to ask her. I loved her, you see.'

'But you didn't even know her.'

'No, duck. I didn't need to. Love at first sight it were for me. I knew there and then that she was the only girl for me. And if she turned me down then I'd be alone for the rest of me life.'

Frankie was now completely swept up in this love story from so many years ago. It was so wonderfully romantic.

'But she didn't? Turn you down, I mean?'

109

'No, duck, she didn't. She just smiled at me—such a lovely smile she had, it lit up the whole village hall—and said yes. And she just stepped into my arms—and off we went.'

Frankie nodded. 'And ... ?'

'And all my pals were jealous. I could see 'em all looking at me and wondering why this beautiful girl had danced with me and not with them. And holding her in my arms was like holding ... oh, I don't know ... like holding stardust and moonbeams all rolled into one. Magical. And she smelled of summer flowers and I knew there would never be anyone else for me.'

Frankie swallowed the lump in her throat. It was all a million miles away from the frenetic, frantic, noisy groping and gesturing of getting-to-know-you on the dance floor these days.

'And—' she looked at him, not wanting the story to end '—you carried on dancing with her, did you?'

'Ah, I did. And we talked when we sat out the more lively dances and got to know one another a bit. I bought her a ginger beer—the village hall weren't licensed—and then we danced some more. And when the night was over I walked her home.'

'Oh, that's so lovely,' Frankie sighed. 'Walking her home. I so wish people still did that.'

He nodded. 'I held her hand, and we walked across fields and along lanes and I didn't know where I was or what time it was or anything. I was just floating along, listening to her talking and laughing—she had such a pretty laugh—and then we stopped at the end of her street and I kissed her goodnight.'

Frankie swallowed again. 'That was brave of you.'

'Ah.' He chuckled. 'I thought she might slap me face, but she didn't. She kissed me back. And I was like a dog with two tails. There wasn't a happier lad in the whole world than me that night.'

'And you asked to see her again? And she said yes?'

'Yes, to both, duck. By some miracle she saw something in me—me, not very tall and not very good-looking and with curly hair and a bit of a squint. And her—the prettiest girl in seven counties. And then I told her I loved her.'

'Wow.' Frankie shook her head. 'And what did she say?'

He chuckled again. 'She said she was right glad because she thought she loved me too. And that was it. We'd be together for ever, we said. And we were. From that day on ... until ... until she died. We courted for four years while we saved up to get wed.'

'And she wore the dress?'

He nodded. 'She was always beautiful, but never more than on our wedding day. In that dress. It means everything to me, that dress. I'll never, ever get used to being without her, duck. Never. My heart broke the day she died and has never mended. All I want is to be with her again. She was my life, my love, my reason for living.'

Frankie dashed away the tears. 'Please, please, have the dress. You don't have to pay for it. I'll wrap it up for you now and you can take it home.'

'I can't, duck.'

'Why? Because you think, um, Thelma and Louise might—?'

'Thelma and Louise is long gone. Back to wherever they came from. They took what they wanted—and there weren't much to take, I can tell you—and then they cluttered off.'

OK. In his grief-stricken mind, Thelma and Louise had taken their gun-toting, mad-car-driving away from Kingston Dapple. That was a relief.

'So, if they've gone, why can't you take it home now?'

'I haven't got a home any more, duck.'

Oh, no ... Frankie groaned. Homeless—at his age! How awful. Surely there must be shelters or something? Or was he even too mad and sad to be housed in a shelter?

He looked hopefully at her. 'So, now do you understand, duck? This was the only thing of my wife's I had left. And Thelma and Louise robbed me of it—and everything else. I don't care about the rest of it, but I care about the dress. It was the most important thing I had left in my life.'

'But you came in here wanting to buy it, didn't you?'

'No, duck. I'm here with it. It brings my Achsah close to me, see?'

Achsah? Frankie frowned. Where had she heard that name before?

'*Achsah*?'

'I thought it was a lovely name.' He nodded and gave a little chuckle. 'Mind, she always hated it. Called herself Betty in private. Her dad was a bit of an old fire and brimstone man. Well known for it over in Tadpole Bridge, he was. All her brothers and sisters had odd Old Testament names too. Poor souls. They all hated them and—'

'What's *your* name?' Frankie interrupted, everything suddenly falling scaringly into place like a tumble lock.

112

'Ernie Yardley, duck. What's yours?'

'Frankie Meredith,' Frankie said faintly. 'And you can't be Ernie Yardley because Biddy came in here a few weeks back and bought an outfit for his funeral. Ernie Yardley's dead.'

'I know I am, duck.'

Frankie felt very sick. And very, very frightened.

'Don't be scared, duck.' Ernie beamed at her. 'I was scared rigid meself when I found out I was dead but not *gone*—if you get my drift.'

Nooo, this couldn't happening. She must be dreaming ...

'You mean, um ...' Frankie closed her eyes in the hope that it was all an illusion, then opened them again. It wasn't. Ernie was still there. 'You mean, you're a *ghost*?'

'I suppose I must be.'

'You can't be.' Frankie looked wildly round the shop. 'I can't be here talking to a ghost. I don't believe in ghosts.'

'Not my problem, duck, if you don't mind me saying. Whether you believe in me or not is neither here nor there, really, is it? I'm here, so are you, and we're having this chat, so one of us must be mistaken, mustn't we? Look, can I just tell you my side of things?'

'NO!' Frankie shouted, angry at her gullibility and still terrified at the same time. 'No, just go home. Stop messing about, stop playing silly games and go home. Oh, you nearly had me fooled with that story.'

'The story ain't a story, duck. It's all true. Exactly how it happened. All I want now is to be reunited with my beloved Achsah. She's waiting for me, and I can't reach her.'

113

'Sorry. This isn't funny any more. You are *not* a ghost! You are *not* Ernie Yardley! Maisie stupid Fairbrother set you up for this, didn't she? Because I said I didn't believe in ghosts, she's sent you along to play at haunting. You might as well drape a white sheet over your head and go "woo-woo-woo" and—'

'Look, duck, I don't like it any more than you do. I don't even understand it. But I left this life in Poundland just as I was getting some nice cut-price things for me tea. And it didn't bother me a jot. I've wanted to be reunited with Achsah for so long, duck. But I'm not. I'm here, with her frock what they stole from me, see?'

'Go away!' Frankie marched over to the door and hauled it open. The thick grey fog swirled in, like ... well, like a whole lot of ghosts. 'Get out! Now! You don't scare me. Not any more. It's just some sort of stupid joke! Go, please!'

'You go and ask Slo Motion if you wants to know the truth.' Ernie looked woebegone. 'Slo Motion did my funeral. They—Thelma and Louise—didn't go along with my plans, duck. They changed everything to the cheapest possible.'

'Stop it! You're just being silly now. All this nonsense about Thelma and Louise.'

'Thelma and Louise are my nieces, duck. My only relations. Pair of nasty bitches they are too. And they had me cremated when I wanted to be buried along with Achsah in the little churchyard in Tadpole Bridge, like we'd always planned. They went cheapskate, duck. They cleared out all my things and got rid of them. What they couldn't sell, they just dumped. Like Achsah's dress here. And that wasn't all—'

Frankie clapped her hands over her ears. 'La-la-la! I'm not listening! Get out! And tell Maisie Fairbrother that this won't work! I-do-not-believe-in-ghosts!'

'As I said, I'm sorry, duck. But it's really not my problem what you believe in. You go and ask Slo to tell you what happened before my funeral. Slo knows who I am and what happened. Get him to tell you about the car journey to Tadpole Bridge. Ask him what happened at the traffic lights. There weren't no one there except him and me and I was dead. Not a living soul knows about that car journey except me and Slo, and I suppose I'm not a living soul, so to speak. Get him to show you a picture of me, and then you'll know who I am.'

'Get out!' Frankie marched to the door and flung it open. 'I'll be fair to you. I'm going to count to ten...'

'OK, duck, off you go.'

'One and two and ...' Feeling very silly, Frankie counted slowly. '... nine and ten. Right, if you don't go now I'm going to call the police. I don't want to, but I will, then you and Maisie Fairbrother are going to look really silly with your trumped-up nonsense, aren't you?'

There was no reply. She squinted round the shop. The 1950s rails stood silent. Achsah's alleged wedding dress was still there.

And Ernie Yardley, or whoever he was, had gone.

How on earth had he managed to slip past her? For his age he must be amazingly light on his feet. Probably ballroom dancing, Frankie thought. He'd obviously been a good dancer in his day. And there'd been a big increase in ballroom dancing

115

in the area since *Strictly*. All the oldies loved it because it reminded them of the days when every village had a little dance hall—just like in Ernie's supposed story—or so Rita had said. However he'd managed it, he'd gone.

Frankie carefully searched every inch of the shop. No, not a sign of him. Thank goodness, because she really would have called the police. Probably ... Silly old fool—telling her such a tale. Just as well Lilly hadn't been here—Lilly would have believed every single word of it. And damn Maisie Fairbrother. She'd have a few things to say to her, too. It would take more than a few mad old pensioners to frighten her ...

Checking everything again, Frankie locked the kitchen, set the alarm, switched off the lights and opened the door. Oooh, it was a really awful night. The fog hung, a sulphurish yellowy-grey blanket, blotting out almost everything in the market place. The thought of heading home to Featherbed Lane, and having a bath, hot chocolate and snuggling into bed with a good book until sleep swept over her, had never seemed so appealing.

'Goodnight, duck.' Ernie's voice wavered from somewhere behind her. 'And please, if you've got any compassion in your soul after what I've told you about me and Achsah, go and see Slo Motion, tell him I said "Whoops, Ern, there you go. Can't have people thinking you can't hold your ale, can we?" and get this lot sorted out for me.'

Frankie swirled round in the darkness. How the hell had he got back into the shop? 'No. No way. Absolutely not. This has gone too far. Get out of my shop!'

'Please, duck. You seem like a nice girl. I miss

116

Achsah so much. I want to be with her again. I can't spend eternity alone like this. You can help me if you want to.'

'Enough!' Frankie slammed the lights on again and marched angrily across the shop, looking between, under and over the rails. 'I like a joke as much as anyone, but this isn't funny any more. I don't know where you are or where you were hiding, but enough's enough! Get out!'

But, despite searching every inch of Francesca's Fabulous Frocks, from top to bottom again, Frankie could find no sign of Ernie Yardley.

The shop was completely empty.

Chapter Eleven

Her heart thundering, Frankie hurtled into the Toad in the Hole. It was, as usual, practically deserted.

Frankie looked round the minimalist decor in despair. There was no one here who could help her. No one she could talk to.

A few couples sat awkwardly on the high stools, and a lone man was picking at what looked like a plate of entrails-in-jus, but there was no sign of Lilly or the others. They must have decided against the Jägerbombs-fest and gone their separate ways. And Dexter had gone out for a night of passion with the nubile Ginny. Even Brian and his kebab van were still touting their Saturday night cholesterol-fest round the villages.

And Ernie Yardley's so-called ghost was possibly still in Francesca's Fabulous Frocks.

117

Not that she believed it for a moment. She didn't, simply didn't, believe in ghosts.

Was someone playing a cruel trick on her? Someone who resented her inheriting Rita's shop and wanted to drive her out? It seemed highly unlikely, but then so did Ernie Yardley's so-called ghost ...

There was only one thing for it. Tired as she was, Frankie knew now she'd never sleep until this was sorted out. She pulled out her mobile phone.

'Oh, hi, Phoebes, sorry to bother you. I mean, I know you said you and Rocky were having a cosy night in and I hope ... What? You're dressed as who? Really? Wow. OK ... A bit too much information there, probably ... Please don't let me stop you ... Oh, yes, I can hear AC/DC in the background. I thought you were seriously into Take That? Does it? OK ... No, no—what I really wanted to ask you is Slo in downstairs? Is he? Oh, great ... And do you think it would be too late ... ? Oh, don't they? Never before midnight? Yes, the late-night films on Sky can be quite ... OK, lovely. No, I don't want to arrange a funeral, thanks. I just need to ask him something. What? Yes, it was. A really great day. Thanks again for all your help, Phoebes. I really couldn't have done it without you. Oh, no, don't worry, I won't pop up tonight. You and Rocky carry on. See you soon ... Bye ...'

Frankie snapped her phone shut, dug into her handbag for her car keys and stepped out of the Toad into the cold, clammy, foggy night.

*   *   *

Thirty-five slow, tortuous minutes later she pulled

118

her bright blue Mini into the parking space outside the Edwardian house in Winchester Road where both Phoebe and Slo had flats. It normally took about ten minutes to drive between Kingston Dapple and Hazy Hassocks but tonight it had been like driving blindfolded. It had been petrifying, not being able to see the road markings, or, in some cases, even the road.

She was still shaking as she carefully locked the Mini, skirted the various cars parked on the driveway, and rang the 'Motion and Rivers' bell just beneath the 'Lancaster and Bowler' one. She could hear the muffled sounds of AC/DC rocking away at the top of the house.

Of course, she thought, as she shivered violently in the freezing fog, it was all nonsense. Slo, bless him, was going to laugh at her, and she still had to drive all the way back to Kingston Dapple in the worst fog Berkshire had seen for years. She must be completely mad. She should have waited until the morning at least and—

'Hello, love.' Essie Rivers, still beautiful in her eighties, elegantly wrapped in a very pretty powder-blue dressing gown and with her hair tied up in a mass of trailing floaty scarves, opened the door and smiled at her. 'Young Phoebe phoned down and said you were on your way. Come along in and get warm. What a filthy night.'

Frankie stared, embarrassed, at Essie. 'Oh, no—I'm sorry. You're ready for bed. I mustn't disturb you.'

'Nonsense.' Essie ushered her into the welcoming, peach-lit hallway. 'I'm just popping in the bath ready to settle down and watch a nice George Clooney film later. Pop your coat on the

119

hook there, dear, otherwise you won't feel the benefit when you go out, will you?'

Frankie shed her coat and scarves and, having struggled with the zips on her long boots, kicked them off and left them by the front door.

Essie shook her head. 'There's no need to take your boots off—you should see the mess that Slo tramps in. I've made some sandwiches and put the coffee pot in the living room. Slo's waiting for you, dear. In you go.'

'Thank you, but—'

'No buts.' Essie beamed, opening the living room door. 'You go and chat to Slo while I wallow nicely in my bubble bath. Might see you later if you're still here, dear.'

'Yes, yes ... thank you so much.'

The living room was cosily snug, with a real coal fire, long crimson velvet curtains closed against the foggy night, and softly lit by red-shaded table lamps.

'Hello, Mr Motion.' Despite her misgivings about the wisdom of this visit, Frankie looked around in delight. 'Oh, what a lovely room.'

'Nice to see you again, young Frankie. And call me Slo, please. Mr Motion makes me feel right old. And thank you, duck. My Essie certainly knows how to make a home homely.' Slo, who had been sitting in a deep and many-cushioned armchair, with the opening of *Ocean's Eleven* frozen on the screen in front of him, stood up. 'Come along in and get warm.'

Frankie sighed blissfully in the warmth, and scuttled towards the fire, holding out her hands. 'I'm really sorry if this is messing up your plans for the evening. I should have left it until ...'

'You're not messing up anything.' Slo indicated

to the television where George Clooney was silently but glamorously poised, ready for action. 'Sky Plus, you see. So clever. We're all ready to go when Essie has had her bath. Now settle yourself down in that chair and grab a sandwich while I pour the coffee. Cheese and chutney. OK with you?'

'Fantastic.' Frankie sank into the billowy cushions and stared greedily at the small mountain of fat sandwiches on the coffee table. 'I didn't think I was hungry, but now I think I'm absolutely starving.'

'Good girl. I like to see a lass with a good appetite.' Slo heaped sandwiches onto two plates and poured two mugs of coffee. 'Now, get stuck in and tell me what this is all about.'

'Well,' Frankie mumbled round her deliciously squishy cheese and chutney, 'it all sounds a bit mad now, but ... but well, I really need to know if you believe in ghosts.'

Slo chuckled throatily, the chuckle turning into a full-blown chesty cough. When he'd recovered, he chuckled again. 'Well, I wasn't expecting that one. And no, duck, I don't. Mind you, I do believe in magic. But that's something else entirely. Me and Essie got together through magic you know.'

'Yes, Phoebe told me. It was a lovely story. So, you believe in *something*? I mean, things that can't really be explained?'

'Ah.' Slo nodded. 'I do. But not in ghosts, duck.'

'I didn't think you would somehow.'

'No one would, not in my business, duck. See, in my line of work I hear a lot of nonsense about ghosts and so forth. But when you're dealing with the mortal remains of the dead, you quickly realise that all that's left of the living person is just that.

121

Mortal remains. A shell. The spirit, the thing that made 'em them, is gone. And hopefully to a better place. And it's over. But I don't believe in ghosts, duck. Never have, never will. But there's plenty of them as does—and you're one of them?'

'No,' Frankie said quickly. 'That's just the point.'

Slo looked puzzled. 'It's lovely to see you, but did you come all this way tonight in this weather to ask me if I believed in ghosts?'

'No, well, yes . . . Oh, look, this is probably going to sound really weird, I want to ask you about someone you, er, buried . . . that is, cremated recently, but, thinking about it, I don't suppose you'll be able to tell me anything because of client confidentiality.'

Slo spluttered cheerfully through his sandwich. Crumbs mingled with the cigarette ash lingering on the front of his dark-red sweater. 'Not much of a problem in our business, client confidentiality, given that most of our clients are dead. Mind you, if it's something to do with money, or funeral costs of a particular person, I can't tell you, of course, but— well, you try me, duck. If I can help you, I will.'

Frankie, toasting her toes in front of the fire and making inroads into Essie's exquisite sandwiches, explained that she wanted to know about Ernie Yardley—leaving out the fact that he was now, allegedly, hanging around in Francesca's Fabulous Frocks, of course.

It all sounded pretty lame now, Frankie thought, especially with the muffled sounds of AC/DC interspersed with laughter from upstairs, and the sensuous wafts of apple-blossom-scented steam drifting from the bathroom. Normal life going on as, well, normal.

But she'd started so she might as well carry on.

'What I really want to know—' she leaned forward, 'is if you can maybe show me a picture of him. Oh, and tell me if his nieces were really called Thelma and Louise, and if they insisted that he was cremated rather than buried.'

Slo nodded, wheezing cheerfully. 'Ah, that's easy enough. I've got the photo we used for the order of service somewhere—I'll dig it out for you later, duck. And yes, you're right about Ernie's nieces— nasty pair they were. Mean as weasels. Wanted the cheapest possible funeral. I happened to know Ernie had put a bit away so he could be buried in Tadpole Bridge churchyard with his Achsah, being a mate, he'd told me, but, of course, dying sudden like he did, and leaving nothing written down, it was left to them nieces to sort out the final arrangements.'

'So he was cremated?' Frankie reached for another delicious sandwich. 'He is definitely dead?'

'Oh yes.' Slo nodded. 'And his ashes were just left at the crem. Them nieces wouldn't listen to me when I told them I knew what Ernie wanted. They wouldn't even pay for the ashes to be interred in Achsah's grave. At least poor old Ernie would have been with her as he'd always wanted. But no, they just left 'em at the crem. I picked 'em up a few days later and brought 'em back to the chapel of rest.'

'So—' Frankie lifted her mug of coffee '—Ernie Yardley's ashes are still here, or rather, wherever you keep them?'

'They are, duck. Such a shame. Poor old Ernie not laid to rest proper like. I wasn't happy with that Thelma and Louise right from the start. I knew they were after whatever he'd left. You see it a lot in my business. Money—' He shook his head. 'You wouldn't believe what the relatives get up to ... Anyway, duck, I still don't see why you're that interested in Ernie Yardley. Nice bloke, one of the best, and never happy since Achsah passed on, poor soul, but really—'

Frankie swallowed a mouthful of hot, strong coffee. The fire crackled and hissed. She took a deep breath. 'Can you tell me about a car journey? Something to do with a car journey and the traffic lights.'

Slo coughed, then stared at her, his sandwich suspended. 'You can't know about that.'

Frankie felt the shivers run down her spine. Despite the heat from the fire she was suddenly cold. 'You mean, there was something?'

Slo put down his plate. 'Aye, duck, there was. But there's no one in the world what knows about it. I've not breathed a word to anyone. More than my life's worth. Not even to Essie. And certainly not to Constance and Perpetua—my cousins, duck, and co-directors in the business, you know them, don't you? They'd have me guts for garters, they would. How the devil did you get wind of it?'

Frankie tried to stop the goosebumps crawling across her flesh. 'He told me.'

'What?' Slo leaned forwards. 'Who did?'

'Ernie Yardley.'

'Ernie Yardley's dead, duck.'

'I know. But, OK, maybe the person who told me isn't really Ernie Yardley. In fact—' she stared at Slo '—he can't be Ernie Yardley, because he's dead. But, this ... this ... person who says he's Ernie, told me that something happened after he was dead—with you and a car and ...'

124

Slo shook his head. 'Now you're scaring me, duck. Now you're really scaring me. Go on, tell me what Ernie, er, this person told you.'

'OK. Look, I know you're obviously not going to believe this, but ...' And haltingly she told him everything.

'Well, blow me down.' Slo exhaled nosily, his chest sounding like a symphony of bellows. 'I don't know what to say and that's a fact. Now you've got me right mixed and muddled.'

'And,' Frankie said quickly, 'there's something else. He, Ernie, or whoever he is, said I had to tell you something. I know it sounds daft, and you'll probably laugh, but he said I had to say, "Whoops, Ern, there you go. Can't have people thinking you can't hold your ale, can we?"'

'Dear Lord in heaven!' Slo sank back against his cushions. 'Dearie, dearie me.'

'Did you say that? To Ernie Yardley?'

'Not to Ernie Yardley as he lived and breathed, no,' Slo said faintly. 'OK, Frankie, duck, I'll tell you what happened, but you must promise me you'll never, ever repeat it.'

'Promise. Cross my heart and hope to, er, well, you know. And will you promise me you'll never tell anyone anything about our conversation tonight, either?'

'You have my solemn word on that, duck.' Slo nodded.

'Thank you. And when it's all, um, sorted out I'll tell you, OK?'

'Righty-ho. And I hope you're not squeamish—I'm going to just give you the plain facts, I'm not going to dress it up in any sort of pretty Disney-fied way. OK?'

125

Frankie nodded.

Slo took a deep, wheezy breath. 'Right, after Ernie died in the shop, the paramedics took his body to Winterbrook Hospital where he was certified as dead on arrival. Cardiac arrest. Plain and simple. The hospital contacted me as the local funeral director, and I collected him from the mortuary and brought him back to the chapel of rest. That's normal. Happens all the time. With me so far?'

Frankie nodded again.

'Some nosy-parkering do-gooder from the seniors group was quick off the ball and contacted Ernie's nieces to tell them he'd died, and they came hot-footing down to see me to arrange the funeral, and, if I'm not mistaken, to start raking through whatever he had left, but that's neither here nor there. As there wasn't a will, that's when the nasty nieces, Thelma and Louise, said they wanted the quickest and cheapest send-off possible at the crem. Still OK?'

'Yes, thank you.'

'Right, now for a body to be cremated there needs to be two death certificates issued. Ernie had the one from the duty doc at the hospital, and as he'd been seeing his own GP regularly for his heart problems there wouldn't be no need for a coroner nor none of that stuff, but his own doctor had to certify, to put it bluntly duck, that Ernie was Ernie and that he was dead, and issue the second certificate. Am I making sense?'

Frankie nodded again. It all sounded a bit long-winded to her, but she didn't want to interrupt.

'Good, duck. So, I rang the crem to book a slot—sorry, I know that sounds right disrespectful

126

to anyone not in the business, but really you have to get in as quick as possible otherwise the funeral can be delayed for ages and them nieces wanted it done and dusted—and then phoned old Doctor Harman at the Tadpole Bridge surgery. He was Ern's GP. Well, he runs a one-man-band practice, so he's everyone's GP out there. Anyway, I told him I needed him to get over here to the chapel of rest and certify Ernie as dead then and there, so as I could get the paperwork to the crem that day and make sure the funeral was going ahead as planned.'

Slo paused and Frankie nodded again.

'Right, duck. Well, blow me, old Doc Harman waffled and puffed and said he was off duty and couldn't drive over to Hazy Hassocks because he'd had a "hearty lunch" with some pals and was over the drink–drive limit.'

Frankie frowned. 'Oh, that was a bit unfortunate. Did that mean you had to delay everything?'

Slo shook his head. 'Not an option, duck. It happens. Not often, but if the nieces wanted the cremation to go ahead without waiting nearly two weeks I had to have the right paperwork that day. So, I thought, we'll have to go down the old Mountain and Mohammed route.'

'Sorry, I don't understand.'

'If Doc Harman couldn't come to Ern, then Ern would have to go to Doc Harman.'

Slo stared at her in the firelight. Frankie stared back.

'You mean, you had to drive him in his coffin? To Tadpole Bridge?'

Slo shook his head and wheezed sadly. 'Not in the coffin, duck, no. That's illegal. Can't fasten down a body in a coffin without the appropriate death certificate, see? So, I took him—Ernie, that is—to Tadpole Bridge in the Daimler. In the passenger seat.'

'No way!'

'Sorry, duck. Told you it weren't pretty, and it's not something I'm proud of, but needs must. Anyway, I made sure Ernie was fully dressed and I thought no one would notice.'

Frankie suddenly wanted to laugh even though it wasn't remotely funny. 'You mean, you drove to Tadpole Bridge with a dead body—Ernie's dead body—belted into the passenger seat of your car? In broad daylight?'

'Yes, duck. That's exactly what I mean. See now why I can't have a word of this getting out? It would finish us as a business if anyone knew. Oh, I treated Ernie right respectfully, and I chatted to him all the way there.'

Frankie pulled a face. 'But, er, wouldn't he have been, um, stiff?'

Slo shook his head. 'Rigor mortis goes off pretty quickly. Just as well, really, or we'd never be able to do the laying-out and embalming and stuff.'

Frankie winced.

'Sorry, duck. But you did ask.' Slo coughed apologetically. 'Anyway, we got to Tadpole Bridge with no mishaps, and old Doc Harman staggered out of his cottage with his stethoscope and said, "Yes, that's Ernie Yardley and he's had a dicky ticker for ages and he's dead", and he wrote the certificate and that was that.'

'And then you and Ernie came back here, to the chapel of rest, and ... ?'

'Going out there we were lucky with the traffic lights, and no one took no notice of us at all.

128

Coming back, we got caught by a red light on the junction to Bagley-cum-Russet and Fiddlesticks. And there was some old dears waiting to cross the road and they waved at me and looked in the car...'

'No!'

'Yes, duck. Sadly. And poor old Ernie had slumped a bit in his seat belt—so, in case they could hear me, I just said the first thing that came into my head...'

'Which was "Whoops, Ern, there you go. Can't have people thinking you can't hold your ale, can we?"'

Slo nodded. 'And then the lights changed and off we went. And I got the death certificates to the crem that same afternoon and Ernie Yardley's funeral went ahead as planned—not by him, but by the nasty nieces—and see, there isn't anyone in the world who can know what I said to him that day, except him and me... and he was dead.'

The fire crackled in the silence.

Frankie exhaled, her skin crawling. 'What about the old ladies crossing the road?'

Slo shook his head. 'No, duck. The windows was tight shut. They couldn't hear me, but they could see I was chatting to him. Even if they got a glimpse of Ernie they wouldn't have twigged that he were dead. He was pale naturally, so they might think he looked a bit ill. But they couldn't hear me, I'm sure. They just thought we was talking. No, I'd swear on my Essie's life they weren't aware of anything odd going on at all.'

Frankie sat in silence, staring at George Clooney, a million thoughts racing round her head.

'So, what does it mean? All this? Is Ernie really

129

haunting my shop? Is he a ghost?'

'I've got no darned idea, duck. But you've got me spooked now, and no mistake.' Slo stood up and walked slowly over to a walnut desk in the corner.

After a minute or two of rummaging, he returned with a folder. 'Here we are, duck, all the bits and pieces from Ernie's funeral. Them nasty nieces didn't want any of it as a memento of poor old Ern, naturally, so I kept it in here out of respect, really.'

He sat down again, pulled out a photograph and passed it to Frankie. Feeling cold and more than a little frightened, she really didn't want to look at it.

'Go on, duck,' Slo encouraged her. 'Take a peek. This is Ernie. Now, is this the same man who—?'

Reluctantly, Frankie gazed down at the photograph and swallowed.

The elderly man smiling up at her was wearing an old-fashioned shiny suit, with grizzled hair and a cheerful-goblin wrinkled face.

'Oh my God,' Frankie whispered. 'Yes, that's him. That's the man in my shop.'

Chapter Twelve

Cherish had always hated Sundays. Well, at least since she'd been living here alone. Having worked in Miriam's Modes in Winterbrook since leaving school, Sundays back then, shared with her parents, had been lovely. Sundays back then had always been a busy day of housework in the little bungalow, and cooking economical meals to pop into the tiny fridge-top freezer compartment for the week ahead, along with the traditional Sunday roast, and washing and ironing her work skirts and blouses, all to the accompaniment of lovely sing-along songs on the radio.

Now, Sundays were just another lonely day. Just like every other lonely day.

It had been all very well, Cherish thought, as she dusted the Royal Doulton figurines in the Hazy Hassocks bungalow that had hardly changed for five decades, giving up her job to care for her parents; giving up any chance of meeting someone and marrying them and having children; dedicating her life to her parents until they had passed away. They'd loved her, and she'd loved them and been dutiful, and hadn't minded the duty one jot.

But now, with no parents, no job and no one in the whole world who needed her, it was a very forlorn existence.

Of course she had Biddy who'd been her friend since school days, and Biddy was single too. But Biddy enjoyed her own company. Probably because Biddy was always so miserable. Always wanting the see the bad side of everything. Biddy, Cherish thought, as she folded her duster and placed it neatly beside the polish in her cleaning-tidy, was very mean and sometimes downright depressing, which was why she still had no real friends. Apart from Cherish, of course.

But even in late middle age, Biddy still didn't seem to mind being alone, because Biddy had always been a loner, really. Even at school, Biddy had managed to alienate most people by her barbed comments. Cherish, for some reason, had never been the target of Biddy's bile. Both only children with elderly parents, they had formed an unlikely alliance. And Biddy, always totally happy with her own sniping company, simply didn't understand why Cherish craved the companionship of others, then or now.

Which is why, on Biddy's advice—"Well, if you really want to meet other people, although Lord knows why you should, then you might as well make some money out of it and as you're pretty useless at most stuff, why don't you resurrect that colour advising thing you used to do?"—Cherish had started the colour-palette advisory service as a home-run venture.

She'd always had a feel for colours indicating people's inner vitality, somehow. Even as a child. Her mother had called it a gift. Cherish's mother had been a beige person, as was Cherish now. Her father had been more of a lovat green or heather mixture. As a family, none of them had been remotely what you'd call *gaudy*.

The colour advising was something she'd always done at Miriam's Modes. There had been a certain class of lady who shopped there and they'd always seemed to welcome Cherish's advice on the most suitable colour for their new season's shirtwaister or costume.

Funny, Cherish thought, no one said costume these days. It was always suits. Suits, in her day, had been strictly for men. Ladies always wore two-piece costumes.

It would have been lovely, Cherish thought, if she could have carried out her colour-advising in that lovely vintage frock shop yesterday. Not that she needed the money, whatever Biddy said, because Cherish had never really needed money. Her parents had been very astute with their endowment policies leaving her a healthy nest egg, and, even after she'd stopped working, Cherish's own insurance premium, saved for since childhood, had matured nicely on her fiftieth birthday. She'd always managed to live well within her means.

No, money was no objective, but it would have made such a difference, knowing that she had somewhere to go, someone to see, a purpose in life, when she stumbled out of bed each morning to switch on the kettle first, followed by the radio on the kitchen windowsill.

It was sad, she felt, in her mid-fifties, to live her life regulated by the radio programmes during the day and the television programmes at night. But at least she hadn't gone down the daytime telly route like so many others of her age.

The television remained switched off until the six o'clock news, as it always had in her parents' day, when Cherish had her supper on a tray. The tray-on-lap had been a daring innovation brought in after her parents died. When they were alive, they all sat round the dining table for their meals, and discussed the day's events. After their deaths, close together, Cherish had found a dining table set for one a very dismal thing.

So now the radio presenters and television announcers were her daily friends, and were more real to her than any real people. She felt they were all talking just to her, and she talked back to them. And she hated it when they went on holidays and a stranger took over their programmes. It totally ruined the symmetry of her day.

It had taken her months and months to recover from Terry Wogan's retirement.

There. Cherish looked at the cabinet full of Royal Doulton ladies. They all sparkled in their

133

crinolines, staring imperiously at her from their pale blank eyes. Her mother had loved the crinoline ladies, but Cherish hated them. She thought they were all in the wrong colours, and frequently told them so. If she hadn't felt so guilty about it, she'd have packed up the entire collection and donated it to Biff and Hedley Pippin's charity shop. Like most things in the bungalow, really. But, because the bungalow was a shrine to happier times with her parents, she simply couldn't bring herself to get rid of a single item.

Ten o'clock. Cherish sighed. The day stretched endlessly ahead. And it was still so foggy and cold outside there wasn't even much point in wrapping up and taking a stroll down Hazy Hassocks High Street. There'd be no one about on a day like this. Hazy Hassocks was ambivalent about Sunday opening hours, too. Big Sava would be open, of course, but because she shopped cheaply and cooked simply, as her mother had done, Cherish didn't need any groceries, and the rest of the Hazy Hassocks shops held very little interest.

Unlike Francesca's Fabulous Frocks in Kingston Dapple.

Oh, how she'd loved just looking at all those beautiful frocks, imagining the previous owners, speculating on who might buy them next, and for what special occasion. And Frankie was a very nice girl, too, despite what Biddy had said about her. Even if she wore those garishly bright colours when she really should be in grey.

And how wonderful it would be to work in that shop with Frankie and chat to the customers, and touch those gorgeous fabrics—fabrics made with love into stunning dresses long before cheap

134

clothes were imported by the container-load from other countries—and advise them on which colours would suit them best.

Cherish shuddered suddenly, remembering the debacle in Dorothy Perkins in Winterbrook the previous day. That had been Biddy's fault, of course. Biddy was always so caustic.

She shook her head, trying to erase the awful memory.

She looked at the clock again. Was it too early to make a cup of coffee? Yes, definitely. Coffee was for elevenses and it was nowhere near that time yet.

Oh, dear … Cherish wandered to the window and stared out at the swirling grey gloom. How on earth was she going to fill all those long hours before it was time to go back to bed?

Chapter Thirteen

By half past nine on Monday morning, Frankie had restored Francesca's Fabulous Frocks to some sort of order after the jumble-sale rush of her first day's trading. The rails were restocked and tidy; the purple and gold bags were neatly stacked; the float in the till was replenished; Michael Bublé had been replaced by a selection of easy-listening from Jack Jones, Matt Monroe and Andy Williams; the counter had been polished and the floor swept; and Dexter's rainbow bouquet had been topped up with fresh water and still looked and smelled ravishing.

Frankie looked around her with pleasure—relishing the array of sumptuous fabrics, rich colours and varied designs—and not a little relief.

135

After a sleepless Saturday night—a combination of exhaustion, followed by driving through the pea-souper fog twice, but far, far more because of Slo Motion's revelations about Ernie Yardley—all Frankie's plans for spending Sunday in the shop had been abandoned.

Eventually falling asleep at somewhere around dawn—just as Lilly had stumbled in from her night out in Winterbrook—Frankie had dozed fitfully, woken properly at lunchtime and felt pretty groggy all day. Deciding that she'd do a far better job of tidying the shop and restocking the rails on Monday when she'd had a good rest, and convincing herself it had nothing whatsoever to do with the thought that Ernie Yardley's ghost might just be *real*, she'd spent the day half-listening to Lilly's raptures over her latest 'cutest man in the entire world' and mulling over what Slo had told her.

It simply couldn't be true.

Of course, she hadn't mentioned any of it to Lilly. Mainly because Lilly might just have believed it and made matters a whole lot worse, but also because a loved-up Lilly was even less use as a listener than a dishcloth. So, Frankie had kept everything about Ernie Yardley to herself, as she'd promised Slo she would.

And it had ruined her Sunday.

However now, with the fog gone and the low winter sun streaming through the festive windows on this bright, extremely frosty morning, she almost laughed at her gullibility. Ghosts! No way. It was, Frankie was sure, still something to do with Maisie Fairbrother playing tricks—although the photograph was pretty damning evidence, not to mention the incident at the traffic lights ...

136

And why would anyone want to play those sort of tricks on her anyway? She wasn't aware of having any enemies, and she was pretty sure everyone had loved Rita. So, who? And why?

Because, if it wasn't a trick, then it had to be real, didn't it?

No. She shook her head as she ran her hand across the top of one of the 1960s rails. It was all nonsense. Although, it had to be said, she'd opened up earlier that morning while the market square was dark and still deserted and early-morning drowsy with a feeling of huge trepidation. And, she admitted to herself, she had called out to Ernie Yardley—just in case . . .

But the shop had been completely empty. Achsah's frock was still on the 1950s rails, without anyone small, elderly, grizzle-haired and goblin-faced in ghostly attendance.

It was all some sort of silly, but cleverly organised stunt to unsettle her. And she'd find out who was behind it and deal with it.

As she looked out through the large double windows at the market square where the moisture left by the fog had frozen in crystal feathers, turning everything white like snowfall beneath the bluebell sky, she couldn't understand why she'd allowed herself to get so agitated. There just had to be a simple and rational explanation.

There were no such thing as ghosts. Fact.

Shoppers were cheerfully going about their Monday-morning business, stepping carefully across the icy cobbles, and Dexter, occasionally blowing on his hands, his breath pluming into the sub-zero air, was busily arranging huge buckets of red and white flowers on the decking outside the stall, and replenishing the stocks of holly wreaths and mistletoe garlands.

She watched him for a moment. The jeans, boots and leather jacket were the same, and this morning's sweatshirt was turquoise: a splash of vivid colour against the rich darkness of the greenery. Frankie smiled to herself. She was wearing a short, flared turquoise frock today, with navy tights and boots. Together, they'd look like a matching pair.

Not, of course, that there was going to be any *together* as such. Not in that way. She didn't want any more complications of that sort—even if Dexter hadn't already been involved with Ginny and the home-service ladies. But he was, she admitted to herself, absolutely gorgeous just to look at in a sort of detached kind of way.

The door flew open and three women, muffled against the frosty morning and clutching shopping baskets, bustled in and, after calling out cheerful 'good mornings' and humming along with 'Born Free', headed for the 1980s rails.

Francesca's Fabulous Frocks was up and running once again.

By eleven o'clock, the shop was packed. Frankie had hardly had time to breathe. She was desperate to go to the loo and to have a coffee. She worked as quickly as she could, packing the dresses and chatting at the same time, taking money and zapping cards, but the queue at the counter seemed to grow ever longer.

'Here.' Dexter manoeuvred his way behind the counter, and handed her a mug of Greasy Spoon coffee. 'You look like you could do with it.'

'Life saver.' Frankie grinned, carefully wrapping a grunge outfit in tissue paper. 'Thank you so much.

I'd hoped to get out to you with a cup this morning but—' she looked at the never-ending queue of women who were now looking hungrily at Dexter '—there's been no chance.'

'Great, isn't it? I'm really busy too. I'd better get back before some bugger nicks the mistletoe.' He grinned at her. 'And snap on the colour co-ordinating. Great sartorial minds at work?'

Frankie giggled. 'Oh, the turquoise—yes, I know. I, er, saw you earlier and thought we looked a bit Howard and Hilda.'

'Who?'

'They were in an old sit-com. Always wore the same clothes. A running joke.'

'Oh, right.' Dexter looked blank. 'I must have missed that one.'

'Maybe more Torvill and Dean, then?'

Dexter brightened. 'Oh, yeah, I know them. She's got incredible legs.'

Frankie laughed.

'Anyway—' Dexter ran his fingers through his silky hair '—how are you fixed for lunch?'

Frankie hadn't even thought about lunch. 'Lord knows. I don't think I'll be able to have any. It doesn't matter—it'll be great preparation for the Christmas bloat-out. Sorry?' She leaned across the counter to a diminutive woman in a huge tweed coat, a balaclava and mittens. 'Yes, I've got several peasant dresses on the 1970s rails. Yes, I love those little peeps of lacy petticoat, too.'

'You need help.' Dexter laughed as the woman trundled across to the appropriate frocks.

'In a medical way?'

'In an assistant sort of way. So do I. I don't know how Ray managed on his own at busy times.'

'He always used to co-opt Brian in to help him during December and other hectic periods.' Frankie looked longingly at her rapidly cooling coffee as she reached for a midnight-blue satin shift dress and a Visa card. 'Maybe you could ask him?'

Dexter nodded. 'Yeah, I'll do that. He's a nice bloke. Thanks. But what about you?'

Frankie shrugged. 'No idea. I think I'm going to have to advertise for a part-timer. I hadn't even thought about it, but I do need someone else in here. There was always me and Rita, and we weren't always busy, so it hadn't occurred to me that I might need help.'

'Plenty of students looking for Christmas jobs,' Dexter said over his shoulder as he squeezed out through the throng. 'I could ask Ginny if any of her friends are interested if you like.'

Frankie sniffed. She somehow didn't want one of Ginny's college chums giving her chapter and verse about Dexter's prowess and, although it made her feel very, very old to even think it, neither did she want to spend hours and hours with someone saying 'like' and 'random' and 'awesome' every third word and ending their sentences in an Antipodean upward lilt.

Yep, no doubt about it. She was now officially Methuselah. 'I think someone older would be better in here, actually. A lot of the customers are middle-aged—I think they might prefer it. I'll give it some thought later.'

'OK. Your call. From what I've seen, there are certainly enough, er, more mature ladies around here to pick from. You should find someone pretty easily. And if it quietens down a bit, why don't you close up for half an hour and we could grab a

140

sandwich next door?'

Close up? Shut the shop when there might still be paying customers lurking? Frankie shook her head. Rita would have a fit. Rita had never, ever shut the shop. But then, there had been two of them, hadn't there? Always one of them there to hold the fort.

'We'll see. Nice idea—can't see it happening somehow. Thanks again for the coffee, though.'

She watched as Dexter left the shop. So did everyone else. Andy Williams wasn't the only one sighing a sort of soft collective sigh as Dexter closed the door.

In a brief lull just after midday, Frankie flew to the loo and annoyed herself by eyeing the 1950s rails dubiously on her way back. Ernie Yardley, or whoever he was, was nowhere to be seen. She grinned to herself as she walked behind the counter. She wouldn't be seeing him again—Oh, damn it ...

Frankie stared down at the floor. Trying to avoid the stack of purple and gold carrier bags, she'd kicked over the overflowing wastepaper bin. Another job she'd overlooked from manic Saturday. There was so much to do, so little time to do it in and no help at all.

Making sure that her current handful of customers were still happily browsing and didn't want serving, she bent down and scooped up the detritus to the accompaniment of Andy Williams now proclaiming, rather ungrammatically she felt, that he couldn't take his eyes off of her.

Among the ripped tissue paper and torn price tickets, a handful of battered business cards were

141

strewn across the floorboards.

Cherish's business cards.

Frankie picked one up and stuffed the rest into the bin to be emptied later. She studied it carefully and thought. And, forgetting all Lilly's rules on hygiene in the workplace, tapped the card against her teeth and thought again.

Then she picked up her mobile.

*   *   *

Cherish stared at the black Bakelite phone sitting on the lace-trimmed telephone table in the bungalow's hall. Who on earth would be ringing her at this time on a Monday morning? Cherish had very few phone calls and made even less.

She hoped it wouldn't be one of those eager young people trying to sell her double glazing or a new kitchen or a mobile phone. She always let them talk to her because she felt sorry for them and it was sometimes nice to hear another voice, and never understood it when they seemed so abrupt and impolite at the end when she said it had been lovely chatting but she was well suited, thank you.

Warily, she picked up the receiver. 'Hello … Who? Oh, hello, dear. Yes, of course I remember you. How nice to hear from you. Would you? Really? Oh, yes, that would be lovely. No, I can get the bus easily enough, thank you. There's one due in a few minutes and we've got a stop at the corner of the road. Sorry? Oh, right … yes, I'll be happy to discuss things with you face to face, dear. Of course I will. What? As soon as possible, of course, dear. Lovely, thank you.'

Cherish replaced the receiver and clapped her

142

hands together. It was like a dream come true. Frankie wanted to see her. Frankie must have changed her mind about the colour-palette-advising in Francesca's Fabulous Frocks. How absolutely wonderful.

Explaining why she was leaving so abruptly and where she was going to the nice young man on the radio before apologising for switching him off mid-programme, Cherish reached for her best coat and scarf, picked up her handbag, checked that she had enough change for the bus fare, and practically skipped out of the bungalow.

*   *   *

Frankie, not sure if she'd just made another of many possible entrepreneurial mistakes by even making the phone call, didn't have long to wait. Cherish, again in an unflattering taupe coat with matching headscarf, arrived, pink-nosed and damp-eyed from the cold, half an hour later. Mercifully, alone. Frankie knew she'd never have been able to cope with Biddy in tow.

'Hello, dear. Oh, do excuse me for blowing my nose—it's freezing out there.' Cherish sniffled. 'Oh, you're still in paintbox colours, I see. I'd hoped you'd have gone for a nice charcoal by now.'

'Charcoal isn't me, honestly. Nor is pewter or gunmetal or any of the other grey colours you mentioned. I just don't like them. Sorry.'

'Shame, it would make such a difference to your life, a nice touch of grey. You'll never know what it might unleash.' Cherish looked suddenly enthusiastic. 'I'm assuming here, dear, that you rang me because you'd changed your mind? About

143

using my talents for your customers, even if you won't take my advice yourself? I'm free, dear, if you have. Dorothy Perkins in Winterbrook showed us the door, sharpish. Mind you—' she looked woebegone again '—it didn't help with Biddy telling 'em they weren't the shop she'd known in her youth when you used to be able to get a nice two-piece or a twinset for next to nothing. Then she had a few harsh words to say about new fangled boutiques. They didn't like it. They didn't like it at all.'

'No,' Frankie said diplomatically, 'I can imagine they didn't. And actually, no, I didn't want to ask you about your colour-advisory service. It was about something else altogether ...'

As job interviews went, it was pretty odd, Frankie thought afterwards. She had to ask questions and explain things like how the till and the credit card machine worked while serving customers, and Cherish said nothing, but kept nodding and blowing her nose.

Eventually Cherish spoke. 'It all sounds lovely, dear. Thank you. I've done shop work before. I've got references too. I'd be ever so happy to help out. I'm fifty-five, you know, and I haven't worked for some time, apart from the colour palette advisory service—and that's a bit slow sometimes, dear. Well, to be honest, it's more or less ground to a halt. And working from home can be very lonely. You tell me what hours you'd like and I'll be here. And maybe I could advise people on their soul colours and—'

'No,' Frankie said firmly. 'No colour advising at all. You can carry that on at home, of course, but not on my premises.'

'Maybe I could just pop one of my cards into the

144

bags?'

Frankie thought guiltily of the wodge of cards in the bin and shook her head. 'No, sorry. Conflict of interests, you see?'

'Yes,' said Cherish, who patently didn't. 'Whatever you say, dear. You're the boss.'

Yes, Frankie thought with a momentary fizz of pride. I am. And it's lovely.

She looked hopefully at Cherish. 'So, if you're agreeable, I'll get all the P45 stuff and salary and employment paperwork sorted out with Rita's accountant and solicitor, and we can work out some suitable hours and—'

'I'm happy to work whenever you need me.' Cherish eyed the customers milling round the rails. 'You look as if you're going to be quite busy all the time. I'm very pleased for you that it's going so well, but don't let Biddy know I said so.'

Frankie had no intention of letting Biddy know anything. Someone as mean-spirited as Biddy could put the mockers on Cherish's embryo employment before it even got started.

'I thought you and Biddy were friends?'

'We are, but she always sees the dark side of everything. She's very complex, you know. You see, I've told her she's a natural spring person, which means really she should be forward-thinking and happy in her outlook.'

'Mmm, she did tell me that you'd suggested she wears spring colours.'

'Exactly—' Cherish blew her nose again '—but so far they don't seem to have worked as well as I'd hoped. They don't seem to have touched the inner blackness at all.'

Frankie thought that it was definitely better to

145

say nothing more about Cherish's well intentioned but clearly erroneous colour advice. She smiled. 'Right, so shall we say you work from ten until two from now and through December, just to see how it goes? If it slackens off in the new year we can discuss altering your hours to suit.'

'That sounds lovely, dear. Thank you.'

'Good, that's wonderful. I'm so glad you're happy. I hope we'll be able to work well together.'

'I'm sure we will, dear. You're a sweet girl and you've made everything quite clear. Now, where shall I hang my coat?'

'In the kitchen—through there—but do you mean now? You mean you want to start straight away? I haven't got anything sorted out yet ... legally, I mean. It's all new to me—I'll have to talk to someone.'

'Course you will, dear.' Cherish started unbuttoning her unflattering coat to reveal an equally unflattering beige frock underneath. 'But let's say this is a just a trial period, shall we? I'd like to get a feel for the place.'

Frankie, who throughout the interviewing process had still not been one hundred per cent sure that inviting Cherish to work in the shop had been such a great idea after all, grabbed the lifeline with grateful hands. 'That would be lovely, actually. I haven't had a break yet, so if you wouldn't mind holding the fort for half an hour I'll pop next door to the Greasy Spoon and grab a sandwich. Can I get you something?'

'No, thank you, dear.' Cherish was already heading towards the kitchen with her coat. 'I had a bowl of muesli and an oatmeal biscuit earlier. That'll keep me going nicely until I have my chicken

146

supreme with the news later.'

Frankie, wondering bemusedly if Cherish's colour palette advice extended to her menu and therefore meant she only ate beige food, smiled as she grabbed her own vibrant coat and scarves. 'OK—lovely. I'll just be next door if you need me.'

'I'll be perfectly all right, dear.' Cherish's face split into an unexpectedly warm smile. 'As I said, I worked in Miriam's Modes in Winterbrook for years. I'm right at home in a proper dress shop. You go and have your lunch, dear. Your little shop is in safe hands.'

Chapter Fourteen

'You've employed *who*?' Dexter looked shocked across the top of the shiny red Formica table in the Greasy Spoon about ten minutes later. 'Isn't she the maddest of the lot?'

'Possibly.' Frankie played with the fat plastic tomato on the table top. Ketchup threatened to erupt in a volcanic rush at any moment. 'Probably, in fact. But who isn't mad round here? There wasn't a lot of choice.'

'True,' Dexter chuckled, 'but that was pretty damn quick off the mark.'

'Oh, I don't hang around. Sometimes those spur of the moment decisions are better than ones you agonise over, don't you think? And I'm sure Cherish will be fine. She knows people in the village, she's the right age, she says she's worked in a dress shop before, and she's available. What's not to like there?' Frankie inhaled the Greasy Spoon's

147

delightful fragrances of all-day breakfast and fresh coffee and hoped her stomach wouldn't rumble. 'I'll have to sort out the employment details, of course, then I'll just see how she goes. She seems much nicer without Biddy hanging around—if a bit morose.'

'As long as she doesn't have sticky fingers.'

'I'm sure Cherish is very clean.' Frankie was shocked. 'I wouldn't employ anyone who didn't wash.'

'Metaphorical sticky fingers.' Dexter stirred his coffee. 'Those that are always in the till. I've been caught out by those before.'

'Have you?' Frankie tried hard not to sound too interested. It was, after all, the first time Dexter had volunteered any sort of information about his past. 'Really? That sounds nasty.'

'Yes, it was. Very.' Dexter smiled up at the waitress who'd just arrived with their bacon rolls. 'Thanks.'

Frankie opened the bun, liberally squirted ketchup, bit into her bacon roll and tried not to drool. She waited for Dexter to carry on with the revelations, but he just concentrated on his own bacon roll. She sighed and looked around the Greasy Spoon. The staff today were all middle-aged. No sign of the nubile Ginny. Ah, no—she only worked on Saturdays, so she'd be at college today studying Meeja or Beauty Therapy or whatever it was she did, of course. Thank goodness.

Dexter finished his roll and wiped his hands on the bright red paper napkin. 'That was fabulous. I could eat at least three more, but I know Marguerite needs to be off on the school run soon.'

'Marguerite?' Frankie finished her own roll and

148

reached for her napkin. 'Who's she?'

'The lovely lady out there.' Dexter indicated the flower stall through the window. 'She's kindly standing in for a few moments.'

Frankie squinted through the café's steamy windows, through the Kingston Dapple shoppers and across the market square. A tall glamorous woman with tumbling auburn hair and a mock-fur coat was manning the flower stall.

'I thought you were going to ask Brian?'

'Oh, I am. Marguerite happened to be passing just after you came over to see if I was free for lunch. She's one of my home-delivery customers.'

Frankie shook her head, laughing. 'And she owes you a favour or twenty?'

'Something like that.' Dexter grinned back immodestly. 'My home-service ladies are very grateful.'

'And you're very bad.'

'Actually, I've been told I'm very good.'

Frankie leaned across the table and punched him.

'Anyway,' Dexter said, still grinning. 'Enough about my extra-curricular activities ... Did you have a good weekend?'

'Um, yes, I suppose so.' Well, if you didn't count being scared witless by Ernie Yardley's so-called ghost of course, not to mention the hair-raising visit to Slo. And until she was absolutely sure that Ernie *was* a ghost, Frankie had no intention of sharing either of those fascinating details with anyone. Not even Dexter. 'What about you?'

'Er, it was different. Hardly saw the inside of the lonely bedsit at all.'

Oh, yippedy-doo-dah.

149

'That must have been nice for you.'

'No it wasn't, not really. I took Ginny clubbing on Saturday night, which was fun, and then she took me to meet her parents the next day, which wasn't. I had a proper Sunday roast. With the entire family.'

'Blimey. There'll be an announcement in the court circular soon, then?'

Dexter pulled a face. 'Hardly. It was all pretty scary, actually. Ginny's a sweet girl, and very pretty, but far too young for me. She's only eighteen and loves rap and hip-hop and singers with names I've never heard of.'

'You poor old soul.'

'Don't mock. It was embarrassing.'

'And you,' Frankie said sternly as she reached for her coffee, 'shouldn't mess around with people's emotions. If you felt like that you shouldn't have accepted her invitation for lunch with her family.'

Dexter shrugged. 'No, I shouldn't. But it was just too tempting. And like Oscar Wilde, I can resist everything except temptation.'

Frankie, no literary scholar, was, however, intrigued by the quotation. Was it another clue to Dexter's past? 'Did you, er, study English at Oxford?'

'No.' Dexter laughed. 'I left school after fairly average A levels and went straight to work. I just loved the Stephen Fry telly series about Oscar Wilde. Sorry to disappoint you.'

'You haven't. OK then, if you don't want to have a proper relationship with Ginny, why on earth go to lunch with her parents?'

'Because I've missed being part of a family and having a proper meal and ...' He stopped.

150

'Whoops—almost too much weepy confessional stuff there. Very bad for my image, what with me supposed to be a hard-hearted bastard according to you.'

'I didn't call you that. And I'm sorry if you miss your family. I miss mine, too. And they only live in Reading.'

'Mine might as well live on the moon.'

'Don't you see them very often?'

'Never now. You?'

'Not often enough. I mean, we phone and text and email all the time but it's not the same is it? We just all seem to be so busy.'

'Have you got brothers and sisters then? A big family?'

'Big enough.' Frankie smiled, thinking nostalgically about her noisy, happy family. 'I've got two brothers who are married with two kids each, and a very much younger sister who still lives at home with Mum and Dad. I really miss them. I'm going home for Christmas though and I can't wait.'

'Lucky you.'

'What about you? Are your parents still married? To each other, I mean? Because so many aren't, are they? Lilly's divorced when she was only five and both remarried and she now has masses and masses of step-brothers and sisters.'

'My parents are still together. I've got one brother. Older. Divorced. No children.'

Frankie looked at him, hoping he'd say more, but again he just sipped his coffee.

She sighed. 'I just hope you'll let Ginny down gently then, if you don't want a long-term relationship. At eighteen she's very vulnerable and probably thinks she's in love. And you, being older,

151

shouldn't lead her on. It isn't fair.'

Dexter surveyed her steadily over the rim of his coffee mug. 'And there speaks the voice of experience?'

'Maybe.' Frankie knew she was blushing. 'Maybe not. Whatever. I just think that you should be careful not to hurt her. You're obviously a huge commitment-phobe who knows he's dead attractive and plays around and doesn't give a damn about anyone else. Actually, I reckon that's why you had to leave Oxford and why Ray bailed you out. What was it? Too many clinging ladies, or too many jealous partners?'

'Whoa!' Dexter looked annoyed. 'That's one hell of a character assassination coming from someone who hardly knows me.'

'I don't need to know you. I know your type. And I've watched you in action.'

Dexter shrugged. 'And you've formed your opinion and condemned me out of hand? Fine. And what about you? What do you think I've sussed out about you?'

'I have really no idea.'

'That you're, what, late twenties and gorgeous? That you're clearly not dating anyone, not even casually, and that you have no apparent interest in men? So, you're either gay and not out of the closet, or someone broke your heart and you're not over it. Which one is it?'

'Neither.' Frankie flushed crossly, although secretly a little bit pleased with the 'gorgeous'. 'And you shouldn't jump to conclusions.'

'That makes two of us. And my guess is it's the latter.' Dexter suddenly grinned. 'One day, we'll have to tell one another our life stories then we

152

might understand each other a bit better, but right now we ought to be getting back to work.'

'Fine.' Frankie stood up. 'I'll go and pay.'

'Already done.' Dexter stood up and stretched. Frankie tried not to stare. All the other women in the café didn't even try. 'My treat. Have a good afternoon.'

'You too,' she said, rewinding her scarves round her neck. 'And thanks for lunch.'

'My pleasure.'

Dexter held the door open for her. The icy air hit her like a cold shower after the lovely steamy heat of the Greasy Spoon.

Dexter shuddered. 'Oh, God, it's freezing. I wish Ray had sold flowers in some sort of hot house, with umpteen heaters and wall-to-wall glass.'

Frankie giggled. 'You won't think that in the height of summer.'

'I won't survive until summer at this rate.'

'Because of the freezing weather?' Frankie glanced over at the glamorous Marguerite who had perked up considerably on seeing Dexter emerge from the Greasy Spoon. 'Or the wrath of hordes of broken-hearted ladies?'

'The ladies, of course.' Dexter laughed. 'As you obviously know only too well.'

*   *   *

By the end of the afternoon, Francesca's Fabulous Frocks was finally empty. The last customer had just left, delightedly clutching a gorgeous 1960s lemon frou-frou dress in her purple and gold carrier bag. Frankie, exhausted but very happy with Monday's trading, turned the sign to CLOSED and locked the door.

She'd soon have to start sorting out the piles of frocks upstairs to restock the rails if business carried on like this. She'd do it tomorrow while Cherish served in the shop.

Cherish, Frankie thought as she cashed up, had been surprisingly brilliant. Away from the dour Biddy, she'd blossomed. She seemed to thrive in the frock shop environment, saying it took her back to her happiest days, and was hard-working and friendly. Just like one of those old-fashioned shop assistants you saw in 1950s films. All polite and interested but remaining just the right side of remote. And, as far as Frankie could tell, she hadn't mentioned a word about colour palettes. Cherish, Frankie thought happily, was going to be a huge asset.

OK, now she'd just switch off the lights and go home and put her feet up in front of *Corrie*. She laughed. It meant of course that she'd probably be sharing the sofa with Lilly and Saturday night's cute boy, until giggling, they disappeared into Lilly's neat and minimalist bedroom.

Lilly and Dexter—a right pair of one-night-stand love 'em and leave 'ems.

But, in the Greasy Spoon, Dexter had shown her a glimpse of his previous life, hadn't he? And Frankie, who'd had far too much time in the past to ponder on the motives of men who weren't what you thought they were, had been intrigued. Why didn't he see his family? Why didn't he—?

The tap on the door made her jump. For a second her skin prickled. There had been no sign of Ernie. She'd already checked every corner, and especially Achsah's frock which still hung in all its

154

lustrous glory on the 1950s rails. Everything had been fine. So, surely not? No, of course not. Ghosts didn't knock on doors, did they?

'Frankie!' Dexter's voice echoed from outside. 'Open the door, please. I'm freezing out here.'

With a swoosh of relief, Frankie hurried across the shop and pulled open the door. It was a wickedly cold night. Stars already glittered harshly in the black sky, and Kingston Dapple's marketplace was silver-rimmed with frost.

'Thanks.' Dexter stepped inside, rubbing his hands. 'Hell, it's cold tonight. I think I preferred the fog. It must be about minus ten already. I just thought I should come and apologise to you before you left.'

'Why? It's very nice of you, but I don't remember you doing anything remotely worth apologising for.'

'Earlier. I was pretty rude, really. You're entitled to your opinion about me, but I did jump down your throat a bit. Sorry.'

'Apology accepted.' Frankie smiled. 'And I'm sorry, too. I know I said some things that I shouldn't. You just hit a bit of a raw nerve.'

Dexter nodded. 'I thought so. Sorry. Again.'

'Oh, let's just forget it, shall we?' Frankie said, picking up her bag from the counter. 'We probably both said things that we should have left unsaid.'

'Story of my life. Er, is Cherish still here?'

'No, she left hours ago. She was great. Why?'

'Because I wondered if you weren't doing any new employee induction stuff, you'd like a quick drink in the Toad before we go our separate ways?'

Frankie thought quickly. Snuggled up on the sofa playing gooseberry with Lilly and the cute boy, or a drink with Dexter. Oooh, tough one.

155

'I'd love to, thanks. But what about Marguerite?'

'What about Marguerite? She's not coming with us.'

'You know very well what I mean.'

'Yep, I do. And she's stunning, true, but she's not really interested in me—any more than I am in her. I shan't be seeing her again. Marguerite will find another bit of rough.'

'Is that what you are?' Frankie giggled. 'A bit of rough? Blimey.'

Dexter grinned. 'To her, yes. I'm not a boring suit, like her husband you see. I'm a bit of a working man, like the plumber or the builder or the electrician. We're all very alluring to ladies like Marguerite.'

'It sounds like a sleazy *True Confessions*.' Frankie was still smiling as she buttoned her coat and wrapped her scarves round her neck. 'Or Lady Chatterley. Actually, now you're working with all that greenery and floristry stuff you'd make a great Mellors.'

'Thanks.' Dexter frowned. 'Is that supposed to be a compliment?'

'Nope. A criticism of your alley-cat morals.' Frankie chuckled. 'Although I always hoped Lady C. and Mellors might have had a bit of love mixed in with the lust, didn't you?'

'I've really no idea. Your reading matter is clearly several stratas above mine.'

'Hardly.' Frankie chuckled, thinking of her shelves and shelves of much-adored chick lit.

Dexter shrugged. 'All I know is that Marguerite is simply bored with being a housewife and mother and having a husband who jets off all round the world earning the money to keep her in designer labels and the kids in private education. There are a lot of Marguerites out there. They enjoy a little dalliance but don't want anything that might rock the fat financial marital boat.'

Frankie shook her head. 'Sad, really, isn't it? Why is no one ever happy with what they've got?'

Dexter grinned. 'Oh, please don't go all philosophical on me again. Let's forget about the Marguerites of this world, and just go and have a drink. I'm way too knackered to have deep and meaningful discussions about anything.'

'Me too.' Frankie giggled, pulling on her purple gloves and picking up the shop keys. 'Right, that's everything. All ready for the morning's rush. Have you had a good day too, business-wise, I mean? I promise I'm not going down the relationship route again.'

'Really good, thanks. Once I get used to being frozen to the bone and pick up a bit more knowledge about the plants, I think it'll be great. I mean, you've obviously heard that I'm a flake in my personal life, but professionally I've always been very dedicated. And I like Ray a lot, and I wouldn't want to let him down. He was very proud of the Valentine flower-selling tradition here in Kingston Dapple, and he was the only one in the family who bothered with me when—What the hell is that?'

'What?' Frankie said, annoyed that yet another revelation had been cut short.

'Over there.' Dexter squinted across the shop. 'I could swear I saw something move. You haven't got rats, have you?'

'God, I hope not.' Frankie shivered. 'Where?'

'Over there. By the Marilyn Monroe picture. I just caught some sort of movement out of the

157

corner of my eye. There! You must have seen that!'

Oh Lordy ...

'Hello, duck.' Ernie Yardley stepped from between the 1950s rails. 'Nice to see you, and your young man, too.'

Oh God ... Frankie shook her head.

Ernie beamed at her. 'You went to see Slo, didn't you? Now you know I'm telling the truth, don't you?'

Dexter laughed. 'Blimey, mate, you're lucky. We're just off out, so you nearly got locked in here for the night. Mind you, you nearly gave me a heart attack.'

'An unhappy choice of words given the circumstances,' Ernie said dolefully, then looked at Frankie. 'You'd better introduce us.'

Dexter shook his head. 'No need. I'm Dexter Valentine, and I think I know who you are. Frankie gave me a really good description of you. It's nice to meet you at last, because I've heard lots about you. You're the guy who wants to buy a frock. Right?'

'Wrong.' Ernie grinned. 'Ever so wrong. Isn't he, duck?'

'Couldn't be more wrong,' Frankie agreed, feeling sick. 'Dexter, meet Ernie Yardley. Ernie Yardley's dead. Ernie Yardley says he's a ghost.'

Chapter Fifteen

Dexter's laughter rang round the shop. Frankie and Ernie didn't join in.

'What?' Dexter stopped laughing and stared from one to the other. 'Why are you looking at me like that?'

Ernie smiled at Frankie. 'You might as well tell him, duck. He seems like a nice chap from what I've seen. Keen on you, too, I think.'

Oh Lordy ... Frankie exhaled. Now she not only had a ghost, but a match-making ghost to boot. Fantastic.

She sighed. 'That's complete rubbish, Ernie, but OK, now you're here and Dexter's seen you—which is a huge relief to me because I thought I might be the only one seeing things—I'll tell him.' She looked at Dexter. 'It's a long story.'

Dexter grinned and hauled himself up to sit on the counter. 'OK, I'm fine with that. I like a good yarn. But don't expect me to believe a word of it. I don't believe in ghosts. And he—' he nodded towards Ernie '—doesn't look like a ghost at all. Where are the clanking chains and the wailing and the walking through walls and—'

'Hold up.' Ernie looked miffed. 'I've been through all that with Frankie here. Don't you go mocking the undead, young man. I've already told Frankie, it isn't like you see on the films, you know. And I'm as unhappy with this here set-up as anyone. I just want to rest in peace with my Achsah. It ain't much to ask now, is it?'

'You're good.' Dexter chuckled. 'You're very,

159

very good. OK, go on then, Frankie. Tell me all about it . . . '

So she did. Leaving out the part that she'd promised Slo she'd never mention, of course, but recounting absolutely everything else.

Ernie, who had listened intently, nodded at the end. 'That's all true. Nicely put, duck. So, you see, Dexter, I'm in a bit of a muddle here.'

Dexter, who'd managed to remain completely silent through the story-telling, looked scathingly at Frankie. 'And you believe he's a ghost? Really, truly?'

'I don't know. Honestly, now I don't know. I didn't. I thought maybe Biddy or Maisie or someone had put him up to it. To scare me off for some reason. And then after I'd spoken to Slo I thought I did believe it was all true. Especially when I saw the photograph. Then I didn't again. And now . . . I really don't know.'

'But—' Dexter slid from the counter '—you're an intelligent, rational woman. You *can't*. I mean, you *can't*.'

'Course she can,' Ernie affirmed stoutly. 'Not that I blame you, mind. I never believed in ghosts meself either, before I was one, that is.'

'You-are-not-a-ghost,' Dexter said firmly.

Ernie shrugged. 'Sorry, Dexter, but I am. And I don't want to be. And that's why I thought young Frankie could help me, see?'

'Yes, yes,' Dexter said tersely. 'I've heard the entire story. And while I'd never accuse Frankie of being a liar—'

'Good job, too,' Frankie said hotly. 'Because everything I've just told you is the absolute truth. It might seem far-fetched to you—it did to me as

160

well—but that is exactly how it happened.'

Dexter looked totally confused. 'But I don't believe in—'

'We know,' Ernie and Frankie chorused.

'I know it's a lot to take in.' Frankie smiled gently. 'But look, Dexter, why don't you just suspend your disbelief for a moment, and just try to accept that Ernie is a ghost. Actually, it's quite easy when you try.'

Ernie nodded his grizzled head enthusiastically. 'Go on, Dexter, lad. I can see you're a decent bloke with a good brain, and no doubt you don't believe in UFOs, or crop circles or guardian angels or anything else that you can't *prove*. And I don't blame you, but please, for my sake, give it a go.'

Dexter was silent for a moment. Then he sighed heavily. 'I'll only believe you're a ghost if you do something to convince me. Frankie may well have been almost convinced by your story with the undertaker—in cahoots, were you?—but I wasn't there, so I'm not. So, you'll have to prove it to me. And, as you can't, can you just clear off now so that Frankie and I can go for a drink?'

'All right.' Ernie beamed benignly. 'You did ask.'

And he vanished.

Frankie stared at the empty space where Ernie had been standing only seconds before, and shivered violently. He hadn't moved, he hadn't walked or run or anything, he'd just, well, gone. She needed no further proof.

'Shit!' Dexter blinked. 'No way!'

'There you are.' Ernie reappeared again across the shop, looking a bit out of place by the 1970s punk section. 'Sorry it weren't more spectacular, but that's about as much as I can manage. I might

161

be an old codger but I'm a very young ghost. We don't do much more than that. Enough to convince you, though, I hope?'

Dexter stared at him, wide-eyed and speechless.

Shaking, Frankie cleared her throat. 'OK ... Um, right ... I'm convinced, Ernie. Honestly. So, what can we do to help you?'

Dexter stared at her. 'You're joking?'

'No.' Frankie shook her head. 'I'm not. There's no way on, er, earth that anyone, um, normal could pull off that stunt. Not even Penn and Teller. And after what Slo told me, and showed me, yes, I do believe that Ernie is a ghost.'

'Thank you. Thank you. Thank you. I'd kiss you, duck, if I could,' Ernie said happily. 'I don't think I can though.'

Still looking bewildered, Dexter pushed his hands through his hair. 'OK—I'll admit I can't see any rational explanation either. Now if someone will just wake me up out of this bad dream, can we get on with our normal lives?'

'If you two can sort me out, Dexter lad, then the rest of your life will be as normal as you want it to be,' Ernie said generously. 'I'll be reunited with Achsah and resting in peace. I won't bother you any more.'

'Sounds pretty damn good to me,' Dexter muttered. 'Look, as long as you don't tell anyone that I'm going along with this charade—it'll ruin my street cred—and it means that this ... this ... so-called haunting rubbish stops, then, yes, OK. So, what do we have to do?' He looked at Frankie. 'Jesus! Hark at me! I'm reasoning with someone who's allegedly dead.'

Frankie laughed. 'I know. That's how I felt.

162

Weird, isn't it?'

'Mad is what it is,' Dexter said darkly. 'Totally bloody completely insane.'

Frankie nodded. 'I know. Anyway, Ernie, you've finally managed to convince us both, I think. So, what do we do now?'

'I don't know.' Ernie looked dejected. 'If I knew then I'd have told you last time. I hoped you'd get some inkling of how to help from Slo Motion once he'd convinced you that I am who I say I am. Now, I'm not sure, but there must be some way to set my spirit free, mustn't there?'

Just as well Lilly isn't here, Frankie thought. She'd be in floods of tears by now.

'Why didn't you mention any of this to me before?' Dexter frowned at Frankie. 'Did it just slip your mind to tell me that your elderly Eddie Izzard had suddenly turned into Jacob Marley?'

'And would you have believed me? No, of course you wouldn't. I didn't even believe it. And I was frightened enough myself—I certainly didn't want to scare people away from the shop by talking about it. Not to anyone. Not Lilly and certainly not Cherish, not even you.'

Anyway, she thought, you've clearly got secrets of your own. Obviously not ghostly ones, but huge skeletons rattling about in your cupboard.

'What we need,' she said thoughtfully, 'is a ghost-buster.'

'That we don't!' Ernie was adamant. 'The last thing I needs is for a lot of loud plinketty-plonk soundtrack and damn Dan Ackroyd and his chums running round here with their fume-filled backpacks blasting me into a vapour. No thank you very much.'

163

Dexter laughed.

Frankie smiled at Ernie. 'Sorry, that possibly wasn't the best suggestion. How about if we tried to get the vicar involved, then? Vicars can lay ghosts to rest, can't they? I'm sure I've read about it. We could get the vicar in and have a sort of exorcism and—'

'Over my dead body!' Ernie looked aghast. 'Literally, in my case. Me and Achsah liked going to the pictures when they had the Alhambra in Winterbrook. Every Saturday night we went. I saw that film as well. Bloody scary it was, too. There's no way you're going to get my head spinning like a damn top and me spewing out green slime and very bad language.'

Dexter laughed again. 'I don't think that's how an exorcism works in real life, does it?'

'Search me.' Ernie frowned. 'I know as much about it as you do. But I'm not prepared to take the risk, if it's all the same to you.'

'What about a seance, then?' Frankie said. 'Does that sound more realistic?'

'Or a Ouija board?' Dexter shrugged. 'Aren't they supposed to put the living in contact with the dead?'

'Not a Ouija board,' Frankie said firmly. 'There was a phase of that over in Lovers Knot some time ago. Lilly told me. One of the girls from Jennifer Blessings' salon was really keen on it. They got a lot more than they bargained for by all accounts. Several people were on medication for months afterwards. And none of them sleep with the lights out even now.'

'Jesus.' Dexter looked horrified. 'We'll leave that well alone then. But a seance sounds OK. Doesn't it?'

Frankie sighed. 'I have no idea, really. I've never believed in any of it, or had anything to do with anyone who does. What do you reckon, Ernie? Should we ask someone with the right, er, powers to contact you, and the rest of the spirit world, and sort out why you're trapped here and unhappy, and maybe they'd be able to free you?'

'Sounds better than your previous suggestions,' Ernie conceded. 'But do you know anyone who might be able to—?'

'Maisie Fairbrother!' Dexter and Frankie spoke together and laughed.

'Dear heavens.' Ernie shook his head sorrowfully. 'She's as mad as a skinned salami that one. But, OK, she does dabble in the spirit world, and even my Achsah—who was a very religious woman—thought that maybe Maisie had *some* sort of contact with the hereafter. And, to be honest, if I'm going to be mediumed into the afterlife, I'd rather it was by someone I knew, rather than a complete stranger.'

'OK.' Dexter exhaled. 'So, you're willing to give it a go, are you?'

'I am, Dexter lad. And the sooner the better as far as I'm concerned.'

*   *   *

Ten minutes later, in the plush warmth of Dexter's luxurious car, Frankie leaned her head back against the soft leather and stared through the windscreen. It was bitterly cold. Outside, everything glittered, and the crescent moon was a white-gold scar on the otherwise perfect black velvet sky.

165

'Shouldn't we have phoned Maisie first, to say we're on our way?' She turned to look at Dexter in the darkness. 'Or asked if it was convenient? Isn't just turning up a bit rude?'

'I know where she lives, having taken her home before, and neither of us know her phone number. And I don't know about you, but the sooner we get this ... this madness sorted out, the better. If she doesn't want to see us tonight she can say so, can't she?'

'I suppose so. Look, I'm really grateful to you for all this. I've been worrying about it for days now, thinking I was going crazy.'

'I'm not surprised.' Dexter smiled across at her. 'It still all seems too far-fetched to be true, but, well, I'm intrigued now. And more than a bit spooked by it. And, OK, he seems like a nice old boy, even if does think he's dead, and if he's just play-acting, then this should flush him out. And if he isn't ... well, if we can help him we should, shouldn't we?'

'We should,' Frankie agreed. 'I also think that we shouldn't mention exactly *who* it is that's haunting the shop to Maisie. I think we should just be a bit vague and say I think she may have been right when she said it was haunted. I'm still not sure she's genuine. Let's see if she actually discovers that it's Ernie, shall we?'

'Devious.' Dexter chuckled. 'But I like it. Yes, I think you're right. If he's a fraud then we can scare him witless. And if she's a fraud, then we don't want to give her any clues, do we? OK, we're here now.'

Dexter pulled the car to a halt outside a neat block of tiny service flats on the Hazy Hassocks road. Lights glowed warmly in the curtained

166

windows, but there was no one about. Hardly surprising, Frankie thought as she stepped reluctantly from the delicious warmth into the searingly cold frosty evening.

'She lives on the ground floor, to the left.' Dexter locked the car and followed Frankie into the flat's small, neat entrance foyer. 'At least Brian and I didn't have to haul her upstairs. It's this one.'

Frankie rang the bell.

After a minute, which, to Frankie, seemed more like an hour, Maisie opened the door a sliver, leaving the chain on, and peered out at them through the crack. 'Yes? Who is it?'

'Maisie, I'm really sorry to bother you.' Frankie cleared her throat. She seemed to be making a habit of impromptu late visits to elderly people. She'd probably be getting some sort of reputation round the villages as a geriatric botherer. 'Um, it's me. Frankie from, er, Rita's shop. And Dexter— Ray Valentine's nephew.'

'Ah, lovely, sweethearts.' The chain rattled free and the door opened. 'How nice to see you. Come along in.'

Dexter and Frankie stared up at the towering Maisie who was wearing a pink and orange quilted housecoat wrapped round her considerable bulk, with her cauliflower hair in a spike of multicoloured rollers, and teetering on high-heeled diamante and fluffy pink mules.

'Thank you.' Frankie stepped into ankle-deep plum shagpile carpeting, followed by Dexter. 'Oh, what a lovely flat.'

Well, it was. To her. To anyone not given to clutter and clashing colours and twinkly, sparkly things—clearly like Dexter—it would be a hellhole.

167

Maisie hadn't just decked the halls with boughs of holly, she'd decked everywhere with everything. It was like a grotto but without the pixies.

'Come through, sweethearts.' Maisie swayed into her tiny living room. 'Make yourselves comfy. I was just watching a bit of telly, but never mind that. I can pause and save.'

Sky Plus, Frankie thought, had opened a whole new joyous world to the older telly addict.

A Christmas tree, flouting any rules of colour co-ordination or style, dominated the hothouse room. It drooped under the weight of far too much tinsel and far too many lights and dozens and dozens of mismatched baubles.

'Oh! Fabulous tree!' Frankie clasped her hands together in delight.

Dexter looked at her with deep pity.

'Thank you. I love Christmas, don't you? I did the tree at the end of November. I know it might be a bit early to have the decs up, but I do so love them. Now, can I get you something to eat? Drink?'

They both shook their heads and proclaimed they were fine, thank you.

Maisie settled herself on a pink dralon chair amid a lot of slithery cushions, once they'd seated themselves side by side in amongst even more cushions on the matching sofa. 'So, not that it's not lovely to see you, but what can I do for you?'

They looked at one another, then Frankie leaned forwards. 'It's about the ghosts, in my shop . . .'

'Ah.' Maisie's eyes sparkled almost as much as her Christmas tree. 'I told you you'd be needing me, didn't I?'

'You did.' Frankie nodded solemnly. 'And you were right. I'm sorry that I doubted you.'

Beside her, Dexter stifled a snort.

Maisie wriggled excitedly. 'So, what have you seen? What have you felt?'

'Er ...' Frankie, crossing her fingers, hesitated and avoided Dexter's eyes. 'Well, I haven't actually *seen* anything, but there's a sort of presence. Um, a cold feeling? A sort of feeling that when I'm alone, I'm not. Does that make sense?'

'Perfectly.' Maisie beamed. 'Sounds like a classic case of a haunting to me.'

Relieved, Frankie exhaled and uncrossed her fingers. Dexter snuffled. She still didn't look at him.

'So, sweethearts, what are you asking me to do?'

'Um ...' Frankie faltered.

'Well, more or less, just get rid of it, er, them,' Dexter put in quickly. 'That is, we're not sure how you do your, er, mediuming, but if you could sort of find out if there is anything there—'

'Oh, there is!' Maisie said triumphantly. 'I felt it the minute I stepped inside, didn't I, Frankie?'

'You did. Quite dramatically.'

'Yes, so,' Dexter continued manfully, 'if you could, er, lay the ghost—I mean, ghosts—for Frankie, it would be a great help.'

'No problem at all.' Maisie preened. 'I'm just glad you've seen sense and asked me. Right now, sweethearts, we've established that you have spirits and need to be rid of them, but what exactly are you looking for?'

Frankie frowned. It was like being asked questions by a party-planner. Balloons? Streamers? Music? A table magician? A nice cake?

'Actually, I don't really know. I thought you'd tell us. That is, I agree with you that the shop is haunted and I don't want it to be, but I have no idea what you need to do or what you need us to provide, so I'll—we'll—leave it to you.'

'Lovely.' Maisie rubbed her chubby much be-ringed hands together. 'I'll have a little one-to-one session then. I can come into the shop one night and talk to the unhappy, restless spirits and see what their problems are and ask them to leave you alone. Does that sound about right for you?'

They both nodded.

'Super, sweethearts. I like it when clients have open minds.'

'My mind is pretty closed, actually.' Dexter was still trying to balance on a very slippery candyfloss-pink satin cushion. 'I'm afraid I don't believe in ghosts.'

Maisie tutted loudly. 'You're not alone there, sadly. I find so many people don't believe. But you must have *felt* something otherwise you wouldn't be here, would you?'

'I'm here for Frankie. It's her shop and her problem and I want to help her.'

Frankie had a little warm glow of happiness moment.

'Ah, sweetheart, how lovely.' Maisie smiled. 'Okey-dokey. What I'll need is an empty shop. Preferably late at night. I don't want any confusing auras around, do I?'

They shook their heads.

'Right, and I'll need you there too, as the haunting may be linked to you rather than the premises, but as I've already picked up that you're both *sceptical*—' Maisie made it sound as if they were suffering from some unspeakable antisocial disease '—it would help if we could have someone

170

who has no such blocking emotions in place—just in case I need to go through a third party.'

Dexter and Frankie looked at one another.

'Um, I could ask Lilly, my housemate,' Frankie said doubtfully. 'She believes in fairies and the Easter Bunny and Father Christmas and aliens and well, everything.'

'Perfect, sweetheart.' Maisie nodded the myriad rollers. 'She sounds just the ticket. So, how about this Saturday night coming? Just before midnight? Then if it all gets too exhausting we'll have the Sunday to recover, won't we?'

'OK by me,' Frankie said, 'and I'll make sure Lilly is free. Dexter?'

'Oh, I'm sure I can cancel whatever hot date I may have planned for a spot of spook-spotting.'

'Don't mock,' Maisie said severely. 'It's not funny.'

'No, sorry.' Dexter tried to keep a straight face.

'Right, sweethearts. That's all fixed then. I'll bring the few things that I need, and if you could just make sure there's a nice carafe of iced water available—it can be very thirsty work—and, if you could keep it a secret I'd appreciate it. I don't need a lot of negativity building up and confusing the auras, if you get my drift?'

They nodded again.

Dexter lost the struggle with the cushion and stood up. 'And I'll come and collect you, shall I? I know you have transport problems getting from here to Kingston Dapple.'

'That's very kind of you, thank you.' Maisie stood up too, teetering slightly on the vertiginous mules. 'So, if we say you'll collect me at about eleven thirty next Saturday night, I can have a little afternoon nap to gather my strength. And we'll have your spirit problem sorted out in a trice, sweetheart.'

Frankie, reluctantly letting go of her own clutched collection of cushions—they would look fabulous in her bedroom—stood up, too. 'That's wonderful, Maisie, thank you. Oh, and do we pay you now, or, um, afterwards?'

'Afterwards will be fine, sweetheart. I do piecework. Charge by the hour. I'll prepare an invoice and send it in.'

Dexter and Frankie exchanged amused glances as they all waded towards the door through the shagpile.

'Until Saturday, then,' Maisie said cheerfully, waving them goodbye. 'Crikey, it's cold out here, sweethearts. Heck of a frost, isn't it? Looks like we might be getting a white Christmas. Mind how you go now. Nighty-night.'

'Don't you dare laugh,' Frankie hissed, her breath spiralling into the freezing night air, as they hurried towards the car. 'At least wait until she's closed the door.'

'I'm not laughing.' Dexter pressed the key fob's zapper, and the car made a reassuring clicking noise. 'I think we both need certifying. And I can feel a migraine coming on. All those colours! All those sparkly things! How can anyone live comfortably in all that glitter?'

'I thought it was really lovely.' Frankie snuggled pleasurably into the car's soft leather seat. 'And not at all over the top. Blimey, if, you think that's bad, you should see my bedroom.'

'Well, thanks for the invite, Miss Meredith.' Dexter grinned as he pulled the car away from

172

Maisie's flat. 'I was beginning to think you'd never ask.'

Chapter Sixteen

Cherish stood at the bus stop and shivered inside her fawn raincoat. Even with the nice thick sheepskin lining buttoned in, the north-easterly wind whistled from Siberia, across Kingston Dapple's marketplace, and straight through to her woolly vest.

'Oooh, hurry up bus,' Cherish muttered, blowing on her beige mittens. 'I want to get home and make a nice cup of tea.'

It was Wednesday afternoon. The end of Cherish's third day working at Francesca's Fabulous Frocks. And she could honestly say she'd never been happier. Well, not since those early days at Miriam's Modes, anyway.

It really was a lovely little shop, and she'd had so much fun working with Frankie—who wasn't at all like she thought she'd be—and serving the customers with their chosen dresses. And this afternoon, she and Frankie had taken it in turns to go upstairs to the stockroom and start sifting through all the dresses that had been donated to the shop but not yet dry-cleaned and put out on the rails. Cherish had absolutely loved it. All those beautiful designs in all those gorgeous vintage fabrics. Frocks made when dressmakers were worthy of the name and crafted one-offs rather than the current conveyor belt churning out of masses of cheap replicas.

And it hadn't mattered at all that she hadn't been able to suggest any colour advice to the customers. In fact, Cherish thought now, stamping her fur-lined ankle bootees, she may well give up the colour-palette advisory service altogether. Hopefully, Frankie might even increase her hours in the shop, then there simply wouldn't be any time for sidelines, would there?

How lovely it would be, to be too busy *working* to take on anything else?

Cherish shivered again. She hoped the bus wouldn't be too crowded. She disliked having to stand all the way to Hazy Hassocks. And no one these days gave up their seat for a lady, did they? Cherish sighed. It was a whole new world with a whole new set of values and, despite what Biddy said, they'd have to move with it or get left far behind. She smiled to herself. She, Cherish, was becoming a New Woman.

Across the square, the Christmas lights all swayed and danced in the gale, and the marketplace's Christmas tree was nodding so violently it looked as though the angel on the top, made by Kingston Dapple's Mixed Infants, was in dire danger of tumbling head first onto the cobbles.

The angel, Cherish thought, having peered up at it closely the previous day, actually looked a lot like Bruce Forsyth. She wasn't sure if this was intentional on the part of the Kingston Dapple Mixed Infants. But she'd smiled at it anyway. She'd always liked Brucie.

Several other people joined her at the bus stop. They all managed to avoid one another's eyes. Cherish didn't mind. She didn't want to talk to anyone. Her life was working out really nicely thank

174

you.

She wasn't even dreading Christmas now. Frankie had said she was going home to spend Christmas with her family, and the shop would be closed for three days: Christmas Day, Boxing Day and the day after. Then she'd open up again because there might be a rush of customers looking for a nice frock for New Year's Eve. Would that be all right or would Cherish prefer to take the whole week off and come in again after the New Year?

Cherish, who had been wondering how on earth she'd mange to fill those awful lonely days when the whole world seemed to stop and everyone appeared to indulge in frantic family festivities, had said the three days would suit her perfectly.

She could cope with three days alone in the bungalow. Just her and the radio and the television.

She had no presents to buy—well, she'd bought for Biddy for ages, as Biddy had for her, mainly bath cubes or hankies, but they'd knocked that on the head some years earlier when they realised neither of them actually wanted the presents—and was expecting none. Her Christmas cards, such as they were, had been written and posted two weeks previously. And her Christmas dinner—a selection of chicken portions—was already in the fridge-top freezer, with a Big Sava Christmas pudding for one safely in the store cupboard. She'd have a glass of sherry from the bottle that had been in the sideboard since Millennium Eve to go with it, and maybe she'd treat herself to a small box of chocolate biscuits to dunk while she watched her favourite soap opera omnibuses.

The chicken pieces would do nicely cold with some bread and butter on Boxing Day, and the

175

third day would possibly mean whatever was left with a tin of baked beans.

Cherish nodded happily to herself. Christmas was all organised.

There was still no sign of the bus and people were stamping their feet and grizzling loudly now. Cherish huddled deeper into her coat and looked up at the sky. Steely grey, it really did look as though there would be snow before too long.

Cherish hoped not. She actually loved the snow because it changed the boring vista from the bungalow's windows, and there was still a childlike magic about watching the snowflakes tumble and dance. But if it snowed heavily, the roads might be blocked, and the buses wouldn't run and then she might not be able to get to work ...

Get to work ...

She played the words over again in her head. How lovely they sounded.

'Oi!' Someone shouted from the road.

Cherish ignored them. No one ever shouted cheerfully to her. It must be for one of the others in the ever-growing bus queue.

'Oi! Wanna lift?'

Cherish looked expectantly at the rest of the queue, wondering which of the lucky shivering travellers was going to be whisked away from the icy blast. None of them moved.

'Cherish, gel!' the voice continued. 'Gorn all hoity-toity, have you?'

Cherish turned her head and blinked at the kebab van.

'Gotcha!' Brian opened the passenger door and beamed across from the driver's seat. 'You were miles away, weren't you? Come on, gel. Jump aboard. I'm off to Hazy Hassocks. Going right past your door.'

For a moment Cherish hesitated. The kebab van—lovingly if inexpertly liveried by Brian—wouldn't normally have been her mode of transport of choice. The red and green capsicum peppers painted on the sides looked like misshapen irradiated slugs, and the pitta breads resembled a pile of dead beheaded fish. And as for that pinkish grey length of meat—well ... Cherish averted her eyes.

She was proud to say she'd never had a kebab in her life.

'Come along, gel.' Brian held the passenger door open wider for her. 'You'll be waiting there for ages. Bus broke down coming out of Fiddlesticks so I've heard. You'll freeze your assets off in this cold.'

The queue groaned and looked mutinous. Cherish didn't hesitate. She clambered inelegantly up into the van.

'Lovely, gel.' Brian beamed happily at her as he leaned across and pulled the passenger door tightly shut. 'We'll have you home in no time.'

'Thank you,' Cherish said faintly. 'It's very kind of you.'

Brian nodded along to some indecipherable tune on the radio and pulled away from the bus stop. His hair, Cherish noticed, was even wilder than usual, and his duffle coat had some sort of earth clinging to the sleeves. And he smelled faintly of herbs and onions. But the van was lovely and warm, with a little heater playing nicely round her booteed toes.

'Just finished at the shop, have you?' Brian asked chattily, as he confidently negotiated the traffic. 'Frankie said you was working there. Enjoying it?'

'Very much so, thank you,' Cherish said primly, drawing the hem of her raincoat away from any threatened contact with Brian's disreputable jeans and boots. 'And isn't it a bit early for you to be out selling kebabs? I thought that was an evening thing?'

'Ah, 'tis. I'm doing what you're doing. We're two of a kind, you and me, Cherish, gel.'

Was Brian working in a frock shop? Cherish looked askance. Surely not?

'You're helping out Frankie, and I'm helping out young Dexter,' Brian informed her as they left Kingston Dapple behind and headed out through the grey and frozen countryside towards Hazy Hassocks. 'Nice lad, Dexter. I always helped out his uncle Ray on the flower stall round Christmas time, so I was pleased when he asked me. I've got a load of holly and a couple of Christmas trees for customers out Hassocks way in the back of the van.'

Cherish could only hope that some sort of hygienic sanitary arrangements had been made in the back of the van to prevent Brian's two businesses, well, mingling. At least it explained the earth on his duffle coat.

'Got yours yet, gel?'

Cherish shook her head. 'I don't bother with any decorations or a tree. It's only me. There doesn't seem to be any point.'

'That's terrible.'

Brian whizzed them round a corner and Cherish brushed against him. She righted herself quickly.

'No, seriously—' Brian looked at her through his unkempt hair '—that's sad. You should put some decs and things up. Just for yourself. I've got mine up. You know I was dead lucky because Rita left

178

me her bungalow? Well, this is my first year away from my nasty old ma, and I'm going to have the time of my life.'

'Are you?' Cherish looked at him in surprise. 'What? With other family members?'

'Lord bless you, no, gel. On my own. I can't wait. I'm going to have the best Christmas ever.'

'Really? Didn't you have nice Christmases when you were little, then?'

'Miseries they were.' Brian pursed his lips. 'Right miseries. Never a happy word spoken in our house over Christmas. Not enough food, no presents to speak of, always cold because we couldn't afford any coal, and damn all festive cheer.'

'Oh, I'm so sorry. My childhood Christmases were lovely. I think that's why I don't bother now. I can't compete with the memories.'

'Nor do you want to, gel. You can look back on your happy times gone by, and you know you'll never recapture them, but you can make these Christmases special too. Have a little tree and some garlands and some carols playing on the radio. Nuts and sweets by the fire. Buy yourself a few treats to unwrap Christmas morning and cook yourself up a proper feast with all the trimmings for your Christmas dinner. That's what I'm going to be doing.'

'Buying your own presents?' Cherish was shocked. 'And spending money on lots of rich food? Just for you? Isn't that very wasteful?'

'It's fun, gel.' Brian looked at her sadly. 'My life's been mighty short on fun—apart from the time I spent with Rita, and that came to nowt—and if I'm not speaking out of turn, I'd say yours hasn't been a bed of roses lately, neither. No, I'm right looking

179

forward to Christmas. I'm even getting a Christmas stocking to put at the foot of my bed.'

'Oh, yes! I always loved my Christmas stocking when I was a girl!' Cherish clasped her mittens together in remembered happiness. 'Waking up to see if "he'd" been, and then, when "he" had, just feeling all those exciting lumps and bumps and hearing the crackle and rustle of the wrapping paper and trying to guess what "he'd" brought me, and then snuggling into bed with my parents while I opened everything and showed them. Ah yes, they were blissful times. You must remember those?'

Brian shook his head, slowing the van down as they entered the queue of traffic heading for Hazy Hassocks. 'I never had a Christmas stocking when I was a kid, gel. Not one. This'll be me first.'

Cherish looked across the van in horror. 'Oh, Brian, I had no idea. I mean, of course, I know, from what people have said, that your mother wasn't ... isn't the, um, gentlest or most generous soul in the world, but even so—'

'My ma was, and still is, a cruel bitch and my dad was a drunk and a bully.' Brian shrugged cheerfully. 'Can't put a gloss on that, gel. Them's the facts.'

'Oh dear.' Cherish stared down into her lap and tidied the folds of her raincoat just for something to do.

'Don't you go all soft on me, gel,' Brian said kindly. 'I didn't mean to tell you all that stuff. You're just very easy to talk to.'

'Am I?' Cherish was surprised. Nobody ever really bothered to talk to her at all. Well, Frankie had over the last few days, which had been lovely, but before that, there really hadn't been any great soul-sharing moments with anyone. Not even her

180

parents. 'Thank you.'

'It's been my pleasure, gel. But you heed what I says. Don't you go scrimping and scraping unnecessarily because you think Christmas is a waste of time. You splash out a bit and enjoy yourself. Give yourself some treats.'

'Do you know,' Cherish said slowly, smiling to herself, 'I might just do that. I mean it doesn't have to cost a fortune, does it? But it would be nice to have a few days of luxury.'

'Exactly, gel.' Brian grinned cheerfully through his wild hair that had now fallen across his face. 'You and me both. Having a happy Christmas. Treating ourselves in the comfort of our own homes. There's plenty who won't be able to do that, you know.'

'Oh, I know.' Cherish nodded. 'I suppose we should be very grateful.'

'Ah.' Brian nodded, turning the corner into Cherish's street. 'That's a fact. Here we are then, gel. Delivered to the door. Safe and sound.'

'Thank you very much. I'm very grateful.' Cherish opened the door, and shuddered again as the icy air rushed in. She slid her feet carefully to the pavement. 'Take care, Brian. And thank you again.'

Brian grinned, waved and drove away.

Cherish, still shivering and feeling in her handbag for her door key, watched him until the van had turned the corner and disappeared.

How very odd, she thought, as she quickly unlocked her front door. She'd just had the longest and most interesting conversation she could ever remember having for years, with mad Brian from the kebab van.

How very, very odd.

Chapter Seventeen

Getting Lilly to give up her Saturday night out—the latest cute boy seemed to have lost his appeal, as they all did sooner rather than later—had been far easier than persuading Cherish not to hang around on the night of the planned seance.

Frankie quickly realised that telling Cherish she needed to have a good Saturday night sort out of stock and drag down any hidden festive frocks that may be lurking upstairs to fill the rails in the last frantic shopping days before Christmas had been a big mistake.

Cherish, who'd loved sifting through the newly donated taffetas and silks and voiles and laces throughout the week, thought it sounded like a great way to spend her Saturday night.

'I'd love to help you. I can miss *Casualty* for once, dear.'

'No, I wouldn't dream of it,' Frankie had said in desperation. 'In fact, I think it might break your employment contract. Overtime and all that.'

'But I'd do it for free, dear.'

'Well, that's very kind of you, but it's more the hours, you see,' Frankie had improvised wildly. 'The new EU directive. You're not covered by the insurance for working out of hours.'

Eventually, Cherish, who luckily had no more knowledge of EU directives on working practices than Frankie, gave in with a huge air of disappointment.

Lilly, bless her, had listened wide-eyed to the story of Maisie holding a cleansing seance in the shop and agreed happily to be there.

'But you haven't really got ghosts, have you?' she'd asked while attaching huge featherlike false eyelashes in emerald green. 'It's only like a game?'

'Sort of,' Frankie had said, reluctant to actually tell any more lies. 'It's just in case, really. Maisie was convinced there were ghosts in the shop, and I want to make sure there aren't. It'll be like having a good clean even when you know there's nothing nasty lurking. For peace of mind.'

'Sounds like fun.' Lilly had concentrated on her eyelashes. 'And it makes sense. Jennifer Blessing has the pest control people in twice a year to make sure we've got no creepy-crawlies in the salon even though we keep it immaculate. It must be the same sort of thing, mustn't it?'

'Exactly,' Frankie had said.

Slo had phoned to ask how things were going, and Frankie had told a lot of half-truths—she'd already promised herself that she'd only tell Slo that Ernie had gone when he really had—and Slo had wheezed cheerfully and said so long as no one ever got to hear about that car journey he was happy. And Frankie, delighted to be able to tell the truth at last, had assured him she would take that particular piece of information to her grave.

And Ernie, when he'd next appeared just as she was shutting up on the Wednesday night, had been equally as enthusiastic about Maisie's forthcoming visit.

'Can't wait, duck, and that's a fact. Only a few more days and me and my Achsah will be together again. Let's just hope Maisie Fairbrother's up to

183

the job, eh?'

And Frankie had fervently agreed.

*　　*　　*

So, here she was, at a quarter to midnight, two Saturdays before Christmas, with Lilly all dressed in spectral black for the occasion, waiting for Dexter to arrive with Maisie.

The ice-cold weather continued across Berkshire, but the clear skies had given way to sullen low clouds and a biting north-easterly wind. Everyone was forecasting a white Christmas.

'Oooh, it's quite shuddery, just thinking about it, isn't it?' Lilly prowled round the rails. 'What if there is a ghost, and it comes out all howling and dripping blood from its fangs?'

'That's vampires,' Frankie said, also pacing up and down. 'And it won't be scary, Lilly, I promise you.'

'Oh, I'm not scared, just curious. I watched *Paranormal Experience* all on my own. Twice. I wouldn't mind meeting a ghost, actually. Do you think I'd look OK in this lime-green shifty thing?'

'No.' Frankie shook her head. 'You'd look like a runner bean. Put it back, Lill. It'll get all creased. Ah, here they are.'

The door opened and Dexter, incongruously pulling a tartan shopping trolley, stood back to allow Maisie to step inside.

Frankie pressed her lips together tightly to prevent any laughter escaping. Lilly didn't.

Maisie was wearing a marquee-sized kaftan in a multicoloured geometric print, skyscraper heels in green and lilac and adorned with tinsel bows, and a

184

bright blue woolly bonnet over the curls.

'Hello, sweethearts—oh, my goodness!' She did the head-hitting-with-the-back-of-the-hand thing again. The bonnet fell off. Maisie slumped backwards against the door. Dexter, manoeuvring the shopping trolley, skipped niftily out of the way. 'I may need a chair. Oh, I can feel them immediately. Everywhere ... They're draining my energy. You have a very serious problem here.'

Lilly grabbed a chair and Maisie overflowed onto it with a sigh.

'If you just tell us what we have to do,' Frankie said, now pretty sure, given Maisie's repeat Oscar-winning performance, that this was going to be a complete waste of time, 'we'll get you anything you need.'

'Lovely. Thank you.' Maisie spoke faintly. 'This is amazing. I can actually hear them calling to me already. Dexter has my bag of tricks—and that's just a figure of speech, not an indication that this is a magic act—' she looked sternly at Lilly '—so if I could have a little table just beside me, here.'

The table was fetched, a jug of water and a glass set on it, and the tartan shopping trolley placed beside the chair.

Delving into it, Maisie brought out two small bowls of what looked like potpourri but smelled like Bombay mix, a small brass filigreed lantern, two bunches of dried herbs and a greying lump of something that defied description, and arranged them on the table.

'For cleansing the negative auras,' Maisie said shakily. 'I still feel a lot of negativity.'

'Can't imagine why,' Dexter chuckled.

'We don't need the lights,' Maisie whispered.

185

'Just my cleansing candles for illumination. In my bag, sweetheart. I'll have the big orange calendula one on the table here, and the little jasmine ones along the counter over there … and then the patchouli and ylang-ylang ones in a circle round my feet, evenly spaced, it's vital there should be no gaps in the geometry, er, symmetry.'

Making sure there was no danger of igniting any of the precious frocks, Frankie and Lilly eventually managed to place the candles to Maisie's satisfaction and light them. Dozens of little flames danced and guttered.

'Aren't they pretty. So many of them! And don't they smell lovely?' Lilly inhaled.

Frankie nodded. 'Great, as long as they don't burn the shop down. I'll get the fire extinguisher out of the kitchen, just in case.'

'And turn the lights off.' Maisie's voice was still very faint. 'We don't need any artificial lighting. The spirits don't like it.'

'Bugger the spirits,' Dexter said, following Frankie into the kitchen, 'I need to see where I'm going at the moment. Quite an actress, isn't she?'

'And bossy with it.' Frankie nodded. 'Well, at least Lilly's impressed anyway. Oh God, what are we doing?'

'Laying the ghost,' Dexter said firmly. 'Once and for all. It'll all be fine, you'll see.'

Frankie wasn't so sure.

They'd discussed it endlessly throughout the week. Over hearty fat-filled food in the Greasy Spoon, and twice over rather weird cocktails in the Toad in the Hole. Then, they'd both agreed it was the only thing to do. At least they'd be giving something a try.

186

Now it was actually happening, it seemed like something else altogether.

It was very odd, Frankie thought, unclipping the fire extinguisher from the wall, that she and Dexter had fallen easily into meeting up at lunch times and after work simply to discuss Ernie's exorcism. They hadn't touched on anything personal at all, but having a shared secret had brought them closer in some way.

'Are we still not telling Maisie that it's Ernie who's our resident ghost?' Dexter hefted the fire extinguisher. 'Are we going to let him come as a surprise?'

'Definitely.' Frankie looked around the kitchen. 'I still think Maisie's a fake, so I'm not intending to give her any help at all. We know Ernie can materialise at will, so let's see what she does with him *if* she manages to communicate with him at all. Right, let's go.'

With the lights out, and the shop illuminated only by the multitude of flickering candles, shadows danced eerily up the walls, around the rainbow rails of frocks, and across the low ceiling.

'You stand here to my left,' Maisie whispered shakily to Lilly, 'because you believe in the spirit world and will increase the positivity. And you, Frankie and young Dexter, must stand to my right. And no one say anything. Not a word. Whatever happens. Promise me, sweethearts?'

They all nodded. Lilly giggled. Frankie could feel her heart thundering under her ribs.

'Are you OK?' Dexter whispered.

She nodded.

'Good,' he said softly, and took her hand in the darkness and squeezed her fingers.

187

Her heart thundered even more.

Maisie leaned back in her chair and fumbled under the neck of the kaftan. Producing an oddly shaped pendant on a thick chain, she held it between her thumb and forefinger.

'Are you here?' Maisie whispered hoarsely. 'Are you here with us?'

The pendant jerked wildly.

Dexter squeezed Frankie's hand.

'And do you want to be free?' Maisie croaked. 'Are you unhappy?'

The pendant swung from side to side.

'That's a yes on both counts,' Maisie informed them. 'Shall I release you?'

'Is she talking to us or them?' Dexter whispered in Frankie's ear.

'Them I hope.' Frankie tingled, feeling Dexter's lips close to her skin.

'Shhhh.' Maisie looked cross. 'Don't speak.'

The pendant whirled round and round.

'Can't even see her fingers moving,' Dexter murmured. 'It's impressive.'

'Show yourselves to me,' Maisie demanded, sweeping her hand across her forehead. 'Show yourselves! Now!'

They all held their breath.

The pendant seemed to take on a life of its own, swinging violently backwards and forwards.

Maisie gave a little scream and slumped sideways.

'Is she dead?' Lilly whispered.

'God, I hope not.' Frankie peered at Maisie. 'It would take a hell of a lot of explaining.'

'Of course I'm not dead,' Maisie groaned. 'They're coming through. It exhausts me. And stop talking.'

Dexter nudged Frankie. 'Over there,' he whispered. 'By the fifties frocks.'

In the dancing shadows, Ernie was leaning nonchalantly against the rails, grinning cheerfully. He gave them a little wave.

Frankie waved back, then frowned. 'Did she do that?'

'Doubtful, seeing as we know he appears like that without Maisie here,' Dexter said softly. 'But let's see what she does now. If we can see him then she must be able to.'

Maisie gave a jerk and shook her head. 'I can't hear you all at once, I need to hear one voice only. I can't see you, but I can sense you. Make yourselves appear.'

Frankie and Dexter looked at one another.

Lilly peered across the shop towards Ernie. 'Isn't that something over there?'

'Ssssh!' Frankie and Dexter hissed together.

Maisie, her eyes wide open, looked wildly round the shop. 'No, no, this is all wrong. I'm hearing too many voices. I need a spokesperson. I need just one of you to materialise and talk to me. I need guidance.'

'She needs glasses,' Dexter said quietly, 'if she can't see Ernie.'

Frankie sighed. 'I knew she was rubbish. Maybe we should give her a bit of a clue?'

'Please.' Maisie glared at them. 'Don't talk any more. I'm communicating.'

Ernie had strolled into the middle of the shop and stood looking sadly at them.

'There!' Lilly shrilled. 'Maisie! There's someone over there!'

'Quiet!' Maisie snapped as the pendant went into frantic overdrive. 'This isn't going to work if I don't have complete silence.'

'I'm here, Maisie, duck,' Ernie said helpfully. 'Right in front of you. Now, if you could just say whatever you needs to say to get me back to my Achsah I'd be right grateful.'

'That's better.' Maisie subsided back into her chair. 'Total silence.'

'She's crap,' Dexter said firmly. 'She can't hear Ernie or even see him. She's never going to reunite Ernie with his wife at this rate.'

Lilly jiggled up and down on her stilettos. 'Maisie, there's someone here. I can see him. You've magicked up a ghost!'

'It's not magic, you silly girl, and no one has materialised yet—you're imagining things. Too much imagination can kill the sightings as much as too much scepticism.'

Ernie sighed heavily. 'Look, Maisie, duck, I ain't one to complain, but I'm here and everyone else knows I'm here and you must know that I'm here and—'

'I've got someone!' Maisie suddenly screamed. 'I've got someone coming through the rabble and chaos!'

'Thank God for that,' Dexter sighed. 'At bloody last.'

'I must insist on complete silence, and far less blasphemy and profanity,' Maisie gasped, reaching for a glass of water. 'I'm drained here. Drained. That's better. Now, if you could just show yourself to me.'

'Ta-dah!' Ernie did a little mocking jiggling dance.

'She's telling me that she wants to be reunited,' Maisie said triumphantly. 'That she won't rest until she's reunited.'

'*She?*' Dexter and Frankie looked at one another.

'Hold up, duck.' Ernie stopped jigging and frowned. 'You seem to have got the drift of what I'm after, but I ain't no she.'

'It looks like a man to me,' Lilly said doubtfully. 'He's really sweet.'

Ernie beamed at Lilly.

Maisie suddenly let out a banshee wail. Frankie clung even more tightly to Dexter's hand. Lilly whimpered.

The shop grew icily cold and a wind, gentle at first, seemed to waft through the darkness, rippling through the half-lit dresses on the rails, making them dance and shimmer like rainbows in the candle glow. Growing in intensity, the wind became a howling, roaring gale, like a live thing, unseen, running amok.

Then, just as suddenly as it had started, it stopped.

There was absolute silence.

'She's here!' Maisie said hoarsely. 'Oh, dear Lord and all the saints, she's here.'

'Jesus!' Dexter blinked as a shadowy figure emerged from the gloom. 'What the hell is happening here?'

Frankie felt very sick. She was shaking from head to toe. Even Lilly was silent.

'Speak to me.' Maisie's voice was guttural now. 'Speak to me.'

'I'll speak to you all right, you daft old bat.' A very angry-looking woman, with her fair hair in a 1940s snood, and wearing a white petticoat, strode

191

across the shop. 'What the devil you think you're doing, disturbing us, I've no bloody idea. But now you have, I'll thank you to undo whatever hokum you've just done and let us go back to where we came from.'

Maisie gave a scream, followed by a wistful sigh, and conveniently fainted.

'Christ Almighty!' Dexter shook his head. 'Look at them.'

Frankie looked.

The shadowy shop was suddenly full of women: women of all shapes and sizes and ages, all in various states of undress, all shrieking happily and eagerly raking through the rails of frocks.

'I'm going to be sick.' Lilly clutched her mouth and flew towards the kitchen.

'A right bloody how's-yer-father balls-up this is,' Ernie snapped. 'Now I'm still here, and I'm not alone. Now I'm sharing me haunting space with a lot of flaming half-dressed dead shopaholics.'

Chapter Eighteen

'Maisie!' Frankie shook the kaftan-clad shoulder and shrieked in the cauliflower-curl-covered ear. 'Maisie! Wake up!'

Maisie just grunted.

'Hang on.' Dexter deftly moved the candles away from Maisie's sprawled designer-clad feet. 'We've got enough problems. We don't want to turn the place into an inferno as well, do we?'

'I don't see why not,' Frankie said faintly. 'We've got hell on earth here already.'

192

'I'll put the rest of the candles out and switch the lights on,' Dexter said, clearly trying to keep some sort of control. 'The, um, well, ladies might all disappear in the light.'

He did, and they didn't.

The woman in the white petticoat frowned at Frankie. 'Who are you? Where is this? And what century are we in?'

'I'm Frankie Meredith,' Frankie mumbled, not taking her eyes from the apparition. 'This is my frock shop, in Kingston Dapple, in Berkshire, and it's the twenty-first century.'

'Twenty-first century.' White Petticoat frowned. 'Is it? Crikey. And anyway what the blazes did you think you were doing here, meddling with things you clearly don't understand?'

Frankie, petrified, just stared at her. Across the shop, the women were still shrieking with girlish excitement, but now also tugging frocks from the rails, struggling into them, and admiring one another.

It was like Saturday afternoon in Primark.

'Come on, one of you,' White Petticoat said tersely. 'Speak to me. Tell me exactly what's going on.'

'They're scared witless of you, duck,' Ernie said helpfully. 'And I can't say I blame them.'

'Oh, heaven preserve me.' White Petticoat looked Ernie up and down. 'Now we've got a bewildered newly dead. They drive me mad, you know. All lost and confused and insisting they're still alive. Get over it, love. You're dead.'

'I know that,' Ernie said crossly. 'And I'm dead happy to be dead. I just don't want to be here.'

'That makes two of us.' White Petticoat patted

193

her snood. 'I was more than happy where I was until she—' she jabbed a finger towards Maisie '—dabbled. Saints preserve me from a bloody dabbler.'

Ernie nodded. 'Exactly what I said, myself.'

'Tell me I'm dreaming,' Frankie said, trying not to cry. 'Please tell me I'm dreaming.'

'I wish.' Dexter looked totally bemused. 'What the heck do we do now?'

'Wake her up—' White Petticoat jabbed a finger at Maisie again '—and get her to send us back to the afterlife.' She turned her blazing glare to Frankie. 'Was this your idea? The seance? A bit of a giggle, was it? Well, let me tell you, it's far from funny to disturb the dead. I do wish people would leave the spirit world well alone. Stupid, absolutely stupid.'

'Now you just hang on.' Ernie stepped forwards. 'Young Frankie and Dexter here didn't cause this. It's more my fault than anyone's. They were just trying to help me pass over. I want to rest in peace.'

'Which is what we were all doing nicely, thank you.' White Petticoat sighed. 'And who are you, anyway?'

'Ernie Yardley, duck. And you?'

'Bev Barlow.'

'Nice to meet you.'

'And you.'

'Christ.' Dexter shook his head.

Maisie snored.

Frankie rubbed her eyes. 'This is crazy. We've got to do something. No, correction, Maisie's got to do something.'

She picked up the jug of water and flung it into the large, flabby, comatose face.

Dexter applauded.

'Whooooo!' Maisie screamed, sitting up and shaking herself, with several cauliflower curls now dripping into her eyes. 'Did you chuck water over me, Frankie? Oooh, that was very nasty of you.'

'Maybe it was, but I don't care,' Frankie said angrily. 'What the hell have you done, Maisie? You said you knew what you were doing. You said you could help me to un-ghost my shop! Now look at it!'

'Crikey, sweethearts.' Maisie gazed proudly round the spirit-filled shop. 'Did I really do all this?'

'Yes, you bloody did.' Dexter leaned over her. 'And now, please reverse it.'

'Well I never.' Maisie mopped her face with a massive hankie and beamed cheerfully. 'I've never managed to raise anything or anyone before. Ever.'

'What?' Frankie sighed. 'You mean, you're a fraud? One big fake? Like we suspected all along?'

'I'm not a fraud. I do have some powers—some very special powers. It's just that, so far, they've not had very spectacular results.'

'Well, they have now,' Bev snorted. 'And hopefully you'll be able to summon up your clearly limited powers to send us back to where we came from.'

'Which is where?' Maisie asked interestedly. 'It's always fascinated me.'

Bev tucked a stray hair under her snood. 'The afterlife is far too complex to describe to you now. And while I obviously have the time I certainly don't have the patience. Just accept that there are various layers, and most of us are more than happy to be where we are. We certainly don't want to be dragged back into a world we hardly recognise with

195

people we don't know, by the likes of you.'

Dexter and Frankie exchanged glances. But any further explanations were halted by a lot of screaming and scuffling.

A fight had broken out round the 1960s rails.

'Here!' Ernie strode across the shop. 'Stop that! This is a lovely little shop, and young Frankie's trying to make a living. It ain't a bloody bun fight! You leave them frocks alone.'

The women stopped squabbling and fell back, looking abashed.

'And that's fine for you to say—' a figure with close-cropped hair and wearing long johns, sashayed forwards, clutching a floaty purple minidress and pouted '—but some of us haven't seen a decent bit of material for simply *ages*.'

'It's a man!' Frankie blinked. 'Isn't it?'

'Oh Lordy,' Dexter muttered. 'It's the Louie Spence of the spirit world. Fantastic.'

'OK.' Frankie took a deep breath. 'This is madness. Maisie, do something. Now.'

'I don't know what to do, sweethearts, and that's a fact. You'll have to give me some time to think.'

Bev snorted. 'Well, being dead, I've obviously got all the time in the world, but I'm guessing these living people haven't. So I suggest you get a bit of a shift on, all right?'

'Just give me a minute.' Maisie took several deep breaths. 'Let me see what I can come up with. But, when you were coming through, didn't you tell me you wanted to be reunited? I'm sure I heard you say you wanted to be—'

'I didn't say anything, and I certainly don't want to be re-united with anyone down here, ta.' Bev sighed heavily. 'I've got all the chums and family I need back there in the afterlife, thanks very much.'

'But I could have sworn you said you wanted to be reunited,' Maisie looked confused. 'I'm sure someone wanted to be reunited.'

'Me, duck,' Ernie said. 'Me. And you even managed to get that wrong. What a bloody palaver this all is.'

Maisie ignored Ernie and closed her eyes again. 'Well, I'm very sorry I'm sure if I misunderstood you, er, Bev. The signals must have got crossed somewhere. I'll try to sort out my earthly auras from my spiritual ones. Just let me concentrate. Right, I'm getting a clearer picture now.'

'Sounds like my damn old telly,' Ernie said. 'And that only worked properly when you gave it a good whack with your fist.'

'Don't tempt me,' Dexter muttered.

Frankie who was still shaking and absolutely sure she'd wake up in her pink and purple bedroom at any moment, cleared her throat and looked at Bev. 'Look, while Maisie sorts this lot out, can I ask you a question?'

'Ask away.' Bev looked bored. 'I'm not going anywhere.'

'I know it sounds rude, but why are you all, um, not properly dressed?'

'Because when we died, a very long time ago in most cases, the fashion for bedecking the corpse in all its earthly finery was seldom heard of. Especially among the lower orders. The men always used to be buried in their best suits if they had one, but not the ladies. We got nightdresses or petticoats to cover our dignity if we were lucky. Some of the poor souls just got shrouds. Most of them haven't seen a dress for over sixty years. That's why they're so excited by the frocks.'

'Oh dear.' Lilly had teetered unsteadily out of the kitchen, looking green. 'That's a bit unfair. Whatever happened to equality?'

'There weren't no equality back then,' Ernie chipped in. 'Men and women had separate roles and were treated very differently.'

'I'm glad I'm alive now, then,' Lilly said, watching the women still sifting excitedly through the clothes rails, but with more decorum since Ernie's rant. 'Oooh, is that one with the purple frock a *man*?'

'I am, dear heart. Thanks for noticing. I'm Jared.'

'I'm Lilly.'

'Pretty name for a very pretty girl.' Jared, now with the purple minidress over his long johns, gave a twirl and a curtsy.

'Faggot!' Bev sniffed.

'You can't say that!' Frankie was horrified. 'Not even if he's dead and you're dead. That's so non-PC!'

'What's PC got to do with it?' Bev frowned. 'What does it mean? Postcard? Police constable?'

'Don't bother,' Dexter advised. 'She's from a different era, and so is he by the look of it. Jesus, Frankie, what are we going to do?'

'Are they all *dead*?' Lilly looked worriedly at Frankie. 'Really, truly dead?'

'Afraid so. But they seem friendly enough.'

'And I'm really, truly talking to *dead people*?'

'Yes, unfortunately you are.'

'Wow—cool.'

Frankie managed a wan smile. 'I'm glad you can see a good side to all this. And—are you *drunk*?'

'Only a little bit.' Lilly giggled. 'I was a bit scared ... OK, a lot scared—it was much, much worse than *Paranormal Experience*—but I opened that bottle of champagne in the fridge and had a good few glugs.' She smiled lopsidedly. 'Nothing like a bit of fizz to put the sparkle back.'

'My Krug?' Frankie frowned. 'Dexter's Krug? You've drunk the Krug? I was saving that for a special occasion. Dear Lord, Lilly.'

'I didn't drink all of it, well not quite, and this is pretty special in my book, and anyway, you never said there'd be *ghosts.*'

'There weren't supposed to be.' Frankie sighed. 'I don't believe in ghosts.'

'That's not really true,' Ernie said miserably, 'now is it?'

'OK, I believe in Ernie,' Frankie corrected. 'And I'm so sorry that this has gone so wrong.'

'Me too, duck.' Ernie looked sadly across the shop. 'You know, once they'd all appeared, I really, really hoped my Achsah might be among 'em, and that we'd be together again, even if we were sort of earthbound, but no. She ain't there. It was like losing her all over again.'

'Oh, Ernie.' Frankie shook her head. 'I'm so sorry. Oh, I could kill Maisie!'

'And that wouldn't help much, would it?' Dexter smiled gently at her. 'We've got enough dead people already. We need Maisie alive and kicking and sorting this bloody mess out.'

'Exactly.' Frankie glared at Maisie who now had her rather damp head in her hands. 'After all, we only wanted her to return Ernie to his rightful, um, place in the life after death, er, structure, and—'

Maisie looked up. 'You *knew* you had a ghost, sweetheart? You *knew* the shop was haunted by *someone*? A particular person? You never told me that, now did you? Things might have been very different if you'd told me what I was supposed to be doing. Why didn't you tell me?'

'Because,' Frankie hissed, 'you said you *knew* what you were doing. You said you could sort out any haunting problem. There was no way I was going to give you a clue that it was Ernie who was hanging around the shop. I wanted to believe in you. I wanted you to prove that I was wrong, and you could manage to lay my ghost. But I was right, wasn't I? You're totally useless.'

'Harsh, duck, but true.' Ernie nodded. 'And I'm thinking she still can't see me, can you, Maisie?'

'Anyway,' Maisie carried on, 'you'll just have to give me a little bit more time to gather my powers and I'll try to get rid of all these ladies.'

'And me?' Ernie asked plaintively. 'Don't forget me.'

'I'm disappointed in you, Frankie, sweetheart, really I am.' Maisie swept her hand dramatically through her bedraggled perm. 'Now, just leave me alone. I need to concentrate.'

Dexter sighed heavily. 'She can't see or hear Ernie at all, can she? Only the ghosts she's conjured up. What a bloody waste of time.'

'And what about me?' Jared stopped admiring himself in the cheval mirror. 'She only said she'd get rid of the women, didn't she? What about me?'

'She probably thinks you're a girl as well,' Lilly said kindly. 'You look lovely in that colour. It really suits you.'

Jared simpered and pranced round the shop, holding out the hem of his purple skirt.

'Why are you all women?' Dexter dragged his eyes from the now pirouetting Jared, and looked at

200

Bev. 'How come Maisie managed to raise a whole crowd of women ghosts, oh, and Jared?'

'Search me. Luck of the draw? Tuning into the right auras at the right moment? Or the wrong one in my case? I've really no idea.' Bev again looked bored by the question. 'We certainly weren't all together "up there", if you like. We don't know each other. And I can't speak for the rest of them, but I died in nineteen forty-three and I've never materialised before, never felt compelled by anyone calling me from "down here" before.' She gave Maisie a withering look. 'Whatever powers she has, they're sadly misrouted if you ask me. One minute I was just, well, enjoying the afterlife, the next, I was being rushed away, against my will, down some dark tunnel all sprinkled with stars, and ended up here.'

'Wow.' Lilly was open-mouthed. 'That is sooo spooky. I can't wait to tell—'

'You must never breathe a word of this,' Frankie interrupted fiercely. 'Promise me, Lilly. This stays between us here tonight. If any of this got out— well, one we'd be a laughing stock, and, two, I'd definitely go bankrupt and three, we'd probably all be sectioned. So, promise me—you'll never, ever tell anyone about this.'

'Bummer.' Lilly frowned. 'Oh, OK. Whatever. Yeah, I promise.'

'Lilly telling all and sundry is the least of your worries at the moment, I'd say.' Dexter stared again at the hordes of women, still chattering nosily round the frock rails. 'Getting rid of this lot is far more important.'

Frankie nodded and looked at Maisie. 'Come on, you must have some idea what to do. When you, er, materialised them you did it with that pendant thing, so surely you can put it into reverse, can't you?'

Maisie bit her lip. 'I don't think so.'

'Why on earth not?'

Bev folded her arms and tapped a bare foot. 'We're waiting.'

'Because,' Maisie said reluctantly, 'the pendant isn't special, sweetheart. It's not an ancient artefact. It's just for effect. I bought it in Claire's Accessories.'

'Jesus Christ!' Dexter rubbed his eyes.

Jared had found a lilac maxi-dress and had draped it round his shoulders like a stole and was now strutting camply round the floor.

Ernie and Bev watched him in disgust. Lilly hiccupped and clapped her hands.

'So,' Frankie said, feeling very close to tears, 'you honestly don't know how to undo what you've done?'

Maisie looked sulky. 'As you've already guessed, I've never managed to get through to anyone before—not like this—let alone try to send them back again, so, no, sweetheart, I don't. But despite you withholding information from me, I'll try for you. I'll try. Can we have the candles lit again and the lights out, please, and I'll see what I can do.'

'Stay there!' Frankie said firmly to Lilly as Dexter quickly relit the candles. 'Stand there, next to Maisie and don't move. You're all giggly and wobbly and I don't want you setting fire to yourself. And don't speak, please.'

'OK.' Lilly looked excited. 'This is brilliant, though, isn't it? Like when we went to see that illusionist in Winterbrook and all the lights went out and someone nicked the takings. Do you remember?'

'Stop talking,' Maisie said as Dexter turned out the lights and Francesca's Fabulous Frocks was once more plunged into darkness. 'Please, please, stop chattering.'

Some hope, Frankie thought.

Maisie closed her eyes. 'Ladies ...'

'And gents,' added Ernie, 'although I know you can't hear me, you silly old so-and-so.'

'And me!' Jared piped up from the gloom.

'All right then, if you have to be picky—spirits all.' Maisie sounded grumpy. 'Spirits all, listen to me. Listen.'

The rabble round the rails fell silent.

Ernie moved closer to Frankie. 'Look, duck, if the daft old bat actually manages to get us all back over to the other side, I just wants to say sorry for causing all this trouble and thank you for your help. You've been more than kind.'

'You're welcome,' Frankie whispered back, wiping away a tear. 'And I hope you and Achsah live, well, no, but you know what I mean, happily ever after.'

'Ah, me too, duck.' Ernie nodded his grizzled head. 'And you and young Dexter, too.'

'Oh, I don't think so, but ... anyway, good luck. And hopefully, goodbye.'

'Goodbye, duck. It's been a pleasure knowing you.'

Frankie swallowed the lump in her throat. It was like waving someone who was emigrating off at the airport, knowing you might never see them again.

Maisie threw her head back and started to mutter some sort of incantation.

The air was exotically filled with the mingled scents of calendula and patchouli and ylang-ylang and the shop suddenly seemed much, much colder.

'Go back!' Maisie screamed unexpectedly, making them jump. 'Go! Go back to your other life!'

The shop was icy now and there was an even deeper darkness.

Maisie's head slumped forwards and she mumbled something else unintelligible. It sounded like a poem.

The cold increased. Lilly snivelled a bit. Dexter moved closer to Frankie and slid his arm round her, pulling her against him.

Maisie stopped mumbling and suddenly shot upright in the chair. 'We need noise! Noise! Lots of noise! Noise can disperse the spirits from their earthly bonds!'

'What sort of noise?' Lilly giggled. 'Should we all go wooo-wooo-wooo?'

'Clap you hands and stamp your feet and shout loudly,' Maisie said sharply. 'All of you.'

Feeling totally ridiculous, Frankie, Dexter and Lilly clapped and stamped and shouted.

'That's the ticket.' Maisie nodded. 'Louder! Keep it up, sweethearts. Now, be gone! Be gone! Spirits, go! Rest in peace! Rest in peace! For ever!'

The shop's darkness turned to impenetrable blackness. A tearing wind roared round them, making the candle flames dance higher and higher and then extinguishing them, plunging the shop into nothingness.

Then a roll of thunder boomed round them, and someone screamed, and carried on screaming, a thin, blood-curdling scream that spiralled away, upwards, ever upwards.

The wind rushed and danced and seemed to suck the life out of the room. There was no air, no feeling. Just a vacuum.

They all stopped stamping and clapping and shouting.

The screaming intensified.

Frankie, terrified and clutching tightly to Dexter, hoped it wasn't her.

Maisie, after howling out a further garbled incantation, gave a sob and a sigh, and then collapsed.

Immediately, the wind stopped shrieking, the blackness lightened slightly, and everything was quiet.

Deathly quiet.

'Er—' Dexter eventually gulped in Frankie's ear. 'I think she might have managed it. I think she might actually have done it. Stay there—I'll put the lights on.'

'Don't go,' Lilly whimpered. 'Please don't go.'

Frankie held Lilly's hand and worked some saliva into her mouth. 'It's OK, Lill. It's OK. You'll see when Dexter puts the lights on. It's all over now. There, see.'

The shop was bathed in the lovely, friendly, warm glow of joyous electricity.

'See?' Frankie squeezed Lilly's hand. 'It's perfectly all right now and ... Oh shit.'

Chapter Nineteen

The dozens of ghostly women had disappeared. Well, mostly.

Bev and Jared still stood in the middle of the shop staring at one another. And two elderly women who had earlier been arguing over a pink strapless empire-line evening dress, wandered dejectedly between the clothes rails.

And Ernie was standing beside Frankie looking morose.

'Bugger.' Dexter shook his head. 'What went wrong there?'

'Looks like we missed the spiritual bus, angel boy.' Jared pouted flirtatiously.

'Nooo!' Bev shouted. 'No! I can't still be here. I want to go home!'

'So do I.' Ernie sighed. 'And now I've got no damn chance.'

'And what about them?' Frankie looked at the women still kicking their heels disconsolately by the 1970s frocks. 'Who the heck are they? Why are they still here?'

'Don't look at me.' Maisie sat up, looking very pleased with herself. 'I did my best. And I've got rid of most of them, haven't I? And could someone get me a drink of water, please?'

'Get it yourself,' Frankie said wearily. 'A fine mess this is now. I started off with one ghost and now I've got five. You'll have to try again, Maisie. You've managed it once. You can do it again.'

'And you, sweetheart, have got to be joking. I'm like a limp rag. Completely drained. I haven't got enough energy hardly left to breathe, let alone use my powers.'

'Powers!' Ernie snorted 'Powers, she calls 'em. Huh!'

'You're not leaving this shop until you've got rid of all of them.' Frankie knew she was losing control. 'I can't cope with five bloody ghosts.'

'Language, please.' Bev frowned. 'Ghosts, yes we are, but bloody, no. Mind you, there are some pretty gory sights up there, I can tell you. Specially them what were beheaded back in the olden days.'

'Don't tell me that.' Lilly gulped. 'I saw *Night of the Living Dead*.'

'Sounds about right.' Dexter sighed.

Maisie hauled herself unsteadily to her designer-clad feet and teetered on the high heels towards the kitchen. 'As you're clearly not going to help me, I'm going to get myself a drink of water. When I've had a drink of water, I wish to be taken home.'

'I don't care what you bloody wish,' Frankie flared at the retreating wobbly kaftan. 'You can't go home and leave these, um, well, them here.'

'I'm happy, loves,' Jared squeaked, stroking his purple ensemble and gazing blissfully round the shop. 'More than happy to stay. So many frocks, so much time.'

The two women by the rails stared at him, then at each other.

Jared waved at them. 'Looks like we're all in a bit of a pickle, doesn't it, girls? I'm Jared.'

'Ruby,' said the one in the droopy grey nightdress. 'Nice to meet you.'

'Gertie,' said the elder of the two who was a very pale grey, and looked like she was wrapped in a

207

sheet. 'Lovely little shop, isn't it? Pretty dresses. I like pretty dresses.'

'Aaaargh!' Frankie screamed. 'Enough!'

Everyone looked at her.

'Sorry, but I can't cope with this. This is total madness.'

'It's not, Frankie. Chill. It's been much more fun than clubbing on a Saturday night,' Lilly said and then yawned. 'But I'm dead tired now. That's the trouble with champagne, isn't it? You get a lovely bubbly high, then whoosh it's gone.'

'And I'm not likely to know now, am I?' Frankie glared at her. 'Seeing as you've drunk it all.'

Lilly giggled. 'Soz. I'll buy you some more for Christmas. Anyway, now you've only got a few ghosts left and they seem quite happy, can we go home now?'

'No!' Frankie stared at her in disbelief. 'I can't go home and leave them here. I need the shop to be de-ghosted before I open again on Monday morning.'

'You'll be waiting a long time for Maisie, then,' Dexter said dolefully. 'I've just checked on her and she's bedded down on the coats in the kitchen and is dead to the world.'

Bev sighed. 'Looks like you're stuck with us— same as we're stuck here—for the time being. Such a darn nuisance. You don't want us here and we certainly don't want to be here.'

'I do, loves,' Jared chirruped.

'Shut up!' Everyone chorused.

Jared flounced off into a corner and started talking to Ernie.

Bev shrugged. 'As I was saying, looks like we'll all have to make the best of it until you can

208

find a proper medium who can return us back to the afterlife. You seem like a nice girl with good intentions. After all, this schemozzle only happened because you thought you could help Ernie out of his predicament. Look, we'll try to keep out of the way when your shop's open. We'll be ever so discreet. You won't know we're here, and hopefully neither will your customers. And there must be loads of people out there who can contact the dead properly, unlike that useless pudding snoring her head off out there.'

'Oh, yes!' Lilly looked slightly more awake. 'There are! They're all over the telly! Loads of them. Really famous spiritualists and mediums, and there's all sorts of programmes on haunted houses. We can contact one of them and get them to do a proper session, can't we?'

'No.' Frankie shook her head vehemently. 'We tell no one about this. No one. I've only got two weeks trading to go before Christmas. I certainly don't need to scare away customers at the busiest time of the year. I'll just have to make the best of it until the new year. I'll think about what to do, then.'

'You could use it as a selling point.' Lilly said, yawning again. 'Jennifer Blessing always says that you can always turn a disaster into a selling point. Like the time—'

'Shut up!' Frankie snapped. 'I am *not* turning my shop being haunted into a selling point. And please, please, promise me you won't mention this to anyone.'

'I've already promised.' Lilly looked sulky. 'I'm good at keeping promises. Promise. Oooh, and now I need the loo.'

'Too much champagne,' Frankie said crossly. 'And while you're through there, do something useful and see if you can wake Maisie up then we can all go home.'

'Don't mention going home, please—' Bev tucked more fair wisps of hair into her snood '—it's painful. But there's something you can maybe do for me before you go.'

'Is there?' Frankie looked at her. 'Go on then. Try me.'

'Find us something to wear.' Bev indicated the rails. 'Jared will probably spend all his time down here trying on everything, but it looks as though me, Ruby and Gertie could do with something decent. Just in case.'

'In case of what?'

'In case we appear at an inopportune moment. Like I say, I've never been earthbound before, so I don't know when we're invisible and when we're not. I'll make sure we try to stay unseen, but I'm not sure how it works. And I'm thinking you won't want three ladies in various states of undress mingling with your Christmas shoppers.'

'She's right.' Dexter nodded. 'Ernie's OK, he's fully dressed in his suit, he's even got a shirt and tie and nice polished shoes on, so if anyone spots him they'll think he's a shopper, but the one over there in the sheet—' he made a face in Gertie's direction '—she'd scare the pants off anyone.'

Frankie sighed, then smiled at Bev. 'I'm afraid the frocks I've got only date back to the nineteen fifties at the moment. We haven't had any real vintage stuff. They might be a bit, um, modern for you.'

'They might,' Bev agreed. 'But they'll be even

210

more modern for those two.'

Ruby and Gertie were looking disconsolate.

'OK.' Frankie tried not to think that this was the maddest thing she'd ever done in her life, and took a deep breath. 'Let's pretend you're all normal customers—go and have a look and see what might suit you.'

Gertie and Ruby immediately homed in on the strapless pink evening dress again.

'Not that.' Frankie shook her head. 'Sorry. It has to be daywear only. Otherwise you'll stick out like sore thumbs.'

'And you don't think they might do that anyway?' Dexter asked kindly. 'Being as they're dead?'

'Bev doesn't look dead. Nor does Ruby in a good light. I'm not so sure about Gertie.'

'I was always pasty.' Gertie grinned at them in a rather scary manner. 'Even when I was alive. Pale and pasty. Proper little pasty face my dad used to call me. I don't look that much different now, actually.'

'Jesus,' Dexter muttered.

Frankie, suddenly wanting to laugh and sure that if she started it'd turn into hysterics and she'd never stop, ignored him, and hurried across to the rails of dresses.

'Blue would suit you,' she said to Bev. 'What about this?'

Bev surveyed the 1950s blue frock with its white collar and cuffs and nipped-in waist. 'Mmm, I quite like that one. Can I try it on?'

'Be my guest,' Frankie muttered, raking through the frocks to find something—anything—that would do to cover Ruby and Gertie's obvious, er, deadness.

'This would be nice for you.' She pulled out a crimson wool dress in a very small size and showed it to Ruby. 'You're very petite.'

'I used to be a right big lass,' Ruby said conversationally, lovingly stroking the crimson dress. 'Until my last illness.'

Frankie whimpered. It was one thing *knowing* they were dead, it was quite another having to face *why*. 'I'm really sorry, I didn't mean to upset you.'

'Oh, you haven't,' Ruby said cheerfully. 'It was smashing being thin for a while at least. And now I'm always thin and I love it.'

She slid enthusiastically out of the greying nightdress and stood stark naked in the shop.

Dexter, Ernie and Jared quickly averted their eyes.

'Oh God, you haven't got any underwear,' Frankie gulped. 'I'm afraid I don't do undies.'

'Not a problem for ghosts,' Ruby assured her, slipping on the crimson dress which fitted her perfectly and giving a twirl. 'There! How does that look?'

'Really nice.' Frankie nodded. 'It could have been made for you. Shame none of you have got any shoes on. Shoes would set off the frocks beautifully.'

'It's not damn *Gok's Clothes RoadShow*,' Dexter said testily. 'They're dead, Frankie, not off to some huge red carpet event. They don't need matching accessories. Just get them dressed and let's get out of here.'

'Yes, but,' Frankie hissed, 'if they're *seen* wandering around the shop barefooted in the dead of winter, people will *notice* won't they?'

'Mmm, suppose so.'

212

'Oh, I do wish Rita hadn't donated all her shoes to Maisie now.'

'Maisie will just have to un-donate some then, won't she?' Dexter said. 'I'll pick some up when I take her home. Although they might not fit that well, I suppose. What size was Rita?'

'Six,' Frankie said. 'Ladies? Will size six shoes do you? I can't guarantee that they'll match your frocks, but—'

'Any shoes will be most acceptable,' Bev said. 'I'm a six anyway. I don't know about them two, though.'

'I think I was a five,' Ruby said, 'but I've only ever had hand-me-down shoes so I can stuff the toes with newspaper.'

'I'm a size seven,' Gertie added. 'But I can tread the backs down. I always had to do that when I borrowed my sister's shoes. She were a size six so they'll be fine for me. And I'm not fussy about style or colour.'

Frankie heaved a sigh of relief. Shoes, it seemed, didn't have that much importance in the afterlife. She wouldn't mention it to Lilly.

'We'll manage with whatever you can get, thank you. And I do like this dress.' Bev pirouetted in her blue frock. 'I had something similar before we got bombed out. It takes me right back.'

'It really suits you,' Frankie said. 'Er, is the, um, bombing how you, um, passed over?'

'Died,' Bev said, admiring herself in the cheval mirror. 'Yes. We don't use euphemisms. No passing over, passing away, going on before, shuffling off the mortal coil. None of that old baloney. We died and we're dead. Fact.'

'Er, right.'

213

'Can you find a dress for me now?' Gertie asked plaintively, trailing her sheet behind her. 'Don't forget me.'

'As if,' Dexter said.

Frankie shot him a look.

'What about a nice bright yellow? Something cheerful.' Frankie rattled the hangers back and forth. 'Yellow always brings a bit of sunshine into the dullest day, I feel, don't you?' Oh heavens, she was turning into Cherish. 'Ah, now this is lovely and looks as if it might be your size, doesn't it?'

She flourished the lemon cotton dress, its full skirt randomly splodged with deeper yellow sunflowers.

'Oh, yes!' Gertie clapped her greying hands. 'Lovely! So pretty! I was always one for a pretty frock!' She cast a coquettish simper at Dexter. 'The boys all loved my pretty frocks.'

Dexter, Frankie noticed, looked slightly sick. Ernie and Jared still had their eyes closed.

Shedding the raggedy wrapped-round sheet and displaying her all-over greyness to its full advantage, Gertie shrugged the vibrant yellow frock over her head.

'Zip me up, love, will you?' She grinned at Frankie. 'I can't wait to see meself in a dress after over eighty years.'

Frankie zipped, avoiding looking at the withered grey skin.

'Oh! I love it!' Gertie elbowed Bev and Ruby away from the mirror. She looked anxiously at Frankie. 'Thank you so much—but when we go back, can we keep the dresses on? We won't have to go back to wearing the other things, will we?'

'I shouldn't think so,' Frankie said, not having a

clue. 'I'm sure if you're wearing the dresses when, well, whenever whoever can return you to, er, the afterlife, then you'll go, er, back in whatever you're wearing at the time. You're more than welcome to keep them.'

'Lovely.' Gertie looked delighted. 'Thank you. I can't wait to show this off to my old man when I get back. It'll be like our honeymoon all over again.'

Dexter chuckled.

Frankie winced.

'Right.' Dexter ran his fingers through his streaky hair. It fell beautifully and silkily back into place 'I'm totally worn-out. So, now we've established that Bev and Ernie and co. will hang on here, as discreetly as possible, until we can find a real medium to release them, are you OK with that?'

Frankie, who'd watched the fingers-running-through-hair movement with the sort of longing she'd thought had long since vanished, rubbed her eyes. Oh Lordy ... Big mistake. The panda look was never a good one.

'Um, actually I don't see what choice I have, so yes.'

'Great. Then I'll go and load Maisie into the car and take her home and collect three pairs of shoes for the, um, ladies. OK?'

Wearily, Frankie nodded. 'And I'll get Lilly—goodness knows where she's gone—and worry about all this again in the morning.'

'Look on the bright side,' Dexter said as they walked towards the kitchen, 'at least tomorrow's Sunday. We can all have a lie-in and you won't have to pop down here to feed them and change their litter trays or anything, will you? It'd be much more troublesome if it were kittens, wouldn't it?'

215

Frankie laughed. 'Yes, I suppose so. Although I will worry about Ernie. He's so disappointed.'

'Yeah, poor bloke, he's pretty down about all this—Oh God, Frankie, listen to us. We're getting emotional over a *ghost.*'

She giggled. 'But a very sweet ghost. And I really do want to help him. Still, bizarrely he seems to be getting on OK with Jared, so maybe he won't be too lonely until we can sort something out with a proper medium. I'll have to check the internet and see if there's anyone local.'

'Someone with proper mediuming credentials this time.' Dexter nodded. 'Someone with A stars in all aspects of things spiritual. No more amateur dabblers like—Oh, great . . .'

They stood side by side in the kitchen doorway. Maisie was still snoring happily on the pile of coats, but now Lilly was curled up beside her, murmuring in her champagne-fuelled sleep and sucking her thumb.

'All right for some.' Frankie sighed. 'Oh, what a hell of a night this has been.'

'You can say that again—no, please don't.' Dexter smiled gently at her. 'Just a figure of speech. And honestly, I know it hasn't gone the way we planned it, but I wouldn't have missed it for anything.'

'Wouldn't you? Are you mad or a masochist or something?'

'Neither of those.' Dexter suddenly hugged her. 'It's just been so completely insane, it's made me forget, well, things I thought would haunt me for ever. So thank you for that.'

If she hadn't been so tired, so confused, so totally bewildered by practically everything, Frankie might

216

have asked further questions. As it was, she was just delighted to feel Dexter's arms around her. He was warm and alive and real—very, very real—and right now she needed all the reality and normality she could get.

'You're welcome. And thank you for helping me so much with all this rubbish. Although I'd have thought anything would be preferable to discovering that there really are ghosts. I bet you didn't bargain on that when you left Oxford, did you?'

Dexter shook his head. 'No. But then I didn't bargain on a lot of things when I left Oxford.'

She looked at him as he stared at her. They were merely inches apart. Her heart lurched. Oh, he was so beautiful. And so untrustworthy.

Just like Joseph Mason.

'Really?' She wriggled away from him. 'Sounds fascinating. We really must have a chat about it sometime. Well, now we've got the dead sorted, we'd better wake the living and go home for what's left of the night.'

'OK.' Dexter shrugged, clearly getting the message, and bent down to shake Maisie's massive kaftan'd shoulder. 'Whatever you say.'

Damn it, Frankie cursed to herself as she grabbed Lilly's thin hand and pulled her thumb from her mouth with a plop. How stupid am I?

'Go 'way,' Lilly mumbled. 'Leave me alone.'

'We're going home, Lill.'

'Are we?' Groaning, Lilly sat up, stared in some surprise at the still-snoring Maisie, then looked groggily from Frankie to Dexter. 'Oh ... Where am I? Who am I? Oh, thank goodness I'm awake. God, Frankie, I had such a bad dream.' She hiccupped cheerfully. 'Do you know, I dreamed your whole shop was full of ghosts. How mad is that?'

Chapter Twenty

Noddy Holder and the rest of Slade were raucously wishing everyone a merry Christmas. Less than two weeks to go until Christmas, and Frankie had given in and shelved the easy-listening music.

Francesca's Fabulous Frocks was rocking.

On this bitterly cold Monday morning, Frankie, in her short red wool dress and matching tights and boots, felt almost festive. Almost. The events of Saturday night still weighed heavily, and she'd opened the shop with some trepidation.

Everything seemed normal enough. The rails were still a little askew, some of the frocks still hung untidily, and the scattered candles and small table and chair that Maisie had used were still in situ, but apart from that, there were no signs that anything untoward had taken place.

Of Ernie, Bev and the others, there was no sign at all.

Frankie, hoping that maybe Maisie's cack-handed exorcism had worked with some sort of delayed reaction and therefore they'd all been returned happily to the afterlife, still called out a cheery good morning—just in case.

No one answered her.

So she'd put the *Greatest Christmas Hits* CD on the stereo, quickly removed Maisie's accoutrements, tidied the rails, and turned the shop door sign to OPEN.

She was just restocking the pile of slithery purple and gold carrier bags beneath the counter when the door opened.

'Morning, fellow ghost-buster,' Dexter called loudly over Roy Wood and Wizzard wishing it could be Christmas every day. 'Nice music. Are we alone?'

Frankie straightened up and laughed. Dexter was wearing a bright red sweatshirt under the leather jacket. 'Snap! Again. We really should text each other about our wardrobe choices. And yes, no sign of the, um, ghostly residents—at least, so far.'

Dexter looked round the shop. 'Weird, isn't it? Did we imagine it all? It all looks so normal now. Anyway—' he flourished a large Big Sava carrier bag '—just in case we weren't the victims of some mass hallucination, I've got the shoes.'

'Brilliant, thank you. I'll put them into the far fitting room and, um, just announce that they're there and hopefully . . . ' Frankie trailed off.

'I know,' Dexter finished. 'It does seem crazy, discussing the footwear of people who are dead. I just grabbed what I could. Maisie was very reluctant to let any of them go, but I persuaded her in the end.'

'None too gently, I hope.' Frankie peered into the bag. 'Oh, lovely, all nice low-ish heels which is good—I mean, if they haven't worn shoes for decades we don't want them staggering about and drawing even more attention to themselves, do we? But you've got four pairs in here.'

'I brought some for Jared as well. I'm guessing he'll stay in his frock as he seemed very fond of it, so I thought he ought to have suitable footwear too.'

219

'Purple slingbacks.' Frankie nodded. 'Perfect. Thank you.' She leaned her hands on the counter. 'And does this all seem completely insane to you?'

'Pretty much,' Dexter agreed. 'But I spent yesterday doing quite a lot of internet research into ghostly sightings, and hauntings, and all things to do with the paranormal, and even if I hadn't seen it all with my own eyes, I'd believe in it all a lot more now. There are some things that simply can't be explained. Some really intelligent, sensible, down-to-earth people have had very similar experiences to ours. So, let's just say I'm no longer a sceptic.'

'And while you were surfing, did you find anyone even slightly likely to be able to sort out our, er, little dilemma?'

'Not really. All the really famous names have great websites, of course, but they only seem to do television shows or theatre tours. I'm assuming that they're too big and too expensive to take on a single private spiritualist session or whatever it is we need. As for anyone else lesser known—they all sound good, but they could be as useless as Maisie, couldn't they?'

Frankie nodded. 'They could. And another Maisie is the last thing we want. I'll try to make some discreet enquiries. Word of mouth round the villages is always a good way to go when you want to find out stuff.'

'OK. And I'll keep on searching, too. But are we agreed that we're not going to do anything about ghost-laying until the new year?'

'Yes. Definitely. I want to get Christmas out of the way first.'

'Fine. Suits me. Anyway, before we're

interrupted by living customers or dead incumbents, there was something else much more important I wanted to ask you.'

Frankie groaned inwardly. It was bound to be about the childish way she'd behaved on Saturday night. Her own Sunday had been taken up with mulling over her growing feelings for Dexter and the reasons why they must never, ever become anything more.

'Really? Is it how to spell Mississippi?'

'No.' Dexter looked puzzled. 'Why should it be?'

'Because Lilly and I had a stand-up fight over that one once when we were doing a charity pub quiz. It's a standing joke.'

'Oh, right. No, it's far more boring than that. It's about our calorie-laden and cholesterol-filled bad food habits.'

Frankie frowned. Dexter had always struck her as a blokey bloke. Not a faddy healthy-eating freak. Was this something else she didn't know about him?

'What about our bad food habits?'

'Well, since I've arrived in Kingston Dapple, I've lived off snatched bacon rolls and the occasional all-day breakfasts in the Greasy Spoon, along with some fabulously gooey cakes brought in from Patsy's Pantry, and I've gone home to something indistinguishable that takes about thirty seconds from the freezer to the microwave. And I'm guessing your diet has been much the same.'

'It has,' Frankie admitted. 'But I'm not going to embark on some slimming campaign now. There's no point. I'll be going home for Christmas and my mum always believes in fattening us up. We sort of roll from the table to the sofa and back again.'

221

Dexter laughed. 'Sounds like the perfect Christmas to me. And you don't need to diet—that wasn't what I was inferring at all.'

'Good. So what?'

'Melissa, one of my customers—well, one of my home-delivery ladies, actually—mentioned that she'd been to this fabulous new restaurant, in the middle of nowhere, and they only serve fresh produce, locally sourced, and—get this—it's totally vegetarian.'

Fighting the urge to say she didn't give a flying fig about what his home-delivery floozies ate, or where, Frankie forced a smile. 'How interesting, and very healthy. And?'

'I'd like to take you there.'

'What?'

'I'd like to take you out to dinner. Somewhere nice. Somewhere where we can have a proper meal made from fresh ingredients, and be alone—without anyone alive or dead interrupting—and actually talk to each other.'

'Why?'

Dexter laughed. 'Why don't you just say no?'

'Sorry, I know that sounded really ungracious.' Understatement, Frankie thought, giving herself a severe mental shake. 'I mean, I just wondered . . .'

'I'm not going to try to add you to my tick-list of local conquests, if that's what's bothering you. You've made it quite clear what you think of me, and also that you're not interested—and I never chase lost causes.' Dexter shrugged. 'I just thought, because we've been through all this ghost stuff together, and we're sharing the being new business owners thing as well, and we're friends, it might be nice to go out together—as friends—without

222

hordes of other people. But if you don't want to, then—'

'I do,' Frankie said quickly. 'Honestly. Thank you. I'd love to.'

'Good.' Dexter looked far more jaunty. 'I'll book a table then. Wednesday evening suit you?'

'Perfectly.' Frankie nodded. 'And sorry again— it's just … well, I haven't been out on a date for ages, and I've become very wary of people's motives.'

'No need to worry about mine, then, is there? It's not a proper date, and I've just laid out my stall. Talking of which, I suppose I ought to go and open up. We're doing a roaring trade in Christmas trees at the moment. Everyone seems to want real trees this year. Brian's been a great help on the delivery side of things.'

Frankie laughed. 'Don't tell me Brian has taken on the, um, duties with your home-delivery ladies? He'd never get out of his duffle coat in time.'

'Cruel.' Dexter laughed, heading for the door. 'I'll let you know what time I've got the table for, shall I?'

'Please. And, Dexter, sorry I behaved so churlishly.'

'I'm sure you have your reasons.' Dexter grinned at her. 'And I'm looking forward to finding out what they are.'

Frankie was still smiling stupidly at the closed door when Ernie appeared at the end of the counter.

'See, duck, I told you he liked you.'

Frankie sighed. 'Oh, Ernie. Yes, he does, and I like him, too. But that's as far as it will go for all sorts of reasons.'

223

Ernie chuckled. 'We'll see, duck. We'll see.'

'We're not going to be another you and Achsah, so don't even think about it.' Frankie tried to look stern. 'And it's not that I'm not pleased to see you, but I'd really hoped that you'd, well, gone. Are the others still here, too?'

Ernie nodded. 'Sadly, yes. But we've had quite a pleasant time, duck. Once you're dead you don't measure time in hours or days or anything so I'm not sure how long it's been, but we've all been chatting and getting to know one another. I must say, if I do have to be suspended down here for a while longer without my Achsah, it's quite nice to have a bit of company.'

Frankie peered round the shop. 'And where are they now?'

'Oh, they're all here, duck. But we promised we'd keep out of the way as much as possible and we will. None of them blame you for the mess that Maisie woman caused, and they don't want to make things more difficult for you now.'

'Thank you.' Frankie heaved a sigh of relief. 'Oh, and I've got the shoes for them. I'll put them in the end fitting room, so if you could just let them know. I'd give them to you but I'm guessing you can't hold things.'

'Sadly, no, duck. But they'll be pleased with the shoes, I'm sure.'

'Let's hope so. Oh, and there's one other thing I meant to ask you—do you know if everyone can see you when you materialise? Or is it just people who are a bit more in tune with otherworldly things?'

Ernie shook his head. 'No idea, duck, sorry. None of us knows very much about the niceties of being haunters or who becomes hauntees or why, really. It's all a mystery to me. Why, duck? Are you worried about the customers?'

'Well, yes, but mainly because Cherish works here part-time and she'll be in at ten o'clock. And I think she knows you—she's a friend of Biddy's, and Biddy definitely knows you because she went to your funeral.'

'And a mean-mouthed baggage she is and all.' Ernie frowned. 'Biddy, that is, not Cherish. Cherish never went to the seniors day group. Shy, she is by all accounts. Not a joiner. But yes, Cherish would know me by sight, definitely, and Biddy certainly would. Thanks for the warning, duck. I'll keep meself out of the way, just in case Cherish spots me. I can just imagine what Biddy would make of it if she knew I was undead.'

Frankie nodded over her shoulder as she headed towards the cubicles. 'Especially as she made such a big deal about giving you a good send-off.'

'Garn!' Ernie scoffed. 'Biddy don't give a tuppenny damn about any of the dearly departed. She only went along to my funeral, and all the others, for the free food and drink afterwards. She's not a very nice woman.'

'Sounds about right,' Frankie admitted, placing the four pairs of shoes neatly on the floor of the farthest fitting room, and pulling the curtain across.

Ernie was standing by the 1950s rails, his little happy goblin face looking sad again. 'Can I ask you a favour, duck?'

'Of course.'

'Achsah's frock. Can you promise me that you won't sell it? Not until I'm gone for good. I feel close to her as long as I can be near her frock.'

'Of course I won't sell it. Shall I take it off the

225

rails and put it up in the stockroom to make sure no one wants to buy it? I know several people have looked at it.'

Ernie shook his head. 'Could you just leave it here, duck, please? I seem to be stuck down here in the shop. I'm not sure I could materialise upstairs, and then I wouldn't be able to see it at all, would I?'

'Oh, Ernie. I'll leave it wherever you want it to be, and I promise you, it won't be sold.'

Ernie's face split into a beatific smile. 'Thank you, duck. You're a lovely girl.'

'And you're pretty lovely yourself, Mr Yardley. Achsah was a very lucky woman. Anyway—Oh, you've gone ...'

'Who's gone, dear?' Cherish trotted happily into the shop. 'Have I missed a customer?'

'No ... no, definitely not. It's just me talking to myself.'

'I do that all the time.' Cherish unbuttoned her beige woollen coat. 'When I'm at home I chat to the radio and telly presenters as well, you know, and sometimes I know I do it to myself when I'm out. That's why I love those mobile phones.'

Frankie frowned. 'I don't quite see the connection.'

'Well, dear—' Cherish neatly folded her taupe gloves and scarf together '—everyone has mobile phones these days, don't they? And they all walk about *talking*. So, when I catch myself having a conversation out loud I just put my hand up to my ear and everyone thinks I'm on the phone and no one thinks I'm doolally. Shall I put the kettle on, dear?'

'Yes, yes please,' Frankie said with a laugh. 'And you're very early this morning.'

226

'I got a lift in.' Cherish blushed slightly. 'Brian picked me up. He's working with Dexter all day and he goes past my bungalow and it saved me having to wait for the bus in this bitter weather.'

'Oh, that's kind of him. Brian's a lovely chap.'

'He is, dear. I might have misjudged him, you know. I'm afraid I was guilty of judging by appearances. I'm learning a lot, dear.'

Frankie smiled to herself as Cherish tripped happily into the kitchen. Cherish was blossoming more with every day. Maybe one day she'd turn up wearing some bright colours rather than the all-over bland beige, then Frankie would know the transformation was complete.

But, she thought to herself, smiling as three women, red-nosed from the cold, came into the shop, why on earth would Cherish's bungalow in Hazy Hassocks be on Brian's route to work? Now that Brian lived in Rita's ex-bungalow, he was already *in* Kingston Dapple, and therefore Hazy Hassocks was actually miles out of his way. How very strange ...

'Shall I make coffee for the boys as well, dear?' Cherish called cheerily from the kitchen doorway. 'They must be freezing out there.'

Boys? Oh, Dexter and Brian. 'Yes, of course. Please do. I'll pop out with them.'

'No need, dear. I'm more than happy to do it. I can see we've got customers.'

Several more women, all shivering, clattered in and declared that it was far, far too cold for snow and whatever happened to global warming, and then joined the first three rattling through the rails.

Chris Rea was now driving home for Christmas.

'I'll take this one, please.' One of the first

227

customers placed a black lace over red satin evening dress on the counter. 'It's a proper one-off classic. It'll be lovely for my husband's works' do at the weekend. You've got some lovely dresses here, dear. Lovely. I'll tell all my friends to come in here. It's nice to know you won't fetch up at some local function and bump into someone wearing the same frock.'

'Thank you.' Frankie smiled, taking the red and black frock over the counter. 'And did you want to try this on first?'

'It's a fourteen so it should be OK.' The woman frowned. 'Maybe I should just try it ... are the fitting rooms over there?'

'Yes.' Frankie nodded to the curtained-off cubicles. 'Give me a shout if you need a hand with the zip or anything. There's a mirror in there, but you can come out and use the cheval if you'd prefer.'

'Lovely, thanks. It's so nice to have proper customer service.' The woman retrieved her chosen frock from the counter and headed towards the cubicles. 'I really appreciate it.'

From the corner of her eye, Frankie saw the curtains of the end cubicle twitch. 'Oh, could you not use the far end one, please,' she called quickly to her customer. 'Er, I think there's someone in there.'

The woman veered off to another fitting room.

Phew. Frankie exhaled.

'What's going on over there in the fitting rooms, dear?' Cherish put a tray with four steaming coffee mugs on the counter. 'How many people have you got in that end cubicle? The curtain's going nineteen to the dozen. Looks like quite a kerfuffle.'

228

'Oh, um, I think it's OK.'

'Shall I just go and check, dear? It might be someone being a bit light-fingered, if you get my drift. We had that happen at Miriam's Modes once. A lady trying one frock on over another and attempting to walk out with them all. Shocking, it was!'

'Yes ... yes,' Frankie said distractedly, her eyes on the end cubicle's fluttering curtains, 'it must have been. No, Cherish, leave it, please, I'll sort it out. You can serve these customers for me and— oh, sod it!'

Cherish had already bustled busily across the shop floor.

Frankie held her breath.

Cherish rattled back the end fitting room curtain and screamed.

'Sorry, dear heart,' Jared said coyly as he simpered out, still in his purple get-up but now with the addition of the matching slingbacks, and sashayed towards the counter. 'Didn't mean to make you jump.'

Cherish was standing, transfixed, simply staring, her hands to her mouth.

Oh, bloody hell ... Frankie glanced quickly at her other customers. Busily admiring various frocks and humming along to Greg Lake being rather dismal about disappointing Christmases, they didn't appear to have noticed anything amiss.

'Jared!' Frankie hissed. 'Please! You promised!'

'I know, sweet, but I got carried away. So sorry. The shoes are just *darling*. Thank you so much.'

'You're welcome. Now, please, just disappear.'

'Harsh woman!' Jared pouted, before pirouetting prettily and executing perfect points with the purple

229

shoes. 'Never fear, darling girl. I'm going.'

And with his hand on his hip, he exaggeratedly swayed across the shop floor, between the clothes rails, and vanished.

'Goodness me!' Cherish trotted back to the counter, still flapping her hand across her face. 'She gave me the fright of my life. I didn't expect her to appear from the curtain just like that. Poor lady, though, such terrible hair loss. Alopecia do you think, dear?' She giggled. 'Mind you, she more than made up for it on her legs. They were very hairy, did you notice? I always shave mine when I have my weekly bath, don't you? But she looked very nice in the purple, didn't you reckon? Right, dear, now I've got over my shock I'll just put our mugs on the counter, and take the coffee out to the boys before it gets too cold to give them any benefit.'

Open-mouthed, Frankie watched Cherish—who had rarely ever spoken more than two sentences in an entire hour—calmly carry the tray out of the door.

'That was a close shave, if you'll pardon the pun.' Bev, perched on the end of the counter, chuckled. 'Fancy her thinking Jared was a woman.'

'Oh, Bev, please don't manifest now. You all *promised*.'

'I know.' Bev shrugged and looked down at her elegant navy-blue soft leather Patrick Cox shoes. 'And I was trying, honestly, but I think, like Jared, it was the excitement of having shoes on again. Maybe it's *excitement* that makes us appear? Or any sort of emotion? Sorry, love, I'll try to calm down and vanish. Ah, maybe not just now though. It might look a bit odd.'

The black-lace-on-red-satin lady had emerged

from the fitting room clutching the frock.

'No more odd than you sitting on the counter in a snood—although it goes well with the dress style,' Frankie said grudgingly before smiling at her customer, crossing her fingers and hoping that the red-and-black lady wouldn't think someone looking like an extra from *Blitz* perched on the counter was even slightly strange. 'Did it fit?'

'Perfectly, thank you. I'll take it.' She flourished a credit card. 'This is a wonderful shop. I shall pop in again for something for my New Year's Eve party.'

'Please do.' Frankie zapped the credit card. 'We'd be delighted to see you.'

'She can't see me, can she?' Bev said. 'Or hear me?'

Frankie shook her head as she folded the black-lace-on-red-satin carefully into a carrier bag.

'Wonder why not?' Bev slid to the floor. 'Funny business this haunting. Wonder why we appear to some people and not to others?'

Frankie simply shrugged as she smiled goodbye to the customer.

'Okey-dokey, I know you can't talk to me. I'll toddle off now then—' Bev smiled, still admiring her shoes '—and ta for these, Frankie. They're lovely. Ruby and Gertie are thrilled to bits with theirs, too.'

'You're welcome,' Frankie whispered in case anyone should hear her. 'Now, please go away. Oh Lordy—' She sighed, suddenly catching sight of Gertie and Ruby wandering happily round the 1980s frocks and prodding the shoulder pads. 'And please take them with you.'

'Will do,' Bev said cheerfully. 'And have you

231

had any joy in finding someone who can sort us out yet?'

'Not yet,' Frankie hissed as yet more customers trudged, shuddering with cold, through the door. 'But we're working on it.'

'Good girl.' Bev smiled. And disappeared.

Frankie heaved a sigh of relief just as Brenda Lee started rocking around her Christmas tree.

'Goodness me,' Cherish said as she fluttered back in, her cheeks pink and her hair all wispy, 'it's absolutely bitter out there. The wind is screaming across the market square and that flower stall offers very little shelter. The poor boys are shrammed. I've told them they should both be wearing fingerless mitts. And thermal underwear.'

Frankie blinked. Cherish was discussing *underwear* with Dexter and Brian? The transformation was rattling on far more quickly than she'd even imagined.

'And,' Cherish continued, 'can I just say how lovely you look in that scarlet? I'm not afraid to admit that I might have got it a teensy bit wrong about you being a *grey* person, dear. I'm beginning to wonder if I should maybe add a splash of colour to my life, too. Actually, I was wondering about buying some orange cushion covers for my sofa.'

'Are you?' Frankie said, amused both by Cherish's admission and her conspiratorial tone. 'Well done. I'm sure they'd look lovely.'

'Yes, I think they'd cheer the room up a lot, although my mother would have hated them. She was very partial to her oatmeal.' Cherish picked up her mug of coffee. 'But I think I should have realised a long time ago that you can't live in the past, you see. The past lives with you inside your

232

heart, dear, doesn't it? But we must make the most of now, mustn't we?'

Frankie blinked, wondering if Cherish had been taking advice from a life coach.

'Brian says—' Cherish warmed her hands on her coffee mug '—that whether our past has been happy or sad, it's over and it's now that counts. Brian's very clever, you know, dear.'

'Er, Brian? Clever? Right ... Yes, I suppose he, um, might be.'

'He's sensible.' Cherish nodded. 'And very kind. Now, dear, what would you like me to do today?'

Frankie, trying not to look too shocked, quickly thought that keeping Cherish out of the shop as much as possible would be a good thing. Just in case anyone, er, dead put in an appearance.

'Oh, um, well, when you've had your coffee, would you like to carry on organising the stock upstairs this morning? I've had another load dry-cleaned so they need to be put into decades. And Mitzi Pashley Royle from Lovers Knot has been really generous and given us masses of her old cocktail frocks. If we get really busy down here I'll give you a shout. Is that OK?'

'Lovely, dear, thank you. I do enjoy the sorting out, as you know. And cocktail frocks, you say? How gorgeous ... I'll take my coffee upstairs now, dear, and make a start.'

And with a spring in her step, pale, wispy, faded Cherish, disappeared happily towards the stockroom.

Frankie leaned against the counter and shook her head. Cherish and Brian? Brian and Cherish? No, surely not ...

Chapter Twenty-one

'So where's he taking you tonight?' Lilly asked on Wednesday evening, watching with amusement as Frankie ripped everything from her wardrobe and hurled it onto the pink and purple flounced bed.

'Some place called Hideaway Home,' Frankie muttered, trying to sort out her clothes and manipulate the hair straighteners on her fringe at the same time. 'It's a new restaurant out in the wilds somewhere round here. They do vegetarian Farmhouse Feasts or something. Dexter thought it was time we ate healthily.'

'Of course he did.' Lilly giggled. 'I'm sure your badly treated digestive system was the only motive he had for suggesting it, and—' she plonked down on the bed dislodging half a dozen dresses '—I know all about Hideaway Home.'

'Do you? Really? Have you been there?'

Lilly shook her head. 'No, but it's owned and run by those people who won *Dewberrys' Dinners* last year. The telly cookery programme? You know? We watched it together.'

'Oh, yes, I remember them. Is it? Really? Wow.' Frankie grinned. 'They were great.'

'Especially that chef—Ace? Ash? How hot was he?'

'Very,' Frankie agreed. 'So it should be good, then?'

'Apparently it's totally brilliant.' Lilly stood up. 'Jennifer Blessing and her husband have been there. She says it's amazing. You'll have a great time. And when you've decided what you're wearing come and give me a twirl. I'd better get on; I've still got loads of packing to do.'

Frankie switched off the straighteners and peered at her reflection framed by the ropes of little rosy fairy lights. Her hair looked fine, and her make-up was OK. Now, should she dress up or down? Or somewhere in the middle? Should she wear rare black for sophistication or a bright colour for fun?

'Packing?' She looked at Lilly through the mirror. 'You're not going away until the day before Christmas Eve.'

'I know, but I can never decide what to take and what not to. I have to start packing early because I keep changing my mind, you know what I'm like.'

'Only too well, but what I never know is how you can bear to go somewhere *warm* at Christmas and New Year. It seems all wrong, somehow.'

'What seems wrong,' Lilly said with a grin, 'is spending my Christmas with Mum and Dad and their new partners and all the step-brats. It's hell on earth, believe me. They love it; it drives me insane. It's not natural for everyone to get on so well—and to have so many kids. And then they do it all over again only at the *other* house for New Year. It's totally gruesome. No, me and the girls will have a really kicking time in Cyprus and we'll think of you freezing to death over here.'

'We'll certainly be doing that,' Frankie said, listening to the north-easterly wind howling outside. 'We'll probably be twenty feet deep in snow by the time you get back in early January.'

'Which means the airports will be closed and we'll have to stay in Cyprus for ages longer.' Lilly shimmied happily out of the bedroom. 'What a bummer.'

Pink, Frankie thought when Lilly had gone. Pink would look nice tonight. Less vibrant than her usual daytime colours, and feminine and pretty, but not looking as though she'd made too much of an effort. She didn't want Dexter to think she was *trying*.

She pulled out a clover-coloured frock from the heap on the bed: short, swirly and long-sleeved. Perfect. And she had a pair of darker pinky-purple tights somewhere ... She started rooting through the drawers, discarding unsuitable items over her shoulder. Ah! Got 'em! OK, now the purple boots ... Great ...

'Oooh, you look fabulous!' Lilly nodded in approval when Frankie eventually presented herself in the bedroom doorway. 'He won't be able to keep his hands off you.'

'He better had.' Frankie laughed. 'This isn't any sort of romantic date, Lill. We're mates and we're just going out together to chat about stuff.'

'Yeah, right. What sort of stuff?'

Frankie shrugged. 'Business, business, business, oh, and probably ghosts.'

'You could talk about all of that in the Greasy Spoon or the Toad,' Lilly said prosaically. 'You don't need to be going to some smashing restaurant to talk about any of that. And—' she grinned at Frankie '—despite me being blown away by what happened on Saturday night, I haven't mentioned anything about the ghosts. Or about your shop being haunted. Not a word. Not to anyone. Not even when I've been a little bit drunk. I'm dead proud of myself.'

'And I'm amazed.' Frankie laughed. 'But very

236

grateful.'

'And they're still all there?'

Frankie nodded. 'Unfortunately, yes. We're just leaving everything alone until the new year by which time hopefully we'll have found a proper medium to sort them out.'

'Sad to think they'll be there over Christmas on their own.'

'They're dead, Lilly. They won't mind. I don't think they do Christmas in the afterlife.'

'Course they do,' Lilly said scornfully. 'That's what it's all about, isn't it? Christmas? Jesus being born? And living in heaven and everything? Which is where they've come from, isn't it?'

'I don't know.' Frankie shook her head. 'Neither do they. And I'm not getting into any deep religious arguments about the afterlife. I don't even want to think about it.'

'Well you should. They're your ghosts after all.'

'Hardly. Most of them are down to Maisie.'

'OK, but not Ernie.'

'Not Ernie, no. And I do want to help Ernie. And I will try.'

'Good, because he's sweet. Oooh—is that a car stopping outside?' Lilly skittered to the window and looked out into Featherbed Lane. 'Yep, it's Dexter. Cool. Have a great time.'

'OK, thanks. And you enjoy your serial packing and unpacking. Bye.'

Frankie grabbed her bag, struggled into her coat, wound her scarves round her neck and ran downstairs, annoyed to find that she had tummy-dancing butterflies. Get a grip, she told herself. It's not a date. You've spent loads of time alone with him before. This is no different to eating

237

at the Greasy Spoon—except it'll be posher and less, er, greasy.

She hurried quickly down the path. It was a desperately dark night, and the bitter wind seemed to cut right through her coat and stab viciously at her face.

'Hi.' Dexter opened the passenger door for her. 'Right on time. Impressive.'

'So are you.' Frankie smiled as the car purred away into the cold, dark night. 'On time, that is. Not impressive.'

Dexter laughed.

Frankie undid her coat in the car's warmth and relaxed back in the seat. It was OK now. No butterflies. No problems.

'You look lovely.' Dexter glanced across the car. 'Really fantastic. And I'm delighted to say that I'm not wearing pink tonight.'

'Thank you. I'm glad we're not a matching pair for once.' Frankie looked at his pale-blue shirt and black trousers under the leather jacket. 'And you look pretty neat yourself.'

'Neat? I'm devastating,' Dexter said and laughed. 'So, have you had a busy day, today? I haven't seen much of you.'

'It's been really hectic. And you?'

'Manic. And I've loved it. I think I might have found my true vocation at last. I've got loads of ideas for the spring. I was thinking we might somehow join forces and promote both businesses—you know, Easter weddings, frocks and flowers—that sort of thing.'

Frankie, delighted that Dexter was planning to stay in Kingston Dapple, and then annoyed with herself for being delighted, nodded. 'Sounds

238

brilliant. Yes, I can see all sorts of things we can combine on. And by then we'll have got rid of our other problem.'

Dexter negotiated the narrow streets out of Kingston Dapple. There were few cars on the road and no pedestrians. The night was far too cold for anyone to venture very far.

'The ghostly incumbents? Yes, let's hope so. Are they still behaving themselves?'

Frankie smiled in the darkness as they headed through the buffeting gale towards Bagley-cum-Russet and Fiddlesticks. 'Mostly. They do appear at odd intervals but so far no one seems to have taken any notice of them. And Cherish, bless her, after her one close encounter with Jared, is totally unaware of them, so there's no danger of her blabbing to Biddy or anyone.'

'I'm surprised—' Dexter stopped at a deserted crossroads '—that Maisie hasn't been in touch this week.'

'Me too,' Frankie admitted. 'Actually I'm a bit worried about Maisie. She knows too much. I just think she's biding her time before going public. Perhaps we'll have to pay her another visit and make sure she doesn't say anything.'

'And what about the undertaker bloke? Has he asked you anything more since you told him that Ernie, who he knew was dead, actually wasn't quite.'

'Oh, Slo—love him. No, he's kept his side of the bargain. He's got a lot to lose, er, well, professionally if any of this gets out. I promised I'd tell him when it was all over and I will.'

'And Lilly? Has she managed to keep quiet?'

'So she says, and I believe her. And anyway she's

239

far to busy thinking about her Christmas trip to Cyprus with her oldest school friends to worry too much about anything else. Lilly, bless her, is fairly single-minded. Right now her whole time is taken up with packing and wondering if she can drink a different cocktail in every bar on the Strip in Protaras and still be standing at the end of it.'

Dexter laughed as they left Bagley-cum-Russet behind. 'Sounds like a plan to me. I might think about jetting off somewhere warm for Christmas myself.'

'Really?'

'Nah. Not really. Not this year. I'm already sorted for Christmas, actually. And anyway—' he yawned '—working for a living is turning me into an "early to bed, early to rise" bore. I was up at three this morning to go to the flower market to pick up a new consignment of Christmas roses. And they've gone like hot cakes. I'll have to get more tomorrow.'

'Three o'clock! You must be wiped out. We could have rescheduled tonight if you're too tired.'

'I'm running on adrenaline, and if I hadn't got the table tonight we'd have had to wait until well into January, and I don't want to do that. They're booked for weeks and this was a cancellation. Anyway, if I fall asleep in my uber healthy and nutritious soup you can drive me home, can't you?'

'Drive this?' Frankie snorted. 'I doubt it. I've never driven anything bigger than a Mini in my life. And is this a BMW?'

'You're really not a petrol-head, are you?' Dexter said kindly. 'It's a Mercedes.'

'Well, whatever, it's massive and powerful and scary.'

'It's lovely,' Dexter said as they left the last signs of habitation behind them and plunged into the dark, bleak, windswept Berkshire countryside. 'And practically the only thing I have left of my previous life.'

Frankie said nothing. She wanted to know, but she didn't want to pry. Not yet.

'Now—' Dexter glanced at his satnav '—I've been told that maybe we'll need radar to find this place, so you can navigate if we get lost. Apparently we have to turn off on the Fiddlesticks road, then past the turning to Lovers Knot and carry straight on, ignoring all other turnings. We have to find a road called Cattle Drovers Passage and it's at the end of there.'

'Easy-peasy.' Frankie chuckled. 'And it's certainly out of the way. Did you know it was owned by the people who won *Dewberrys' Dinners* last year?'

'Brian told me this morning. I didn't see the show. I had other things going on at the time, but I do know about it. I'm impressed.'

'As impressed as Cherish is with Brian?'

'What? I mean, I know they're friends—and an odd couple they make—but are you suggesting that there's something more?'

'I'm not suggesting anything at all—Ooh, wasn't that the Lovers Knot turning? Were we supposed to ignore that or turn down it?'

'Some navigator you are.' Dexter laughed. 'We're dead on track. So go on—about Cherish and Brian.'

'There isn't anything to go on about, really. But Cherish is positively blooming and never stops talking. And Brian gives her lifts to and from work

241

even though he has to go out of his way to do it. And she always beats me out to you with the coffee since Brian started helping you out.'

'Do you mean she fancies *Brian*?' Dexter sighed. 'Is that why she's become the deliverer of my morning coffee? And I was under the illusion that, just when I need defrosting with scalding caffeine delivered by a gorgeous lady in a short dress and long boots, and all I get is mumsy Cherish in all-over beige, it's because she's madly in love with me.'

Frankie chuckled. 'Get over yourself. Not every female in the world fancies you, you know.'

'Don't they?'

'No.'

'Damn.' Dexter slowed down and peered through the windscreen. 'I'll have to work on my technique. It's nice if Cherish and Brian have formed a friendship, I guess. Two lonely people. Two lonely very nice people at that.'

'They are,' Frankie agreed. 'Brian had great hopes of his romance with Rita, I know, and was very hurt after it ended. And Cherish just seems to have been used by everyone she's ever known. But I don't expect it'll develop into the romance of the decade, do you?'

'Probably not. And maybe they wouldn't want it to, anyway. Maybe they'll be more than happy to settle for friendship and companionship, and good for them. Maybe they won't. Maybe they are right for one another, and then again, maybe they're not. Who knows? But in my experience, falling in love with the wrong person causes an awful lot of problems. Right, any idea where we are?'

Frankie, soaking up yet another snippet of

information about Dexter's past, stared vaguely through the windscreen, and then shook her head. 'It's so dark out there and I haven't seen any signs or road names or anything. Still, we haven't turned off anywhere, so we must be on the right route. Oh, look, there are lights over there, and the tail lights of cars up ahead. So maybe that's it?'

It was.

After negotiating the narrow and winding Cattle Drovers Passage, they drove along a well-lit gravelled track, which ran beside a beautiful old farmhouse, and eventually pulled into a spacious and well-filled car park.

'Wow.' Frankie blinked at Hideaway Home restaurant. It was a huge and traditionally converted barn, softly illuminated by dozens of strategically placed lights. 'It looks fabulous.'

'Doesn't it?' Dexter switched off the engine. 'And I'm starving. I could eat a horse.'

'Horse,' Frankie said with a chuckle as she unfastened her seat belt, 'is definitely not on this particular menu.'

They hurried through the bitter, blustery, ice-dark night into the glorious golden warmth.

Inside, Hideaway Home glowed with discreet lighting, rumbled with conversation and laughter, and smelled divine. A towering Christmas tree stood in one corner of the entrance, covered in hundreds of pinprick white lights, and carols played softly over the sound system.

Frankie looked around her, delighted that they'd just let the massive converted barn speak for itself. There were no deliberately placed ploughshares or cartwheels or other kitsch farming implements to accentuate its barn-ness. Instead, the original

243

slatted wooden walls had been lovingly restored and towered dizzily upwards to where the ancient thick, knotted beams criss-crossed the ceiling, supporting the tile-and-slate roof. The decor was pale and natural, with scrubbed wooden tables, comfy farmhouse kitchen chairs, heavy polished cutlery and fat cream candles.

Perfection.

'Good evening, I'm Poll, and I'm delighted to welcome you to Hideaway Home,' a tall woman with amazing cheekbones, and wearing a long flowing frock, lots of beads, and with her hair tied back with matching ribbons, said and smiled at them. 'Can I have your name, please?'

'Valentine. A table for two.'

'Ah yes.' Poll checked her clipboard. 'Lovely. Follow me, please.'

'I know her!' Frankie hissed as they made their way through the dozens of well-spaced tables, amused to notice yet again that almost every woman in the restaurant had stopped eating to stare at Dexter. 'Well, no, I don't, but I recognise her from the television show. Oh, how brilliant—it's like celeb spotting! And look at that open-fronted kitchen—you can actually watch them cooking— that's brave.'

'It is.' Dexter smiled at Poll as she showed them to their table and handed them the menus. 'Thank you.'

'Here's the wine list—' Poll beamed '—and tonight's menu. All our food is fresh and locally grown. Take your time to choose. Would you like some breads while you make up your mind?'

'Yes, please.' Frankie nodded enthusiastically as they shed their coats. 'I'm starving.'

244

'Good.' Poll laughed. 'I can guarantee you won't be by the time you leave. I'll get my husband Billy to bring you a selection of his home-made bread straight away. And what would you like to drink?'

'White wine spritzer for me, please, as I'm driving. Frankie?'

'The same, please.'

'Shall I bring you a bottle of our house white and some soda? Then you can top up as you go?'

'That'd be great, thanks.'

'Lovely. I'll get them for you. Enjoy your evening.'

'Wow,' Frankie said again as Poll swept away, and she looked around. 'Everyone's food looks fabulous, and the smells are incredible ... and oh, look, there's the boy chef that Lilly fancied—Ash? He's even hotter in real life. I can't wait to tell her he's actually cooking tonight. Oh, and the pretty girl—can't remember her name ... Ellie? Ella?— she's cooking, too. Now—' she screwed up her eyes '—we just need to spot Poll's husband Billy, the one who made all the bread and things—Ah! There he is! Just coming over with a basket. Blimey—this is soooo cool.'

Dexter laughed. 'I'm glad you're enjoying it. And that's before we even eat anything.'

Beaming her thanks at Billy, then at Poll with the wine and soda and ice to make their spritzers, and groaning with delight at the scent of warm bread and the little pats of golden butter, Frankie wanted to clap her hands with total happiness.

'Right,' Dexter mumbled round a mouthful of home-made granary bread, 'now what to choose ... No, seriously, what to choose? Have you looked at the menu?'

Frankie, relishing the exquisite delight of a hot cheese-topped roll, nodded. 'I'll never be able to make up my mind. So much lovely, lovely food.'

Eventually, having chosen their starters and mains and placed their order, Frankie leaned back in her chair and looked at Dexter. He was such good company, and so beautiful. She was delighted simply to be with him, and yes, OK, delighted that other women were staring at them and being *jealous*. Not that they had any need, of course, but they weren't to know that, were they?

She smiled at him. 'Thank you so much for suggesting this. This is the best night ever.'

'You're welcome. You deserve it. You've been working flat out from the minute I met you. I can't believe you even have time for a social life.'

'I don't much any more,' Frankie admitted. 'Well, certainly not since I took over Rita's shop. But that's not a problem, honestly. And I'd hate to admit it to Lilly, but I'm getting too old for all-night clubbing and far too many cocktails. I enjoy my nights out—or in—with my girlfriends and I also like my solo nights in with the telly or a good book.'

'But you never go out? With anyone?'

'You mean anyone male? Well, I'm out with you, aren't I?' Frankie wrinkled her nose at him. 'Stop ferreting. You said before you knew why I was single. Well, you were right. Once bitten—very, very badly mauled, actually—and never again.'

Their first course arrived then: goat's cheese and onion pastries accompanied by herby red onion marmalade and a huge portion of Hideaway Home's farmhouse salad.

'Dear me.' Frankie looked at her heaped plate in astonishment. 'I know I said I was hungry, but perhaps I should have gone straight to the main. I'll never eat all this.'

'Course you will,' Dexter said, unfolding his napkin. 'And anything you leave just pass over this way. It looks and smells amazing. So, go on, then. This mauling—who and when?'

Frankie groaned greedily over her first delicious mouthful of goat's cheese, and shook her head. 'You don't want to hear about it.'

'I do if you want to talk about it. I want to know what makes you you. If it's still painful, then, of course, I understand that you won't want to tell me, but if it helps.'

Frankie shrugged. 'Oh, I'm over it—well, *him*. It's been three years. But I can't forget how it practically wrecked my life. I was truly devastated. Humiliated. I lost everything. Home, job, self-respect . . .'

'That was some mauling.'

'Yep. And it's made me afraid to ever trust anyone again.'

Dexter met her eyes across the table. 'Ah, trust, or the lack of it. I can relate to that only too well.'

'Really?'

He nodded. 'Oh, yes. But this is your therapy session, not mine.'

Frankie sighed. He was never going to tell her anything about his past, was he? So should she really be about to tell him all about hers? Hmmm, tricky one.

The starters were being quickly devoured. Frankie thought she had never tasted anything quite so divine.

She looked at him across the table. 'OK, if you're sure you want to hear this, but don't say you weren't

247

warned—just stop me if you start to nod off.'

'The snoring will do that.'

Frankie laughed. 'Right, are you sitting comfortably? Then I'll begin ...'

'My gran used to say things like that.' Dexter smiled at her. 'I like it. It's cosy. Like *Jackanory*.'

'I can assure you that this,' Frankie said quickly, 'is *nothing* like *Jackanory*. OK, when I left school I wanted to do fashion retailing. So I joined Masons'—they're the big department store in Winterbrook—as a trainee. They're an old-fashioned family firm, and they set up really good training courses, with college day release. I loved it. I was good at it, too—not bragging, but I was. Anyway, after a couple of years I thought I'd use what I'd learned at Masons' in other outlets, so I left and moved away and became a fashion buyer at another even bigger store in Reading, then manageress of an exclusive one-off boutique in Newbury, then four years ago I heard they were looking for a manager for the ladieswear department at Masons'.'

'Where you'd started?' Dexter was spooning herby marmalade onto his pastry. 'Fine. I'm not bored yet.'

'I applied and got the job and rented a flat in Winterbrook. Masons' had moved on quite a bit since my early days, and had expanded hugely and added various really fashionable departments with one-offs from up-and-coming designers as well as the chains, and I loved running them all. Then I met Joseph.'

'The mauler?'

Frankie nodded.

'Would you like me to kill him for you?' Dexter

248

scooped up salad.

'Not now, thank you.' Frankie laughed. 'Sorry, this must sound really tedious to you.'

'Not at all. Just don't tell me if you don't want to.'

'I've never told anyone all of it. Not even my parents.' Frankie swallowed the last mouthful of pastry and looked in surprise at her empty plate. 'Crikey, I've eaten it all.'

'So you have,' Dexter said miserably. 'Sod it.'

She laughed. 'I promise I won't eat all my main. Oh, thank you.' She smiled at the young pretty waitress who was removing their plates.

The young pretty waitress smiled back at her, but clearly only had eyes for Dexter.

'So, this Joseph?'

'Arrived when I'd been back at Masons' for a couple of months. Not only was he drafted in to be my opposite number in the menswear departments, but he was also the Masons' son and heir.'

'Ah.' Dexter nodded, topping up their spritzers. 'The family golden boy learning the ropes from the ground up?'

'Exactly.' Frankie sighed. 'He was a couple of years older than me, and when I first started as a trainee he was away at university, and he lived in London, and although I'd heard about him, we'd never met.'

'And it was love at first sight?'

'More or less. Or at least, I thought so.' Frankie sighed. 'God, I was so gullible.'

Dexter leaned across the table. 'I think I can guess the rest. You don't have to tell me.'

'No one can guess how stupid I felt,' Frankie said hotly. 'I'd had plenty of boyfriends before and

249

thought I'd been in love, but it was nothing like this. I was three million per cent besotted and I assumed he was too. He certainly appeared to be. At least when we were on our own.'

Dexter pulled a face. 'But not at work?'

Frankie shook her head. 'At Masons', Joseph and I worked as equals, and went to fashion shows together, and had meetings with designers together. Ostensibly as colleagues. Nothing more. Only we knew. Our lives were completely entwined, and I really thought he felt the same way as I did. So when he suggested that he should move out of his flat in London, and move into my flat to save the commute, I was the happiest person in the entire world.'

The pretty young waitress returned, expertly carrying several dishes.

'Mushroom and spinach open ravioli?' She looked seductively at Dexter.

'For the lady.'

'Oh, right.' She put the massive bowl in front of Frankie, still looking at Dexter. 'So you're the polenta, blue cheese and red onion pie?'

'I am.' He smiled at her.

She placed the second huge bowl lovingly in front of him. 'And here's the creamy country baby vegetables, and a portion of steamed potatoes with garden herbs, and some of Billy's famous Ballater scones. Enjoy.'

'We will—thank you,' Dexter said softly as the waitress skipped away.

'Stop it.' Frankie laughed. 'She was blushing.'

'She was sweet—and we will never in a million years eat all this. And if we do we'll never move again.'

250

Frankie inhaled the delicious fragrances rising from the bowls of incredible food. 'Woo—this is all amazing. But you're right—we should have ordered one dish and shared. OK, let's see how far we get.'

'While you tell me more about Joseph the bastard.'

'You're right—it's like being in therapy. Are you sure you really want to hear the whole sorry tale? Oh, wow, this is incredible.'

'Mine too,' Dexter agreed. 'And yes, I do want to hear the rest. So, he moved into your flat and . . . ?'

'We played happy families,' Frankie murmured round her ravioli. 'I was in heaven. I loved sharing my entire life with him. And because of Masons' pretty old-fashioned attitude to inter-staff relationships we still kept it quiet at work, so not one person knew or guessed about us, which added an extra *frisson* to the whole affair. We had a blissful time for nearly a year.'

Dexter spooned more creamy baby vegetables onto both plates.

Frankie shook her head. 'I'll pop if I eat all those.'

'No you won't. And it would be a sin to leave any. So, go on.'

Frankie swallowed. So far it had been easy. Not quite so now. 'This particular day, the Masons' hierarchy were visiting. Joe Mason senior, Joseph's father, was the MD and he had an office in the store, but his two brothers, Joseph's uncles, were also joint majority shareholders, held the purse strings, and didn't often visit Winterbrook. So them being in the store was a really big deal. We all had to make sure everything was perfect. Joseph and I had been stocking our departments, making

251

sure everything was just so, and had been down in the basement collecting some point of sale things advertising our new lines . . .'

Frankie stopped and took a gulp of her spritzer.

Dexter helped himself to more potatoes and looked across the table. 'OK, now stop. Please don't upset yourself.'

'I'm not. Honestly. Well, we piled all these placards and posters and things into the service lift, knowing we only had about an hour to get everything in place for the uncles' visitation. And we were laughing and messing about, the way you do. And I . . .' Frankie stopped and laughed. 'And I just grabbed him and kissed him.'

Dexter paused in eating, his fork suspended. 'Right? And kissing is against the law in Masons', is it?'

'No, but as I said, I'd never, ever even given any hint at all that Joseph and I were an item at work, so it seemed sort of madly daring.'

'Yeah, OK, but you were in the lift. Alone in the lift. So . . . ?'

'Our departments were on the second floor, but the lift suddenly stopped at the ground floor. The doors opened and there was Mr Mason senior and the two uncles who'd arrived early.'

Dexter chuckled. 'Getting a full-on view of an X-rated floor show?'

'Getting a full-on view of me and Joseph kissing, yes.'

'And they all had mass heart attacks, or fits of the vapours? They sound like a lot of old maids.'

'They all laughed.' Frankie swallowed. 'Laughed. And made a lot of weird remarks about keeping up the family tradition and everything.'

'OK,' Dexter said slowly. 'And ... ?'

'Oh, and OK, to cut the rest of it mercifully short, Joseph laughed too and pushed me away and said something really strange about it being the way he'd been brought up. And he was keeping a tally of all his shop-girl conquests. And that he didn't even remember my name.'

'What?' Dexter frowned. 'Was he mad?'

'No, just a cowardly bastard. He denied knowing me. He kept referring to me as the ladieswear manager, that's all. We lived together, he'd tumbled out of my bed that morning, and he still made me sound like some silly cheap tart.' Frankie stared away across the restaurant, watching Ash and Ella in the kitchen laughing together, clearly madly in love, as they cooked. 'I felt like he'd slapped me in the face in public. I couldn't believe it. The Masons all crammed into the lift and started talking about business as if I wasn't there. And Joseph carried on ignoring me. When we got to our floor, he was still talking Mason business and walked away with them, and left me and the point of sale stuff just, well, there.'

'Wow.' Dexter exhaled. 'And you thought I was bad.'

'Oh, I'm sure you've had your moments.' Frankie smiled sadly. 'But I doubt even you could behave like that. Anyway, that was it. I was walking about in a daze. When the uncles did their royal tour, Joseph was with them, and they all sort of sniggered at me. I didn't know what was happening. I mean, I knew that our relationship was secret, I just hadn't realised quite how secret.'

'And once the uncles had gone?'

'Joseph just said he was moving out of the flat

and that I mustn't ever tell anyone that he'd lived there or that we'd ever been lovers. If I did he'd deny it. He was in a real panic and talked like someone out of the nineteen thirties ... He said, as heir to the Mason fortune, he could never consider settling down with someone who worked on the shop floor. He actually said his father wouldn't allow him to marry anyone in *trade*.'

'Christ. He'd been got at? By the whole family.'

'Big time. He, apparently, was all lined up to marry someone else. The daughter of another department store king. He also said his father had suggested I was paid off, to avoid any complications.'

'Bloody hell. It's like something out of the Victorian era. They couldn't do that, surely?'

'Oh, they could, and did. They trumped all sorts of falling sales figures in my departments, and several misdemeanours, and all sorts of rubbish. I didn't care. All I cared about was that Joseph, who I loved with all my heart, had been lying to me all along. We had a row, of course. In private. Later. He actually told me I was nothing to him. My flat was just a handy bolt-hole to save him commuting to and from London each day, and I was, well, a bit on the side. A dalliance, I think he said. And that I had to be mad to think he'd even consider marrying a shop girl.'

'Who the hell wrote his script? Noël Coward?' Dexter took her hand across the table. 'But didn't you fight it?'

Frankie shook her head. 'I was so confused, so hurt, so bloody heartbroken, I just wanted to get as far away as possible. I never wanted to see Joseph or Masons' again. So, I took the pay-off and left.

254

Joseph sent someone else to clear his stuff out of my flat—a friend he could trust, I suppose—straight away. And I holed up in my flat for the worst weeks of my life, and then, when the money was running out and I knew I had to stop crying and start eating and get a grip on reality and look for another job, well, I saw Rita's advert for an assistant in the *Winterbrook Advertiser*, and she said she knew Lilly was looking for someone to share her house.' She looked down at their hands entwined across the table and smiled. 'And here I am. Bloodied but unbowed or whatever it is they say.'

Dexter said nothing for a moment. Then he sighed. 'Right, I *am* going to kill him.'

'You'll have a long trip,' Frankie chuckled. 'The other-store heiress was from Sydney. Apparently they live in amalgamated post-continental entrepreneurial bliss in Australia.'

'Global village.' Dexter sniffed. 'Only twenty-four hours away. I can still get him.'

'Leave 'im, Dexter—he ain't wurf it.' Frankie giggled.

He shook his head. 'OK, now I understand a lot more, and I don't blame you for not trusting anyone, but, honestly, men like Joseph-the-slimeball are rare. It was awful for you that he was clearly one of the worst, but there are decent men out there. Plenty of them. Haven't you been out with anyone since?'

'Oh, yes, a few. But only on a very casual basis. Men I've known were safe and weren't likely to hurt me—certainly no one serious, and no one that I really cared about. It's the only way I can cope with relationships, you see.'

255

'Yes, but you shouldn't let—'

The waitress arrived to clear their main course dishes. She and Dexter did the flirty thing again as she handed them the pudding menus and shimmied away.

'I absolutely can't eat anything else, which is such a shame.' Frankie gazed down at the list of delicious and incredible desserts. 'Oh, look it says they're all made by Ella—she was the pudding queen on *Dewberrys' Dinners*, I remember now. Oooh, the hazelnut and Irish cream meringue sounds pretty scrummy, doesn't it? Actually I think I might just be able to manage that.'

'You'd better not be sick in my Mercedes.'

'We could do one pud and two spoons?'

'OK.'

'You are such a pushover.' Frankie laughed. 'Anyway, now I've bared my soul, it's your turn.'

Dexter shook his head. 'No way. Not tonight. And I hope you're not still beating yourself up over it. None of it was your fault ...' He paused and, with the same flirting with the pretty waitress, ordered the required pudding.

When she'd gone, he looked at Frankie again, then he reached for her hand. 'And anyway, as I know only too well, none of us can help who we fall in love with, can we?'

Chapter Twenty-two

'You're such a clever girl,' Brian said admiringly to Cherish as they pushed their way through the last-minute Christmas shoppers in Winterbrook, late on a grey and bitterly cold afternoon. 'This is a much better idea than mine.'

Cherish, snuggled warmly in her faded mink-coloured coat and with her brown and fawn knitted pull-on hat pulled down low over her forehead, blushed. She'd not been called a girl for years, and had never been called clever before. Not even by her parents.

'It just seemed to make sense,' she said, being buffeted backwards and forwards by the crowds who all just wanted to buy something—anything— for their nearest and dearest and get home, out of the Siberian weather, before proper darkness fell. 'I mean, if we're both having our Christmases alone, and buying ourselves gifts, then I thought buying each other's made much more sense. At least, that way we'll have some surprises on Christmas morning, won't we?'

'We will, gel,' Brian said cheerfully. 'So, we're both spending exactly the amount of money we agreed on? No more, no less? What was it? A quarter on the Christmas stocking fillers and three-quarters on the other things? And we've got an hour before we meet up again?'

Cherish nodded. She hadn't had so much fun for absolutely ages.

'And we'll meet up in the coffee shop in Masons', gel?'

257

'In exactly one hour,' Cherish said happily. 'Shall we synchronise our watches?'

'Uh?' Brian looked a bit startled. 'Oh, right, check the time, you mean. OK, gel, let's go for it. We have exactly one hour starting from ... now.'

Cherish watched Brian, tall and dishevelled in his duffle coat, his wild hair looking like candyfloss in the wind, as he pushed his way across Winterbrook's main street. She laughed to herself, wondering what nonsensical presents he'd buy for her. She knew exactly what she was going to buy for him. She'd planned it all carefully, as she planned everything.

It was so exciting, choosing presents for someone who might actually appreciate them, and, Cherish thought, frowning as several teenagers barged into her without even saying sorry, Brian deserved to have a really happy Christmas.

Making sure he was well out of sight, she took a deep breath and plunged into the heaving crowds in the first shop.

*   *   *

Forty-five minutes later, Cherish, carrying masses of bags and feeling happier than she could ever remember, inhaled the rich exotic scents in Masons' ground-floor perfumery department. She'd never worn scent. Well, her mother had favoured Tweed, and she'd sometimes had a little spray of that, but it wasn't something she'd ever really indulged in. No, her nice lily of the valley bath cubes and matching talc did her very nicely. Perfume, she'd always felt, was completely wasted when there was no one else there to enjoy it.

Cherish loved Masons'. She'd been to Masons' with her mother when she was a girl and it had hardly changed. Well, it was much bigger now, of course, with many more departments, but inside it still looked the same. Masons' had retained their acres of polished dark wood and chandeliers and curving richly carpeted staircases with the brass balustrades and large customer-friendly counters with polite, uniformed assistants.

And today, Cherish noted with approval as she pushed and shoved her way through the manic-eyed shoppers, Masons' Christmas decorations were very tasteful in traditional red and green, with lovely classic Christmas songs playing discreetly in the background: 'White Christmas', and 'Winter Wonderland' and 'Let it Snow'. Proper songs by proper singers—not that bouncy, noisy modern Christmas pop stuff that Frankie played in their shop and sang along to all day long. Not that Cherish would criticise Frankie in any way, shape or form. Oh, dear me no. Frankie could do no wrong in Cherish's eyes. Frankie had given her a whole new lease of life, and for that she'd be forever grateful.

Funny, Cherish thought fondly as she headed for the lifts, Frankie had seemed much happier in the last few days, too. Not that Frankie had ever been *downbeat* as such, of course, but there had been a definite change in her recently. Almost as if some sort of weight had been lifted from her shoulders.

Waiting with several other tired shoppers by the lift to be whisked up to the top-floor coffee shop, Cherish now tapped her feet to Nat King Cole crooning 'The Christmas Song'. She loved that one. 'Chestnuts roasting by an open fire' always sounded

259

wonderful. She wondered if they'd work just as well in front of a two-bar electric. Possibly not.

Of course she'd arrived at Masons' early because she'd known exactly what to buy for Brian. She didn't expect him to be on time, so she'd probably treat herself to a buttered scone to go with her tea. She'd buy one for him too, of course. Brian deserved that. He'd completely refused to take any money towards petrol for all the lifts back and forwards to work. Cherish smiled to herself. She was pretty sure now that Brian wasn't passing her bungalow every day making deliveries when he said he was, but she was happy to go along with the pretence.

The lift arrived. Lots of people with lots of bags poured out, and Cherish joined the similarly loaded rush to get in. Three floors later—quite long enough to be squashed in close proximity with total strangers—they arrived at their destination and Cherish followed the flow towards a nice sit down and much-needed refreshment.

The rich smell of freshly ground coffee was immediately evocative. Cherish inhaled greedily, and was instantly whisked back to the childhood days out shopping with her mother when they'd always had lunch in the Cadena and she was allowed to have a thick strawberry milkshake in a tall, fluted glass and two pink straws—but had always been forbidden to blow bubbles or make any sort of slurping noise with the ice cream at the bottom.

Happy days.

After queuing and buying a pot of tea for two and two large scones, Cherish peered round the coffee shop for a vacant table. Ah, yes! There was one for two just over there, not far from the door.

Carefully manoeuvring her tray and her shopping, Cherish slalomed quite niftily through the maze of tables and chairs in case someone else got there before her. Triumph! Cherish plonked her tray down and arranged her carrier bags on the second chair. Then she unbuttoned her coat, removed her hat and started to butter her scone.

The coffee shop was warm, and tinkled comfortingly with the sound of china and lulled chatter and some pleasant festive jingle bells type music.

Cherish looked around her. She wasn't far from the entrance, so Brian should spot her easily. She poured her tea and flexed her cold and aching feet inside her sensible brogues. Oooh, lovely.

'Cherish?' A piercing voice shattered the bliss. 'Cherish? What on earth are you doing here?'

Cherish groaned and returned her buttered scone to its plate. 'Hello, Biddy.'

'I'll just move these, shall I?' Biddy started to tug at the carrier bags on the chair. 'I've got my tea, so I can plonk it down there—if you just move yours up a bit.'

'Actually,' Cherish said rather timidly—Biddy in full-flow always made her nervous—'I'd prefer it if you left the bags there, if you don't mind. That seat is taken. I'm waiting for someone.'

'Are you indeed?' Biddy's nose twitched. 'And is that *someone* why I haven't seen hide nor hair of you for *weeks*?'

'Not at all,' Cherish said robustly, although she was still quivering inside. 'I'm working now, Biddy, as you well know. There simply hasn't been the time.'

'I *always* make time for my friends. But then, that's because I'm a loyal person. Unlike some I could mention.'

Biting back the urge to point out that apart from her, Biddy didn't actually have any friends, Cherish shook her head. 'That's a bit uncalled for, Biddy, if I may say so. After all, it was your idea that I went to work in Francesca's Fabulous Frocks in the first place, wasn't it?'

Biddy was still standing, clutching her tea tray and eyeing the bag-filled chair. 'That's as maybe, but I meant as a colour advisor. Not as some damn sales assistant. Got your feet nicely under that particular table without telling me, didn't you?'

'Oh, do stop being so cross, please. And pull up a chair from that table there. I'll just make room for your tray. And I'm not doing the colour advising any more, so—' she looked at Biddy in her mother-of-the-bride lilac coat and matching headscarf as she scraped a third chair up to the table '—if you want to stop wearing those spring colours, you can.'

Biddy, clearly very put out, plonked herself down on the extra chair. 'And why would I want to do that, may I ask? I happen to like my pale pastels. They suit me. For the life of me I can't see why you'd want to give up the colour advising and become a skivvy.'

'Working with Frankie is *not* skivvying. It's my natural calling. Now, I can see you've got one carrier bag there, so have you finished your Christmas shopping?'

'What Christmas shopping?' Biddy gulped gratefully at her tea. 'Since you and I don't exchange presents any longer, I don't have to waste time or money on that nonsense, thank goodness.'

'Oh, so what have you been buying?'

'Damn secret Santa rubbish for the seniors group Christmas Eve party. You know, pick a name and buy something suitable for a fiver. I got Alf Braintree.'

'Oh, dear—difficult. What did you choose for him?'

'Bath cubes.'

Cherish took a small bite from her scone. Alf Braintree was not renowned for his personal hygiene. 'Er, I didn't realise they did bath cubes for men.'

'They don't. I bought him Black Rose in the knock-down shop. Like I used to do for you.'

Cherish chewed her mouthful of scone. There really was nothing she could say.

'So—' Biddy peered over the rim of her teacup '—who are you waiting for?'

Cherish, who had always been brought up to tell the truth, saw no reason not to now. 'Brian.'

'*Brian?* Brian from the *kebab van*? Mad old *Brian?*'

'Brian is neither old nor mad,' Cherish said vigorously. 'Brian is a very nice man.'

Biddy gave a shrill chuckle. 'Well, Rita Radbone certainly seemed to think so for some time before she took up with fat Ray Valentine. I suppose if you don't mind having other people's cast-offs.'

'Biddy!' Cherish knew her cheeks were flaming. 'That's a wicked thing to say. Brian and I are friends. Just friends.'

Biddy nodded her headscarf. 'Of course you are. Even mad Brian would have to be completely insane to want to be anything more than friends with a Miss Mouse. Especially after sampling the

263

loose morals of Rumpy Pumpy Rita.'

'Biddy!' Cherish was very angry now. She rarely lost her temper, and certainly never in public. Her mother had always said a lady *never* lost her temper in public. 'That's enough! I really think you should stick to the maxim of "if you can't say anything nice then say nothing at all". And as soon as you've finished your tea then I'd like you to leave.'

Biddy laughed. 'Before Brian arrives? In case you discover that I'm speaking the truth? Oh, Cherish, you know me, I always call a spade a spade. Anyway—' Biddy leaned forwards across the tiny, crowded table '—there are more important things I need to tell you than wasting time talking about Rita Radbone's ex-lovers. Goodness, we'd be here until well into the new year on that particular topic.'

Cherish sighed heavily.

Biddy continued, unabashed. 'It was really handy, meeting you here. I was going to call round this evening anyway.'

Cherish frowned. In her world, no one called on anyone without making arrangements first. 'Were you? Why?'

'To warn you to be careful in that shop.' Biddy's eyes sparkled with malice. 'That shop that you think is the be-all and end-all. And not to trust that Francesca Meredith—who you clearly think is the bee's knees. You want to watch your step, Cherish.'

'Why on earth would I want to be careful about the shop and Frankie?' Cherish frowned. 'Really, Biddy, you are very unpleasant sometimes, you know. Why on earth would I need to worry about either Frankie or the shop?'

'Because, and I have this on the best advice, it's

264

haunted.'

Cherish, despite always being careful not to show any public emotion, laughed out loud. 'Oh, Biddy! You're a scream. No, don't tell me—you've been chatting to Maisie Fairbrother, haven't you?'

'Yes I have, actually. So, does that mean you *know*?'

'Know what?'

'That Frankie called Maisie in to do a sort of seance or exorcism or something not so long back?'

Cherish sighed. 'No, I didn't know. And neither do you. But we both know Maisie. And she, well, she does tend to exaggerate things like that, doesn't she? Sorry, Biddy, but I think it's just one of Maisie's tall tales. She rarely goes out of that flat and has far too much imagination, not to mention time on her hands. We both know she has never actually managed to contact anyone, well, dead, don't we?'

'Until now,' Biddy said with relish. 'From the minute she stepped inside it on the night your precious Francesca was clearing out Rita's old tat, Maisie knew that shop was haunted. She had a spiritual turn. Had to be taken home.'

'For goodness sake. Maisie had a *spiritual turn* in Big Sava by the deep freeze dessert section, didn't she? Said the Mivvis were possessed? Tried to exterminate the trapped souls inside the ice cream? It took four people to clean up the mess and three assistants to carry her out. And she got a lifetime ban.'

'That's as maybe, but you ask your precious Frankie what happened that night. You just ask her.'

'I will not. If there had been anything like that

265

I'm sure Frankie would have told me. Goodness me, Biddy, you're just jealous, aren't you? Jealous that I've found myself a little job, and other friends, and am happy for the first time in goodness knows how long. Jealousy is a very ugly emotion, my mother always said.'

'Jealous?' Biddy clattered her empty cup into her saucer. 'Of you working for a pittance in a shop that's haunted? And counting mad Brian from the kebab van among your so-called friends? Jealous? Me? I most certainly am not. But—' she leaned across the table again '—Maisie is completely shattered by what happened in the shop. She said there were spirits everywhere. She said—'

'I don't actually care what she said,' Cherish said quickly. 'Because I don't believe her—or you.'

'Your mistake. Don't say you weren't warned. And—' Biddy's eyes glittered as she collected her solitary carrier bag and stood up '—if you don't believe me and you won't ask Frankie, then ask your precious Brian.'

'Brian? What does Brian have to do with it?'

'He took Maisie home that first night when she had her turn. Him and Ray Valentine's no-good nephew. They practically had to resuscitate her all the way back to Hazy Hassocks. Oh yes, your so-called friends Frankie and Brian have been keeping big, big secrets from you. Right, anyway, as I won't see you before, have a lovely Christmas. Bye.'

Feeling slightly numbed by the whole encounter, Cherish watched Biddy make her triumphal exit from Masons' coffee shop.

'Oh.' Cherish stabbed her knife into her butter and applied it rather viciously to the remainder of

266

her scone. 'Oh, sod her!'

'Blimey, gel—' Brian, his hair wilder than ever and his face glowing from the cold outside, loomed over her table carrying several bags '—I've never heard you swear before. Sorry I'm late. I couldn't make up my mind on one or two things. Ah, lovely, a cuppa and a scone. Thanks, gel. You're a proper gem, Cherish, and that's a fact.'

Cherish blushed and watched him as he moved her bags and sat down. Was he keeping things from her? Was Frankie keeping things from her, too? No, it was impossible. It was just Biddy being, well, Biddy.

'Sorry about the bad word.' She smiled across the table. 'I've just had a bit of a run-in with Biddy.'

'Really?' Brian mumbled round his scone. 'I thought I caught a glimpse of her just now, but I thought I was mistaken.'

'No, you weren't. Biddy was spreading her usual festive cheer.'

'Was she? Blimey. I didn't think she were ever cheerful?'

Cherish shook her head. 'No, I was being ironic. Anyway, she told me something, well, lots of things actually, and she made me cross.'

'Sounds like Biddy.' Brian added three spoonfuls of sugar to his tea and stirred it noisily. 'You don't want to let her upset you, gel. She's just a misery guts.'

'I know, but—Oh, can I ask you something?'

'Course you can. Ask away. Oh, unless it's what I've bought you for Christmas. That's a secret.'

So many secrets … Cherish shrugged. 'Oh, look, I know this is going to sound silly, but did you and Dexter take Maisie home the night that Frankie

267

started to clear out Rita's shop?'

Brian beamed. 'Ah, we did. But you don't want to get no ideas in your head about it, gel. Is that what Biddy was telling you? That I've got a soft spot for Maisie Fairbrother? Never on your life! She's a troublemaker that Biddy.'

'No, no, it wasn't anything like that. She just said that Maisie, well, that Maisie said Frankie's shop was haunted and came over all funny and had to be taken home.'

'Ah.' Brian nodded. 'That's right. She did. And me and young Dexter were going out that way so we shovelled her into the car and took her back to her flat. No more nor less than that.'

'But Maisie said the shop was *haunted*?'

'Yes, she did. Made a right how-d'you-do about it an' all. But crikey, gel—' Brian finished his scone with obvious delight '—you knows as well as I do that Maisie thinks everywhere's haunted. Do you remember that time in Big Sava?'

'Yes, yes, I do. But why didn't you tell me?'

'About taking her home after she'd come over all funny? Nothing to tell, gel. Nothing at all. Just typical Maisie.'

'So,' Cherish said carefully, 'you don't know anything about Frankie asking Maisie to come back and do a seance to get rid of the ghosts?'

Brian's laugh roared round the coffee shop. People from a wide radius of tables stopped and stared over at them. Cherish, who hated making a *show*, lowered her head.

'No way on earth!' Brian chuckled. 'There ain't no ghosts in Kingston Dapple! Why would young Frankie believe Maisie more than anyone else? It's just Biddy stirring up trouble, gel, that's all. She's a mean-minded woman, that Biddy. And if she can drive a wedge between you and Frankie and your little job where you're happy, then she will.'

Cherish nodded. Brian was right, of course. Brian was very sensible about things like that. And Brian would tell her the truth, wouldn't he? Brian didn't have any sort of hidden agenda, not like Biddy.

'You listen to me, gel. Biddy just wants you to be as miserable as she is. She's just got a touch of the green-eye because you've made a nice little life for yourself now. She's just trying to scare you away. And if there'd been a skeeance—or whatever you called it—then we'd have heard about it, wouldn't we? No one can keep a secret in Kingston Dapple, can they?'

Cherish smiled. Yes, they would have, and no, they couldn't. And of course Brian was right—again. It was just Biddy trying to cause trouble.

Reassured, she smiled at Brian. 'Thank you. You're right of course. I was just being silly. I, of all people, should know Biddy by now.'

'Yes, you should. And another thing—just to put your mind at rest—have you ever seen a ghost in your shop?'

'No, of course not.'

'Exactly. And does young Frankie seem scared at all?'

'No, not at all.' Again, Cherish shook her head.

'So.' Brian beamed. 'There you go. There ain't no ghosts. Never have been and never will be. Happier now?'

'Yes, thank you. So, on a much more cheerful note—' she nodded towards Brian's carrier bags '—did you get everything you wanted?'

'I did gel, yes. And wrapping paper and gift tags too. And proper lovely it were, too. Real Christmassy. Shopping for surprises. What about you?'

'The same.' Cherish smiled warmly. 'I enjoyed it, too. Oh, shall we have another pot of tea?'

'Good idea.' Brian stood up. 'No, you put your purse away. This is my treat this time. Another scone?'

'Oh, yes please,' Cherish said happily, so glad that Biddy hadn't spoiled things with her spitefulness. 'That would go down a treat.'

'Right-o.' Brian stopped and looked down at her. 'And you know that the presents for each other were your clever idea? Well, I've had one of my own.'

'Have you?'

'I have.' Brian nodded seriously. 'I was thinking, well, we've bought the presents for each other, so why don't we watch each other unwrap them?'

'No!' Cherish said. 'We can't unwrap them now. It would spoil the surprise.'

'Not now.' Brian chuckled. 'I didn't mean now. No, I was thinking, Rita's bungalow as was, is smashing and cosy. And I've got me decs up and a lovely little tree that young Dexter sorted out for me, and more food than I know what to do with. I know you've bought some, too, but you've got your little freezer, haven't you? I thought it would be right nice if we could open our presents in front of each other. Oh, I'm making a mess of this ... What I mean, Cherish, gel, is why don't we spend Christmas together?'

Chapter Twenty-three

Christmas Eve. Breathlessly cold and gloomily dark, but none the less Christmas Eve at last. Thank goodness.

Much as she loved running Francesca's Fabulous Frocks, Frankie couldn't wait to go home and relax and see her family and do all the traditional Christmas stuff and be fussed over by her parents and catch up with her brothers' and sister's gossip.

Although, she admitted to herself, as she opened up the shop, she was going to miss Dexter. A lot. Which was stupid. Very stupid. It was only for three days after all. But she'd got so used to seeing him every day. And after the magical night out at Hideaway Home they'd seemed so much closer somehow.

And it had been wonderful to actually tell someone all about the Joseph thing. It was true, Frankie thought as she scooped up the last of the post from the doormat, that talking about your troubles aloud really did help to put them into perspective. And D exter had been a brilliant listener.

All in all, she thought, shivering as she crossed the shop and quickly turned on the lights and the non-stop Christmas pop on the sound system, their evening out had been a huge success. Which, in a way, made things worse on a personal level. Because now there was no way she could kid herself that she wasn't very fond of Dexter. Very fond of him indeed. OK, let's face it, head-over-heels fond of him.

After her confession session in Hideaway Home, they'd moved on to more general topics—none of them, annoyingly, involving Dexter's past or the wrong person he'd fallen in love with—and laughed and joked and teased each other in easy friendship. And then they'd had coffee and she'd had a brandy and had more or less floated out to the car and all the way home.

And once they'd arrived outside her house in Featherbed Lane, she'd resisted doing the 'are you coming in?' bit—because, one, she knew he had to be up ridiculously early to get to the flower market, and two and more importantly, he might have said no and ruined everything—and simply thanked him for a fabulous evening, and he'd kissed her cheek and squeezed her hand and driven away.

And she'd continued the floaty thing until she'd fallen asleep amongst the multitude of pink and purple flounces.

And now they'd be apart for three days and Dexter would no doubt find someone to spend Christmas with because he simply wasn't the home-alone type, was he? He'd said he'd got plans for Christmas. Being Dexter he probably had a short-list drawn up already. She didn't even know if he was staying in Kingston Dapple. He'd said he wasn't going abroad, but maybe he'd change his mind. Maybe, like Lilly had yesterday, he'd be flying off to warmer climes and have a passionate holiday romance with some gorgeously tanned, sarong-wearing, glamorous no-strings woman.

Or maybe he'd really just stay at home in the clearly not-so-lonely bedsit and have relays of festive visits from his multitude of local conquests.

Frankie sighed heavily as she hung up her coat

and scarves.

'Why the long face, duck?' Ernie was leaning against the counter. 'It's Christmas.'

'I know.' Frankie switched on the till and the computer and tried not to listen to Mud being lonely this Christmas. 'And compared to the sort of Christmas you'll be having, I shouldn't even feel a teensy bit miserable. Sorry.'

'You don't need to apologise to me, duck. What's your problem? Not bought all your Christmas presents yet?'

'Oh, they're all done. And packed and piled in my car ready to go. No, I was just thinking about Dexter.'

'And he makes you sad, duck?'

'No, he doesn't. That's the problem. He makes me happy. Very happy.'

'And you make him happy, too, duck. I've watched you, don't forget.'

Frankie shrugged. 'I know, but it's difficult. We've both got so many things in our pasts—and I don't even know what his are, but whatever they are they're pretty bad, I just know it. I've told him mine now but even so, because I *know* what he's like, I know I'll never be able to trust him.'

'Sounds very complicated, duck.' Ernie pursed his lips. 'It was so much easier in my day, I must say. Folks got together younger and stayed together. There wasn't all this—what do you call it— garbage?'

'Baggage.'

'Ah, that's it. Baggage. You just met someone local at a dance or somewhere, like me and Achsah, and you courted for a while and then you got married. For most people, if you weren't married

273

by the time you were twenty-five then you were on the shelf. And very few people got divorced—they couldn't afford it for one thing—so you just shuffled along together, taking the rough with the smooth. Mind, it was mostly all smooth with my Achsah. She was one in a million.'

Frankie reached out to pat his arm, then realised she couldn't touch him and withdrew her hand. 'Oh, Ernie, I'm so sorry. And sometimes I wish I'd been born in your era. It all sounds so much simpler.'

Ernie chuckled. 'Well, it was in one way, but we all only know what we know, don't we? I think young Dexter is a smashing bloke and I think you should trust him. Just my opinion, of course. I don't know what it is that bothers you about him.'

Loads of other women, Frankie thought, and far too many secrets, and something awful that happened in Oxford, and someone he loved madly, truly, deeply, and the fact that he's just an all-round drop-dead gorgeous bad boy who will break my heart—again.

She smiled at Ernie. 'Oh, let's change the subject. I'll drive myself mad if I keep thinking about it. But I still wish I'd been born years ago and met him at a dance like you and Achsah and didn't have all these things to dig away at.'

Ernie sighed. 'I hope it all works out right for you, Frankie, honest I do. Like I hope it works out for me and Achsah. Oh, I ain't complaining. I know you'll get us sorted out before too long. I don't suppose you've had any luck in finding someone?'

'None, I'm afraid. Both Dexter and I have been looking up people on the internet.'

'That's the computer thingy, isn't it?'

'It is. We're trying really hard. It's just finding

274

someone who's genuine and who we can trust. I'm sure we'll find someone. Er, where are the others, by the way?' Frankie looked hopeful. 'Have they— gone?'

'No, duck.' Ernie chuckled. 'They're as earthbound as I am, so they're still here. But, being more developed, spiritually speaking, than me, they're planning to have a bit of a Christmas party. They don't celebrate it in the afterlife, apparently, but I think it's all the lights and the glitter and the excitement down here that's got to them. They're making party things right now.'

Frankie frowned. 'So they can touch things and hold things, and you can't?'

'That's about it. The newly dead are pretty useless at most things to start with, so Bev says. We can do a bit of vanishing and a spot of astral transportation, but not much more than that. One good thing about this haunting business, I've learned a lot of what I can expect, from Bev and Jared. They've been really helpful explaining stuff. Ruby and Gertie have been less helpful. They're still just thrilled to bits to have lots of dresses to look at and, well, between you and me, duck, they scare me.'

'You're a ghost.' Frankie giggled. 'You can't be frightened of other ghosts.'

'But Ruby and Gertie—they look a bit, well, dead, duck, if you get my drift.'

Frankie bit her lip. Ernie was right. He and Bev and even Jared looked relatively normal for dead people, but Ruby, and particularly Gertie, certainly looked rather creepy, even properly dressed. Especially in a full light.

'So, this party,' Frankie asked, 'does it involve

playing games? Murder in the dark?'

'Not even funny, duck.' Ernie grinned. 'And as we don't eat or drink then it sounds pretty pointless to me. Never mind, it'll pass the time until you come back and get me and my Achsah reunited.'

Frankie sighed to herself. Ernie still had this absolute faith in her, and she was beginning to think that maybe it was completely misplaced. Maybe Ernie would never be set free. Oh no, too awful to even think about . . .

'We'll, as long as you don't start partying until this afternoon,' Frankie said, 'I don't mind. I'm closing at two and going straight home to my mum and dad. I don't think anyone will be wanting a frock this afternoon.'

'But they might this morning.' Ernie motioned his grizzled head towards the door. 'Looks like you've got a couple of customers already. I'll just make myself scarce.'

And he did.

Frankie smiled at the two women. 'Hello, Happy Christmas.'

'Happy Christmas,' they chorused. 'Blimey, it's bitter out there—it's got to snow soon. The wind's coming dead from the north-east. Lovely if we had a proper white Christmas this year, wouldn't it?'

Frankie nodded. 'I'd love it, but not until I've shut up shop and driven home this afternoon.'

And then, she thought, it can all thaw again in three days' time so I can get back to Kingston Dapple easily. Which was a pretty silly thought, because Dexter was probably not even going to be opening the flower stall until after New Year anyway, was he?

'Oh, sorry, what did you say?'

The younger of the women chuckled. 'I just said we popped in on the off chance to see if you've got anything really slinky for a last-minute party tonight. We've tried everywhere else—must have done every shop in Berkshire yesterday—and it's all for size zero teenagers. Sadly, we're far too old for knicker-high net skirts.'

Frankie laughed. 'I don't think we have anything like that, although we have some lovely nineteen sixties minidresses. But we do have some really gorgeous cocktail frocks that might be just what you're looking for—they're all on the appropriate decade rails, starting with the nineteen fifties over there—oh, er . . .'

Jared, still in his favoured purple, but now with something in scarlet and embellished with baubles wrapped turbanlike round his head, making him look like a gay Carmen Miranda, was salsaing round the frock rails.

The two women didn't seem to notice, and were soon rattling through the dresses with cries of appreciation.

'Happy Christmas, dear heart,' Jared cried, frolicking across the shop towards her. 'And I must say you look absolutely ravishing in that emerald green. Ravishing.'

'Thanks,' Frankie hissed, 'and please go away while I've got customers—and what are you wearing on your head?'

'It's my Christmas bonnet.' Jared struck a pose. 'Bev said we had to wear party hats, so I made my own. It's from a nineteen nineties frock—I hope you don't mind.'

'No, not really, as long as you're happy, but, please, keep out of sight. They don't seem to be able to see you but—'

'Underdeveloped sensory perception.' Jared pouted. 'So much of it about these days. No one uses all their *lobes* any more, poppet. So sad.'

'Yes, whatever—Oh, look, more customers. Go away!'

'Will do, sweet thing.' Jared blew her a kiss and disappeared.

The two original women, both clutching several frocks, had dived into a fitting room, and three more eager last-minute frock-shoppers took their place.

For a moment Frankie was sorry that she'd given Cherish Christmas Eve off. It had seemed pointless for Cherish to come in, she'd thought, on a day when she was closing early anyway, and surely everyone in the world would be thinking of anything other than buying dresses.

But it seemed not.

Making sure that Cherish realised her days off would be paid for, and handing her a small wrapped present—a pretty diary and notebook set with a rather nice pen because Cherish seemed like the sort of person who wrote things down a lot—the previous day, Frankie had been touched when Cherish had kissed her and, with tears in her eyes, had thanked her profusely for letting her work in the shop.

Then she'd handed Frankie a beautifully wrapped-in-robins-and-holly box. 'Just a small token, dear. Have a lovely Christmas.'

'You too.' Frankie had taken the box which smelled strongly of bath cubes. 'And thank you very much for this. I'll keep it until Christmas morning. Thank you for all your help, I honestly couldn't have managed without you. I'll see you on the twenty-eighth.'

'You will dear. You will.' And Cherish had practically scampered from the shop.

'We'll take these.' The women had just emerged from the fitting room. 'They're perfect, love. Perfect. We'd heard about your shop from a friend and thought it couldn't be as good as she said, but it is.'

'Thank you.' Frankie laughed, then she stopped.

Ernie, looking anguished, was standing at the end of the counter, pointing at the frocks.

Frankie, horrified, looked down at Achsah's wedding dress, then at the customer. 'Oh, I'm really sorry, you can't have this one.'

'Why on earth not?' The woman looked annoyed. 'It fits like a dream. It's exactly what I was looking for.'

Ernie had his hands over his face in abject misery.

'Because, er, it's already promised to someone.' Frankie pulled it across the counter. 'I'm really sorry, it shouldn't even be on the rails.'

'But I want it,' the woman insisted, pulling it back again. 'I've searched high and low for something like this.'

'I'm so sorry.' Frankie grabbed the frock and exchanged appalled looks with Ernie. 'I should have, um, put a sold ticket on it, or put it in the back room or something.'

'Yes, you should,' the woman snapped, tugging Achsah's dress back again. 'What sort of shop is this? A frock shop where you can't buy the frocks? Just when I was thinking I'd become a regular customer. No, it's got to be this one.'

'Sorry,' Frankie said firmly, pulling the frock back across the counter in a sort of tug of war, 'but it honestly isn't for sale. Please, go and have a look for something else. Choose another dress, and you can have it for half price.'

'Can't grumble at that,' the second woman said grudgingly. 'Go on, Rose. Go and try that bright pink one on again.'

'I don't want bright pink.' Rose frowned mutinously. Frankie almost expected her to stamp her foot or roll on the floor having a leg-kicking tantrum at any moment. 'I want that one.'

Frankie sighed. 'I do apologise. Look, I'm delighted that you've found dresses you like, and obviously I want you to come back again—please, try the pink one again, and if you like it, you can have it.'

'Have it?' Rose looked doubtful. 'For free?'

'For free,' Frankie agreed. 'It's the least I can do to rectify my mistake.'

'OK,' Rose said, finally mollified, and with a last lingering look at Achsah's cream shantung frock, headed for the rails again.

Ernie, beaming again, watched happily as Frankie placed Achsah's frock carefully behind the counter.

'Don't worry about her,' Rose's companion said, handing over her own dress of choice. 'She looked much better in the pink, anyway. And I love this shop. It's a cornucopia of delights.'

Frankie laughed in relief as she packed the hour-glass peach satin cocktail frock. 'Thank you. I might have that as my slogan in future.'

'I wouldn't,' Bev muttered in Frankie's ear. 'It sounds like a box of chocs.'

Frankie frowned. Bev was again perched on the counter, still in the snood, but with strands of tinsel wrapped round it now, and had red and gold baubles dangling from her ears making her look very Bet Lynch.

Frankie made frantic flapping 'go away' motions with her hands. Bev just laughed and swung her legs. Fortunately, the customer, unable to see her, took no notice at all.

'Yes—' Rose, also clearly not seeing either Ernie or Bev, emerged from the fitting room carrying a magenta frock, and nodded at Frankie '—it'll do nicely. Mind, I still preferred the cream, but then again, this one for free is a much better bargain. OK, love, your mistake has turned into a nice little early Christmas present for me. I'm happy, and yes, I will be back again.'

Frankie and Ernie exchanged delighted—and very thankful—glances.

By two o'clock, Frankie turned the shop sign to CLOSED. She'd returned Achsah's wedding dress to the rails because Ernie preferred it to be there, had sold another half a dozen dresses, the sky had darkened dramatically outside as the wind began to roar, and the ghosts had started their Christmas celebrations.

'What the hell are they doing?' Dexter tried hard to shut the door behind him. 'God, that wind has got up suddenly. No, seriously, what are they doing?'

'Having a Christmas party.' Frankie laughed. 'Although I did ask them not to start until I left, but it seemed to fall on deaf ears.'

Dexter watched Bev and Jared cavorting round the floor, humming along with Jonah Lewie and

281

his cavalry on the sound system, obviously not knowing the words, their headgear wobbling wildly, and Gertie and Ruby playing some sort of noisy clapping game with each other.

Ernie was leaning against the 1950s rails by Achsah's returned frock, looking on, sad-faced.

'Ernie can't do as much as they can,' Frankie explained. 'And he's feeling even more left out.'

'Poor bloke.' Dexter sighed. 'We really will have to find some way of sorting him out as soon as Christmas is out of the way. So, are you all ready for the grand escape to your family?'

'Yep.' Frankie nodded as she tidied away the last of the carrier bags. 'Lilly left for Protaras yesterday, I've loaded up my car and locked up the house and closed the shop, because I don't think I'll have any more customers now. Especially as it looks as though we're going to have some sort of storm. What about you? Been busy today?'

'Surprisingly, yes.' Dexter leaned against the counter. 'I bought a batch of forced flowers—red tulips mainly—which I don't like because they're not natural—'

Frankie giggled. 'Now you sound like a *real* horticulturalist.'

'Actually—' he looked at her '—I'm beginning to feel like one. Anyway, these flowers had the edges of their petals dipped in some sort of glue and then sprinkled with glitter. I bought five dozen on the off chance, and they've all sold out. And I've sold two last-minute Christmas trees as well. So, I'm more or less done, too. I'm closing up now.'

The Christmas track had changed to George Michael being nostalgic about last Christmas. Bev, Jared, Ruby and Gertie were swaying blissfully with their eyes closed.

'Oh God, last Christmas—' Dexter pulled a face '—don't remind me.'

'Bad one?'

'The worst.' He shrugged. 'Which means this one can only be an improvement. Anyway, I just wanted to wish you, well, whatever you want from the festivities.'

'Thanks, you too. Oh, have you had the Ray-and-Rita card from Mykonos?'

Dexter grinned. 'I have. All bright blue Mediterranean sea and sky, and acres of white sand, not to mention the taverna all flower-decked and laid-back—pretty cruel of them, I reckon.'

'Me too. And did you get the industrial-sized box of baklava to go with it?'

'Oh, yes. I ate them all in one sitting and wished I hadn't.'

Frankie giggled. 'I managed to make them last for two, but I still felt pretty sick afterwards. I'm glad Ray and Rita are happy, though. It must be lovely to be living your dream.'

'Not many people manage that, do they?'

'Sadly, no. Er, so, when are you opening up again?'

'The day after Boxing Day. You?'

Doing mental cartwheels of absolute joy, Frankie tried to rein in her smile. 'Oh, er, the same, actually. I know Rita used to be really busy in the run up to the New Year.'

'I'm not sure if I'll have any customers, to be honest. But anything will be better than sitting in the lonely bedsit between Christmas and New Year thinking about everyone else having a roaring time. Oh, hell, please change that record.'

283

Frankie, feeling very guilty about being delighted that Dexter would be home alone after all, was relieved when George's sad memories were automatically replaced by Paul McCartney having a wonderful Christmastime.

Bev and Jared started prancing again. Ruby and Gertie clapped their hands and shrieked a lot.

'Madness.' Frankie shook her head. 'And poor Ernie is still just on the periphery of everything.'

'So our New Year resolution is to get Ernie and Achsah reunited.' Dexter grinned. 'Which will make a change from giving up unhealthy food and beer and taking up jogging. Anyway, I'll let you get on, and I'll see you in a few days. Oh, and I wanted to give you this.'

Frankie stared down at the small silver-wrapped box.

'Oh no ... I mean, thank you ... but I haven't bought you a present. I mean ... well, I didn't think ...'

'It's not much, honestly. I just saw them and thought of you. If you hate them you can give them to your kid sister or your mum.'

'I won't hate it, er, them,' Frankie said, knowing that even if the silver box contained something totally hideous she'd absolutely adore it or them for the rest of her life. 'Thank you so much. It's really kind of you.'

'And, because I'm something of a traditionalist, there's this as well.' Dexter smiled at her as he produced a tiny sprig of mistletoe from his pocket then held it above her head. 'Happy Christmas, Frankie.'

As his lips brushed hers in the gentlest of kisses, the ghosts all clapped their hands in delight, and outside the first snowflakes started to tumble from the pewter sky.

Chapter Twenty-four

It was still dark when Cherish woke on Christmas morning, but there was something about the air of stillness and the strange pale shadows across her bedroom ceiling that made her blink in excitement.

The snow, which had started falling yesterday afternoon and carried on intermittently all evening, must have settled.

It was going to be a white Christmas.

And, Cherish thought delightedly, sitting up in bed and pulling her covers more closely round her, she had a Christmas stocking at the foot of the bed to open. Obviously, because she'd put it there herself the previous night, this wasn't any huge surprise, but the contents would be. Oh, what a lovely idea this had been.

She and Brian had exchanged their stockings solemnly yesterday afternoon over a pot of tea and hot mince pies in Patsy's Pantry just as the snow had started to fall. And they'd promised faithfully not to peek at their contents until Christmas morning.

Brian, Cherish thought, had seemed even more excited than she was—if that were possible.

She peered at her alarm clock. Seven already. Not too early for a cup of tea. Then she'd bring it back to bed, and open her stocking. After pulling on her camel dressing gown and sliding her feet into her sensible slippers, she couldn't resist squeezing the stocking just to hear the blissful rattle and rustle of the paper inside.

She giggled to herself, suddenly filled with childlike joy, then crossed to the window and pulled back the curtains.

'Oh, how wonderful.'

The snow had stopped falling overnight and was probably two inches deep, covering everywhere in a glittering pristine white mantle. It was bone-chillingly cold, with a hard frost, so the snow had frozen like icing sugar. Perfect, Cherish thought. Just enough snow to make it a proper white Christmas, but not enough to stop her going to Brian's bungalow later, or returning to work after Boxing Day.

She couldn't have asked for anything more.

Cherish practically skipped into the kitchen, quickly made her tea and hurried back to bed.

The stocking, red felt with a jolly Santa appliquéd on the front, was quite small, but fat with tiny presents.

Cherish placed her teacup on her bedside table, switched on the lamp, pulled the stocking towards her and opened the first present with much crackling of reindeer wrapping.

'Oh!' Cherish felt the tears prickle her eyes. 'Oh, Brian, how clever you are.'

The first present was a pack of lavender fragranced drawer sachets. She loved lavender. She'd told Brian this once. He must have remembered.

The second present was equally wonderful: a set of lace-trimmed hankies. Cherish had told Brian she hated the trend for tissues, even if they were more hygienic. She loved her delicate hankies and

286

laundered them all carefully on a Monday morning.

Brian, Cherish thought, as the bed became covered in discarded wrapping paper, must have listened to everything she'd ever said to him.

There was a tiny purse, because she liked to keep her change separate from her notes, and some pretty stretch gloves in a Fair Isle pattern, and a small old-fashioned manicure set with orange sticks for the cuticles, and a little box of sugared almonds, and a wipe-clean cover for her television and radio listings magazine.

Cherish, almost crying with happiness, slid her hand into the toe of the stocking for the last present. As she unwrapped it, she laughed out loud.

It was a very tiny, soft, plush pale-blue teddy bear with a sash across its little chest that read 'Friends Forever'.

'Oh, Brian,' Cherish murmured as she sat the teddy bear on her bedside cabinet. 'Oh, thank you so much. This is my best Christmas since ... well, I can't remember when.'

She wondered if he'd opened his stocking yet, and if he'd be as pleased as she was. She really, really hoped so.

Cherish looked at her presents again in total delight. Then, being Cherish, she put them tidily to one side, and neatly folded all the wrapping paper before settling back on her pillows and sipping her tea, staring out at the winter wonderland outside.

Happy, happy Christmas.

*　　　　*　　　　*

Brian arrived at twelve on the dot as they'd arranged. Cherish was waiting for him in the hall, wearing her best fawn coat and her best brown beret, her handbag on her arm, her presents for him in a carrier bag. She'd opened Frankie's present while she'd had her breakfast to carols on the radio, because, knowing that Brian wouldn't have presents from anyone else, she didn't want him to feel awkward.

It was perfect, Cherish had thought, running her fingers over the diary and notebook and clicking the lovely pen open and shut. How clever of Frankie to give her something so wonderful and so useful. It was exactly what she would have chosen for herself. She really hoped Frankie would enjoy her bath cubes, too.

'Happy Christmas, gel,' Brian said gruffly, stepping into the hall. 'And thank you more'n I can say for my stocking.'

'And thank you for mine, too.' Cherish beamed. 'I loved it all. I couldn't believe it. Everything was just perfect. You must have remembered everything I've ever told you.'

'Ah, maybe I have.' Brian nodded, his wild hair even wilder, his big blues eyes filled with tears. 'But you, Cherish, gel. You couldn't have given me anything nicer.'

'You weren't offended?'

Brian shook his head. 'Offended? How could I be? It was the Christmas stocking I should have had when I was a lad and never did. I'm not ashamed to say I bawled me eyes out. You are wonderful, Cherish. The best.'

Cherish exhaled, blushing. She'd bought all Brian's stocking fillers in Winterbrook's main toyshop and carefully wrapped the colouring book and coloured pencils and stick-on transfers and

288

some small cars and a jigsaw puzzle of 1950s steam trains, and then she'd spent the remainder of her stocking filler money on a festive selection box, a chocolate Santa and some chocolate coins wrapped in gold foil in a small net bag.

'I'm so pleased you liked it all.'

'Liked it—' Brian was still damp-eyed '—I loved it, gel. I can't wait to get stuck into the jigsaw later. This is the best Christmas I've ever had. And the snow ... well, that just takes the biscuit, doesn't it? Are you ready to go, then, gel? I've left me turkey in the oven and the veg is all prepared and the spuds should go in soon, so we ought to get a move on. Your carriage awaits.'

Stepping carefully across the glittering ground, loving the creaking scrunch of the hard-frozen snow beneath her feet, Cherish made her way to the kebab van. Brian opened the door for her, and she clambered up inside.

'All in? Right, gel, off we go!'

*   *   *

Brian's bungalow was simply wonderful, Cherish thought, as she left her brogues by the front door. Although it was much the same size as hers, it seemed so much warmer and cosier. And it looked like Aladdin's cave. Brian had garlands and baubles everywhere, in every colour of the rainbow and then some. A Christmas tree sparkled with multicoloured lights in one corner of the living room, with three presents underneath it, and a coal fire blazed in the hearth.

And, from the kitchen, wafted the delicious scents of roasting turkey and stuffing and ... yes, surely that was the unmistakable smell of a proper Christmas pudding steaming?

Cherish clapped her hands happily. She hadn't smelled anything like it since she'd been a child.

Brian took her coat and beret and handed her a glass of sherry.

'Cheers, gel.' He clinked his sherry glass against hers. 'Happy Christmas.'

'Happy Christmas.' Cherish sipped her sherry. 'And this is such a lovely room. What gorgeous fat furniture—so deep and comfortable—and all those plushy cushions.'

'Ah, Rita did me proud when she left me this place. She knew how to make a homely home, did Rita.'

Cherish still gazed round in wonderment. 'And a real fire—how marvellous.'

'Real gas.' Brian chuckled. 'Looks the part though, don't it?'

'It does,' Cherish marvelled. 'I'd never have guessed. It looks exactly like the real thing. And it throws out so much heat. It makes a nice change from my two-bar electric.'

'Right, you sit yourself down,' Brian said, indicating the pair of huge armchairs on either side of the fireplace, 'by the fire here and get warm. I'll go and see to the dinner.'

'Please let me help you.'

'Won't hear of it.' Brian chuckled. 'I'm having the time of my life out there, gel. I've never cooked for anyone else before.'

And after putting Dean Martin crooning Christmas ballads on the stereo, Brian bustled out of the room.

Cherish sank into one of the deep cushiony

chairs and wriggled her stockinged toes in front of the fire as she sipped her sherry. How simply fabulous this was. A proper Christmas...

*   *   *

They had dinner just before two o'clock. Brian had set the small dining table with red paper napkins, several red candles and a glass vase filled with sprigs of holly. He'd even opened a bottle of sparkling wine.

Cherish stared at her plate—piled high with turkey and all the trimmings—and gasped. 'I can't eat all this! Oh, two sorts of stuffing ... and bread sauce! And chipolatas! And so many vegetables.' She gazed at Brian across the table. 'You're a dark horse, Brian. I had no idea you could cook like this.'

'Neither did I, gel.' Brian laughed. 'It's all been a bit trial and error, but I seem to have got the hang of it pretty quickly. I hope it's all right for you.'

'Brian, it's just wonderful.' Cherish tried to remember her manners and not appear greedy, but it was difficult. The food was so delicious. 'I'll never be able to thank you enough.'

'Just seeing you happy is thanks enough for me,' Brian said gruffly, concentrating on his food. 'Seemed so silly, both of us being alone today of all days.'

Alone, Cherish thought. All those lonely Christmases ... But not any more.

'Now you must let me do the washing up afterwards. I insist.'

'No need,' Brian said cheerfully. 'Rita had a dishwasher. I've loaded it and it's whirring away nicely. All mod cons, see?'

'Luxury,' Cherish said faintly. 'Total luxury. You're very lucky, Brian.'

'I know. Don't think I don't thank my lucky stars every day. And I thought,' Brian said as he poured them more wine, 'that we should be finished eating just in time to go through to the living room for the Queen's speech, and then we could open our presents in front of the fire. Do you think that would be OK?'

'Perfect.' Cherish nodded. 'Absolutely perfect. Like everything else today.'

*   *   *

By three thirty, hardly able to move, Cherish flopped happily in the fireside chair. It had been, without doubt, the most fantastic Christmas dinner she'd ever eaten. Now, she thought, with the standard lamps glowing, the Christmas tree lights twinkling, and the dark December afternoon closing in on the white world outside, it was like a dream come true.

'Right—' Brian looked like an overgrown schoolboy, his hair tousled and his eyes shining '—shall we do the presents now? Then we can settle down and watch the film before we think about tea.'

'Tea?' Cherish squeaked. 'I'll never be able to eat tea!'

'Course you will, gel. Just need to let your dinner go down first. Anyway—' he blushed as he knelt down near the tree '—these are for you.'

'Thank you.' Cherish took the packages. Three of them. Beautifully wrapped. 'And these are yours.

I bought three, too, and they're more sensible than the stocking fillers.' She handed the carrier bag to Brian.

'Thanks, gel.' Brian settled himself into the opposite chair. 'Right lovely this, isn't it?'

'Wonderful,' Cherish muttered as she opened the first small package. 'Oh, Brian! Scent! Anais Anais—ooh, it's gorgeous. How lovely. I never buy myself scent.'

'I know, you said.' Brian opened his first parcel. 'It's only the eaudy twaheltte or whatever they call it, not the real thing. Couldn't get the real thing with the money restrictions you set on me. Blimey, gel, thank you, this is right brilliant.'

Cherish laughed happily as Brian held up the warm woollen tartan scarf. Almost cashmere but not quite, but still soft and perfect to keep out the cold when he was working on the flower stall.

'And these too.' Brian held up the thick fingerless thermal mittens from his second present. 'I'll certainly need them. I've been wanting a pair of these for ages.'

'Oooh,' Cherish squealed with delight, opening her own second present. 'How pretty!' She held up the scarlet woollen scarf, pull-on hat and gloves set.

Brian shrugged. 'I thought you might like a splash of colour to go with your winter coat.'

'I'd never have bought anything like this,' Cherish admitted. 'Not for myself, not in such a bright colour, but you're right—it'll look lovely. Thank you so much.'

'You're welcome. I'm so glad you like it. Funny that we've bought each other nice things to keep us warm, isn't it?'

'Great minds thinking alike?' Cherish said,

293

almost flirtatiously. 'Or maybe we just know each other quite well now?'

'I reckon we do. Oh, Cherish, gel.' Brian opened his last present. 'This is just lovely.'

Cherish smiled to herself. She'd really, really hoped Brian would like the book. She knew he wasn't much of a reader, but it was one of those nostalgia editions, with lots of pictures and snippets of news from the last fifty years.

'Blimey, look at that! That's just how I remember it!' Brian was happily flicking through the glossy pages. 'And that! And this! Oh, I shall have hours of fun with this. You couldn't have given me anything better.'

'Or me,' Cherish said in amazement, gazing at her final gift. 'A Jane Austen box set. I've never had them all, and I do so love them. How on earth ... ?'

'Ah, I cheated a bit on that one, gel. I asked Frankie about what books she thought you'd like. She said you'd told her you was a Janet.'

'Janeite.'

'Ah, that's it.' Brian looked a bit puzzled. 'I wasn't sure what it meant.'

'It just means that I'm a Jane Austen fan. And it was so clever of you to ask her.' Cherish chuckled. 'Oh, aren't we lucky?'

'Ah, we are that. Oh, just listen to that wind roaring out there. And here we are all snug and cosy and warm indoors just waiting to put our feet up by the fire and enjoy a good film. Could there be anyone having a better time than us, gel?'

Cherish shook her head, happily snuggling down in her cushions and hugging *Pride and Prejudice*, which she thought she'd dip into if the film wasn't perhaps to her taste. 'Definitely not. Brian, thank you. Thank you so much for making this the best Christmas I've ever had.'

Brian smiled happily. 'It's mine an' all, gel. And it doesn't have to stop here, does it? We could make a habit of this. We sort of shake along right well together, don't we? No point in us both being lonely, is there?'

Cherish shook her head. 'No, there isn't.'

'So you wouldn't object if we did this again, sometime?'

'No,' said Cherish happily. 'No, I wouldn't object at all.'

Chapter Twenty-five

Frankie rolled over in bed, wriggled her pillows more comfortably, snuggled further beneath the pink and purple flounces, and sleepily touched her earrings. Dexter's Christmas present. Little stud earrings, shaped like pretty 1950s prom-frocks, beautifully enamelled in pink and lilac complete with peeping net petticoats. Unbelievably beautiful. She'd wear them forever. She closed her eyes again and drifted off, smiling.

Then the phone rang. And rang. And rang.

Groaning, eyes still closed, she fumbled and groped across the beside table. 'Hello.'

'Frankie, dear.'

'Cherish?' Frankie raised her head from her pillows and blinked blearily at her phone. 'Is that you? Why are you ringing me? What day is it?'

'It's the twenty-eighth, Frankie.'

'Oh Lord—have I overslept? No, it's not even

295

seven yet. It's the middle of the night. It's still dark. Cherish, are you ringing from a mobile?'

'Yes.' Cherish sounded agitated.

'You haven't got a mobile, have you?'

'No, dear. It's Dexter's.'

Frankie blinked again. Was she still asleep? Why on earth was Cherish ringing her on Dexter's mobile? Why was Cherish ringing her at all?

Frankie had driven back from her parents' house after midnight, carefully negotiating the hard-packed snow, and had fallen gratefully into bed. And she'd only been asleep for about five minutes, hadn't she?

'Er, sorry, Cherish? Are you ill? Is there a problem? Where are you?'

'I'm not ill, dear. Well, there's not a problem if you're holding an early sale at the shop, and I'm in the market square.'

'I'm not planning on holding a sale.' Frankie was mystified. 'Why are you at work so early?'

'I came in with Brian, dear. We were going to have breakfast together in the Greasy Spoon. I've been staying at his bungalow over the festive period. Oh, separate bedrooms, dear, in case that sounds in any way sordid.'

Oh, God. Frankie exhaled. It was getting madder by the minute.

'Cherish, is Dexter there? Can I speak to him?'

'You can, dear. But I think you should get down here as quickly as possible. There are about three thousand people in the market square and they're all wanting to get into your shop.'

'*What?*' With a squawk of horror, Frankie leaped out of bed and scrabbled for her clothes. There was clearly no time for a shower. 'Why? What on earth's going on? Look, OK, hold on, I'm getting dressed. What—Oh, hi.'

'Hi.' Dexter's voice echoed cheerfully in her ear. 'And does that mean you're currently naked?'

'Yes. No. Go away.'

Dexter laughed.

Frankie tucked the phone under her chin as she hopped around, pulling on whatever was nearest. 'Thank you so much for the earrings. They're incredible. I love them.'

'I'm glad. They just seemed, well, you, I suppose.'

'You couldn't have given me anything I'd love more.'

'Good. And are you dressed now?'

'Sort of.'

'OK, now I've lost interest.'

'Dexter! Seriously, what's happening there?'

'No idea. I've only just arrived—the flower market is closed, but I had a deal with another supplier for some more sparkly tulips—so I picked up my stock early, and just turned up here to find Cherish and Brian and a whole load of other people outside your shop.'

'About three thousand, Cherish said,' Frankie muttered, trying to use a face wipe and put on her mascara at the same time.

'More like thirty, I'd say. But enough. Especially as they all look ... well, odd.'

'Oh God, they're not ... um ... dead people, are they? We haven't got more ghosts trying to get in?'

'Oh no, they're very much alive. All muffled up against the sub-zeros and clutching flasks of Bovril.'

'Stop right there. It's all too mad. Don't tell me any more until I get there. I'm on my way.'

She arrived in the market square ten minutes later. It was still pitch dark, and the Christmas lights twinkled merrily. The frozen snow, practically untrodden across the cobbles, looked beautiful, but it was still bitingly cold.

Frankie pushed her way through the crowd, who looked very much like birdwatchers, until she found Dexter. She grinned at him and hooked back her hair to display the earrings. 'See? I'll never take them off. Thank you so much.'

'They look cute on.' Dexter nodded. 'And I'm just glad you're happy with them.'

'Happy is an understatement. They are my best ever present.' She looked round the marketplace. 'What the hell is this all about?'

'Still no idea. Nice Christmas?'

'Great, thanks. Over in the blink of an eye. You?'

'Not really. Quiet. Very. And you look like an Easter chick.'

Frankie groaned. Possibly the short yellow woollen frock under her lemon jacket, the pink tights and the red boots weren't the best colour combo, but she'd hardly been in a position to choose, had she?

'Thanks. And where the heck is Cherish?'

'She and Brian were frozen stiff so they've gone to get a fry-up in the Greasy Spoon.'

'And they spent Christmas *together*?'

'Apparently so.'

'Jesus.'

One of the people crowding outside Francesca's Fabulous Frocks suddenly peeled away and approached her. Due to the puffa jacket, muffler and beanie hat it was impossible to guess the gender.

'Excuse me, but do you know when the frock shop's opening? It says the twenty-eighth on the door—and that's today—but not the time.'

The hoarse voice gave no clues to its owner's sex either.

'Nine o'clock,' Frankie said.

'And are you the proprietor?'

'Yes, but why? Who are you? Do you all want to buy dresses?'

'No, of course not. I'm Jackie Minton, Chair of the Winterbrook Psychical Research Association.'

Female then.

Frankie smiled. 'Well, it's nice to meet you, but I don't see . . .'

'And I'm Alan Bradstock. I run the Willows Lacey Afterlife Group.' Another similarly muffled figure pushed in front of Jackie. 'We're rival societies, see. And I don't want her stealing a march on me.'

Ker-ching!

Frankie shook her head in disbelief. 'You're *ghost-hunters*?'

'We don't actually use that phrase,' Alan Bradstock said tartly. 'It's very dumbed-down. We're far more than that.'

'Exactly,' Jackie Minton agreed. 'Anyway, we've heard that this shop has a *presence* and we're all absolutely agog to get inside and feel for ourselves.'

'But,' Alan said, 'if you're the owner, you must know that you have a visitation.'

Frankie laughed. It sounded very false. 'You mean, you think my shop's *haunted*? I've never heard so much nonsense in my life!'

299

'You might not be aware of it,' Jackie rasped kindly. 'You may be out of tune with the spirit world. We could help you.'

'Yes, indeedy,' Alan said jovially, stamping his feet. 'Just let us inside and we'll be able to commune with any ghosts that may have attached themselves to you.'

'Over my dead body,' Frankie snapped. 'Please go away—all of you. I'm going to have some breakfast now. I'll be opening the shop on the dot of nine o'clock—to sell frocks. Just to sell frocks. If you don't want to buy a frock then please don't come in. There-are-no-ghosts-in-my-shop—OK?'

And she pushed her way through the eager crowd, followed by Dexter.

'Cool,' he said admiringly. 'You're such a good liar.'

Frankie yanked at the door of the Greasy Spoon. 'Who—' she glared at him over her shoulder '—blabbed?'

'Whoa! Don't look at me like that. You're scary. And I haven't breathed a word. And who else knew?'

'You and me. Lilly and Maisie.' Frankie found a table by the window and plonked herself down. 'No one else.'

'So? Lilly?' Dexter pulled out the chair opposite her. 'Oh Lord—Cherish and Brian have seen us.'

'Hardly surprising, seeing as we're the only other people in here.' She waved at them across the café. 'Thanks for letting me know about this, er, influx, Cherish.'

'Is it all OK, dear?'

'Yes, yes, just a bit of a misunderstanding. Don't worry about it. Just enjoy your breakfast. Oh, and you're wearing a touch of red. Lovely. It really suits you.'

'Thank you, dear. It was one of Brian's Christmas presents to me. And I loved yours, dear. Just what I wanted. Thank you so much.'

'Er, you're welcome. And your bath cubes were gorgeous.'

'Thank you, dear. My mother always loved freesia bath cubes. I knew you'd like them too.'

Frankie looked at Dexter. 'I don't think I can cope with them playing geriatric Romeo and Juliet at the moment, can you? It's too weird. And I've got enough to worry about. And no, Lilly promised she wouldn't say a word, and she hasn't. I know Lilly's a bit girly and frothy and stuff, but she's dead straight. I trust Lilly implicitly.'

'So? I haven't told anyone, neither have you, and we've ruled out Lilly, so it has to be Maisie.'

'But why?' Frankie frowned. 'She cocked it all up in the first place. Surely she wouldn't claim bragging rights? Oh—' she smiled at the motherly waitress '—two full English please, and two coffees. Mugs, please. Thank you.'

Dexter glanced through the window. 'There seems to be even more of them arriving now. Do you think they have some sort of grapevine?'

'Sixth sense.' Frankie giggled.

Dexter laughed. 'I've missed you.'

Frankie stopped giggling. 'I missed you, too.'

'Coffee!' The motherly waitress plonked two mugs on the red Formica table top. 'Breakfast in about five minutes, loves, OK?'

*   *   *

301

By the time their breakfast was over and daylight had begun to seep across Kingston Dapple, there was a crowd of about a hundred in the market square. The Greasy Spoon was doing a roaring trade in defrosting those who hadn't come armed with wheat-filled hand-warmers and flasks.

Frankie and Dexter stood shivering outside Francesca's Fabulous Frocks, their breath pluming into the sullen air.

'You're going to need a hand in keeping them out as soon as you unlock that door,' Dexter said. 'I'll act as bouncer.'

'Doorman is the correct phrase.' Frankie looked wearily at the milling crowd. 'Or so Lilly keeps telling me. She's dated loads of them. That's why her clubbing life is so good. Look, I'm just going to open up, and whiz in and see if the ... um, well, if Ernie and co. are around, and then I'll explain to them what's happened and if they don't mind then I think I'll let the ghost-busters in.'

'*What*? It'll be mayhem.'

'Maybe, but it's got to be better than them all standing around out here proclaiming publicly that this place is more haunted than the Tower of London or something, hasn't it? And who knows, one of them might actually be able to do something.'

Dexter looked doubtful. 'Well, maybe.'

'I'm going in now. It's too damn cold to hang around outside, especially dressed as a chicken. You and Brian go and open up your stall before your twinkly tulips wilt. I'll just explain to Cherish that this is all some huge misunderstanding, then we'll see what happens.'

'OK.' Dexter nodded. 'But I'll be watching and

302

I'll be over like a shot if it all goes wrong.'

'Thank you.'

'No problem.' He kissed her gently. 'And no mistletoe. I'm getting very bold.'

She was still smiling as she unlocked the door.

*   *   *

Ernie and Bev listened intently. Ruby, Gertie and Jared hadn't materialised.

'... and so,' Frankie finished, 'it's up to you. Shall I let them in and see if they can undo the damage that Maisie caused you, or not?'

'Can't do any harm.' Bev was still wearing tinsel and baubles. 'To be frank, I'm getting very bored with the restrictions down here. I do feel very trapped. We had so much freedom before.'

'And I just want to be with Achsah, duck, as you know.'

Frankie pulled a face. 'I know. And all I want to do is just make you happy.'

'You're a nice girl.' Bev tucked a strand of hair under her snood. 'One good thing about being stuck here, though, was watching the snow. That took us back. We haven't seen snow for ages of course. We spent a lot of time telling stories about snowy winters. Nice, it was.'

'OK, so I let the ... psychical researchers or whatever they call themselves in, and then what? Do you want to disappear and see what they can do, or would you prefer to stay already materialised?'

'Over to Bev on that one,' Ernie said gruffly. 'She knows far more about it than I do.'

'Oh, I think we'll all vanish and see what happens,' Bev said cheerfully. 'They can't do any

303

more harm than that daft old bat, can they?'

'Let's hope not,' Frankie said with a sigh. 'And if they do manage to ... um ... raise you, could you not let on that you know me. I've lied a bit about all this.'

'Don't blame you, duck,' Ernie said with deep understanding. 'I'd lie through me teeth, too, if I was you.'

'I'll tell the others not to say anything either,' Bev said. 'We won't give you away, Frankie.'

'Thanks—you're really lovely. OK, then, off you go.'

And off they went.

'Goodness me, dear.' Cherish bustled in then. 'What a palaver. So, what's going on then, dear? Shall I put the kettle on?'

'In a minute,' Frankie said. 'Look, Cherish, there's something I need to explain to you first. Those people outside—well, someone's told them the shop is haunted.' She gave what she hoped was a jolly laugh. 'Stupid, I know, but they all belong to ghost-hunting groups, and they think they can come in and find, well, dead people. I have no idea where they got that silly notion from, but—'

'Oh, I do, dear.' Cherish, seemingly unfazed, shed her scarlet hat, scarf and gloves and started to unbutton her coat. 'It was Biddy.'

'Biddy?'

Cherish nodded. 'She's such a silly girl sometimes. Takes everything as gospel, and then of course, she's such a *gossiper*. I told her it was all nonsense, of course.'

'You *knew*?'

'That Biddy was saying the shop was haunted, dear? Yes, of course I did.'

'But who on earth told her?'

'Maisie Fairbrother, dear. You know what a soppy-boots Maisie is—or maybe you don't. But she is, dear. Always thinking she's seen *something*. And, of course, she never has.'

'And Maisie told Biddy my shop was haunted and Biddy told you?'

'Yes, dear. It was too daft for words so I never said anything to you. Of course I told Biddy I'd never seen a ghost in this shop and she was being very silly to believe a word Maisie Fairbrother said, but there you go. So, what are you going to do? Let them in and have some fun?'

Still stunned, Frankie looked at Cherish. Fun? Hardly … 'Well, yes, that's what I thought would be best. I mean, the ghost-hunters are here now, they're not going to go away, and it might just stop all the, um, rumours.'

Or, of course, it might start a whole lot more.

Frankie sighed. 'But Biddy …? Oh, I'll kill her.'

'No you won't dear.' Cherish smiled gently. 'You're much too lovely to have harsh thoughts of that nature. I'll go and put the kettle on now, shall I? And find lots of cups? They'll all be proper shrammed out there, poor things.'

'Er, yes, OK … And, Cherish, when they're in here, you won't say anything will you? About Biddy or Maisie or anyone thinking the place is haunted? Please.'

'Of course not. You have my word, dear. I shall stay as silent as the grave.'

Very, very unfortunate choice of phrase, Frankie thought. 'Thank you … Oh, and you and Brian?'

Cherish blushed, smiled, and shed about thirty years. 'We're good friends, dear. Best friends. We

305

had such a lovely time together at Christmas. I hadn't intended to stay over but his bungalow was so cosy and we were stuck into this jigsaw puzzle after we'd watched James Bond, and Brian said why didn't he run me home to pack a little valise—well, he didn't say valise, of course, dear—for a few days, and then I could make myself comfy in his spare room. Which—' Cherish twirled off towards the kitchen '—is what I did.'

Frankie, staring after her, for once couldn't think of a single thing to say.

Chapter Twenty-six

The ghost-busters, led in their rival factions by Jackie and Alan, streamed into the shop. With cries of joy about the warmth and the mass of lovely dresses, rather than the presence of anything spectral, they fell happily on Cherish's tea trays. Francesca's Fabulous Frocks was very crowded.

Jackie flexed her not inconsiderable arms. 'Ah, I do sense you have an aura here,' she said to Frankie. 'And a feeling of resentment and some unhappiness. The spirits here are here against their will. They feel trapped. They want to be free. Have you had a *dabbler* mucking around with an amateur seance, by any chance?'

'Er, no, certainly not,' Frankie lied quickly.

'Good.' Jackie pursed her lips. 'Because they can be very dangerous. Very dangerous indeed. And terribly unsettling for the spirits. They don't know what's happening to them and then they find themselves somewhere they don't want to be and they can't return to the afterlife and they become, well, restive and disruptive.'

Tell me about it, Frankie thought. She smiled. 'Why on earth would I have held a seance, for heaven's sake? The shop definitely isn't haunted.'

She wasn't going to admit anything about Maisie Fairbrother. Well, not unless it all went very wrong and they ended up in court for some reason and she was put under oath and then she might have to. She really, really hoped it wouldn't come to that.

Frankie smiled in what she hoped was a 'how foolish this all is' girly manner. 'No, seriously, this haunting nonsense—it just seems to be based on some silly local rumour.'

'Oh, I can assure you it's far more than that. I agree with Jackie—there's definitely something here,' Alan said. 'The feeling of discontent is very strong. I'd say, like Jackie, you have a spirit or spirits here who were brought here against their will, and want to be set free.'

Frankie exhaled. It seemed as though Jackie and Alan might be a lot more clued up, ghost-wise, than Maisie Fairbrother. Which, of course, wouldn't be difficult.

'OK,' Frankie said slowly, 'and just supposing there are ghosts here—which I still refute—but just supposing, and just supposing they want to go back to ... well, wherever ghosts come from, is that something you can do for it, um, them?'

'Oh, yes,' Jackie said cheerfully. 'We're always returning the unhappy undead to the afterlife. It's one of our most rewarding missions.'

Frankie felt a little frisson of hope.

The Winterbrook and Willows Lacey groups stood quietly back behind their leaders. So far there had been no head-smiting or wailing or pendant-twirling at all. It was quite impressive.

'What I'd like to suggest now is a little radical.' Jackie raised her eyebrows at Alan. 'But because the presence presenting itself here is so strong, I'd like to suggest that we join forces.'

Alan pursed his lips. 'Well, we do have very different methods, don't we? But, yes, it makes sense to do a joint one-off spiritual cleansing. Just so long as we work as equals. No rank-pulling?'

'Oh, absolutely.' Jackie nodded her beanie hat and turned to the assembled ghost-hunters behind her. 'Right—Oh, please, ladies, leave the frocks alone! We're not here for the frocks, are we?'

Shame-faced, several women shuffled away from the rails.

'Good girls. Now—' Jackie looked rather excited '—we're going to be working with the Willows Lacey people. Alan and I will take joint control. You must all send your vibes to us both to make this work. I want no squabbling.'

Everyone nodded their woolly hats obediently.

'Now—' Alan beamed at Frankie '—if you and the tea lady could leave us and lock the shop on your way out, we'll get to work.'

'No you won't.' Frankie frowned. 'I'm quite happy to lock up to prevent anyone coming in and any of this total nonsense spreading any further and ruining my business, but I'm going nowhere. I'm staying put.'

'But—' Jackie spoke loudly and slowly as if to a slightly dim child '—it might not work with you here. The spirits might take against you.'

Oh, no they won't, Frankie thought.

She shook her head. 'As I don't believe there

are any spirits here, then I'm sure they won't. But I think it might be better if Cherish went. I don't want her to be frightened.'

'I won't be frightened, dear,' Cherish said robustly. 'It's quite exciting.'

'No, really,' Frankie said. 'Please, Cherish. You get wrapped up again and go and help Brian with the flowers, and if you could ask Dexter to come and join me?'

Cherish brightened at the thought of helping Brian. 'All right, dear. Won't be a jiff.'

Once Cherish had been muffled up and slithered across the snow-packed cobbles to Brian and the flower stall, and Dexter had taken her place in the shop, Alan and Jackie removed their puffa coats and started to pace round the frock rails.

A lot of the eyes beneath the assorted woolly hats gazed lustfully at Dexter.

'Concentrate, ladies, please!' Jackie snapped.

Frankie giggled.

'Cherish filled me in,' Dexter whispered as he hauled himself up on to the counter beside Frankie. 'She thinks it's all silly, of course, but then she doesn't know what we know, does she? What do you reckon?'

'They seem to know what they're doing more than Maisie—which wouldn't be hard—and they haven't done any wailing or waved pendants or lit candles or anything, so, so far, I'm quite impressed.'

'But will Ernie be?'

'Oh, I hope so. Obviously I want all the ghosts to go back, but for Ernie it's so important.' She looked at Jackie. 'Sorry?'

'I was just asking for a little hush, if you don't mind. No chattering. If you insist on being here

309

then I'd really like you to be quiet.'

'Bossy,' Dexter whispered. 'Why are all these ghosty people so bossy?'

'Shush!' Jackie admonished sternly.

Frankie and Dexter looked at one another and tried not to giggle.

'Of course,' Alan said, 'it would be more effective at night. In the dark. I've never had a spirit materialise for me in daylight.'

'We're several steps up on him, then,' Dexter whispered.

'Shush!' Jackie, still pacing, hissed.

Alan suddenly stopped by the changing rooms and touched the curtains. 'I feel something here. Oh, yes, definitely. If you're here, trapped soul, then make yourself known to us. We come in friendship to help you.'

'Er, yes,' Jackie put in quickly, clearly not wanting to lose ground to a rival. 'We know you're unhappy. We want to make your crossing-over peaceful and easy. We have the spiritual powers to make this happen.'

There was absolute silence. Then the curtains twitched.

'Peep-bo, dear hearts!' Jared, still in full Christmas garb, pranced out. 'You've found me! And much as I love all these frocks I'd be really happy to leave now. I'm bored.'

Jackie and Alan were open-mouthed.

'Do you reckon,' Dexter whispered, 'that they're shocked rigid because they've got a ghost, or because of the way he looks?'

'The latter.' Frankie chuckled.

'Er . . .' Jackie cleared her throat.

The rest of the group just stared.

Alan strode forwards towards Jared. 'Don't be frightened. I can tell you're a bewildered spirit. We're here to release you.'

'Oh, goody, dear hearts.' Jared clasped his hands. 'I can't wait.'

'And neither can I.' Bev walked out from behind the 1980s rails.

'Oh, my!' Alan looked ecstatic. 'This is the most wonderful day of my life!'

'Yes, that's as maybe,' Bev said, frowning, 'but if you can send us back to our other world please just get a move on.'

Jackie looked as though she wanted to scamper on the spot.

The remainder of the ghost-busters just gaped.

'Going well,' Frankie hissed to Dexter.

'So, restless spirits.' Jackie cleared her throat. 'Our minds are in tune with yours. Our wishes are your wishes. Our powers are attuned and ready to help you. Everyone here wants what you want to send you on your final journey. Don't we, friends?'

The ghost-hunters collective, who were clutching each other in joy, nodded their woolly hats as one.

Alan bowed his head and closed his eyes.

'Is he praying?' Dexter queried.

'I don't know about him, but I am.' Frankie sighed. 'Still no sign of Ernie though. Maybe he's just too new to come through like this.'

'Restless spirits. Unhappy souls,' Alan intoned. 'I feel your sadness trapped here by earthly bonds. I'm cutting those bonds. Now!'

'And you shall be free!' Jackie did a sort of Freddie Mercury flourish with her arms. 'Free to return from whence you came!'

'Go now!' Alan said firmly. 'Leave us and go!

311

For ever!'

Jared gave a little shriek, started to wave goodbye to Frankie and then, in a spiral of multicoloured ether and sprinkling of twinkling stars, vanished, his voice growing ever distant.

'Christ.' Dexter swallowed.

'Now me.' Bev looked bored. 'Don't hang about.'

'Yes—go and be free!' Jackie said loudly. 'Rest in peace for eternity!'

And Bev too, waved and smiled and then, with the same glorious sparkling mist shrouding the shop, simply spiralled away.

Frankie was speechless.

How could it be that easy? Oh, Ernie would be delighted.

Jackie and Alan looked at one another and exhaled. The ghost-busters collective simply beamed.

'But,' Alan puffed, clearly exhausted, 'I'm still getting the feeling that—'

'There's something or someone else?' Jackie muttered. 'Me too, Alan. Come sad spirits—show yourselves and let us set you free.'

The 1960s frocks started to undulate and dance.

'Please God—or whoever—let them get Ernie,' Frankie whispered.

'Oooh dear.' Alan jumped as Gertie, still very grey and withered despite the sunflower dress, simpered at him. 'Ah.'

Jackie, trying not to look too horrified, swallowed. 'Welcome dear, spirit. Let us send you back over to the other side.'

'Nice.' Gertie nodded. 'That'd be lovely, ta very much. I've had a nice time here, but like the others, enough's enough, and I've got me nice frock and

312

shoes to show me old man.'

'And me.' Ruby skipped out from between the rails. 'And me! I want to go too!'

'Lord above!' Alan clapped his hands. 'This is better than when we did Marchants Abbey. We only got two then and we thought we'd hit the jackpot.'

'We got three grey ghosts at Marchants Abbey, actually,' Jackie preened. 'Didn't we, boys and girls?'

The Winterbrook woolly hats all nodded smugly.

'This is no time for boasting,' Alan said testily. 'We need to send these ladies back to a happier place and free them from their earthly shackles.'

The intoning, gesturing and praying were much the same as before.

The mist swirled again, the stars danced and twinkled, the ether spiralled.

And, calling cheery farewells, Ruby and Gertie faded away.

'You know,' Dexter said softly as the ether cleared, 'I think I'm going to miss Gertie.'

Frankie sighed. 'I know. Stupidly, I'm going to miss all of them.'

'There now.' Jackie looked exhausted, but very self-satisfied as she nodded towards Frankie. 'No ghosts in this shop, eh? Well, I must say that was a very impressive session, Alan. Thank you for your help.'

'Not a problem.' Alan, red-faced, was all puffed up like a turkey cock. 'A great joint effort there, Jackie, and one we'll be talking about in our meetings for a long time to come I think.'

Frankie, still slightly stunned, took a deep breath. 'Well, er, I don't know what to say ... Er,

313

clearly you were right and I was wrong. Thank you for, um, setting them free, but I'm sure . . . well, that is, there must be another ghost . . . '

Jackie roared with laughter. 'From sceptic to expert in thirty seconds. Always the same. No, they've all gone now, love. I can't feel anything at all, can you, Alan?'

'No, not a thing. No spiritual presence whatsoever. Your shop is no longer haunted. Although I must say, it was one of the liveliest manifestations I've ever witnessed. We will, of course, keep this to ourselves. We are, as a society, sworn to secrecy about our activities.'

'Absolutely,' Jackie agreed, pushing her chunky arms back into her puffa coat. 'We couldn't do what we do if people chattered about it. So, we won't say what happened here, and you no longer have to worry about people being frightened when they come in to buy frocks.'

'I don't think anyone actually ever was,' Frankie said hotly, 'but are you sure there's no one else here? Really sure?'

The collective were shuffling out of the door, clearly delighted with the morning's successful ghost-hunting entertainment.

'My dear girl.' Alan was now at his most pompous. 'You've just witnessed what we can do. We've freed all your earthbound spirits. In broad daylight to boot.'

'Yes,' Frankie said conversationally. 'Why is that, by the way? Why do all hauntings and ghost-bustings have to be at night? Surely, if a place is haunted, it's haunted. Twenty-four seven. There'd be ghosts there all the time. Ghosts wouldn't know if it was dark or light, dawn or dusk, would they? They'd just *haunt*. As, um, the ones in the shop were clearly doing. But you never see any of those *Haunt My House* telly programmes showing spook-spotters rambling around on a lovely summer's day, do you?'

'Well, er, no,' Alan blustered. 'I don't suppose you do. Not that we associate ourselves with the commercial side of things, of course.'

'So, this dead-of-midnight stuff is all for effect really is it?'

'No it certainly isn't.' Jackie looked a bit uncomfortable. 'It just helps the atmosphere along, that's all.'

Frankie smiled. 'OK, I just wondered. And you're both sure there isn't anyone, um, ghostly left here, are you?'

Alan puffed himself up again. 'As you've seen, we are extremely in tune with all things spiritual— so do you honestly think I wouldn't know if there was a presence left behind?'

'Precisely,' Jackie echoed. 'Your shop is now as clean as a whistle, ghost-wise. And I for one could do with a nice hot bath and a peanut butter bap.'

'Sounds good to me,' Alan said with a smirk.

And the door closed behind them.

Dexter and Frankie looked at one another in dismay.

'Sod and buggeration.' Ernie frowned, appearing from his usual post beside the 1950s frocks. 'Looks like I've missed the bloody boat—again.'

Chapter Twenty-seven

After the ghost-busting session, life in Kingston Dapple went on much as normal. Francesca's Fabulous Frocks did a roaring pre-New Year trade in party dresses, and Dexter was kept busy with customers wanting masses of bright flowers to liven up the gloom of the downbeat post-Christmas period.

The freeze continued and the snow stayed put. Everyone who'd been delighted to see it fall was now heartily sick of slipping and sliding and being cold, and just wished it would melt.

The New Year came and went, and Frankie went to Clemmie, Guy and YaYa's party with all her girlfriends and their partners. She invited Dexter and he said he'd love to go, but had something else that had to be done over the New Year break that couldn't be put off, and he wouldn't be in Kingston Dapple.

Frankie still wore her earrings constantly, and thought back dreamily to the kisses—the one with mistletoe and the one without—and determinedly didn't ask Dexter how he saw in the New Year, or who with, and he didn't tell her. Lilly, tanned and in love with a waiter called Andreas, returned from Cyprus.

Cherish astounded absolutely everyone by putting her bungalow on the market and moving into Brian's spare room. 'No point in shilly-shallying at my age. I'm living for the moment,' she told everyone proudly. 'It's like being reborn. I've never been happier.' And neither, it appeared, had

Brian.

Biddy had, of course, sniffed and said it would all end in tears. And Maisie Fairbrother had announced that her New Year's resolution was to give up mediuming and take up holistic healing instead.

And Ernie still lurked miserably—and now alone—in Francesca's Fabulous Frocks.

*   *   *

'You know,' Frankie said post-work, one very cold and frosty evening in mid-January, as she and Dexter squinted at yet another pair of dubious cocktails in the Toad in the Hole, 'I've just had an idea.'

'Hold on to it then.' Dexter grinned. 'You might need it one day.'

'No, seriously . . . it's about Ernie.'

'Oh, Frankie. I know how you feel, and I know how miserable he is, but we've been over it so many times. We've decided that Jackie and Alan couldn't send him back because he was a newly dead ghost and he just didn't latch on to their vibes. Even Ernie agrees with that now.'

'I know. It's not that. It's something different.'

'OK, go on.'

'Well, I don't think he's here by accident. In my shop. I mean, he could have ended up anywhere, couldn't he? And he'd never been in the shop before—not even when Rita had it—so it isn't the shop he's haunting, as such.'

Dexter frowned. 'Sorry, I'm not really following your train of thought at all here. And I always thought that ghosts—if I ever thought about them

317

at all—haunted the place where they died. So, in that case, Ernie should be hanging around in Poundland, shouldn't he?'

Frankie nodded and stirred the turquoise concoction in front of her with the end of her dead sparkler. 'Well, yes. Maybe—but he's not. He's in my shop because of Achsah's wedding dress, isn't he?'

'I suppose he is, yes. He did say he felt close to her because of the dress.'

'And the first time I saw him, after I'd realised he wasn't a cross-dresser, when he told me, well, everything, he said the dress had been stolen by his nieces and donated to Rita. And I was thinking, as it's the *dress* that's so special, maybe if we could take the dress to a church or something— maybe even the church where Ernie and Achsah got married—and hold some sort of ceremony, it might, well, free him.'

Dexter pushed his unfinished cocktail away and ordered a beer from the bored barman. 'It might, but then we'd need the vicar or someone to be in on it, and maybe communing with the undead doesn't go down very well in churches. I wouldn't know. I'm afraid I gave up going to church after I left primary school.'

'Me too,' Frankie admitted. 'Oh, I don't know. It was just a thought. I really don't know what else to do for him.'

'Oooh, I sooo lurve Skype.' Lilly teetered into the Toad, wrapped in a violet fun fur coat over her skinny jeans and hitched herself onto a stool beside Dexter. 'Me and Andreas have just been talking for *ages*. Oooh, I miss him so much. Still, he's coming over at Easter. Only another twelve weeks to go. If

318

I can live that long without him.'

'I'm looking forward to meeting him,' Dexter said, trying not to laugh. 'Frankie's told me a lot about him.'

'That's because he's been the only topic of conversation since she got back.' Frankie played with her tiny cocktail umbrella. 'And I bet he'll have been replaced by someone local several times over before Easter.'

'No he won't.' Lilly pouted and looked at the discarded cocktail. 'Have you finished with this drink, Dexter?'

'Yes—be my guest.'

'Cool, thanks. Oooh, it's lovely. I'll order another one. And anyway, Andreas isn't just coming over for a visit. He's moving here. He's going to live here. With me.'

'*What*?' Frankie shook her head. 'Since when?'

'Since tonight. We talked about it while I was over there, and he's got a second cousin or an uncle or something who runs a Greek restaurant in Winterbrook, so he's sorted out a job there and I said of course he'd be living with us, well, me—so it's all organised.'

'Well, congratulations,' Frankie said faintly, wondering first if Lilly and Andreas had considered visas and work permits and assumed Andreas had, and secondly how much she really wanted to share the Featherbed Lane house with a madly loved-up Lilly and a permanent fixture.

'Er, yes—congratulations.' Dexter tried to keep a straight face.

'Ta.' Lilly beamed. 'And anyway don't make it sound like I hog all the conversations. The ghost-busting has been talked about just as much as

319

Andreas. I can't believe I missed it. I can't believe they've really gone and I'll never see them again. I really liked Jared.'

'I know, so did I, but they're happy now. And we were just talking about poor old Ernie again,' Frankie said. 'And trying to come up with a decent plan for reuniting him with Achsah. For the umpteenth time. I wondered if we could have some sort of church service.'

Lilly ordered another doubtful cocktail. 'What? Like a funeral?'

Frankie laughed out loud. 'Lill, how do you do it? You're brilliant! Oh, Lilly, I love you!'

'Good.' Lilly blinked her long pink-and-sparkle eyelashes. 'But I'm not sure what I did there.'

'Nor me.' Dexter looked confused. 'Did I miss something?'

'A funeral.' Frankie smiled excitedly. 'Why on earth didn't we think of that before? It's so obvious, isn't it?'

'Is it?' Dexter still looked puzzled.

'Yes, blindingly. Listen. We'll give Ernie the funeral he wanted and never had. Remember I said Slo Motion told me the dreadful nieces ignored all Ernie's requests and went for the cheapskate funeral option and that his ashes had never been buried or scattered or anything?'

'Yes, and—?'

'And so, if we arranged to have Ernie's ashes buried in the grave with Achsah where he wanted to be in the first place, surely, that would mean he'd be laid to rest at last, wouldn't it?'

Dexter exhaled. 'God, Frankie, that's brilliant. Why on earth didn't we think of that before? So, what do we do next?'

'Go and see Slo and tell him what we want to do and ask him to arrange it.'

'Actually, I think—' Lilly twirled her little umbrella '—that the first thing you should do is ask Ernie. Just in case. I mean, if it was me, I'd want to know if someone was planning to bury me somewhere, just in case I didn't want it. It seems rude not ask him.'

Dexter looked at Lilly in astonishment. 'You know, Lilly, you really are very clever, aren't you?'

'Yeah. Sure. For a bimbo airhead. It's been said before.' She leaned across the counter towards the bored barman. 'Hi, gorgeous. Can we have the same again all round? Ta.'

*   *   *

'So,' Frankie said to Ernie in Francesca's Fabulous Frocks, about an hour later. 'That's the plan. What do you reckon?'

Ernie, leaning against the 1950s dress rails, beamed all over his little goblin face and ran his fingers through his grizzled hair until it stood on end. 'Oh, my word, Frankie, duck. That sounds just about perfect to me. I mean, I know I didn't want to be cremated, but what's done is done, but if you could just lay me to rest with my Achsah, I'd be right happy. Then, at last, our bodies and our souls would be together again, and we could rest in peace, together, for ... well, eternity.'

Dexter took a deep breath and tried to steady his voice. 'Um—yes. So, if we go and see Slo, and tell him we want to organise a small ceremony for you—that we'd like him to inter your ashes in Achsah's grave, you'll be OK with that?'

321

'More than OK. I don't want no church service or hymns nor nothing—I had all that at the crem. I just want to be with Achsah. In the churchyard at Tadpole Bridge.'

'Wonderful,' Frankie said. 'And I know it's what you want and what we've been trying to do for ages, but I'll miss you, Ernie.'

'Ah, and I'll miss you an' all, duck. And young Dexter here. You've been like a little family to me, you have.'

Frankie gulped and wiped her eyes.

Dexter cleared his throat. 'So, we'll go and see Slo tomorrow, shall we?'

'I'll ring him and make sure he'll be in and doesn't mind us popping round,' Frankie said, nodding happily. 'And then we'll arrange the funeral for as soon as possible. Ernie, I think we've found the solution at last, don't you? I don't see what can possibly go wrong this time.'

Chapter Twenty-eight

'... so, you see, it ain't as easy as all that. Sorry, ducks.' Slo Motion gazed at them sadly the following evening. 'I know you're disappointed.'

They were once again sitting in his cosy Hazy Hassocks flat, with Essie plying them with coffee and sandwiches.

Frankie sighed. 'Oh, sod it. I thought it was going to be really simple.'

Dexter nodded at Slo. 'So, what you're saying is that you can't just give us the casket, and we can't just bury Ernie's ashes in Achsah's grave, even if we all know it's what he wants.'

Slo coughed wheezily. 'Exactly, Dexter, lad. Look, if it were that simple then I'd have done it meself. I knew what old Ern wanted, and I knew the nieces hadn't given him the funeral he'd planned. It would have been so easy for me, being in the business and having the ashes on the premises so to speak, to have a word with the vicar at Tadpole Bridge, open up Achsah's grave quietly, and pop Ern in.'

'But you can't, and we can't?' Frankie frowned.

Slo shook his head. 'No, duck. The ashes legally belong to the next of kin, you see. It's only the next of kin who can decide on the dispersal or disposal.'

'But the nieces—Thelma and Louise—as far as I can gather—' Dexter leaned forwards '—didn't give a toss about Ernie. So why wouldn't they give their permission for you to do what Ernie wanted?'

'Money,' Slo said simply. 'They didn't want to spend a penny more than was necessary. And it costs to open up a grave and have an interment. And they weren't going to pay for it. No way.'

'But we will,' Frankie said. 'Dexter and I have already agreed we'd pay. You must have Thelma and Louise's contact details. Tell them we'll organise it and pay for it. Surely they'd be OK with that?'

Slo wheezed pleasurably a bit more. 'Ah, duck. Mebbe they would and mebbe they wouldn't. But there are *laws*, lots and lots of laws, to do with burials. And the next of kin have to agree in writing to hand the ashes over to a third party. I'd have to write to them, and they'd have to sign the papers to allow you to take charge of the mortal remains, then return the signed arrangements to me for me

323

to organise the interment. It's complicated.'

'Oh, bugger it then.' Frankie sighed crossly, leaning back in her chair and watching the fire dance in front of her. 'And that will take *ages*, won't it? From taking over Rita's shop I know only too well what legal paperwork is like.'

'This can be done quite quick.' Slo nodded. 'As long as all parties are in agreement. But there's no guarantee that Thelma and Louise will even give a jot about what happens to Ernie's ashes. Why should they? He meant nothing to them. I doubt if they got much, if anything, from his estate, and they certainly won't bother about him resting in peace.'

Dexter frowned. 'You mean, they'll probably just ignore your letter?'

'Ah.' Slo nodded. 'Having met 'em, I'm afraid they will, Dexter, lad.'

'Nooo,' Frankie sighed. 'And I thought we'd really found the answer this time.'

Slo took a mouthful of coffee. 'So, you're still saying that Ernie is *haunting* your shop, are you, duck?'

'I am and he is. And—' Frankie leaned forwards '—I know you don't totally believe me, but it doesn't matter. We—Dexter and I—love him, and want him to be reunited with Achsah, and no, I haven't told anyone about the other stuff, and I never will.'

'What other stuff?' Dexter stopped mid-sandwich.

'Something that Slo told me in total confidence,' Frankie said. 'It just made me more sure than ever that Ernie was a ghost when I was doubting it, that's all.'

Dexter nodded. 'Oh, he's a ghost all right. And

desperately unhappy. And ... well, I think I might have thought of a way round all this.'

Slo shook his head. 'You can't go cutting corners, young Dexter. Not with bodies. There are very strict laws in place for a good reason. There'd be bloody mayhem if people took the law about the dead into their own hands.'

'Oh, I realise that.' Dexter finished his sandwich. 'But what I was thinking was, why don't we—me and Frankie—take the paperwork, letters, whatever it is this pair of nasty nieces need to sign, by hand, and wait until they've done it, and then bring them back to you.'

'Wow! Brilliant!' Frankie was suddenly filled with hope again. 'And that way we could tell them face to face that this isn't going to cost them anything—other than a couple of minutes of their time.'

Slo nodded. 'Yes, that might well work. In fact, I don't see why it shouldn't work. Good thinking, Dexter, lad.'

'And,' Frankie said eagerly, 'you could just ring them and tell them we're on our way, couldn't you?'

'I could, and I will, but you know they're not local, don't you?'

'Aren't they?' Frankie frowned. 'How not local?'

'Northern.' Slo sighed. 'Birmingham, Bolton, Burnley, Blackburn—somewhere like that.'

'Blackpool,' Essie supplied helpfully as she came in with refills of coffee and sandwiches. 'I remember it was Blackpool because I used to go there for holidays when I was a kiddie and I tried to talk to them about it when they were here to organise the funeral, but they were a right dour pair and didn't want to talk about anything.'

325

'Blackpool!' Frankie sighed. 'Oh, but that's millions of miles away.'

'Only a few hours drive,' Dexter said cheerfully. 'We can be there and back in a day.'

'Really? And then we can organise Ernie's funeral?' Frankie said. 'Can't we?'

Slo nodded. 'I'll look up the file and find their contact details. I'll ring 'em and tell 'em what's happening and give you the address—if they agree to see you, of course.'

'You make them agree,' Essie said severely. 'Poor old Ernie deserves the best. And these lovely children are kind enough to want to give him the best. You *make* them agree, Slo.'

'Okey-dokey, Essie, duck,' Slo chuckled. 'I'll give it my best shot.'

*   *   *

And he did.

Three days later, long before it was light, on a cold, wet and windy morning which had turned the snow to slush and made everywhere look disgustingly grubby, Frankie and Dexter set off for Blackpool in the Mercedes.

Frankie had told Ernie everything, and had asked him please not to appear in the shop while she was away—just in case Cherish or any of the customers spotted him and caused another Jackie-and-Alan influx.

Cherish had been ecstatic to be left in sole charge of Francesca's Fabulous Frocks for the day, and Brian had assured Dexter seriously that the flower stall would also be in good hands.

'And you and Dexter can stay over,' Lilly had

said, widening her eyes. 'Can't you? Have a sort of dirty weekend—or at least a mucky night—in Blackpool?'

And Frankie had said definitely, categorically, absolutely not.

'Why on earth not?' Lilly had frowned. 'You are so slow, Frankie. He's the most gorgeous man on the planet, after Andreas, of course. And you go out together all the time.'

'Mostly after work. As good friends.'

'Whatever.' Lilly had sighed. 'He fancies you like mad, you're crazy about him. He's even kissed you. Twice. You said.'

'Yes, and it turned me upside down, but that's as far as it'll go.'

'Why? Neither of you have any ties, and you must be over the heart-breaker and life-wrecker by now.'

'Oh, yes,' Frankie had agreed. 'Totally over. But I have no intention of going back there again.'

'As if Dexter would break your heart,' Lilly had scoffed. 'He adores you. Everyone can see it.'

'Can they? Lill, I know nothing about his past. There are still far too many secrets about why he left Oxford. And most of them must involve women—or one woman in particular. I don't know enough about him, and he clearly doesn't want to tell me. And then there are all those other women here.'

'What other women? OK, he played around when he first arrived, but he hasn't looked at anyone else for weeks.'

'He spent New Year with someone else.'

Lilly's face had fallen. 'Did he? Oh, bollocks.'

327

'Where are we?' Frankie looked across the car. 'Are we nearly there yet?'

'No. For the millionth time.' Dexter grinned. 'We're still on the M40. We've still got the M42 and then miles and miles of the M6 to go.'

'Oh, OK.' Frankie snuggled down in her seat, lulled by the rhythm of the windscreen wipers. 'Wake me up when we can see the sea.'

'Lightweight.' Dexter sighed. 'And I thought we were going to share the driving.'

'I am not driving this car. It's too big, too scary, and I'm not insured.'

'You're covered on my insurance.'

'Am I? Damn. OK, then we're on a strange motorway and I might damage it.'

'The motorway?'

'The Mercedes.'

'You mean you're not up for a challenge?'

'Oh.' She smiled at him. 'I'm always up for a challenge.'

'Good,' he laughed. 'So when we stop at the services halfway up for something to eat, you can have a little test run round the car park, then you can drive us the rest of the way to Blackpool.'

'Which means, if we survive, I'll get the lovely tricky bit of trying to find the right house once we get there?'

'The satnav will take care of that. We've got a full address and postcode.'

'I wonder what they'll be like? Thelma and Louise?'

'Awful,' Dexter sighed. 'We know they'll be a pair of dragons. But it doesn't matter. At least they've agreed to see us and sign the papers. We don't have to become good friends or anything with them, do we?'

Frankie leaned her head back against the soft leather and closed her eyes. No they didn't. It was all going to be OK.

Several hours later, hours when Frankie had been bursting with pride at driving the Mercedes confidently along the latter stages of the motorway in the teeming rain, they were following the satnav's strident instructions and crawling round the back streets of Blackpool, heading for Thelma and Louise's house.

'It's very disappointing.' Frankie frowned. 'I thought Blackpool would be all sun and colour and noise and crowds and kiss-me-quick hats. I didn't expect it to be wall-to-wall grey.'

The sea and the sky just seemed to blend into a mass of gunmetal, the streets were wet, deserted and windswept and all the attractions were closed.

'It's January,' Dexter said reasonably. 'It's pouring with rain and freezing cold. And it's as far out of season as you can get. We'll come back later in the year for the illuminations and ride on all the white-knuckle machines on the Pleasure Beach and eat fish and chips from the paper.'

Frankie laughed. 'Sounds perfect. If we're still friends by then, of course.'

'And why wouldn't we be?'

Frankie shrugged. 'I never assume anything any more. Never plan too far ahead. That way I don't get too disappointed.'

'Oh, I'm definitely planning on coming back here in the autumn to do the full touristy bit.'

'With me?'

Dexter sighed. 'Yes, Frankie with you. Well, that is if you still want me, after—'

'After what?' The light-heartedness of the ping-pong banter had suddenly been snuffed out. 'After what?'

'You've now reached your destination,' the satnav squawked.

Frankie pulled the Mercedes into the kerb outside a row of neat terraced houses.

She looked across the car at him. 'You can't just leave it there. After what?'

Dexter undid his seat belt. 'Something I should have told you a long time ago. And something we can perhaps sort out when we've got Thelma and Louise to sign the papers. It'll keep. Right now, Ernie's the most important thing on the agenda, isn't he?'

As Dexter locked the Mercedes, Frankie shivered in the freezing wind blowing straight from the sea along the narrow street. But it wasn't just the bitter wind and the spattering rain that chilled her. Inside, her bubbling happiness had died.

'Ready?' Dexter smiled gently at her as they stood outside the green front door, patchily faded by the constant onslaught of sun and salt-filled wind. 'For the last stage?'

Frankie nodded. She didn't trust herself to speak. She knew her voice would wobble and then he'd know just how important he was to her.

Dexter rang the bell.

The door was opened almost immediately. Thelma and Louise must have been waiting for them, Frankie thought listlessly, hiding behind the net curtains, peering out.

Oh, get a grip, she told herself crossly. Forget

330

Dexter and his secrets. We're here for Ernie.

'Yes?' A thin-faced woman with narrow lips and a pointed nose, looked at them distastefully.

'Mrs Butterly? Thelma Butterly?' Dexter asked.

'No, she's my sister. I'm Louise Reeves. My sister Thelma's inside. You're the ones who've come about Uncle Ern, are you?'

'We are,' Frankie said. Her voice was croaky. She cleared her throat. 'And we've got the papers. We won't take up much of your time.'

'You'd better not,' Louise said ungraciously. 'Come on in, then.'

Dexter stood back to let Frankie step inside the narrow hall first. It was spotlessly clean but very cluttered with furniture and ornaments.

Louise led them into an equally clean but crammed and cluttered living room. An almost identical thin and ferret-faced woman looked up from the leather sofa.

'You the people from down south about burying Ernie?'

'We are,' Frankie said again. 'It's very nice to meet you, Thelma, um, Mrs Butterly.'

'Ah.'

As they weren't invited to sit down, they didn't. Frankie felt increasingly claustrophobic in the overstuffed room.

'Give us the papers then,' Louise said. 'No point in hanging around. Although why you want to be bothering yourself with Uncle Ern's remains I've no idea.'

And we have no intention of telling you, Frankie thought angrily.

Dexter smiled as he handed over the sheaf of papers and Slo's letters. 'It's something we do.

We work for the undertakers, you see. In a sort of freelance capacity. We, um, deal with unburied ashes. When the chapel of rest starts to run out of shelf space for the caskets, we ... er ... we trace the nearest and dearest and take over the interment of the remaining ashes.'

Frankie stared at him. What a brilliant liar he was! Which, she thought ruefully, was probably just as well, as she hadn't given any thought at all to what they'd tell Thelma and Louise about why they wanted Ernie to rest in peace.

'Like a charity?' Louise gave the papers a cursory glance.

'Yes, er, sort of,' Dexter said quickly.

'Must be mad.' Thelma shook her thin head. Even her hair was thin, Frankie thought. 'Dead's dead. Who cares what happens after? And Uncle Ern left nothing worth having. Couldn't even raise a few bob on most of it. We kept the few bits that might be useful, and dumped the rest of his rubbish.'

Including Achsah's wedding dress, Frankie thought angrily.

'That's not our concern,' Dexter said smoothly, taking out his pen. 'All we want you to do, as next of kin, is sign the paperwork to say you give us, and Motions, the funeral directors, the authority to take charge of the ashes and give your, um, Uncle Ernie a decent burial.'

'Be glad to,' Louise said, snatching the pen.

Phew. Frankie exhaled. It was going to be OK.

'How much?' Thelma looked at them. 'Before I put pen to paper. How much?'

'Oh, it won't cost you anything at all,' Frankie said, trying hard to smile. 'We're taking care of all the funeral expenses for Ernie, er, your uncle.'

'I should bloody hope you are,' Louise snapped. 'We ain't parting with another penny for this pointless funeral. We were out of pocket the first time.'

'No, no,' Dexter said hurriedly. 'Frankie's right. It's all taken care of.'

'You might be do-gooders—' Thelma squinted at him '—but you can't be that simple? We ain't paying you. You're paying us.'

'Exactly.' Louise nodded. 'You want our signatures on this paperwork to say you take care of Uncle Ernie's ashes, then you pay for them, OK?'

Oh shit ... Frankie closed her eyes.

'Er, well, it's not normal ...' Dexter looked frantically at Frankie.

'I don't care what's normal. You don't get nothing for nothing in this world,' Thelma said icily. 'You want us to sign, then you pay us.'

'OK.' Frankie pulled a face, trying to remember how much she had in her purse. She couldn't let Ernie down now. 'We'll give you twenty pounds.'

Thelma and Louise laughed. A lot.

'Forty,' Dexter said.

They carried on laughing.

'Well, how much do you want?' Frankie glared at them. 'Bearing in mind that we're a charity.'

'Soft in the head is what you are,' Louise snapped. 'Bothering yourself with other people's dead relations. We want a hundred.'

'Each,' Thelma added, her eyes glittering greedily.

Oh God ... Frankie shook her head. She had no idea if Dexter had any cash at all on him. She thought she might have about sixty pounds and some loose change.

'Frankie?' Dexter looked worriedly at her.

'Sixty-ish.'

'OK.' He glared at Thelma and Louise. 'You sign and you'll get your two hundred.'

'Let's see the money then.'

Between them, Dexter and Frankie emptied their purse and wallet and pockets onto the coffee table. Louise fell on it and counted it with all the alacrity of Shylock.

'Yep.' She nodded at Thelma. 'It's all here. Sign away, Thel.'

The odious Thelma signed in all three places, followed by the equally odious Louise.

'Thank you.' Dexter snatched the papers away from them. 'And goodbye.'

Thelma and Louise, still greedily sorting out the various notes and coins, didn't even answer.

Dexter slammed the front door so hard behind them that flakes of green paint floated from it.

'Oh my God.' Frankie, her hair blowing wildly across her face, leaned against the Mercedes, gulping in the cold, wet air. 'Oh, my God.'

Dexter, shaking with anger, slid his arms around her and held her close. 'Bitches,' he muttered. 'Complete miserly avaricious scumbag bitches!'

'I can't believe people can be that awful,' Frankie mumbled into the shoulder of his soft leather jacket.

'I can,' Dexter said gruffly. 'Anyway, we've got what we wanted. At least Ernie can have his funeral now, can't he?'

Frankie nodded. 'Yes. And that's all that matters, really. Let's get out of here. As far away as possible. And can you drive home, please? I feel all

334

shaky.'

'No problem.' He held her at arm's length and smoothed her hair away from her face. 'And anyway, we're not going straight home.'

'Aren't we?' Frankie knew they really didn't have any money left to do much else.

'No, we're not. I'm going to do something I should have done a long time ago. I'm going to tell you my equivalent of your Joseph story, and then I'm going to show you why I had to leave Oxford.'

Chapter Twenty-nine

Dexter had driven carefully back down the M6, windscreen wipers on full blast, in a flurry of non-stop spray from the other cars and lorries on the wet road. The sky was dark and threatening and the rain poured in a non-stop torrent, washing away the last vestiges of the snow.

Frankie shivered despite the car's very effective heater. 'What an awful day.'

'On all counts, yes.' Dexter nodded.

They'd talked a lot about Thelma and Louise, they hadn't said anything, yet, about his impending revelations.

Frankie stretched, knowing she had to know, even if it broke her heart, which it probably would. 'OK, then. Tell me. About Oxford.'

Dexter glanced across the car. 'Mmm, I was just wondering where to start.'

'The beginning's usually good.'

'I don't think there was a beginning, not really— Oh, yes there was.' He slowed down and tucked the

Mercedes in behind a large lorry in the left-hand lane. 'My brother, Simon—he's three years older than me—and I started our own business in Oxford as soon as I left school. I think that's where it really starts. We were both mad about cars, you see, big, luxury cars.'

'Like this one?'

Dexter nodded. 'We leased one to start with, a classic Jaguar, and we had the idea that we'd offer a sort of luxury taxi service, or chauffeur people to swish events, that sort of thing. Anyway, it took off slowly at first, the way new businesses do. But gradually it started to do really well. We managed to buy our next two cars and register the business. We called it Dream Drives.'

Frankie nodded. 'Sounds good.'

'Maybe a bit naff now, but we were pleased with it at the time. Anyway, Simon was always keen to make as much money as possible in the shortest amount of time, but I thought we could be doing it differently—oh, still sticking to our original principles of top-of-the-range taxi-driving, which is what it was really, but also maybe using the cars to take people who'd never known much luxury or happiness, out for the day. At very cheap rates. Very cheap indeed. I could see it as a sort of loss leader that gave happiness to people at the same time.'

'Nice idea. But Simon didn't agree with it?'

'Simon thought I was mad.' Deter laughed. 'But he went along with it because we were raking in the cash on the posh company rides, and he was happy by then to diversify into anything that paid anything at all. And it got us loads of good publicity for the company, and even more business as a result. So, I did all of the cheap drives and Simon stuck to the luxury executive corporate end of the market. We bought two more cars and employed two more drivers.'

'Quite the entrepreneurs.'

'We were.' Dexter nodded. 'And the two sides of the business worked really well for several years. We were the first firm the corporates came to for days out—race meetings, Premiership football matches, all the prawn sandwich brigade stuff. We had a great reputation. And by running the other side too, well, I felt that we weren't just cosying up to the people who could afford it, but we were also giving happiness to those who couldn't. It was great to see their faces—especially the kids—when I turned up on some really run-down housing estate in my chauffeur's uniform and whisked them off to the cinema or bowling or just into town. It gave them something special in their lives, which weren't very special at all. I loved it.'

Frankie stared ahead at the pelting rain and the lorry's blurred taillights as they joined the M42. 'Yes, I can understand that. So?'

'So,' Dexter said, 'after a couple more years, still looking to expand the business, Simon bought a pink stretch-limo to hire out for hen parties, and girly days and nights out, and then he employed Cindy to drive it.'

He was silent then, concentrating on the road ahead.

Pennies dropping like coins in an amusement arcade, Frankie glanced across at him. 'And Cindy is—was—your Joseph equivalent?'

'More or less, yes.'

'The one you said you shouldn't have fallen in

love with?'

'Yes.'

Frankie swallowed the lump in her throat. 'OK, so you and Simon were now running a really successful chauffeuring service on three levels, and . . . ?'

'I was madly in love with Cindy. I'd had plenty of girlfriends before, but no one like Cindy. I'd never been head over heels in love before. Like you with Joseph, I was simply blown away by her.'

Frankie decided there and then that she hated Cindy more than she ever hated anyone. Even more than Thelma and Louise. And definitely more than Biddy or stupid Maisie Fairbrother.

'So, it was the love story of the year, was it?'

'Sadly not. Cindy liked me, and was my friend, but Cindy didn't love me. Didn't even fancy me. Cindy was in love with Simon.'

'Right.' Was Cindy *mad*? 'And Simon?'

'Was flattered, and fancied her, and, because he was wildly competitive and knew that I loved her, he married her.'

'Oh, God.' Frankie stared at him. 'And what did you do?'

'I was best man at their wedding.' Dexter gave a short laugh. 'And we all carried on working together and expanding the business, and I dated more women than there were days in the year.'

Frankie frowned at the non-stop rain sheeting from the unrelenting sky. 'So, that's where you got the bad boy reputation from?'

'It was well deserved.' Dexter looked at her briefly. 'I loved and left everyone. I behaved like a complete bastard as far as women were concerned. You went one way—after Joseph you didn't date

338

anyone—I went the other. I had to show them, Simon and Cindy, that I didn't *care*.'

Frankie sighed. 'When really you cared like hell? Oh, why is life so complicated? So, that's why you had to leave Oxford is it? Because you still loved Cindy, who was your sister-in-law, and simply couldn't bear to see her and Simon together?'

'I wish it had been that simple.' Dexter slowed the Mercedes down and indicated to leave the motorway.

'Where are we going?' Frankie frowned. 'Are we taking the scenic route?'

Dexter nodded. 'We'll get back on to the M40 later. We're not far from Oxford. I just need to do this.'

'OK, fine by me. So, what happened next?'

'Are you sure you really want to know?'

'Absolutely, as long as you want me to know,' Frankie said firmly, pretty sure she was just about to hear things that would break her heart for ever. And far, far more painfully than Joseph Mason had ever done. 'After all, you were a star listening to my tale of woe. So, let me guess—you had an affair with Cindy? Your sister-in-law. And Simon found out and—?'

'Again,' Dexter sighed, 'I wish it had been that simple. And Cindy would never have had an affair with me, anyway. She treated me like a brother or a best mate. For her, there was no spark at all. She just didn't feel like that about me.'

Cindy, Frankie decided, was definitely certifiably insane.

'No, it wasn't Cindy,' Dexter continued. 'It was something else entirely. You see, by this time Dream Drives was a pretty substantial business,

339

and we had a fleet of cars and some really good blokes working for us. It was all going amazingly well. I bought a house. Simon and Cindy bought a mini-mansion and all the other trappings. We all lived really well. Then Cindy and Simon took a week off to go on holiday ...'

Frankie had no idea where this was leading so she said nothing.

'And,' Dexter continued, 'I thought it might be a good opportunity to get the accountant in to go through the books—Simon handled all the finances, all the preparation of the books for the accountant and the Inland Revenue so I'd never really looked at them before—because I was thinking maybe we could sort of franchise the idea of the chauffeur-driven cars for the less well off and hopefully turn that into a spin-off. And I didn't want Simon dissing the idea out of hand. And, well, to cut to the chase, the accountant left me the figures to look at, and I discovered that someone had been creaming off money for years.'

'*Cindy?*'

Dexter shook his head. 'No way. I knew it wasn't Cindy. But it was a huge swindle. Really huge. We're talking hundreds of thousands. All our corporate clients had been paying through the nose for trips and services that hadn't existed, for years.'

'Jesus.'

'Exactly.' Dexter was very pale. 'And I just knew it was how Simon was funding his Richard Branson-type lifestyle. I just knew it. And I felt so sick. So, when they came back from their holiday, I tackled him.'

'Bloody hell.' Frankie shook her head. 'And did he admit it?'

'No. Not in so many words. Well, not at first, anyway. But he went completely berserk. We had a fight. Big time. And he said I should have kept my nose out and everything would have been all right and that he was only taking money from the big customers who could afford it.'

'And he thought that was OK?'

'Apparently. And Simon just kept on saying I had to keep my mouth shut, and denying that it could hurt anyone. But it was my business too, you see, and I'd worked so hard to make it successful for years. And, despite my bad reputation—' he smiled gently at her '—I am basically a very straight bloke. I loathe dishonesty. Simon wasn't just ripping off the corporates by his swindle, indirectly he was also cheating me and the less-privileged customers who'd enjoyed the service for so long. And because Simon had been greedy and dishonest, I knew it was only a matter of time before we were investigated, then the whole business was going to fold, and I couldn't let that happen.'

'So?'

'So I begged him to admit everything, to come clean. The accountant must have known the figures were wrong, so it was only a matter of time before the Inland Revenue found out, and so it would be much better for Simon to admit he'd made a mistake with his figures and offer to repay, than to be under investigation and for us to lose everything.'

'And he wouldn't?'

'No. He just kept saying as long as I kept schtum then it would all go away. But I knew it wouldn't. And Dream Drives was really, really important to me and I wanted to save it.'

341

'And Cindy? What did she know about all this?'

'Nothing. That was one thing Simon and I agreed on. That Cindy—and none of our employees—should ever get wind of it. Oh, Cindy knew we'd had a major falling-out, but she didn't know why. And we didn't tell her.'

'So?'

'When it became clear that Simon had no intention of confessing, and every intention of carrying on his scam, I gave him umpteen chances to change his mind but he wouldn't, so then I went to the police, and told them. And Simon was arrested and charged with fraud.'

'Bloody hell. I bet that went down well.'

'It completely ballsed up everything. And then—' Dexter swallowed as they turned into the driveway of a large country house '—it got worse.'

Frankie frowned at the house. There were lights spilling in warm welcome from all the windows. What on earth were they doing here? Was it a hotel? Had they stopped for dinner? It was dark now, and she was hungry, but somehow she'd imagined they'd go straight back to Kingston Dapple. Maybe Dexter felt he needed to take a break after all the awfulness.

'Simon was let out on bail, pending inquiries.' Dexter pulled the Mercedes to a halt behind a row of cars. 'And he came to find me, furiously angry, and said he knew I'd reported him.'

'Well, yes I suppose he would have reached that conclusion.'

Dexter got out of the car and opened the door for her. 'This won't take long. We'd better hurry—it's too wet to hang around outside.'

Frankie stared doubtfully at the huge, beautiful

sprawling house. Suddenly swamped by foreboding, a niggle of fear shivered inside her. She had an awful feeling that this house was immensely important to Dexter and to the secrets of his past. She was convinced now that something horrid awaited her inside.

'Where are we? Is this a hotel? Are we eating here?' Frankie looked at him hopefully. 'I've got my credit card, but no cash at all. Bloody Thelma and Louise had all my cash.'

'You won't need any money, it's not a hotel, and, no, we're not stopping long.' Dexter took her hand, and heads down and feet scrunching on wet gravel, they hurried through the icy wind and rain towards the doorway.

'Then what exactly are we doing?' Frankie shook raindrops from her hair as they stood in the gorgeously warm and luxurious foyer, looking around in astonishment. 'Is this place run by friends of yours or something? Or is it a private house? Do you have landed gentry chums you haven't mentioned? Sorry, Dexter, I'm very confused now.'

'You won't be.' Dexter smiled at her. 'Please, Frankie, I need to do this.'

In the distance, along beautifully decorated corridors, Frankie could hear the muted hum of voices and occasional laughter and the clink of cutlery. She was completely mystified. Were they gate-crashing someone's posh party? Or—her heart sank—was this Dexter's family home?

Was Dexter really the son of the Earl of Warwick or something?

Could today get any more bizarre?

Yes, Frankie thought, her heart sinking even further, as they started to climb a wide, twisting staircase, flanked on all sides by lovely watercolour landscapes, it probably could.

'OK.' Dexter took her hands in his when they'd reached the top of the stairs. 'Frankie, you're very, very important to me, and this may be the stupidest thing I've ever done in my life—and I've done some blinders—but do you trust me?'

She nodded, still mystified, still worried. 'Yes, actually. Totally.'

'Right, that's good, because now I'd like you to meet Cindy.'

Chapter Thirty

The room was large and warm, exquisitely decorated, and tastefully filled with antique furniture.

The tall slender girl with the pale face and the mass of red pre-Raphaelite curls, sitting in the high-backed armchair by the window, was probably the most beautiful woman Frankie had ever seen.

Cindy.

Fabulous, rich and classy. No wonder Dexter loved her so much.

Frankie just wanted to die on the spot.

'Hi.' Dexter grinned across the room. 'Frankie, this is Cindy. Cindy, meet Frankie.'

Frankie, her heart now plummeting like a runaway lift, worked some saliva into her mouth and hoped she was smiling. 'Um, hello, nice to meet you.'

It was anything but.

'And you.' Cindy smiled sweetly. 'He's talked

about you non-stop for ever. I couldn't wait to meet you. And—' she looked teasingly at Dexter '—you lied. You said she was beautiful.'

Bitch, Frankie thought.

Cindy grinned. 'She's not just beautiful. She's simply stunningly knock-out fabulous.'

OK, but then so are you, Frankie thought sadly. So are you, and he loves you, and I can't possibly compete.

Cindy smiled some more. 'Oh, please sit down.'

Frankie and Dexter sat, slightly awkwardly, side by side on a small velvet sofa.

Humiliated beyond belief, Frankie just wanted to stand up and run away. How could Dexter do this to her? How could he invite her into Cindy's palatial home without warning?

At least she'd just *told* him about Joseph, not bloody dragged him across the world to Sydney to *show* him.

Dexter took Frankie's hand and looked at Cindy. 'I've just told her. About Simon.'

'Good.' Cindy nodded. 'About time.' She smiled again at Frankie. 'He was scared to tell you. He thought you'd leave him. I knew you wouldn't.'

'Er ...' Frankie, still completely confused, just stared. 'Leave him? We're not even together.'

'Not what he thinks.' Cindy chuckled. 'Oh Lord, Dexter, you haven't told her how you feel at all, have you? You're so useless.'

'I haven't told her anything,' Dexter murmured, his hand tightening on Frankie's. 'Well, not about ...'

Not about your much-loved ex-sister-in-law— she remembered that Dexter had told her that his brother was divorced—living in a mini Chatsworth

345

and being loaded and drop-dead gorgeous as well, no, Frankie thought bitterly, you sodding well haven't.

'Then I will,' Cindy said quietly. 'How far did you get?'

'To where Simon came and accused me of telling the police.'

'Oh, right, so I get to explain the good bit, do I?' Cindy smiled cheerfully. 'Oh, sorry—my manners are appalling—do help yourself to drinks or whatever. Dexter knows where everything is.'

I bet he does, Frankie thought even more bitterly, desperately trying not to cry and make a show of herself.

'Tea?' Dexter stood up.

'Please,' Cindy said. 'Frankie?'

'No thanks. I'm fine.'

'If you're sure ...'

Dexter disappeared through an archway and Frankie could hear the sounds of kettle, water and cups.

'It's probably better that he's not here to listen to this bit,' Cindy said. 'He's such a softy. And I'm so glad you and he are together, because he ... No, sorry, that's down to him to sort out. I'm not fighting all his battles. Anyway, briefly—yes, Simon accused Dexter of turning him in—which was, of course, the right thing to do—for Dexter to do, I mean, not Simon. And Simon went ballistic—he always had a nasty temper but, well, I loved him, and he was my husband and you sort of get used to things like that. Not that he was ever violent to me, of course ... Anyway, after Si and Dexter had had their fight—again—Simon stormed home and said to get my coat because we were going out.'

Frankie simply nodded politely. She wasn't sure she cared much about the Valentines' family feuds any more.

'I tried to ask him what had happened at the police station—I was there when they arrested him but I knew nothing. Si just said it was a silly mistake, and I believed him. He said it was just some mix-up with the accounts or something. Anyway, we got into the BMW and headed out on the M40. It was a really dark night, and Si was driving like a mad man. He always drove fast, but this was scary. I asked him to slow down, and all he did was laugh and dial Dexter on the hands-free.'

Frankie nodded again. There was nothing she could—or wanted to—say.

'And once Dexter answered, he—Simon—said that if Dexter was taking away everything he'd ever wanted, then he—Simon—was going to take away the only thing that really mattered to Dexter.'

Frankie blinked. 'You?'

'Me.' Cindy smiled.

Whoopee-doo.

Frankie took a deep breath. 'So you always knew that Dexter loved you? But you didn't ever love him?'

'Dexter had a massive crush on me from the minute I joined Dream Drives, yes, I knew that. And he's the most fantastic bloke I've ever met. And I know how gorgeous-looking he is and everything, but, no, he just didn't push my buttons in that way. There was no sexual chemistry at all on my side. I only had eyes for Si. I love Dexter—and I always will—but just as a brother and a friend.'

Definitely mad, Frankie decided.

'And ... and does he still love you?' Frankie

knew she really, really didn't want to hear the answer, but she had to know.

'Oh, you'll have to ask him that one yourself.' Cindy smiled. 'I couldn't possibly comment. Anyway, before he comes back, where had we got to with the other stuff?'

Frankie sighed in irritation. 'Simon driving you away from Dexter on the M40 and going too fast and—'

'Ah yes, and, then, at just over one hundred and twenty miles an hour, Simon deliberately drove into a motorway bridge . . . Ooh, tea, lovely, thanks, Dexter.'

Frankie, completely overcome with far too many emotions, watched as Dexter put his own cup down carefully on a spindly-legged table and then gently held the feeding-cup up to Cindy's lips, wiping her mouth with a tissue afterwards.

'Thanks, that's great. You always make a lovely cuppa.' Cindy looked happily across at Frankie. 'The BMW was a write-off. Simon, being a lucky bastard, walked away—well, stumbled—with concussion and a few snapped ribs and a fractured ankle. I broke my back.'

'Oh, my God,' Frankie whispered. 'Oh, my God, I had no idea . . . I'm so sorry.'

'Yeah, well, it was pretty crap for a while—but I'm doing fine now. You learn to adjust and I can do a million more things than I could a year ago.'

Frankie unashamedly wiped her eyes with her hands. 'And Simon?'

'I divorced him before the trial. And now he's in prison. For a long, long time. Fraud, embezzlement, attempted murder.'

Frankie shook her head as Dexter sat down

348

beside her again. 'Oh, but ... you ... living here?'

'Swish, isn't it?' Cindy beamed. 'A suite in the best private nursing home in the area. Luxury living. Hot and cold medical care at the drop of a hat. I've even got my own lift. And all down to Dexter. Oh, I can see he hasn't even told you that.'

'And I wasn't going to.' Dexter held Frankie's hand tightly. 'That's between us.'

'You shouldn't have any secrets from Frankie.' Cindy looked quite stern. 'Our house—mine and Si's—and every single thing we possessed, was sold and went to pay off the fraud and the debts and the tax man and the lawyers and Uncle Tom Cobley and all, leaving me with sodding nothing. So, yes, Dexter, despite me screaming at him not to, because stupidly he thought this, the accident, my injuries, were his fault, sold up everything he owned—'

'Not quite everything,' Dexter interrupted. 'I kept the Merc.'

'So you did.' Cindy wrinkled her nose. Then she looked at Frankie. 'He sold what was left of his share of the business, which was actually loads, his other cars, his house, and raided all his bank accounts, and set up a trust fund to finance my ongoing care here once the NHS had had enough of me.'

'Oh.' Frankie didn't even bother to stop the tears now. 'Dexter, I can't believe it, but why on earth didn't you tell me? I mean ... it's just amazing and it's why you—'

'Don't say anything nice.' He pulled her against him. 'Please. I'm no bloody hero or kindly benefactor. It's what I had to do. And we live with it. And it was my fault, because—'

349

'No, it wasn't,' Cindy said. 'None of this was down to you. It was just Simon. Stop crucifying yourself. And I'll never, ever be able to thank you enough for all this as you well know. And one day, when I'm up and about and walking and working again, I intend to pay you back—with interest.'

'And will you, um …?' Frankie sniffed.

'Recover? Fully?' Cindy smiled. 'Honestly, I've no idea. Probably not. But I go to physio and rehab in Birmingham twice a week and they're working miracles. And I've met this really neat squaddie there who had his legs blown off in Afghanistan. We fancy the pants off each other, but we're still not sure how to best manage the, er, more intimate side of things—' she screamed with laughter '—but we're having a hell of a lot of fun finding out.'

Frankie laughed then too. It sounded a bit odd and shaky.

Dexter shook his head. 'Poor bloke. You'll probably wear him out.'

'Oh, I do hope so.' Cindy giggled. 'So does he.'

Frankie took a deep breath, then looked at Dexter. 'Thank you for bringing me here. It certainly puts my problems well into perspective, and I understand everything now—well, all except one thing … why did you have to leave Oxford? Surely, none of this was your fault? It was Simon who—'

'Not the way the family saw it,' Dexter said as Cindy nodded awkwardly in agreement. 'Apart from Ray, of course, who was always on my side and who swore he wouldn't breathe a word about it if I wanted to make a fresh start in Kingston Dapple. Ray was … is … has been brilliant. But the rest of them all blamed me. My parents said I

350

should have kept quiet. Should have let Simon get away with it. He was my brother, blood's thicker than water, all that crap. If I'd kept my mouth shut then Simon wouldn't be in prison, Cindy and Si would still be married and probably would have given them grandchildren, Dream Drives would still be raking it in, Cindy wouldn't be paralysed. They said it was all down to me. My parents want nothing more to do with me, but they visit Simon in prison every month.'

'But that's not fair!' Frankie exploded.

'What's fair in this life?' Cindy snorted. 'Stupid sods, they are. Not that they visit me, either, since the divorce, because they think I should have stood by my man. As if! When he was as bent as a ... well, bent thing, *and* tried to kill me into the bargain?'

'My parents,' Dexter said, 'are prats.'

Cindy chuckled. 'And they seem to be living under some sad notion that Simon is financing all this too and that I should still be grateful to him. If they ever came here—which they won't—I'd tell them the truth.'

'No you wouldn't.' Dexter grinned at her.

'Nah, I probably wouldn't. Let 'em stew. Bastards. Oh, drink your tea, Dexter, and then take this fabulous girl home.' Cindy looked hopefully at Frankie. 'Now you know about me and it and everything, you'll come and see me again, though, won't you?'

Frankie nodded. 'I will. As often as possible.'

'Great.' Cindy beamed. 'My mates are pretty good about visiting, and my sexy squaddie goes AWOL as often as possible, with the help of his more able-bodied chums, love 'em, and of course Dexter comes here regularly, don't you?'

Dexter nodded.

Cindy looked at Frankie. 'Poor sod, above and beyond the call of duty, he stayed here in the visitors' quarters at Christmas and again at New Year, when he must have been aching to be with you. Well, I *know* he was aching to be with you because you were the only thing he bloody talked about.'

Dexter made shut-up motions with his hands.

'Don't try and deny it.' Cindy grinned at Frankie again. 'So yes, poor thing, a right bundle of laughs for him that was, being here with me—not. Oh, they try their best to give us a proper Christmas and all that, of course, and the food is fab, but as all the residents are about as mobile as I am, there's not a lot of festive frolicking.'

Dexter stared down at the intricately pattered Aubusson carpet.

'So this is where you were?' Frankie said gently. 'And who you were with? Why on earth didn't you tell me?'

'Because I couldn't. Because, like your backstory, everything had festered and blown up out of all proportion in my head. I was so scared that if I told you any of it, then you'd blame me for ... for, well, all this, like my parents did, and just walk away from me.'

'Never in a million years. You've told me now, and I'm still here.'

He smiled at her. 'Yes, you are. Frankie, you're just wonderful.'

Dexter pulled her into his arms and kissed her. And, floating, she pulled his face even closer to hers and kissed him back.

'Oh, pul-ease,' Cindy chuckled somewhere in the

352

distance. 'For God's sake, the pair of you—get a room.'

Chapter Thirty-one

February fourteenth dawned mild and sunny, with a pearly haze drifting across Kingston Dapple market square.

After the vicious winter, spring had compensated by arriving early in Berkshire.

'Right,' Frankie said to Ernie as she zipped round Francesca's Fabulous Frocks in the early morning sunshine, 'now you're clear about what's happening today?'

'I am, duck,' Ernie said excitedly, looking like a child about to embark for a Disneyland holiday. 'And I just can't wait. Although, I will miss you and our little chats very much. And you've been right kind to me.'

'Stop!' Frankie held up her hands. 'Don't! I will not cry today. Well, not yet anyway. And just think, Ernie, when this is over today, you'll have Achsah to chat to for ever and ever, won't you? You won't need me.'

Ernie shook his grizzled head. 'I'll never forget you, though, duck.'

Frankie swallowed the lump in her throat. 'And I'll always remember you. And I'll put flowers on your grave regularly and make sure it's all tidy and everything.'

'There's no need.'

'There's every need. Right, now we've got about half an hour before we need to go, so I'll just make sure everything's OK here for Cherish to take over while I'm, um, at the funeral.'

She stopped. Even she could see it was very, very odd to be discussing the funeral with the person who was being buried.

Ernie chuckled at her confusion. 'And it's a right lovely day for me and my Achsah to be reunited, isn't it? A day for lovers. Perfect.'

Slo had been rather upset that Tadpole Bridge's vicar could only offer Valentine's Day as the earliest date for the interment. Almost a month after she and Dexter had returned with the paperwork from that very, very weird and emotional day with Thelma and Louise, and, of course, Cindy.

'And we're lucky to get that. It's because it falls on a weekday this year, duck,' Slo had explained. 'If it had been on a Saturday he'd have had weddings, apparently, and couldn't have fitted us in, but if you'd rather wait?'

And Frankie had shaken her head. 'No. Ernie needs to be laid to rest as soon as possible. I still can't believe we've got to wait that long, actually.'

Slo had nodded. 'I know it's a bit of a delay. Vicar runs three parishes, see, duck. Cutbacks, falling congregations. He has to shuffle his duties. And the soonest he can do an interment at Tadpole Bridge just happens to be February fourteenth. Shall I take it?'

And Frankie had said yes without hesitation.

She and Dexter had discussed shutting up the shop and the flower stall as a mark of respect, then decided that as no one else knew about Ernie's second funeral, and also that as Valentine's Day was possibly going to be busy for both of them—

354

Dexter especially—they'd ask Cherish and Brian to hold the respective forts, which, of course, they'd been delighted to do.

So, with her shop windows filled with red heart-shaped balloons and huge overblown artificial flowers, and as many scarlet, crimson and ruby frocks as she could find, and with Dexter's stall simply awash with long-stemmed red roses, Frankie thought their joint entrepreneurial efforts to celebrate the most romantic day of the year were very successful.

Kingston Dapple marketplace, Frankie thought, gazing through the window, had done St Valentine proud.

'Afore young Dexter gets here,' Ernie said, leaning against the 1950s frock rails, 'and Cherish arrives to take over, can I just say something before I go?'

'Of course. Anything. Is there anything that's worrying you? Have we done something wrong—about today?'

'No.' Ernie chuckled. 'Course not. No, duck, it's about you and young Dexter. I told you I knew how he felt about you, didn't I? And anyone with half an eye could see you felt the same way. And you said it wouldn't work out because you both had loads of luggage ...'

'Baggage.'

'Ah, that too.'

'We've more or less sorted out our, um, luggage.' Frankie smiled. 'We've told each other everything. I ... well, I think it might be OK now.'

Ernie beamed at her. 'And thank the Lord for that, duck. Because, once I'm back with Achsah I won't be able to see what's going on here any more, and I just want to wish you all the happiness in the world. Take a word of advice. Don't waste the present because of what happened in the past. Look to the future—together. And be happy, always. Like me and Achsah. That's all, duck.'

'Thank you.' Frankie sniffed. 'You're so lovely. I wish we'd met when you were alive. Oh, now my mascara's going to run.'

'Crying already?' Dexter opened the door and smiled gently at her. 'That'll never do. Are you ready to go?'

Frankie nodded. 'As soon as Cherish gets here.'

'She won't be long. She and Brian are just having a cheesy muffin.'

'Sorry?'

'For breakfast. In the Greasy Spoon.'

Phew.

Dexter nodded at Ernie. 'So, today's the day. This must be the first funeral I've ever looked forward to, but I'll really miss you.'

'Ah, me and young Frankie have just been saying all that stuff.' Ernie nodded his grizzled head. 'You've both been wonderful, seeing as you didn't believe in me at first. You've been right wonderful.'

Frankie shot a look at Dexter. 'Don't cry! Please don't cry. We've just got to hope that it works this time, and Ernie and Achsah are reunited.'

Dexter nodded. 'I know there are no guarantees that this funeral will do the trick, Ernie, but I really hope it does.'

'You couldn't do any more,' Ernie said. 'No one could have done more than you two have done for me. And if it doesn't work then it won't be your fault. You're both right lovely.'

Frankie sniffed again. 'Oh, don't, please, and

here's Cherish on her way. Right, Ernie, for the last time, you vanish now, please. We'll go and get in the car and we'll see you—or rather we won't—at Tadpole Bridge. And, if this funeral is what you need to set you free and we don't ever see you again, then have a really, really happy afterlife.'

'You too, ducks, you too—once you've made the most of this one, mind.'

And Ernie faded away.

'Not late am I?' Cherish bustled through the door. 'Oh, don't you both look lovely. Like Torvill and Dean.'

Frankie groaned.

Inadvertently, she and Dexter had both opted to wear red today: Dexter with a bright red shirt under his grey suit, and her with her short cherry-coloured frock and matching tights and boots.

Red—the colour of Valentine's Day—for love? Definitely. Frankie smiled happily to herself.

Ernie had said he didn't want anyone to wear black for the interment. Especially after Thelma and Louise had insisted on it for the first funeral. Funny, Frankie thought, how long ago that seemed. When this was still Rita's Rent-a-Frock and Biddy had arrived to hire an outfit for Ernie's funeral . . .

So many things had changed since that day, and now they'd come full circle.

'Right, dears.' Cherish beamed at them both. 'Off you go and have a lovely day.'

'We will,' Frankie said grabbing her short red coat and her handbag, 'and thanks, Cherish. For looking after the shop again.'

Cherish flapped her hands. 'I couldn't be happier, dears. As you well know. You go off and have some fun. After all—' she looked coy '—

today's the day for fun, isn't it?'

'What the hell did you tell her we were doing?' Dexter muttered as they hurried round to the marketplace's service road where Dexter had parked the Mercedes.

'Oh, just celebrating the day, you know. I sort of fudged the details. I certainly didn't mention the funeral.'

'So she thinks we're off on some rather debauched jolly, does she?'

'Mmm, probably.' Frankie slid into the car. 'What about Brian?'

'Oh, I told Brian I was taking you out for a special breakfast that might turn into lunch and dinner.'

'So we both lied?'

'Yep.' Dexter nodded and grinned, as the Mercedes purred out onto the main road. 'Looks like it.'

'You look really great in a suit.' Frankie leaned her head back. 'Sort of decent and sexy all at the same time.'

'You just look sexy.'

She smiled to herself. 'Oh, have you got the flowers?'

'What flowers?'

She punched him.

'Yeah, in the boot. Red roses as agreed for Ernie and Achsah, but nothing for you.'

'No dozen red roses for me? Damn.'

'Nothing so conventional.' Dexter reached over and pulled her hand under his on the steering wheel. 'I wouldn't dare.'

They travelled in companionable silence for a while, and Frankie looked out at the Berkshire countryside, all covered in a haze of green and yellow as shoots and buds and leaves started to unfurl.

It was going to be a perfect day for the funeral.

*　　*　　*

Slo was already at the church when they arrived in Tadpole Bridge, standing beside the Daimler, happily smoking a cigarette in the sunshine.

'Please don't put it out on our account.' Frankie shook her head. 'We won't tell anyone. Oh, this is a lovely place.'

Tadpole Bridge's ancient parish church was tiny and four-square, with mellowed brickwork and zigzagging moss-patched paths. The churchyard looked like a wild-flower meadow, with gently spreading chestnut trees and tall waving grasses.

'Have you, um, got everything ready?' Dexter asked. 'I mean, um, the grave?'

'The boys were in early this morning. It's all been done decent like. As it should be.'

'But—' Frankie pulled a face '—we won't be able to actually, er, see anything, will we?'

'Bless you, no. The grave's been opened up and a nice sheet of artificial turf laid over Achsah's coffin. We'll just pop Ernie in beside her, like he wanted and cover it all over again, temporary for now and properly later. There'll be nothing to disturb you, duck.'

'Oh, wow!' Lilly, wearing a vivid clash of yellow and orange, clattered up the church path at that point. 'This is sooo cool. What a pretty graveyard. Frankie, when I die make sure I'm buried here, won't you?'

'If I'm around in about two hundred years' time, yes,' Frankie said, trying not to think of her own mortality. Not when there was so much to live for now.

'Oooh, he's cute.' Lilly brightened, looking towards the church. 'Is he another mourner?'

'He's the vicar,' Slo said, hastily stubbing out his cigarette.

'Really?' Lilly's eyes were huge. 'I didn't realise they had such young vicars.'

'Remember Andreas,' Frankie hissed. 'Do *not* flirt with the vicar.'

'I'm not.' Lilly pouted. 'And I never think of anyone but Andreas. But he is kind of sweet.'

'Right,' Slo said as he and the vicar shook hands. 'I think we're ready to go. After you, Reverend.'

The vicar, who, Frankie noticed, was wearing jeans and boots beneath his cassock, smiled in a gentle and suitably sad manner, and led them through the waving grass and ancient skew-whiff headstones to the far side of the churchyard. Slo followed, his head bowed, carrying Ernie's ashes in a maroon casket.

Dexter held Frankie's hand tightly. 'OK?'

She nodded. 'I think so. I mean, yes, I'm happy for Ernie, but there's still an air of ... well, just remembering that everyone here was like us once.'

'That's why we mustn't waste a minute of it,' Dexter said softly. 'And we won't, I promise you.'

They reached the grave. Everywhere was silent, there was nothing but the gentle rustling of the grass and the distant non-stop hum of the traffic on the A34.

The headstone, slightly crooked and with faded lettering, just gave Achsah's name and the date of her death and the words *Beloved Wife of Ernie. Until We're Together Again*. And there was a space for Ernie's details to be added.

Frankie pushed her hand against her mouth and Dexter hugged her.

'We'll get the headstone done with Ernie's name as soon as we can.' His voice wobbled slightly. 'Then it'll be exactly what they wanted.'

The vicar cleared his throat. 'This isn't a religious service as you know, so I'm not going to say anything very much, just that it's a privilege to be here today to be able to finally lay the mortal remains of Ernest Yardley to rest with his wife.'

Slo stepped forwards with the casket.

'They're not going to open the coffin are they?' Lilly asked in horror. 'I can't look.'

'No,' the vicar assured her. 'That would involve an exhumation order.'

'Would it?' Lilly blinked her emerald eyelashes at him. 'Fancy.'

Frankie nudged her sharply.

The vicar took the casket from Slo and stepped forwards.

'Please stop. It's not right,' Frankie said suddenly. 'He's not here.'

'Sorry?' The vicar frowned at her. 'Are we missing another mourner?'

'No.' Frankie shook her head. 'No, but ... look, please, can you just wait a moment.'

'Well, yes.' The vicar nodded. 'But I'm not sure what we're waiting for.'

Frankie dragged Dexter to one side. 'Ernie's not here! I *know* he's not here. This won't work. It'll just be the same as before.'

'Frankie, you're just letting all this emotion get

361

to you.'

'No, I'm not. I know when Ernie's around. I know him so well by now. I can feel him. And he's not here. He's still at the shop. I know he is.'

Dexter sighed. 'OK, I believe you ... I think ... but we were so sure this was what he wanted. That this would work. Please don't say that we've gone through all this, and it isn't what he needs to let him be reunited with Achsah.'

'It's the haunting thing that's wrong—again.' Frankie frowned. 'Ernie haunted the shop because—'

'Of Achsah's wedding dress,' Dexter finished. 'Of course. We haven't got the dress!'

Frankie stumbled across the uneven grass again and looked apologetically at the vicar. 'We've ... um ... forgotten something. Can you give us, er, about half an hour?'

'Oh dear.' The vicar looked touchy. 'Well, I'm not sure. I'm very busy and—'

'Oh, go on, please,' Lilly fluttered her eyelashes coquettishly. 'If Frankie says she needs something then she does. She wouldn't mess you around. And it's such a lovely day and this is such a pretty place. You could show me round the church.'

Slo frowned. 'Frankie, duck? Dexter? What's up?'

'Achsah's wedding dress,' Frankie hissed. 'We need to bury it with him ... them. It's what Ernie's, um, attached to down here, you know. We won't be long. Promise.'

'Ah, OK, duck.' Slo still looked uncertain. 'It all sounds like a load of old baloney to me, but you've been dead set on this all the way through, so, whatever you say. I'll keep the vicar sweet, you go and get the frock.'

'Thank you.'

Holding hands and running as fast as they could across the tussocky grass, Frankie and Dexter flew back to the Mercedes.

'Back again?' Cherish looked up in surprise as they tore into Francesca's Fabulous Frocks. 'That was quick.'

'Forgot something,' Frankie muttered, swerving round a bevy of customers, as she headed for the 1950s rails. 'Ah! Got it!'

She tore Achsah's dress from the rails and brandished it above her head.

'Isn't that like a wedding frock?' Cherish frowned. 'Oh! You dark horses! You're nipping off to have a secret Valentine's Day wedding! How absolutely lovely, dears!'

Dexter laughed. 'Sorry, Cherish, nothing like that. It's just, um, we'd promised this dress to someone and in all the excitement we forgot it.'

Cherish looked crestfallen.

'Ernie,' Frankie hissed, nodding towards the frock. 'I've got it now. So sorry. Come on, they're waiting for us. And Achsah's waiting for you.'

*   *   *

Slo, Lilly and the vicar looked at them in confusion as they stumbled back towards the grave, Frankie carefully carrying the cream silk shantung dress and Dexter carrying the red roses.

'We need to put this into the grave as well,' Frankie said, indicating the frock. 'It was Ernie's last wish. Is that OK?'

363

'Well, there aren't any ecclesiastical rules against it,' the vicar said, now checking his watch. 'But it's a little unusual. But if Mr Motion has no objections?'

'No.' Slo coughed wheezily. 'None at all. And they're right. Old Ern ... er, Mr Yardley, made it clear that the wedding dress was to be, um, interred with his ashes.'

'A bit of a waste of a frock.' Lilly frowned. 'They won't get much wear out of it down there.'

Everyone ignored her.

'Right.' The vicar took the ashes from Slo. 'Let's start again. It is with great pleasure that I can finally reunite the mortal remains of Ernest and Achsah Yardley here at home in Tadpole Bridge, and their immortal spirits in the sight of God.'

Dexter hugged Frankie tightly. 'Is it OK now?'

She nodded, not even trying to stop the tears. 'He's here and he's happy.'

The casket containing the ashes was placed gently into the grave, followed by Achsah's wedding dress. Slo creakily leaned down and covered the casket and frock with the sheet of artificial turf.

Dexter laid the red roses on top.

Everyone stood back.

Frankie, leaning against Dexter, shivered. Slo, the vicar and even Lilly all had their heads bent in deep respect.

Then the previously silent churchyard was filled with a sweet cacophony of birdsong and a sudden gentle rush of warm breeze, and, somewhere, two voices joined in happy laughter, spiralled upwards and upwards and away into the bluebell sky.

'Wow,' Dexter said huskily. 'Wow.'

'They're together again.' Frankie wiped her eyes.

'We've done it. Ernie and Achsah are reunited at last.'

Chapter Thirty-two

'Close your eyes,' Dexter said.

'Are we playing party games?' Frankie asked, obediently shutting her eyes.

'Nothing so juvenile.' Dexter snorted. 'We're sensible grown-ups.'

'Oh, yeah, I'd forgotten.'

It was the evening of Valentine's Day. After the interment of Ernie's ashes, Frankie and Dexter had followed Slo back to Hazy Hassocks and been treated to one of Essie's lovely lunches in their sheltered courtyard garden. It had been just the right thing to do, relaxing and peaceful after the heightened emotion of the graveside, and Ernie and Achsah's gentle reunion.

Lilly had had to go back to work at Beauty's Blessings and had said a reluctant goodbye to the vicar, but had been much cheered by Andreas sending a Valentine's greeting text just as she was getting into her car, saying that he'd be over in ten days—his uncle in Winterbrook had sorted out all the necessary paperwork, so he'd be starting work in the UK far sooner than he'd thought.

Lilly had clapped her hands in ecstasy, and kissed Dexter and Frankie and Slo and said she'd couldn't wait to move Andreas into Featherbed Lane—and ten days was such a little bit of time to wait, wasn't it?

'Have you still got your eyes closed?' Dexter

asked.

'Yes.'

'Good. Now, I'm just going to take your hand—there are three steps up here, so be careful. I don't want to be spending Valentine's Day eve in A&E. Although all those nurses might be a bit of a bonus.'

Frankie giggled as she followed him up the steps and into the soulless bedsit in Peep 'o' Day Passage for the first time.

'OK,' Dexter said. 'Now open your eyes.'

Frankie did. And whooped with delight.

The living room, large, light and airy, stretched the whole length of the house with big picture windows at one end, opening out on to a balcony. The balcony, in turn, looked out over the tiny, meandering River Dapple and the meadows that undulated towards Hazy Hassocks.

'Oh, it's fabulous!' Frankie gazed round in total joy. 'And you are such a liar! This is certainly no soulless bedsit!'

But it wasn't the cosily furnished room or the stunning view that entranced Frankie most. It was the fact that every surface in the living room was covered with vases of vibrantly coloured gerberas—every colour of the rainbow—the tips of their petals dusted with glitter, which sparkled like a million tiny stars.

'They're amazing.' Frankie stared at the dozens and dozens of flowers. 'Absolutely incredible. So gorgeous—oh, thank you so much.'

Dexter laughed. 'Well, with you being the queen of all things bright and beautiful—not to mention paintbox coloured—I couldn't possibly go down the hackneyed red roses route today, could I?'

366

Frankie sniffed. She'd tried so hard not to cry since they'd left the churchyard, but it had been very difficult.

Dexter frowned at her in concern. 'Are you OK? Cry if it makes you feel better, Frankie, I've had a few moments today, too. I know how you feel.'

'I'm not miserable. Honestly. I'm very happy for Ernie and Achsah, and I'm certainly very, very happy for me. It's the fabulous flowers and you being lovely and everything. Honestly, I'm not crying, I'm just a bit emotional.'

'Understandable. It's been one hell of a day. In fact it's been one hell of a ninety-one days.'

'Ninety-one days?' Frankie stopped stroking a particularly vibrant shocking pink gerbera.

'Since we met.'

'You've *counted* them?'

Dexter nodded. 'Call me sad, if you want to.'

'I wouldn't dream of it. I'm just, well, amazed. I thought . . .'

'Thought what? That I was another bloody Joseph Mason? Not a chance. Frankie, there's not another woman in the world that I'd have wanted to share the last ninety-one days with—or the next ninety-one years, come to that.'

'Not even Cindy?'

'No.' Dexter laughed. 'Certainly not Cindy.'

Frankie stared out of the window. 'She said I had to ask you if you still loved her.'

'Did she?'

Frankie nodded. 'She did. So I am. And do you?'

Dexter walked towards her and held her hands. 'No, I don't. Cindy isn't the love of my life.'

'Isn't she?'

Dexter laughed. 'You know she isn't. You know

how I feel about you. You know I'll never, ever want or need anyone else.'

Frankie smiled at him. 'As long as you live?'

'Oh, way beyond that. Well into eternity. Like Ernie and Achsah. For ever and ever. After all, a girl with a haunted frock shop has to be every man's wildest dream.'

She giggled. 'It's all been a bit strange, hasn't it?'

Dexter nodded. 'You could say that ... Frankie Meredith, you are simply amazing—and I love you.'

'I love you too.'

They stared at one another in delighted surprise.

'And there's something else,' Dexter said, gently tracing her lips with his fingertips. 'A sort of special supper treat for today.'

'You've cooked?' Frankie squeaked. 'When? And, anyway, I thought you only microwaved, and are we eating out on the balcony? With candles?'

'No, I haven't cooked, yes, I normally microwave; and no, we're having supper through here.' He took her hand and led her into the bedroom.

'Oh my God!' Frankie danced with delight. 'Oh-my-God! How did you do that?'

'Magic,' Dexter laughed. 'Well, no not really ... do you like it?'

'Like it? I love it!' Frankie threw her arms round his neck. 'And I love you, but you've never been in my bedroom ...'

'Sadly, no.' Dexter shook his head. 'Despite that early invite, the reality never materialised, so I thought I'd just recreate it here and hope ...'

Frankie laughed. 'Did Lilly ...?'

'Lilly took photos of your room, yes. And gave me all the details I needed. Of course—' Dexter looked at his one-time stark, pale and masculine bedroom with feigned horror '—all this pink and purple, and all these frills and flounces and cushions, and all the little twinkly lights and sparkly candles, means I'm going to be sleeping in a sort of boho tart's boudoir, but, heck, if it makes you happy ...'

Frankie was still jigging with delight. 'Oh, yes, it makes me happy. You make me happy. I'm the happiest person in the entire world. You're an absolute star. Oh, it must have taken you ages and ages.'

'Yes, well, I sort of thought it would make it a home from home for you. Because if Lilly and Andreas are going to be living in Featherbed Lane, it might get rather crowded and you might feel a bit left out.'

Frankie nodded. 'I know. I thought I'd have to look for somewhere else, and now Andreas is arriving really soon I'll have to think about it seriously. It's just so difficult to find anywhere.'

'What about here?'

'Here?' Frankie stopped jigging and stared at him. 'Really? Here with you? Permanently? Move in? Live together? You're asking me to live with you?'

Dexter grinned at the bombardment of questions. 'Yes to all of them. If you'd like to, of course.'

'No, I wouldn't.' Frankie poked out her tongue. '*Like*? Pah! No way! I'd *love* it. We'll have such a lovely, lovely time. Oh, Dexter, you're simply incredible, and ... Wow! Is that a Hideaway Home hamper?'

'Mmm.' Dexter grinned. 'It is. That's our supper. A special lovers' picnic, apparently. But there are

369

rules about eating it.'

'Are there?'

'There are.' Dexter kissed her and started to unzip her scarlet frock. 'Apparently, we have to be in bed and feed each other, otherwise we don't get the full benefits.'

'Oh, no, I can quite see that.' Frankie giggled, unbuttoning his shirt and leading him towards the big, pink and purple frilled bed.

'And we wouldn't want to waste all those healthy vitamins and minerals, would we?' Dexter murmured, pushing her gently into the cushiony satin flounces.

'No, we wouldn't,' Frankie sighed as he kissed her again. 'Oh, happy, happy Valentine's Day, Dexter Valentine.'

'Do you know—' Dexter smiled down at her '—I think it might just be the best ever.'